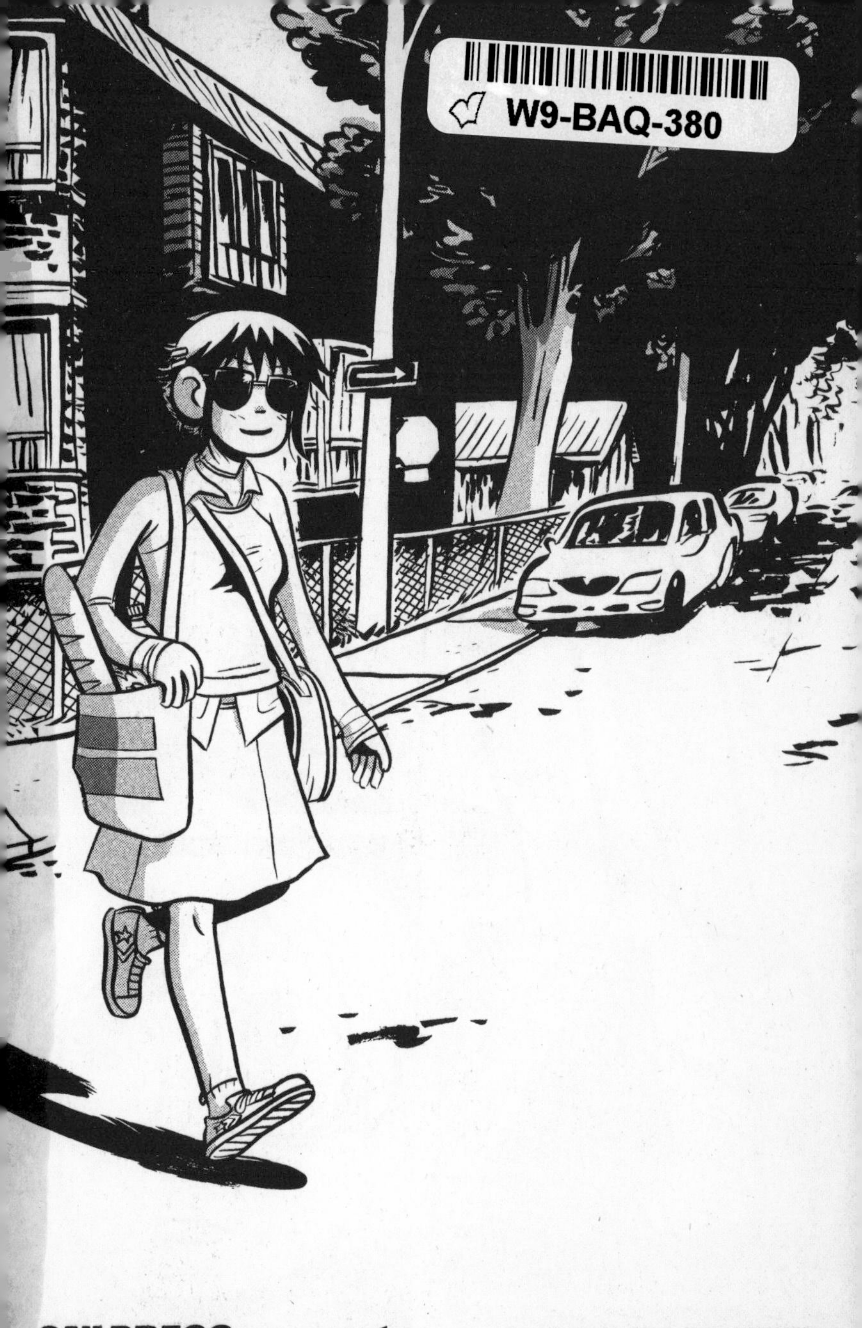

ONI PRESS presents

BRYAN LEE O'MALLEY'S

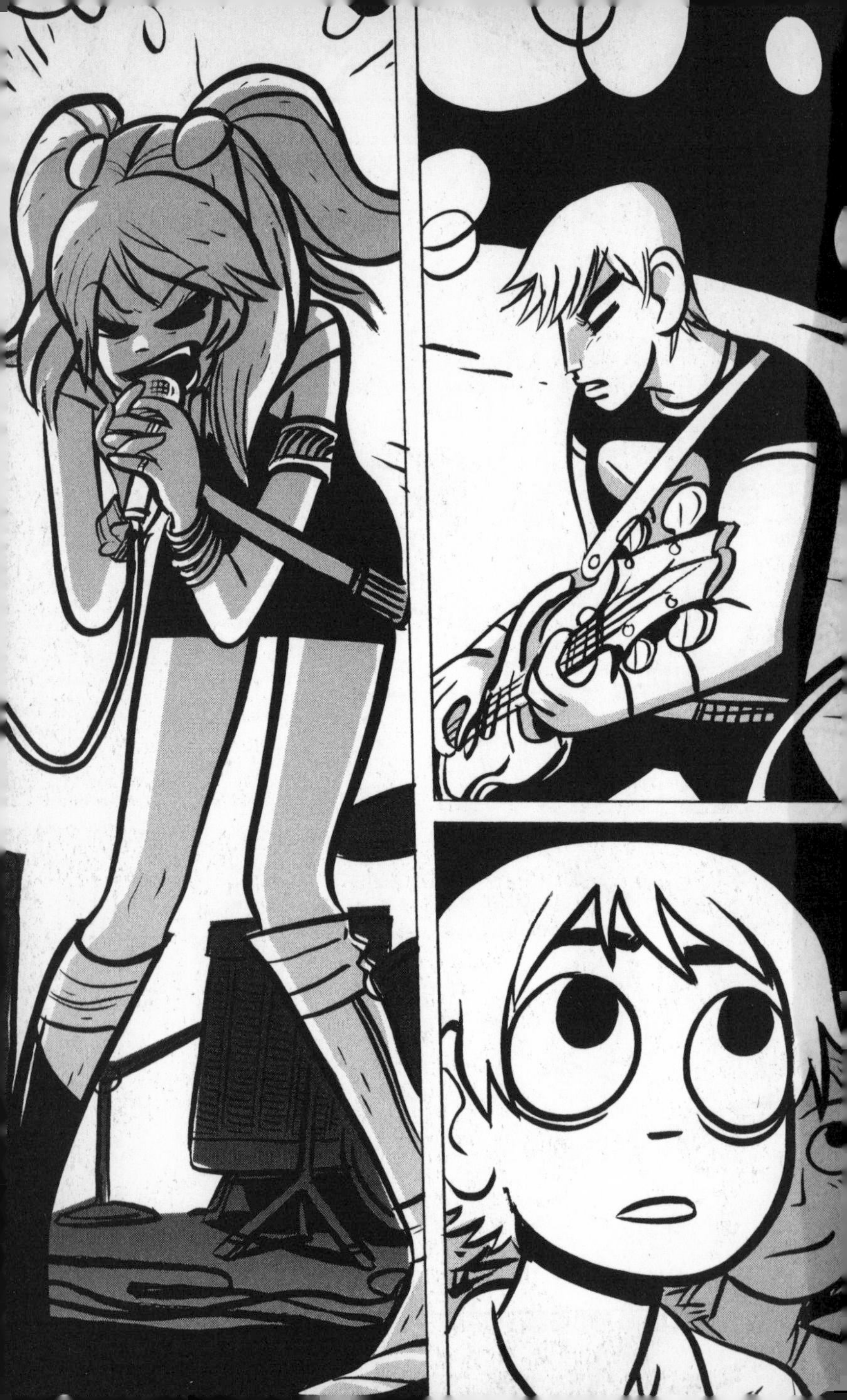

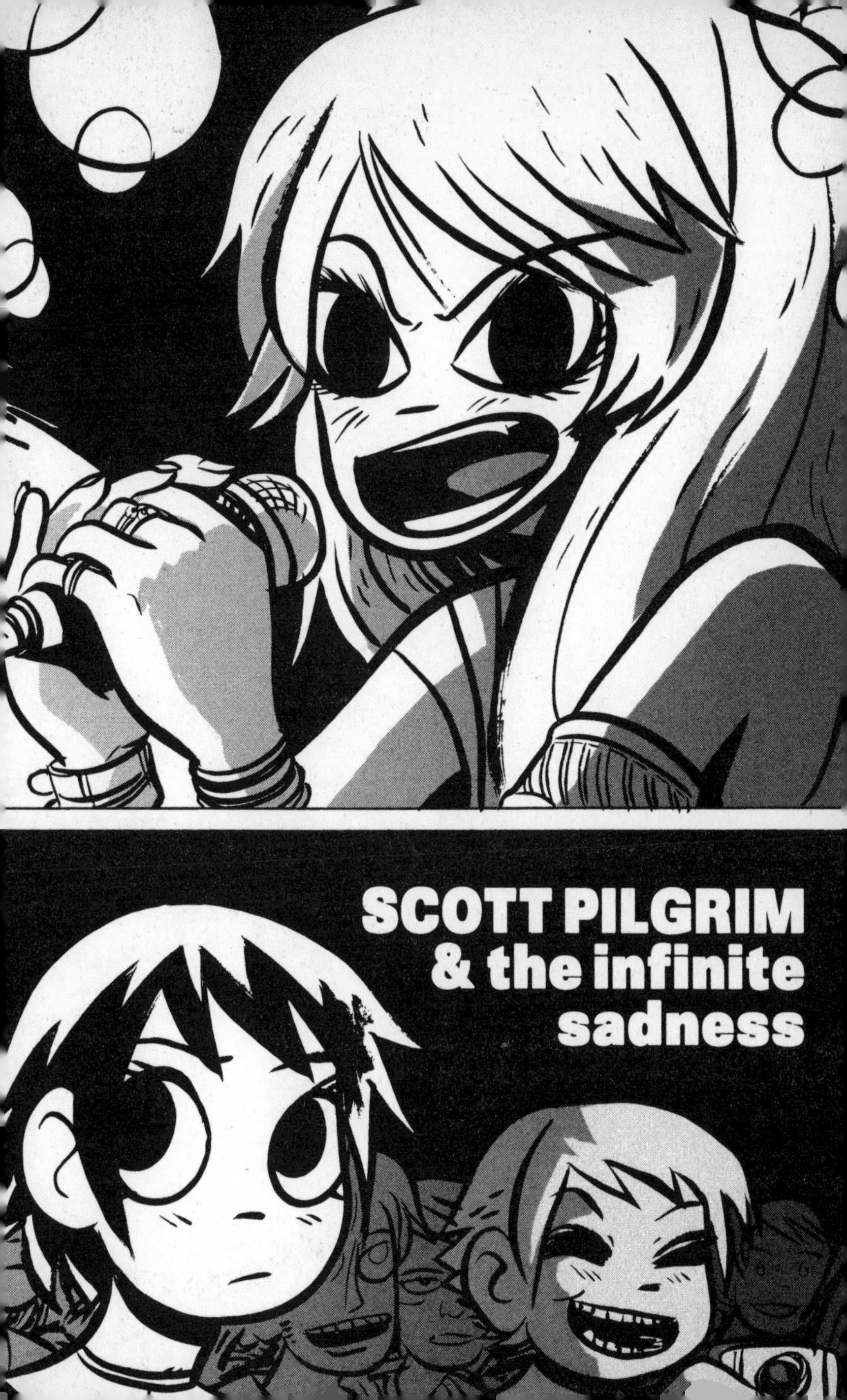
SCOTT PILGRIM
& the infinite
sadness

design by Bryan Lee O'Malley
production by Steven Birch @ Servo Graphics | edited by James Lucas Jones

Published by Oni Press, Inc.
Joe Nozemack, publisher | James Lucas Jones, editor in chief | Randal C. Jarrell, managing editor
Maryanne Snell, marketing & sales director | Douglas E. Sherwood, editorial intern

Scott Pilgrim, Scott Pilgrim & the Infinite Sadness is ™ & © 2006 Bryan Lee O'Malley. Unless otherwise specified, all
other material © 2006 Oni Press, Inc. Oni Press logo and icon are ™ & © 2006 Oni Press, Inc. All rights reserved. Oni
Press logo and icon artwork created by Dave Gibbons. The events, institutions, and characters presented in this book
are fictional. Any resemblance to actual persons or rock stars, living or dead, is purely coincidental. No portion of this
publication may be reproduced, by any means, without the express written permission of the copyright holders. We
should have called it Bryan Lee O'Malley & the Infinite Slowness.

ONI PRESS, INC.
1305 SE Martin Luther King Jr. Blvd.
Suite A
Portland, OR 97214
USA

www.onipress.com
www.scottpilgrim.com
www.radiomaru.com

First edition: May 2006
ISBN 978-1-932664-22-5

10 9 8
PRINTED IN CANADA.

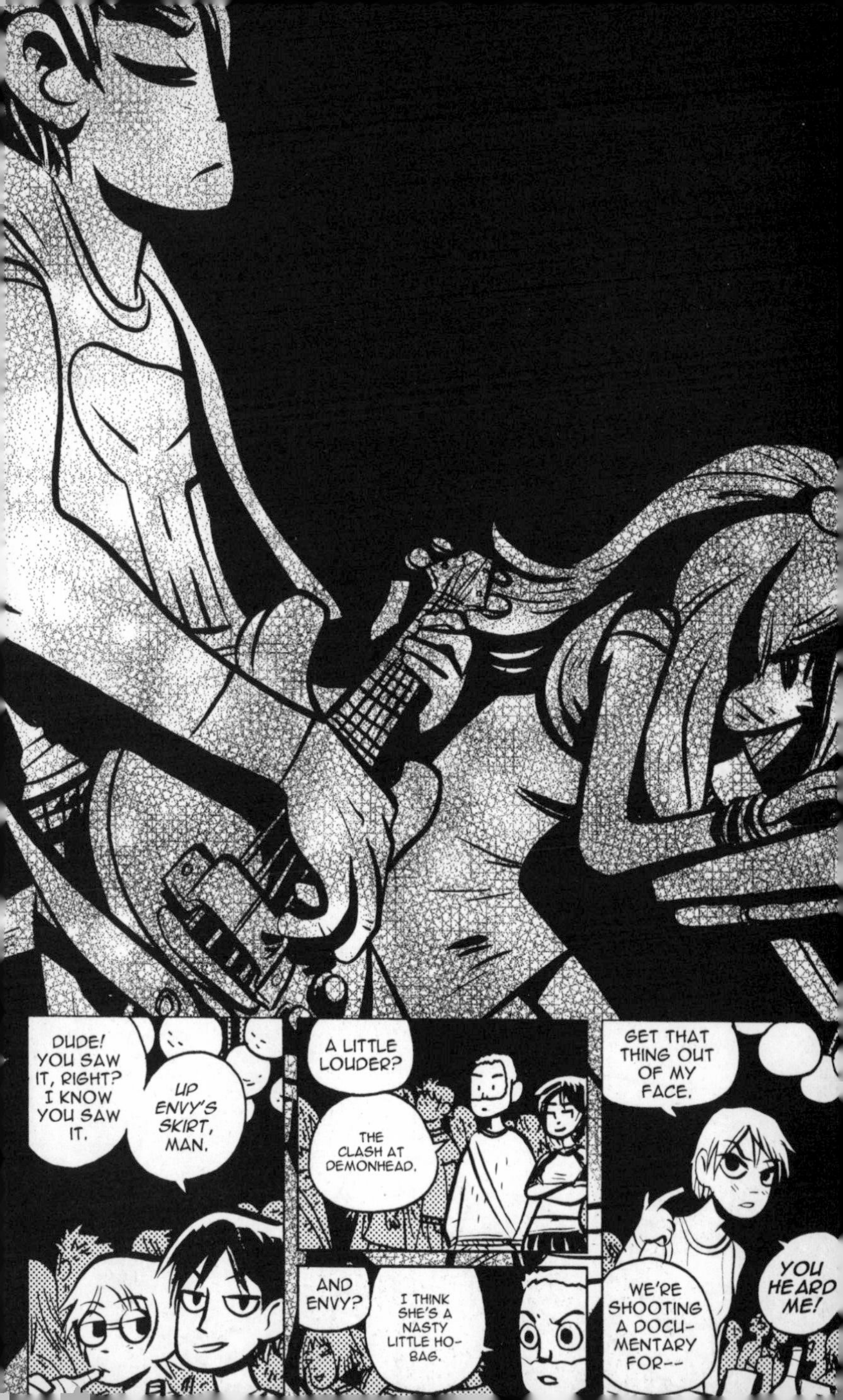
DUDE! YOU SAW IT, RIGHT? I KNOW YOU SAW IT.
UP ENVY'S SKIRT, MAN.
A LITTLE LOUDER?
THE CLASH AT DEMONHEAD.
AND ENVY?
I THINK SHE'S A NASTY LITTLE HO-BAG.
GET THAT THING OUT OF MY FACE.
WE'RE SHOOTING A DOCU-MENTARY FOR--
YOU HEARD ME!

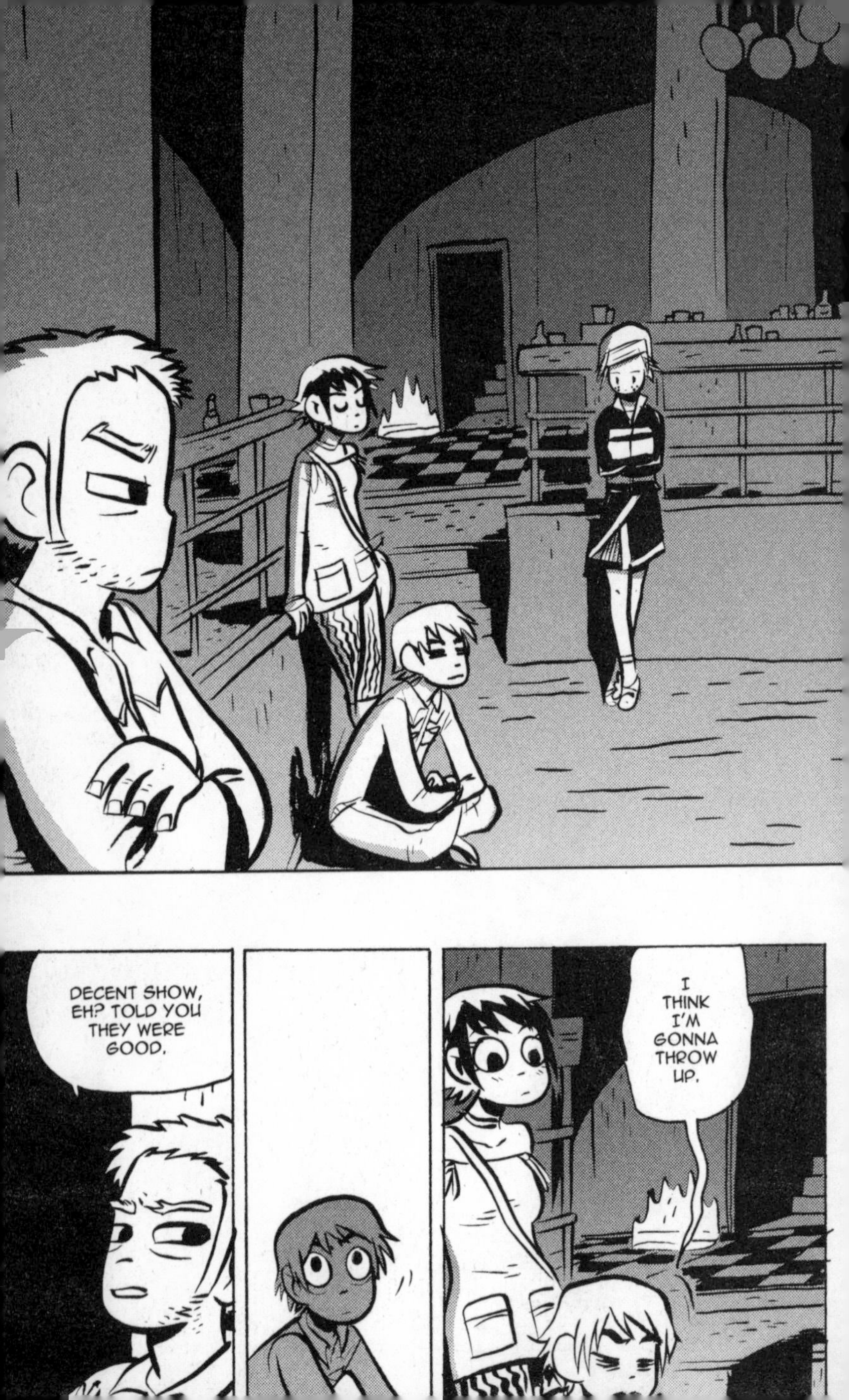
DECENT SHOW, EH? TOLD YOU THEY WERE GOOD.
I THINK I'M GONNA THROW UP.

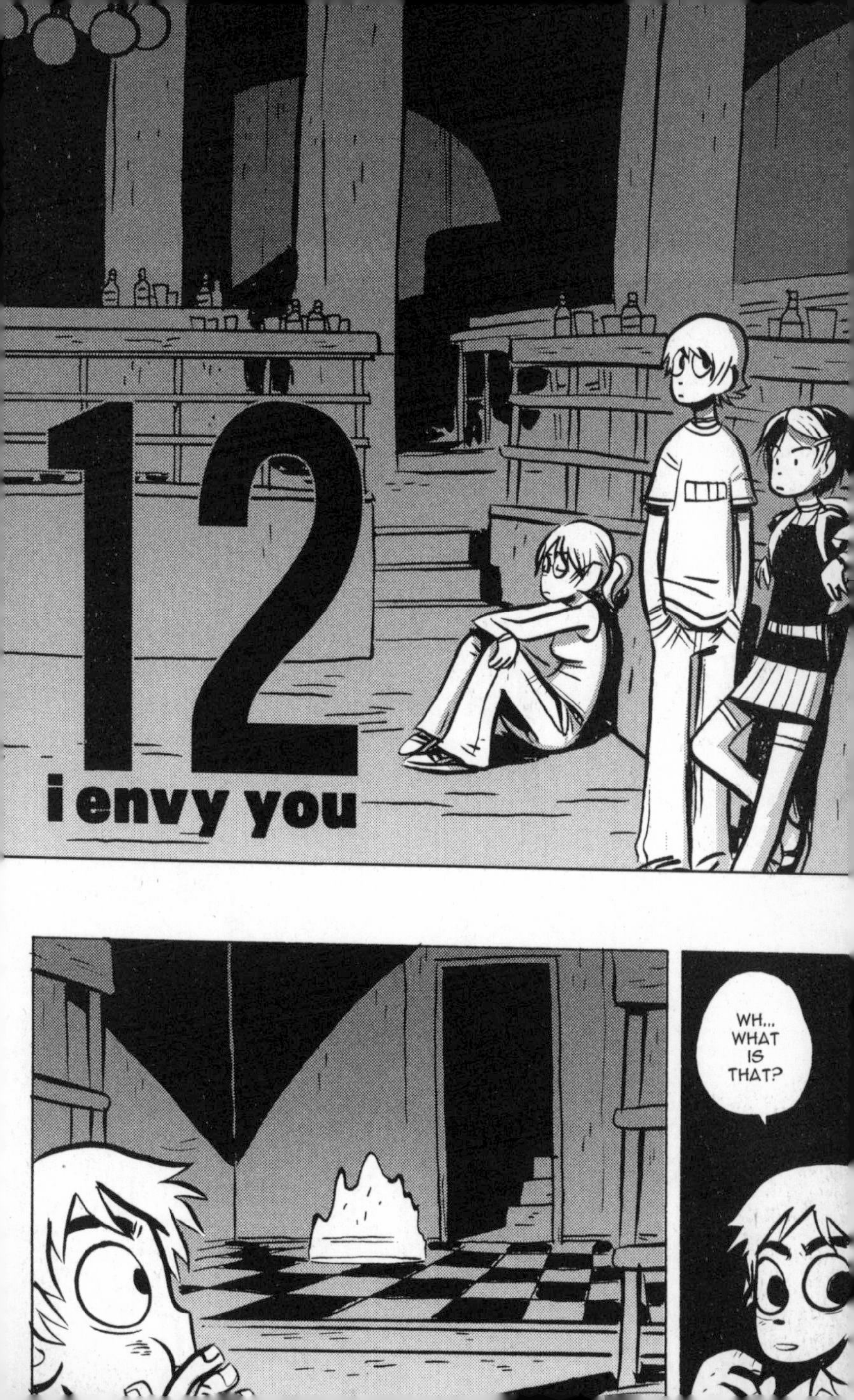
12
i envy you
WH... WHAT IS THAT?

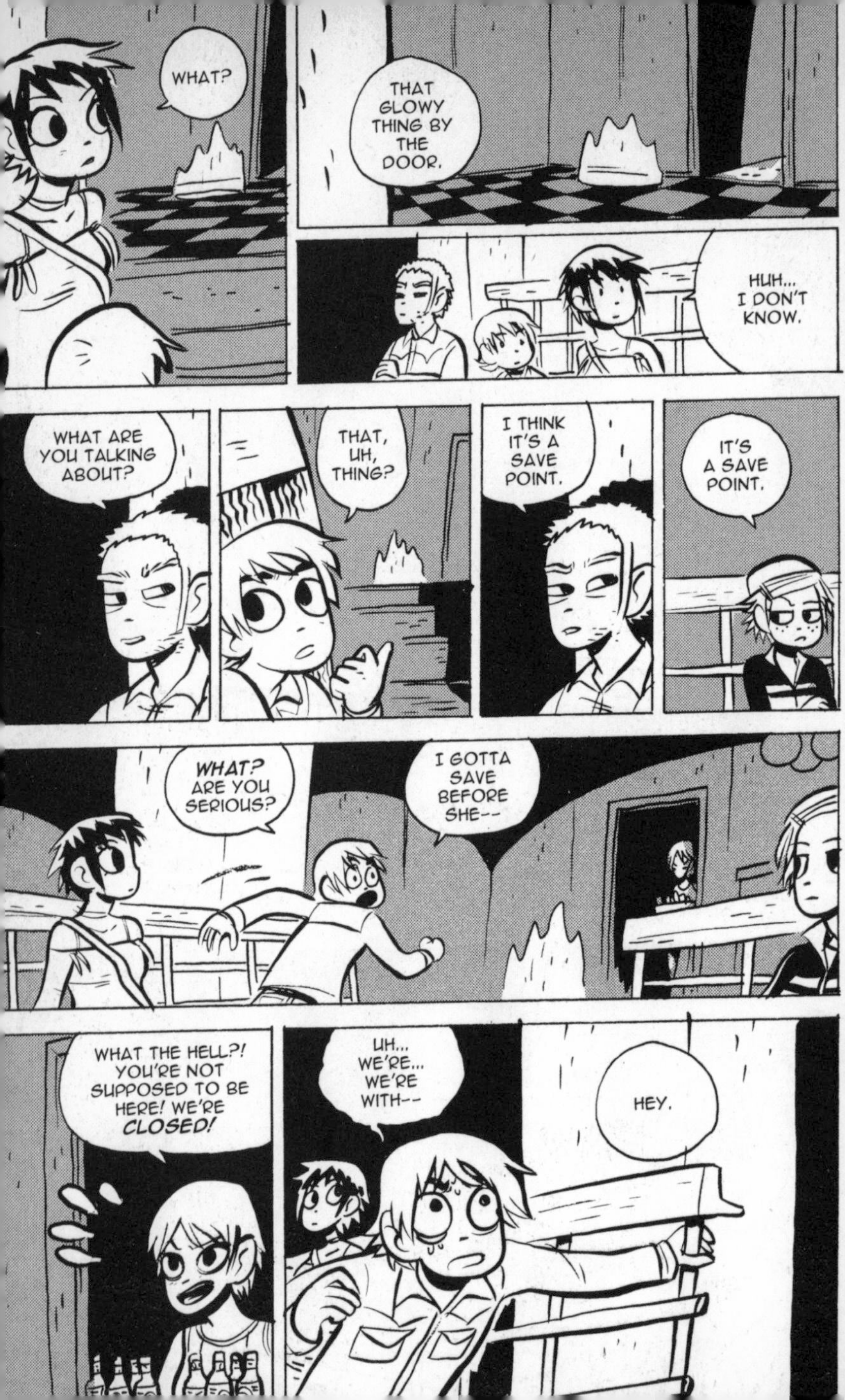
WHAT?
THAT GLOWY THING BY THE DOOR.
HUH... I DON'T KNOW.
WHAT ARE YOU TALKING ABOUT?
THAT, UH, THING?
I THINK IT'S A SAVE POINT.
IT'S A SAVE POINT.
WHAT? ARE YOU SERIOUS?
I GOTTA SAVE BEFORE SHE--
WHAT THE HELL?! YOU'RE NOT SUPPOSED TO BE HERE! WE'RE CLOSED!
UH... WE'RE... WE'RE WITH--
HEY.

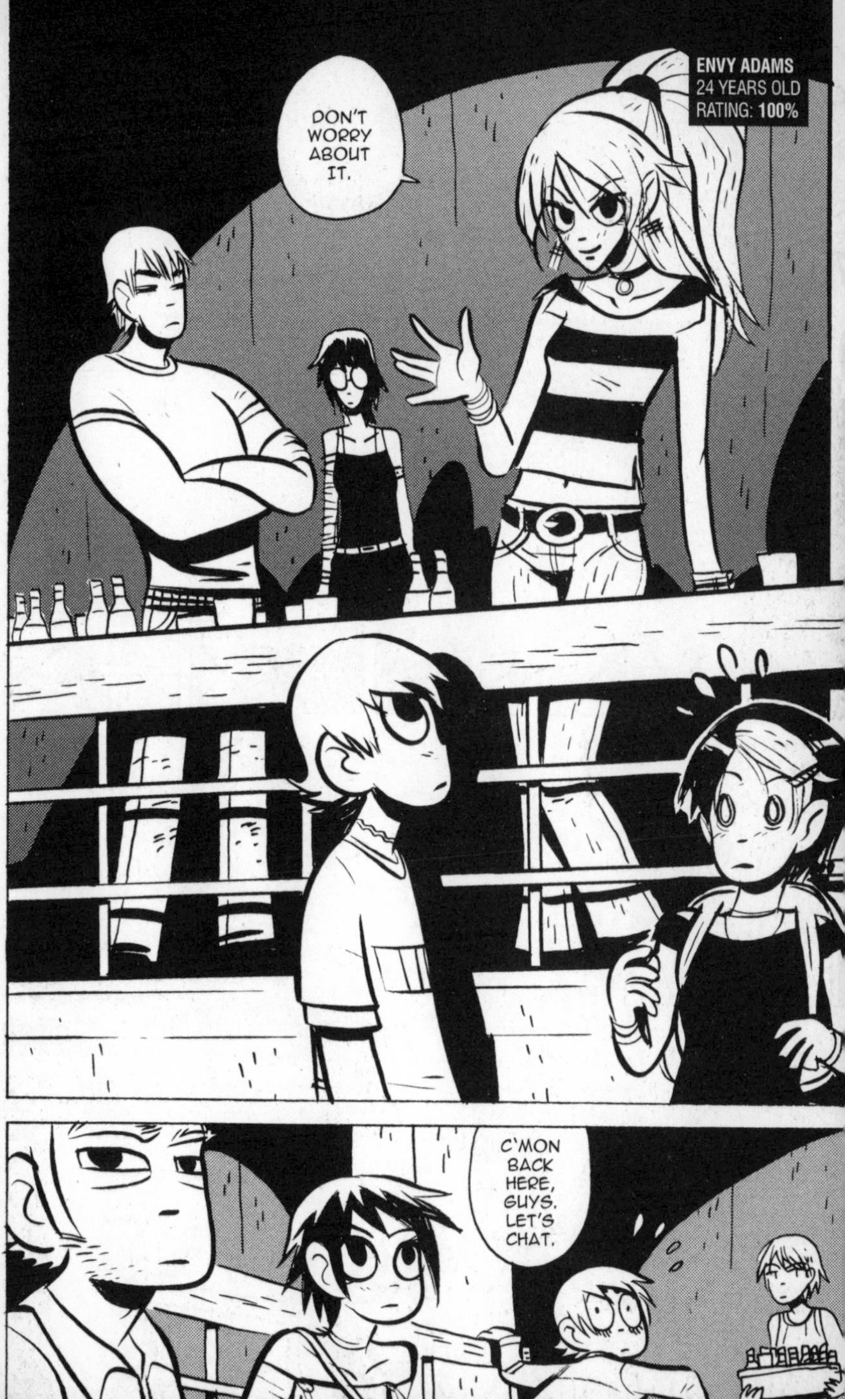
ENVY ADAMS
24 YEARS OLD
RATING: 100%
DON'T WORRY ABOUT IT.
C'MON BACK HERE, GUYS. LET'S CHAT.

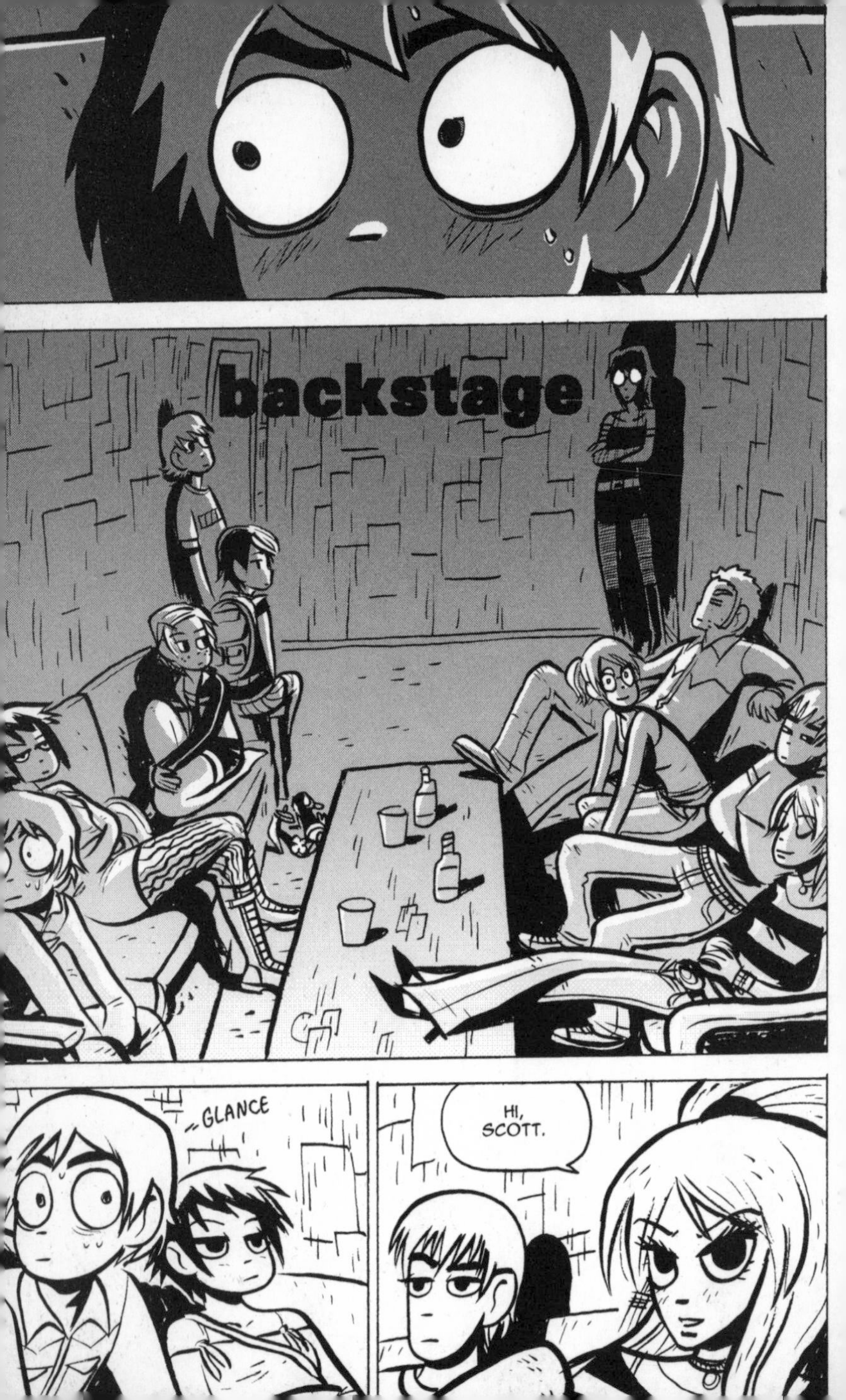
backstage
GLANCE
HI, SCOTT.

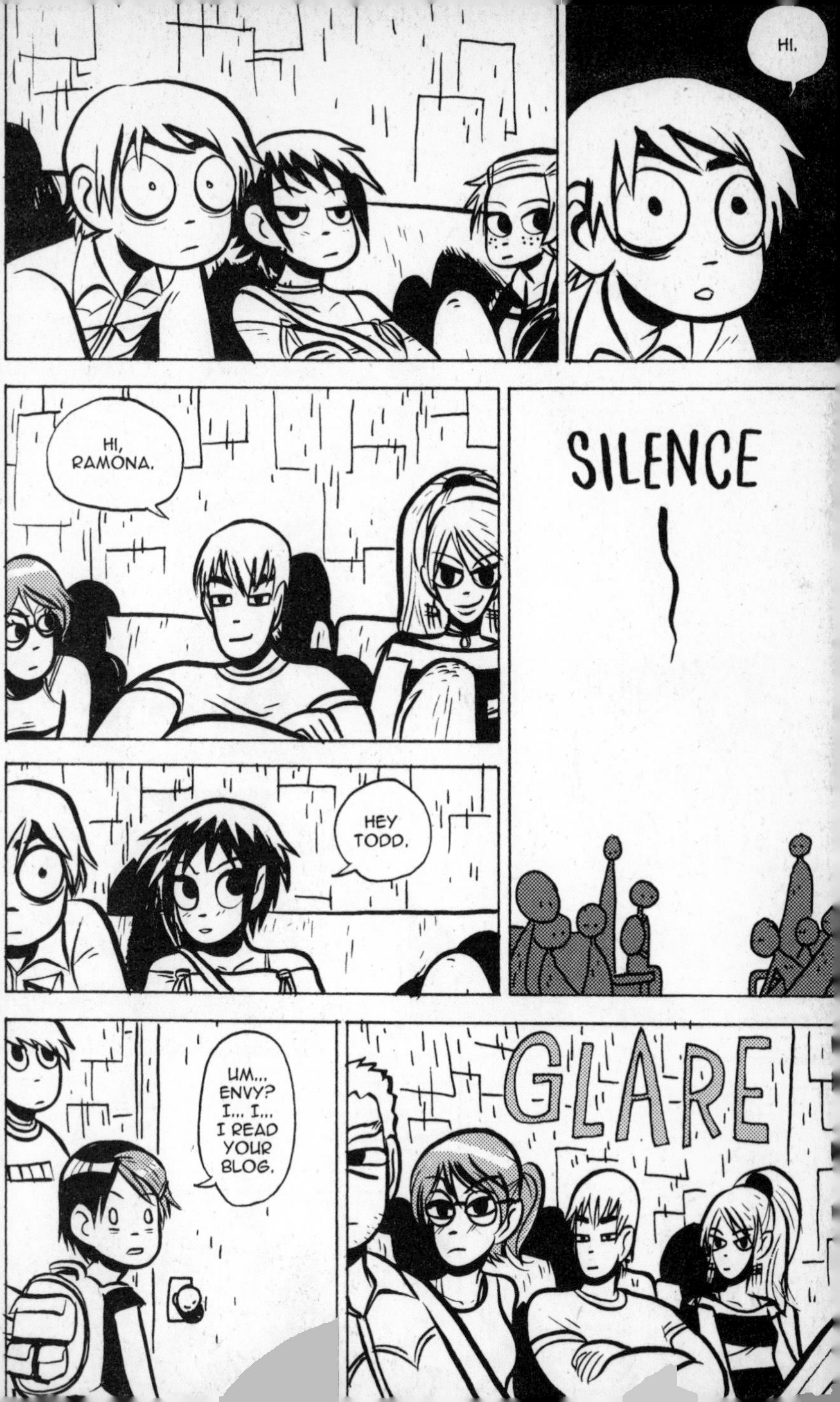
HI.
HI, RAMONA.
SILENCE
HEY TODD.
UM... ENVY? I... I... I READ YOUR BLOG.
GLARE

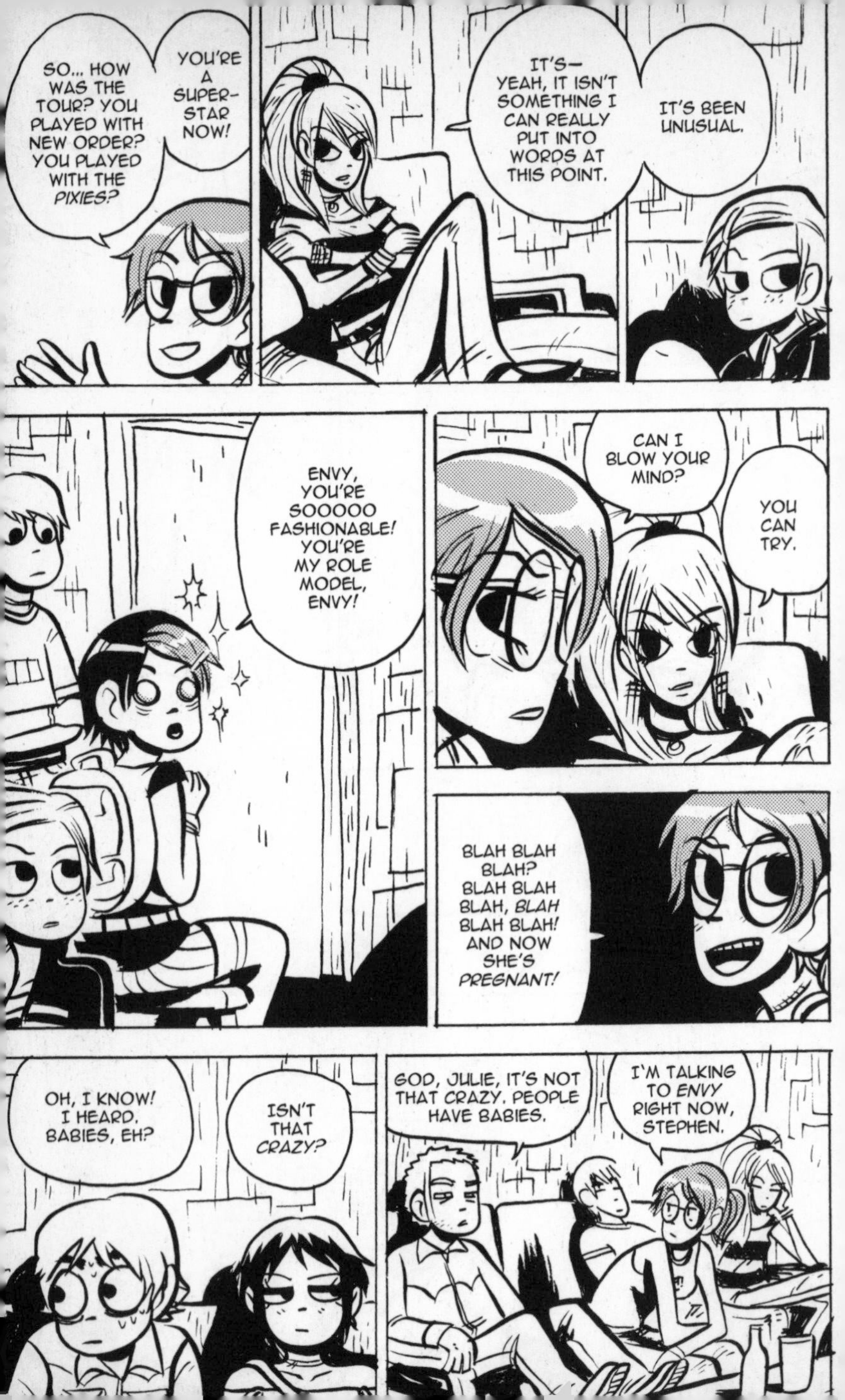
SO... HOW WAS THE TOUR? YOU PLAYED WITH NEW ORDER? YOU PLAYED WITH THE *PIXIES?*
YOU'RE A SUPER-STAR NOW!
IT'S— YEAH, IT ISN'T SOMETHING I CAN REALLY PUT INTO WORDS AT THIS POINT.
IT'S BEEN UNUSUAL.
ENVY, YOU'RE SOOOOO FASHIONABLE! YOU'RE MY ROLE MODEL, ENVY!
CAN I BLOW YOUR MIND?
YOU CAN TRY.
BLAH BLAH BLAH? BLAH BLAH BLAH, *BLAH* BLAH BLAH! AND NOW SHE'S *PREGNANT!*
OH, I KNOW! I HEARD. BABIES, EH?
ISN'T THAT *CRAZY?*
GOD, JULIE, IT'S NOT THAT CRAZY. PEOPLE HAVE BABIES.
I'M TALKING TO *ENVY* RIGHT NOW, STEPHEN.

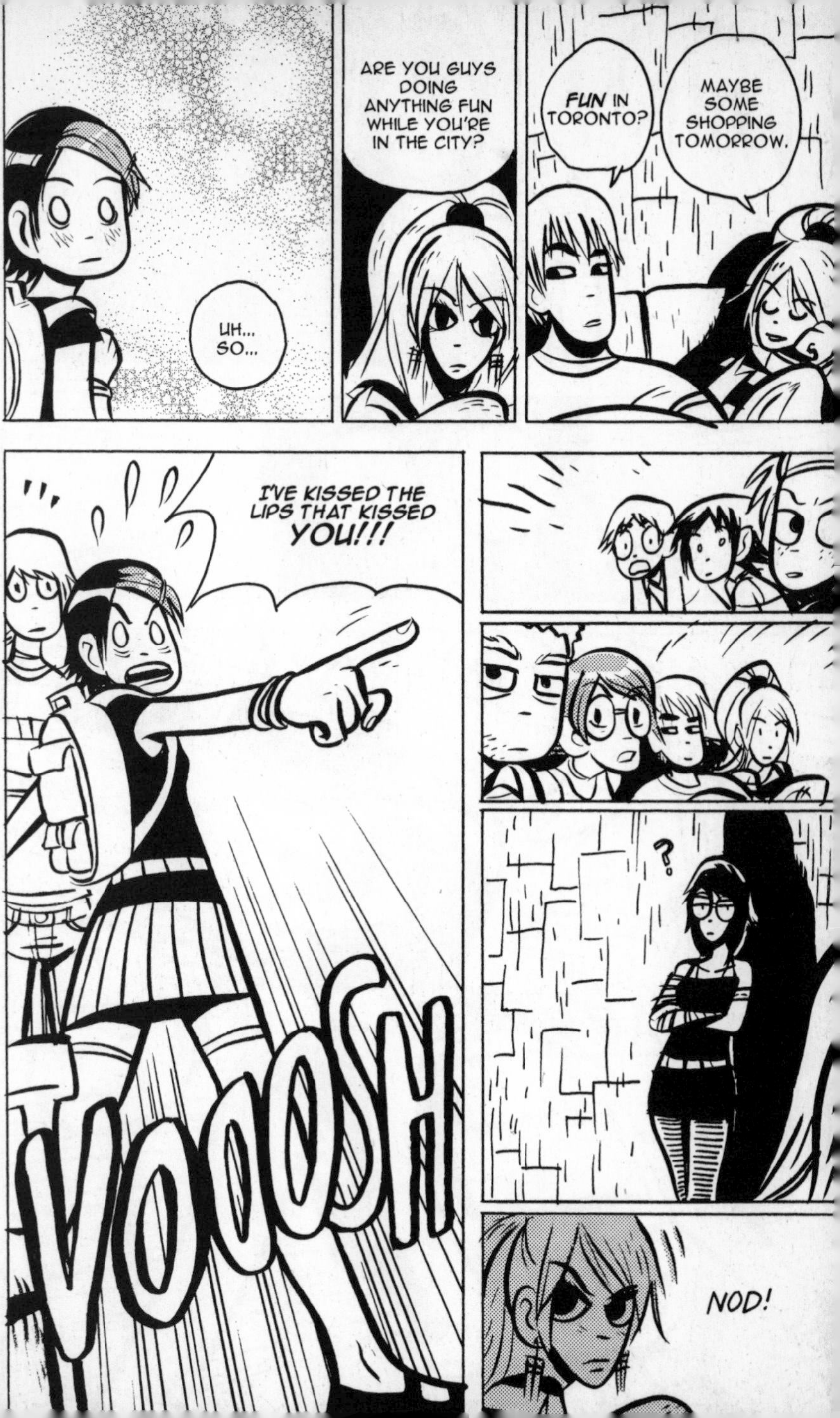
UH... SO...
ARE YOU GUYS DOING ANYTHING FUN WHILE YOU'RE IN THE CITY?
FUN IN TORONTO?
MAYBE SOME SHOPPING TOMORROW.
I'VE KISSED THE LIPS THAT KISSED YOU!!!
VOOOSH
?
NOD!

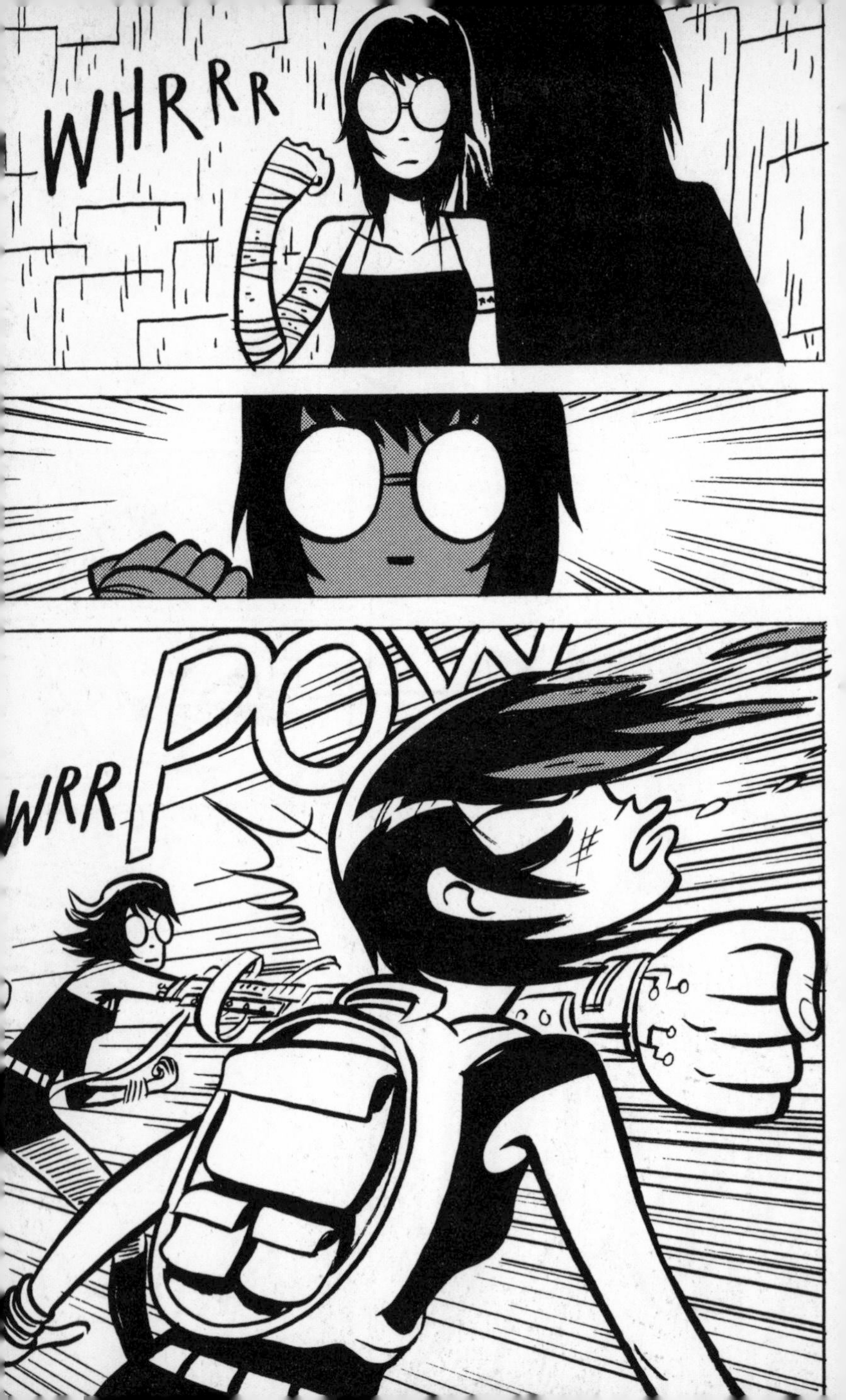
WHRRR
WRR
POW

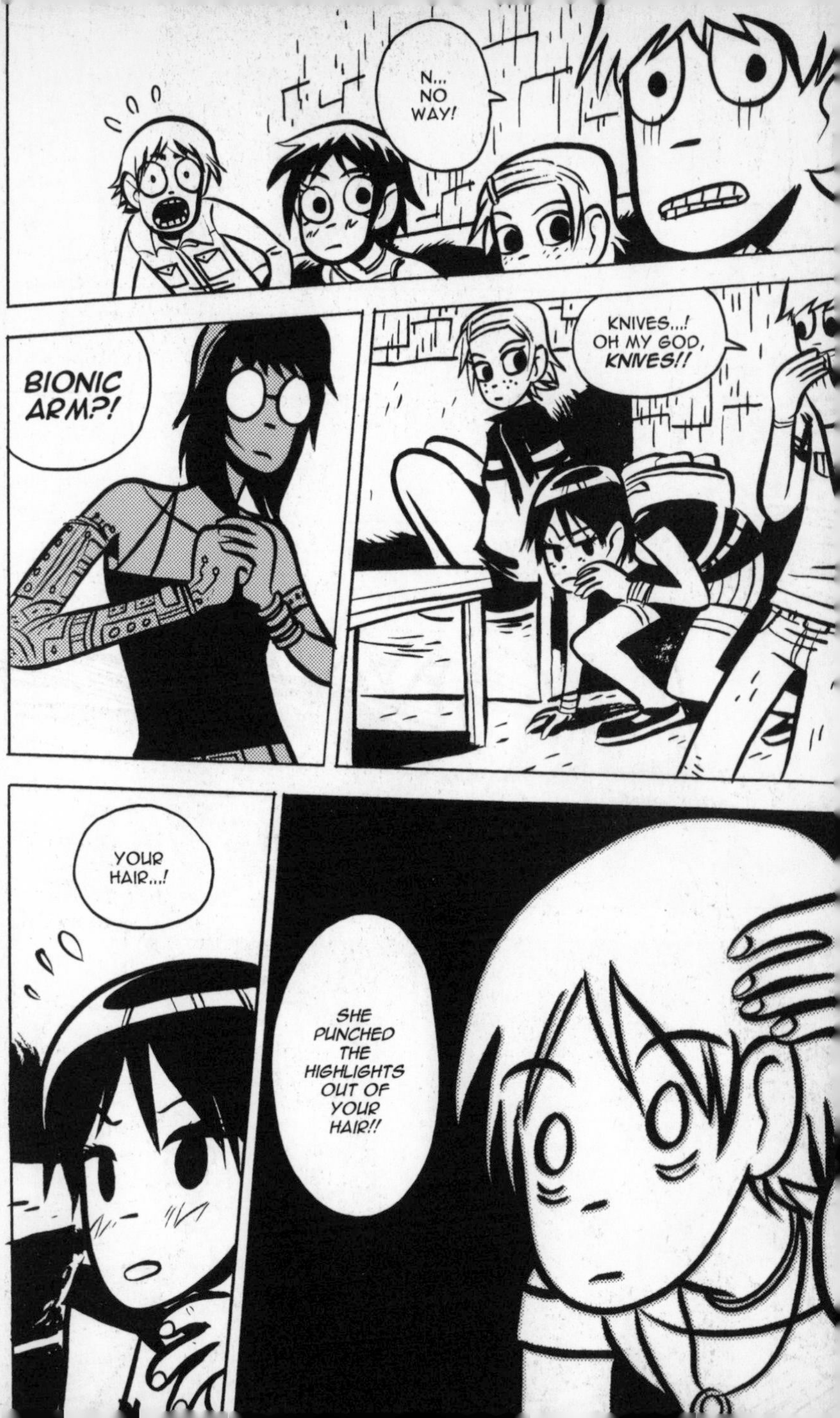
N... NO WAY!
BIONIC ARM?!
KNIVES...! OH MY GOD, KNIVES!!
YOUR HAIR...!
SHE PUNCHED THE HIGHLIGHTS OUT OF YOUR HAIR!!

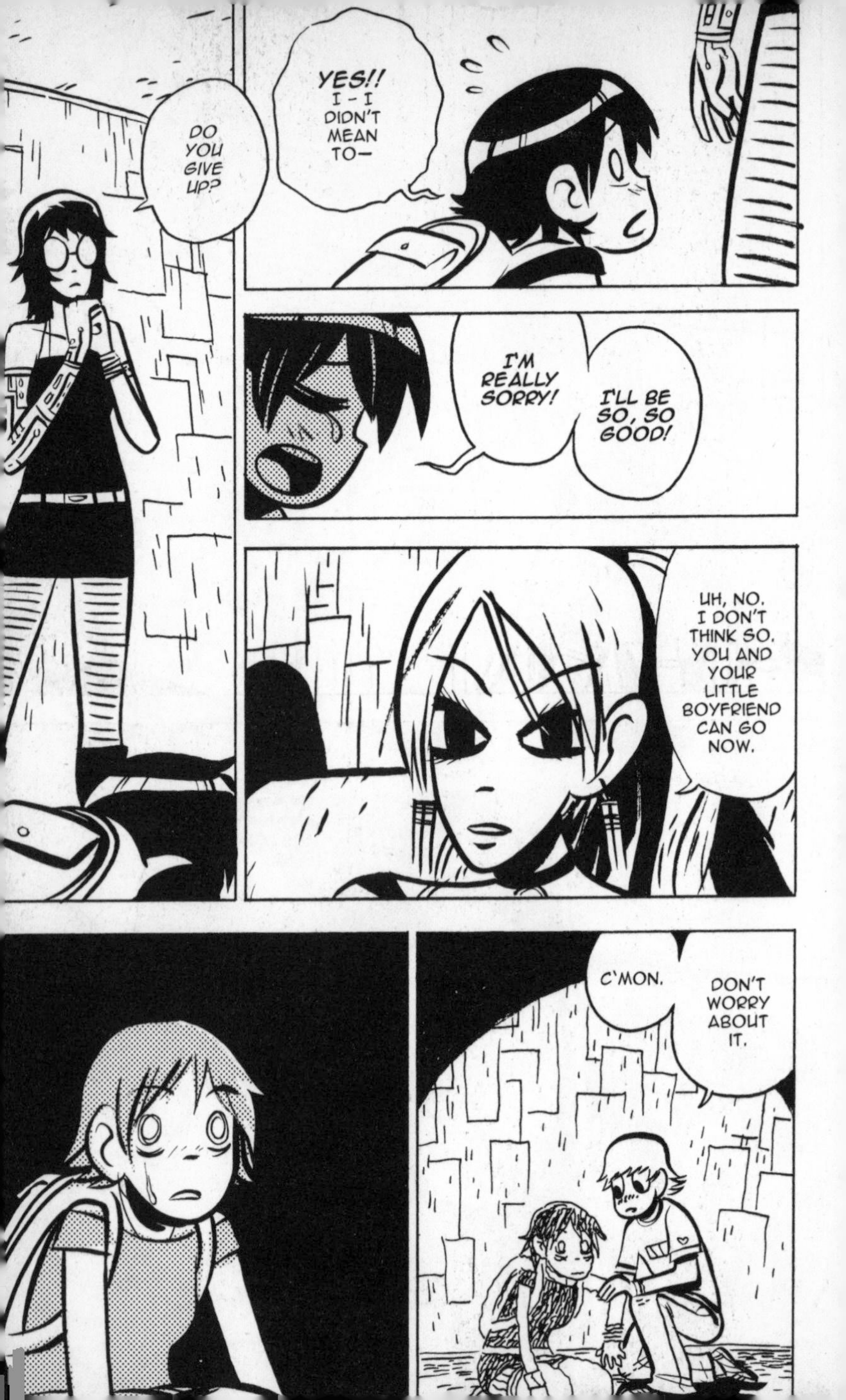
DO YOU GIVE UP?
YES!! I - I DIDN'T MEAN TO—
I'M REALLY SORRY!
I'LL BE SO, SO GOOD!
UH, NO. I DON'T THINK SO. YOU AND YOUR LITTLE BOYFRIEND CAN GO NOW.
C'MON.
DON'T WORRY ABOUT IT.

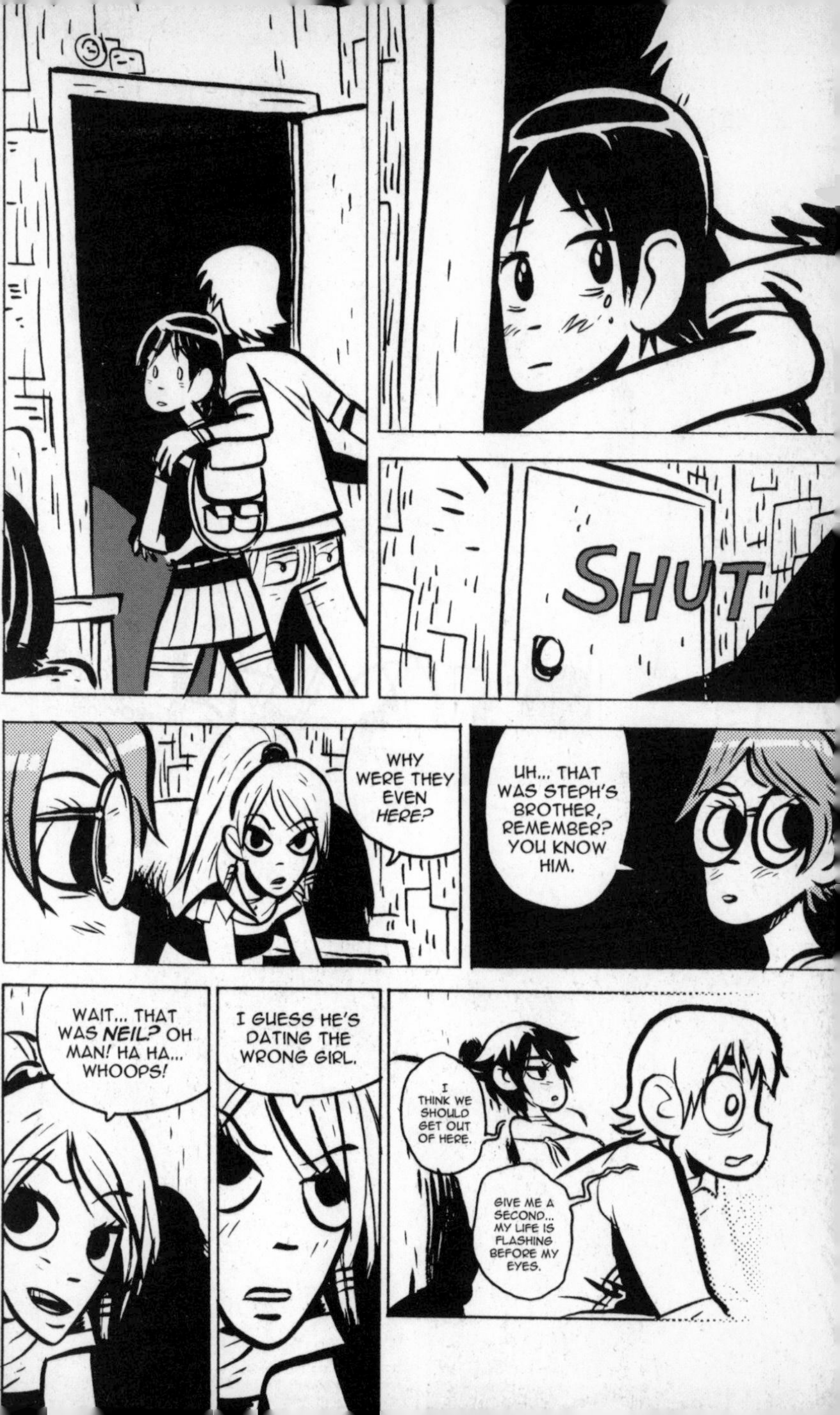
SHUT
WHY WERE THEY EVEN *HERE?*
UH... THAT WAS STEPH'S BROTHER, REMEMBER? YOU KNOW HIM.
WAIT... THAT WAS ***NEIL?*** OH MAN! HA HA... WHOOPS!
I GUESS HE'S DATING THE WRONG GIRL.
I THINK WE SHOULD GET OUT OF HERE.
GIVE ME A SECOND... MY LIFE IS FLASHING BEFORE MY EYES.

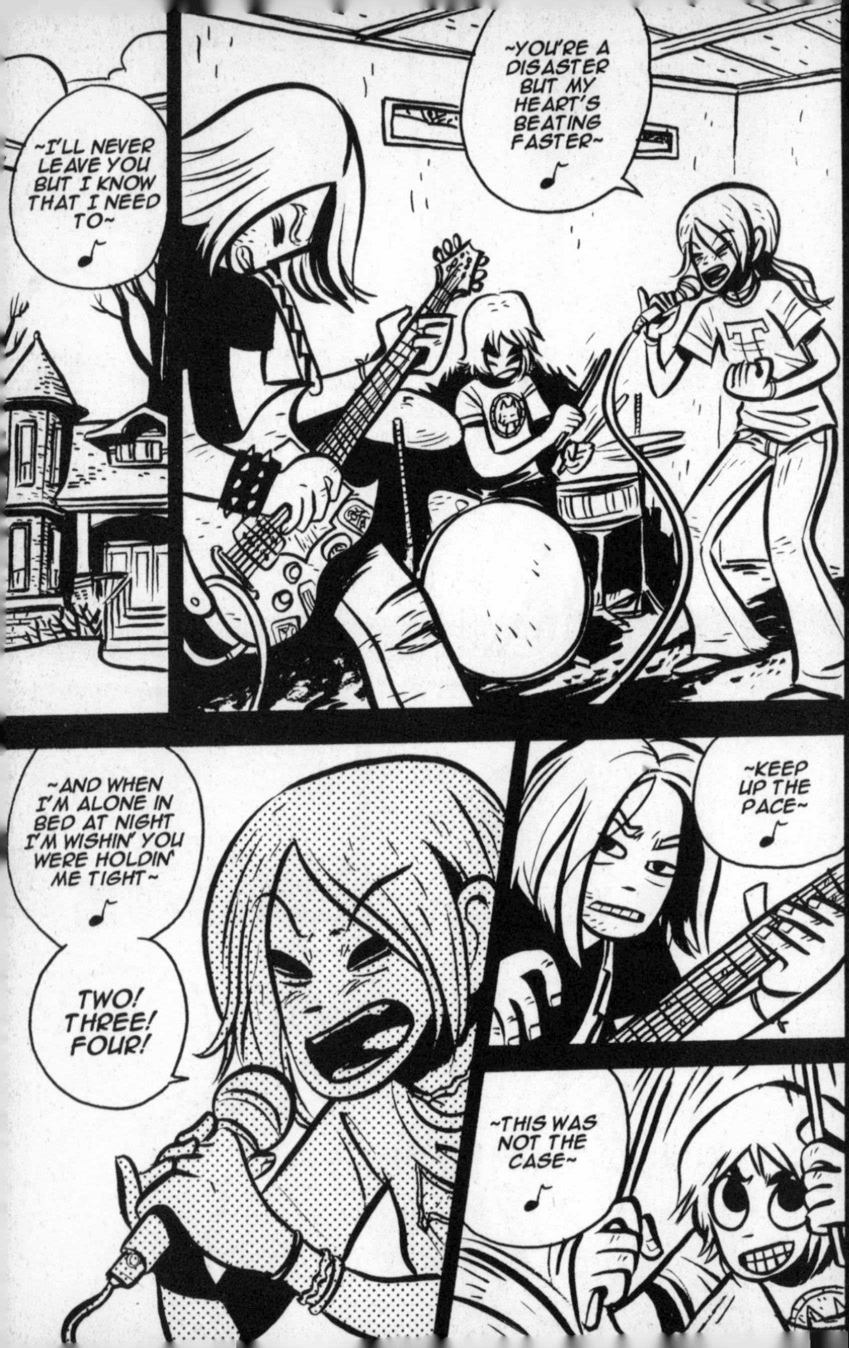
~I'LL NEVER LEAVE YOU BUT I KNOW THAT I NEED TO~
~YOU'RE A DISASTER BUT MY HEART'S BEATING FASTER~
~AND WHEN I'M ALONE IN BED AT NIGHT I'M WISHIN' YOU WERE HOLDIN' ME TIGHT~
TWO! THREE! FOUR!
~KEEP UP THE PACE~
~THIS WAS NOT THE CASE~

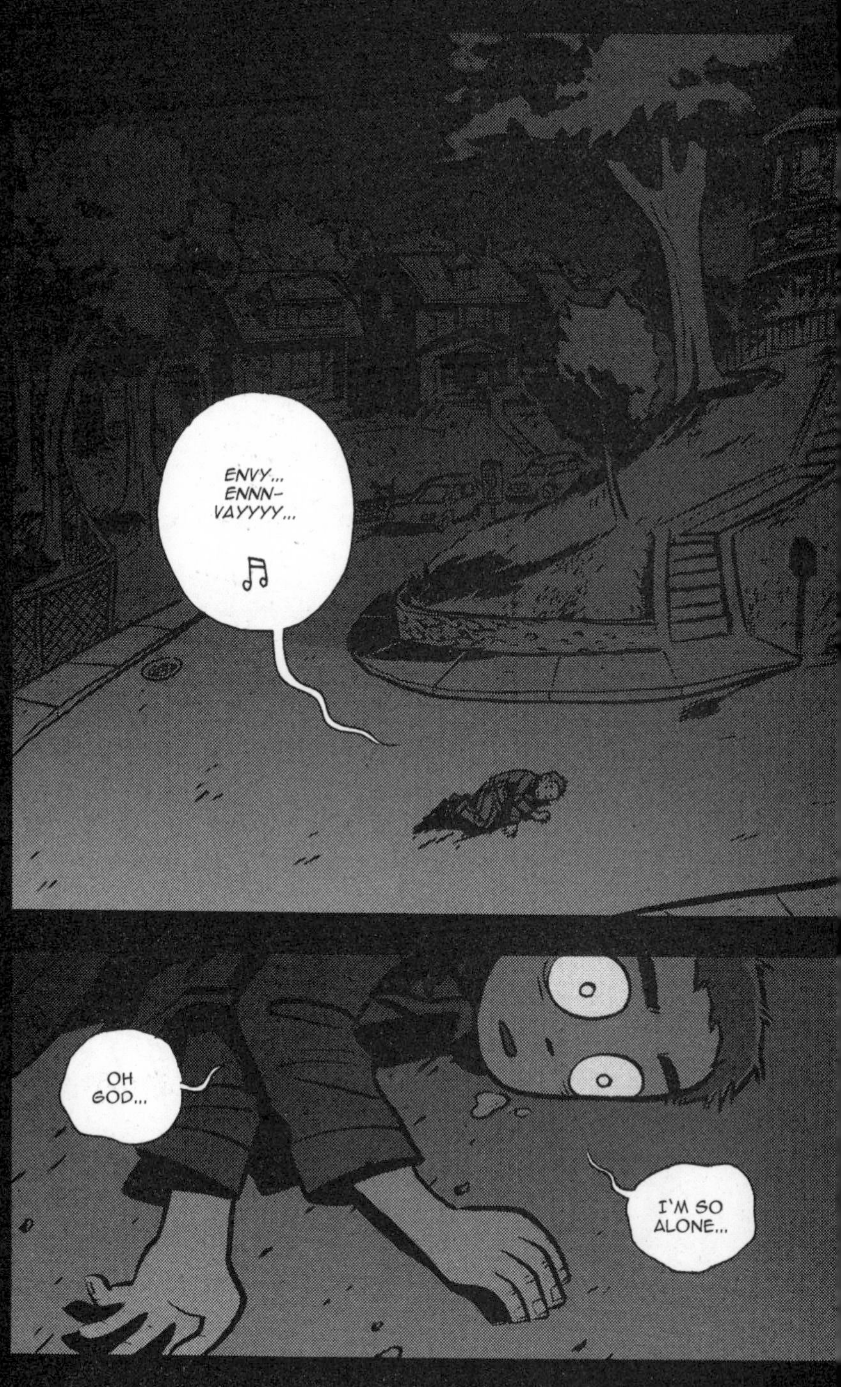
ENVY... ENNN-VAYYYY...
OH GOD...
I'M SO ALONE...

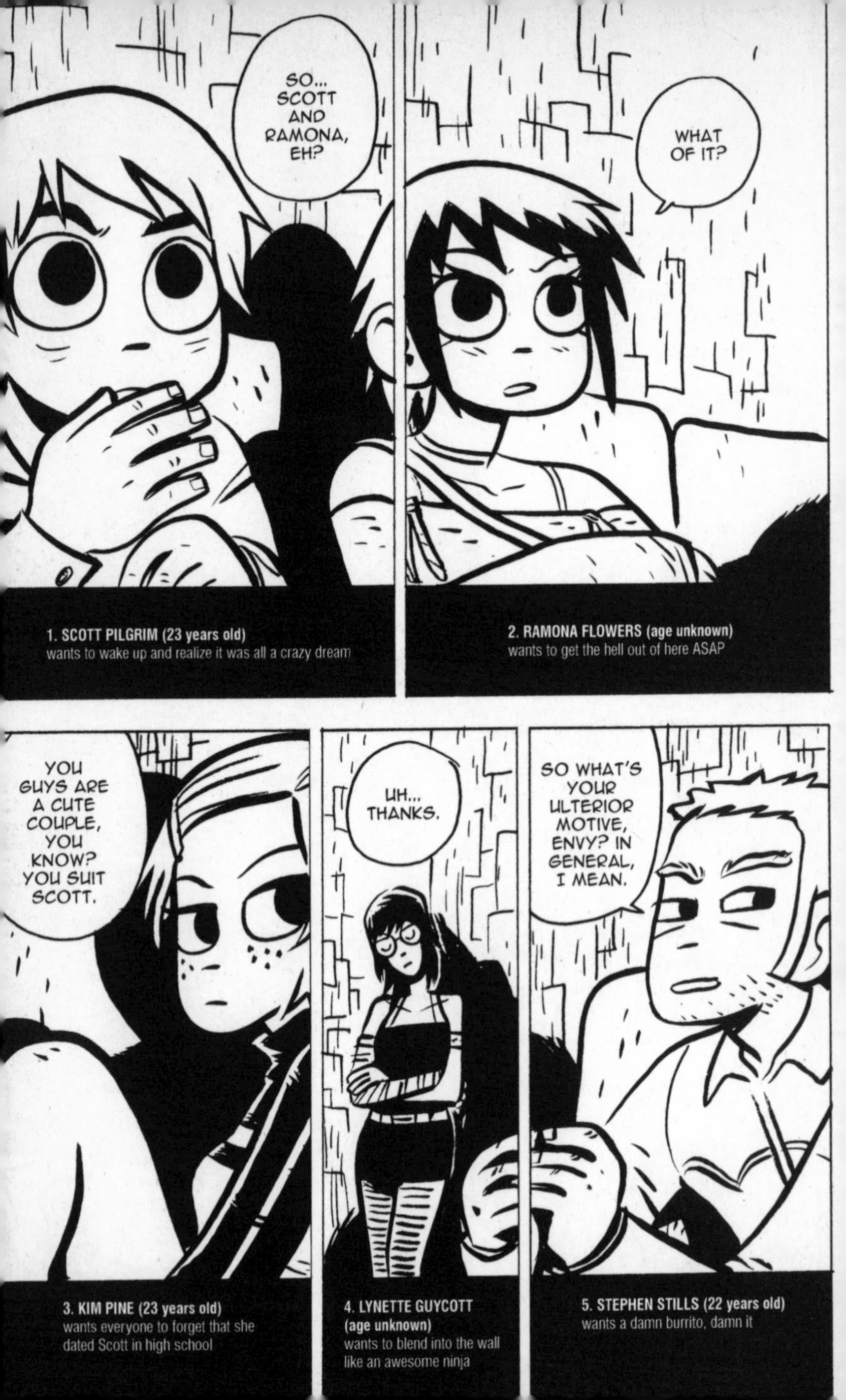
SO... SCOTT AND RAMONA, EH?
1. SCOTT PILGRIM (23 years old)
wants to wake up and realize it was all a crazy dream
WHAT OF IT?
2. RAMONA FLOWERS (age unknown)
wants to get the hell out of here ASAP
YOU GUYS ARE A CUTE COUPLE, YOU KNOW? YOU SUIT SCOTT.
3. KIM PINE (23 years old)
wants everyone to forget that she dated Scott in high school
UH... THANKS.
4. LYNETTE GUYCOTT (age unknown)
wants to blend into the wall like an awesome ninja
SO WHAT'S YOUR ULTERIOR MOTIVE, ENVY? IN GENERAL, I MEAN.
5. STEPHEN STILLS (22 years old)
wants a damn burrito, damn it

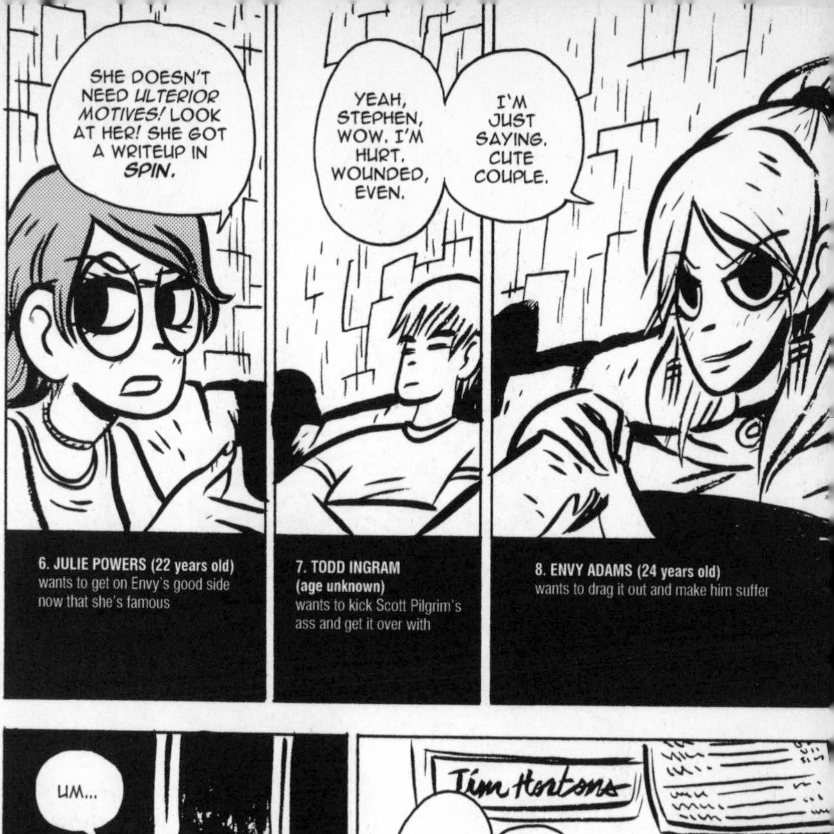
SHE DOESN'T NEED ULTERIOR MOTIVES! LOOK AT HER! SHE GOT A WRITEUP IN SPIN.
6. JULIE POWERS (22 years old) wants to get on Envy's good side now that she's famous
YEAH, STEPHEN, WOW. I'M HURT. WOUNDED, EVEN.
7. TODD INGRAM (age unknown) wants to kick Scott Pilgrim's ass and get it over with
I'M JUST SAYING. CUTE COUPLE.
8. ENVY ADAMS (24 years old) wants to drag it out and make him suffer
UM...
Tim Hortons
JUST... DON'T.
DON'T EVEN TALK TO ME.

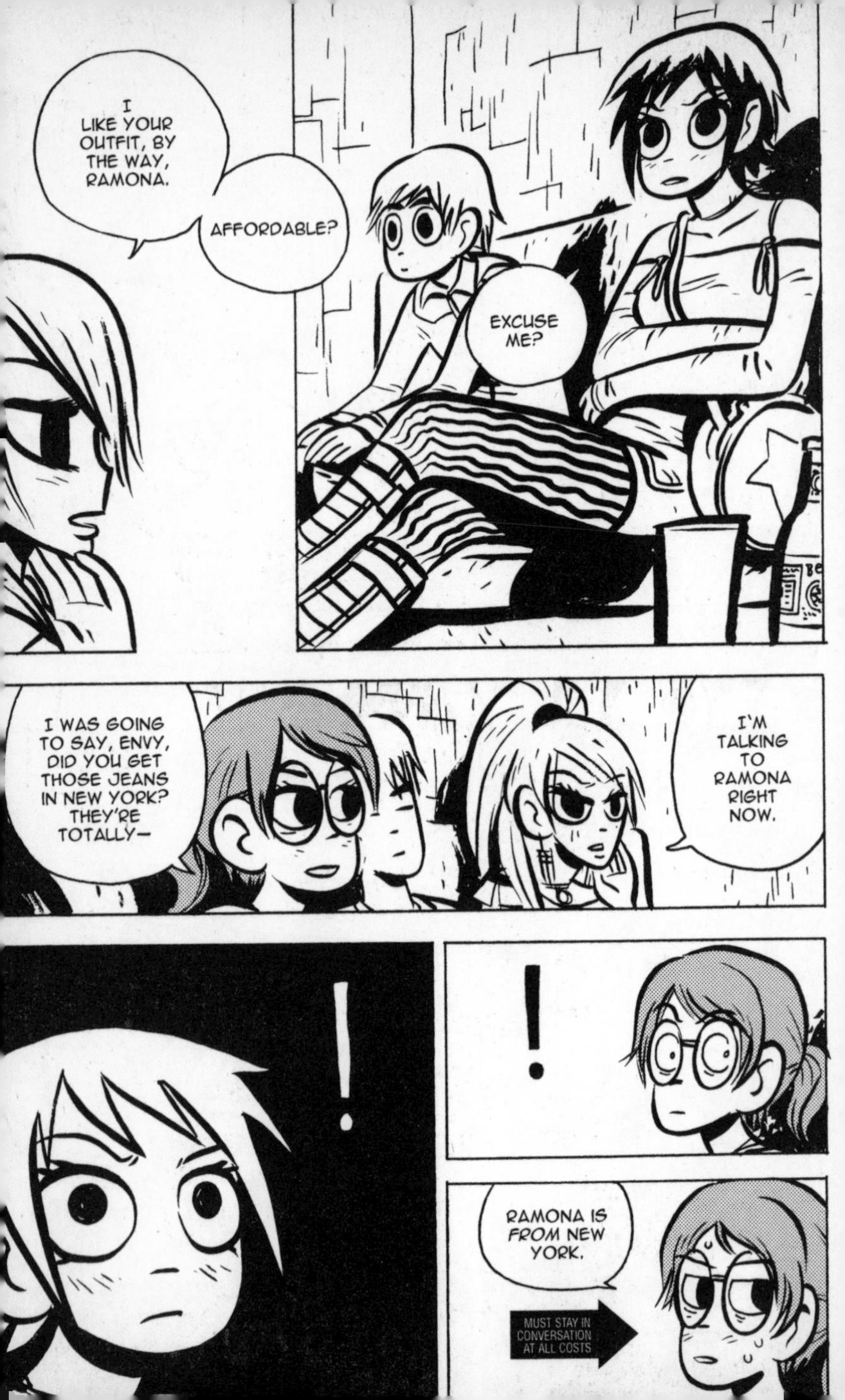
I LIKE YOUR OUTFIT, BY THE WAY, RAMONA.
AFFORDABLE?
EXCUSE ME?
I WAS GOING TO SAY, ENVY, DID YOU GET THOSE JEANS IN NEW YORK? THEY'RE TOTALLY—
I'M TALKING TO RAMONA RIGHT NOW.
!
!
RAMONA IS *FROM* NEW YORK.
MUST STAY IN CONVERSATION AT ALL COSTS

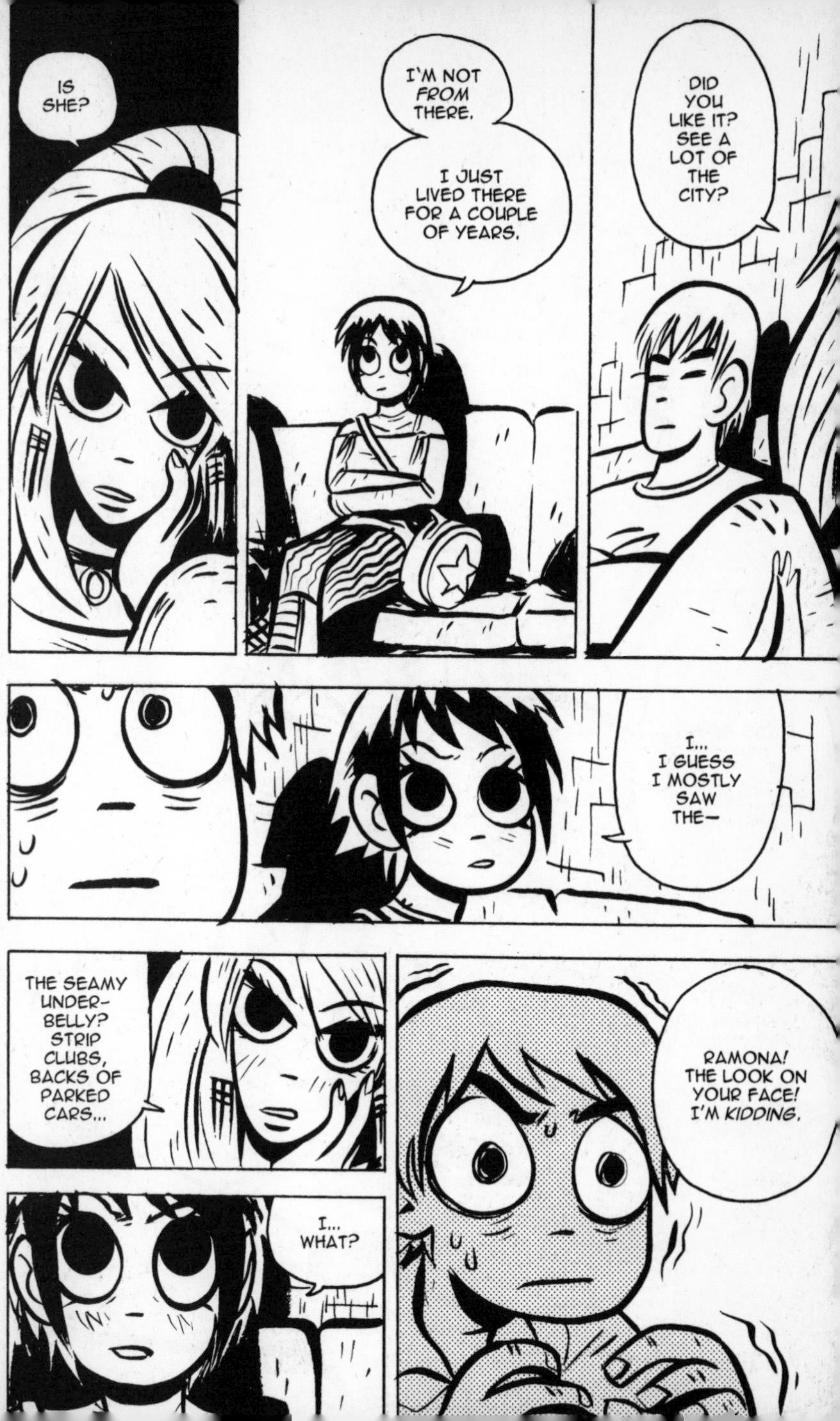
IS SHE?
I'M NOT *FROM* THERE.
I JUST LIVED THERE FOR A COUPLE OF YEARS.
DID YOU LIKE IT? SEE A LOT OF THE CITY?
I... I GUESS I MOSTLY SAW THE—
THE SEAMY UNDER-BELLY? STRIP CLUBS, BACKS OF PARKED CARS...
I... WHAT?
RAMONA! THE LOOK ON YOUR FACE! I'M *KIDDING*.

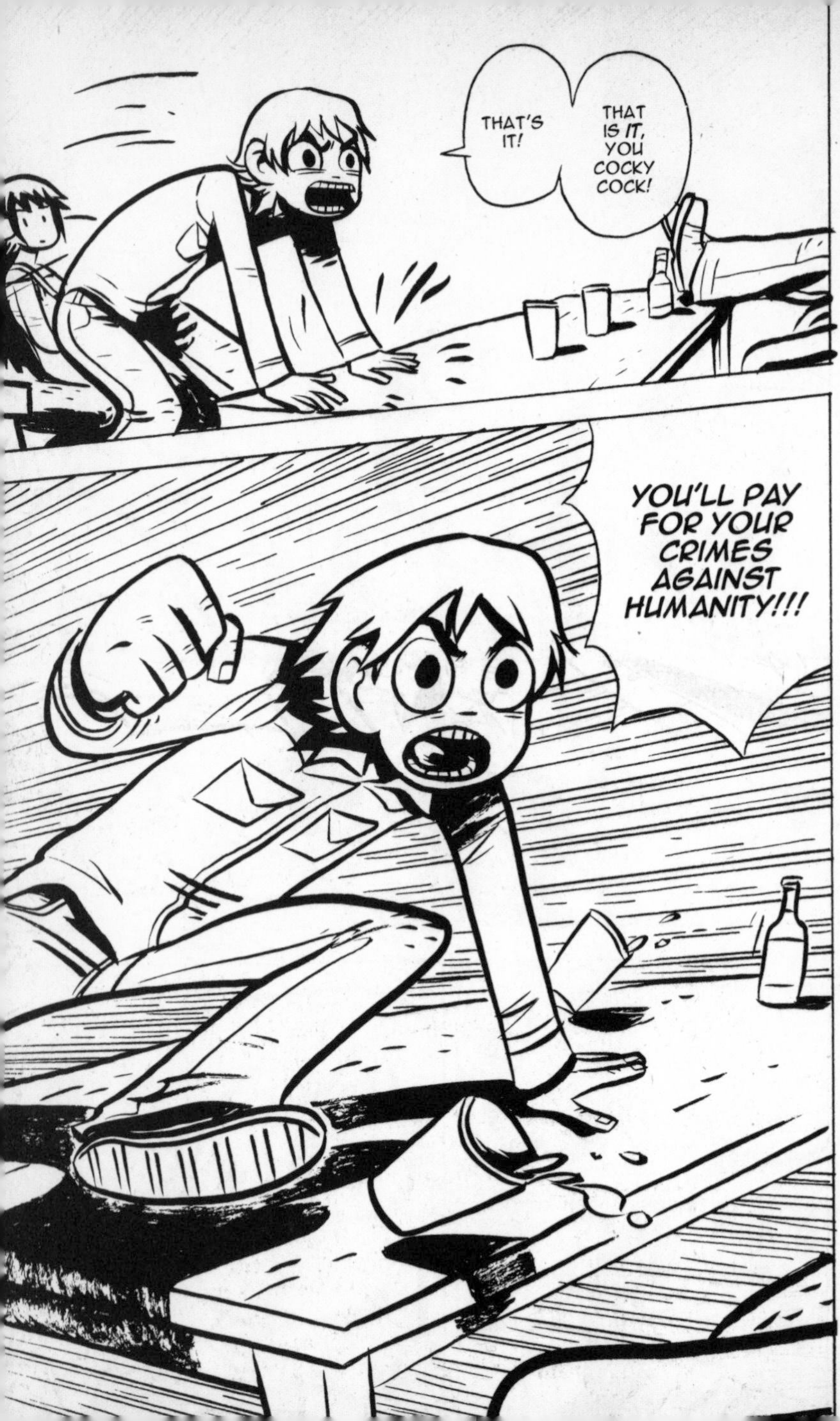
THAT'S IT!
THAT IS *IT*, YOU COCKY COCK!
YOU'LL PAY FOR YOUR CRIMES AGAINST HUMANITY!!!

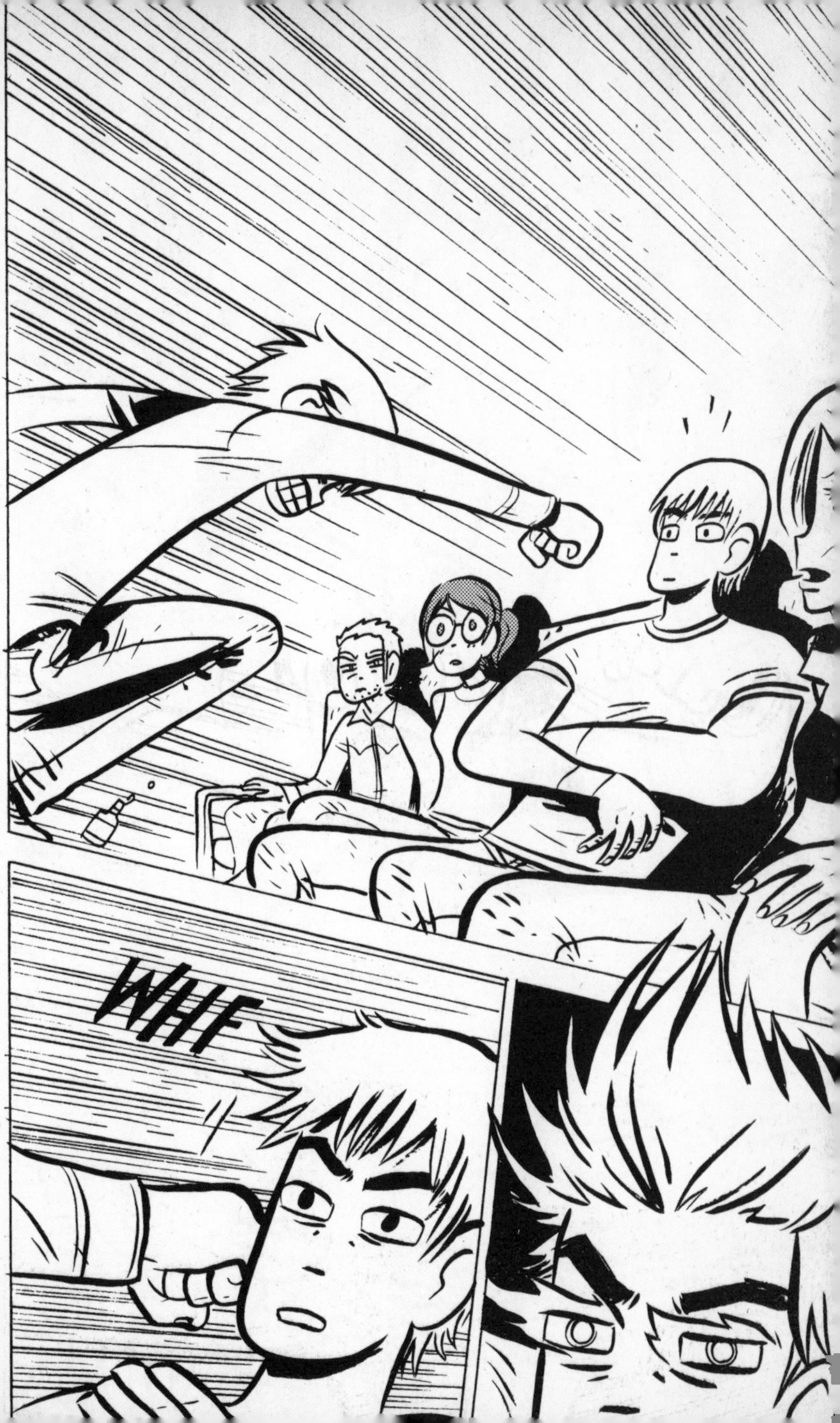
WHF

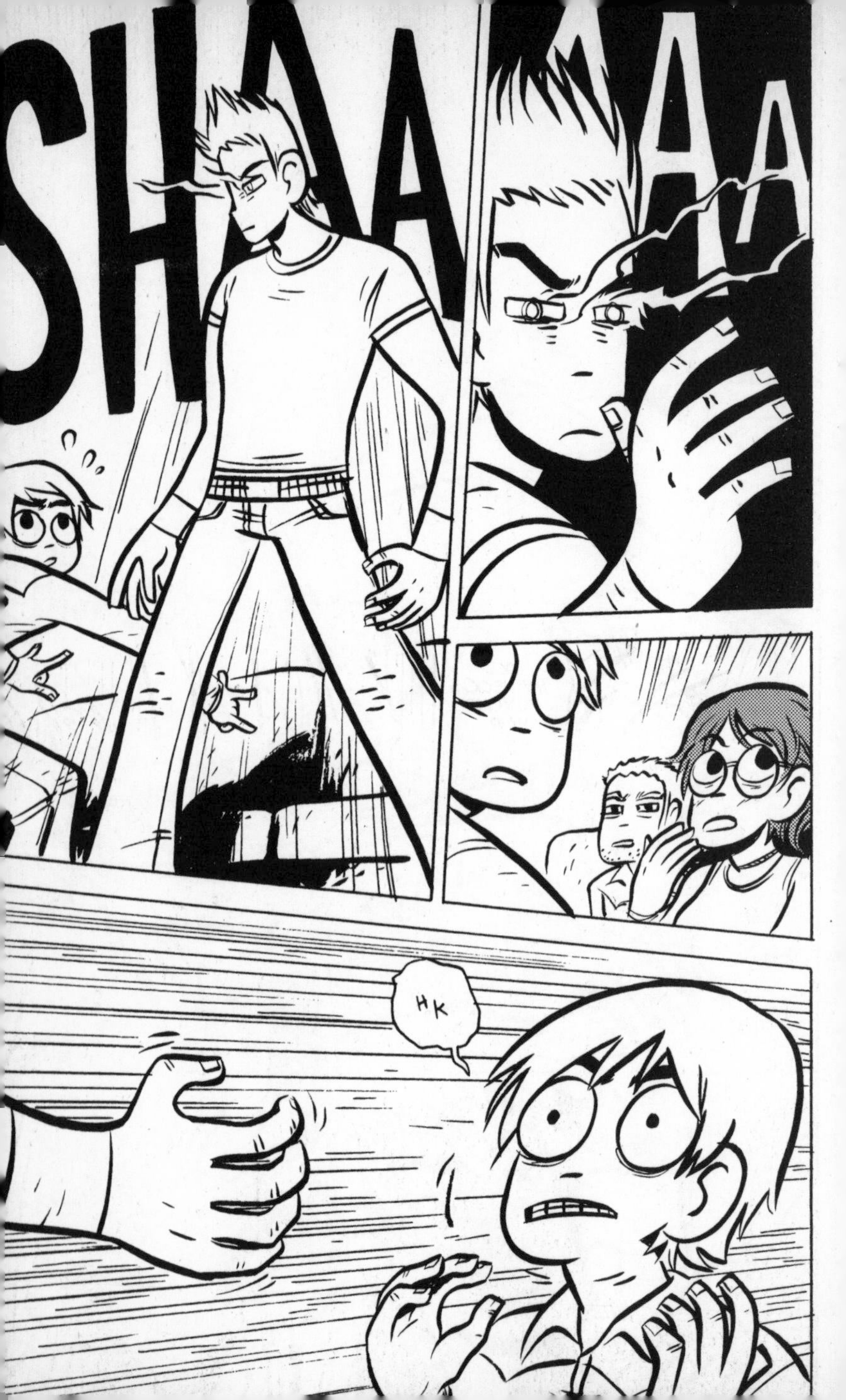
SHAAAAAA
HK

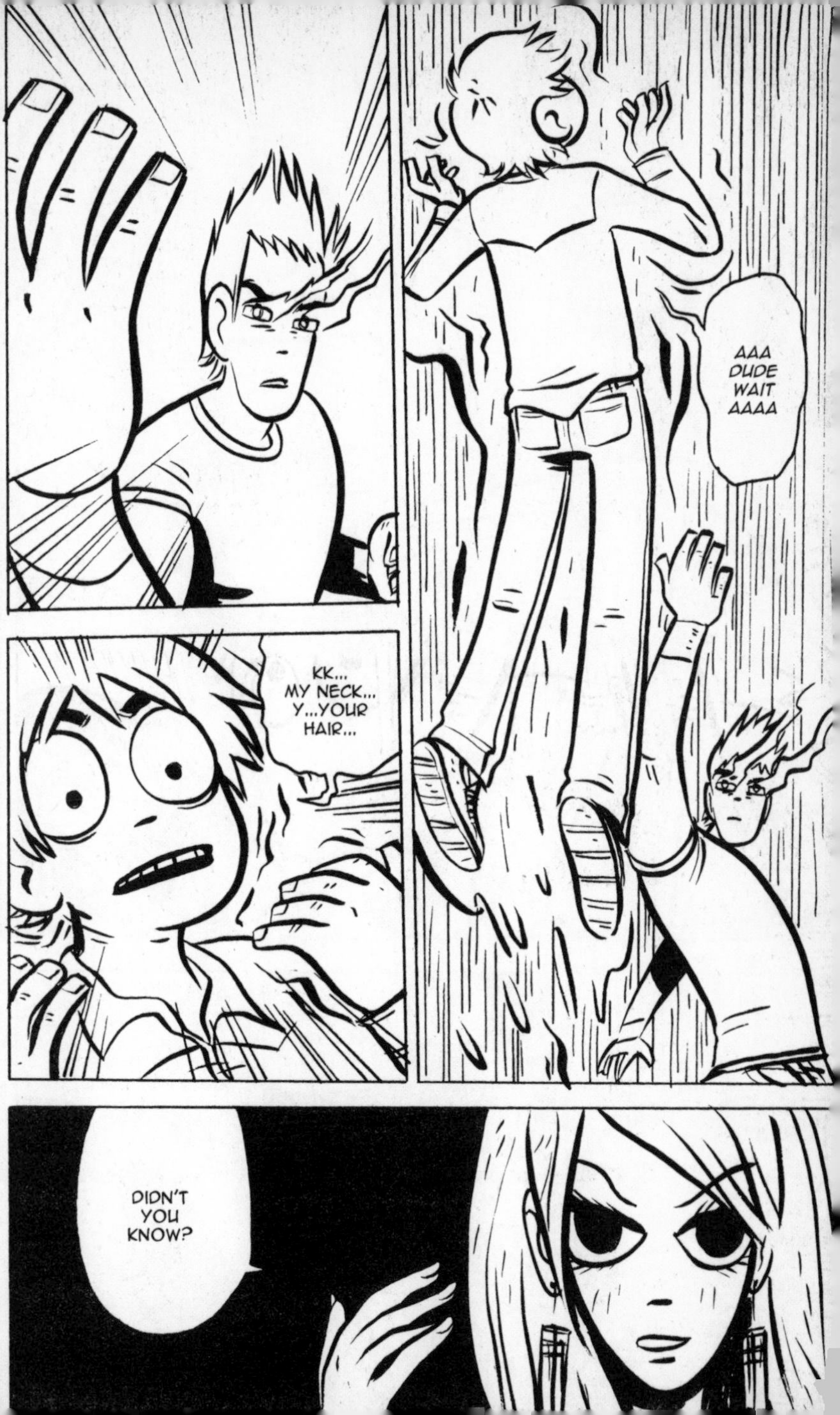
AAA DUDE WAIT AAAA
KK... MY NECK... Y...YOUR HAIR...
DIDN'T YOU KNOW?

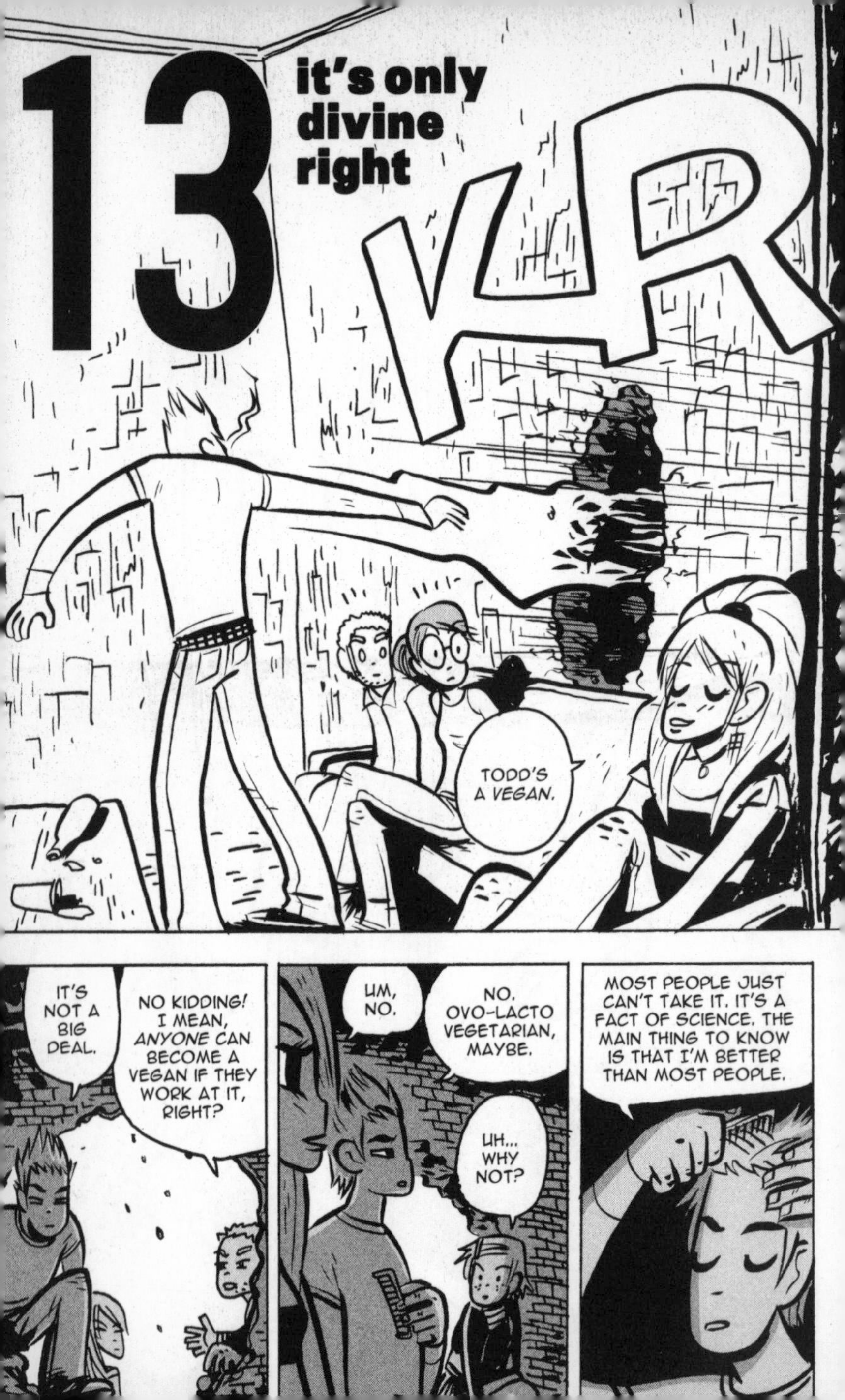
13
it's only divine right
KRR
TODD'S A VEGAN.
IT'S NOT A BIG DEAL.
NO KIDDING! I MEAN, ANYONE CAN BECOME A VEGAN IF THEY WORK AT IT, RIGHT?
UM, NO.
NO. OVO-LACTO VEGETARIAN, MAYBE.
UH... WHY NOT?
MOST PEOPLE JUST CAN'T TAKE IT. IT'S A FACT OF SCIENCE. THE MAIN THING TO KNOW IS THAT I'M BETTER THAN MOST PEOPLE.

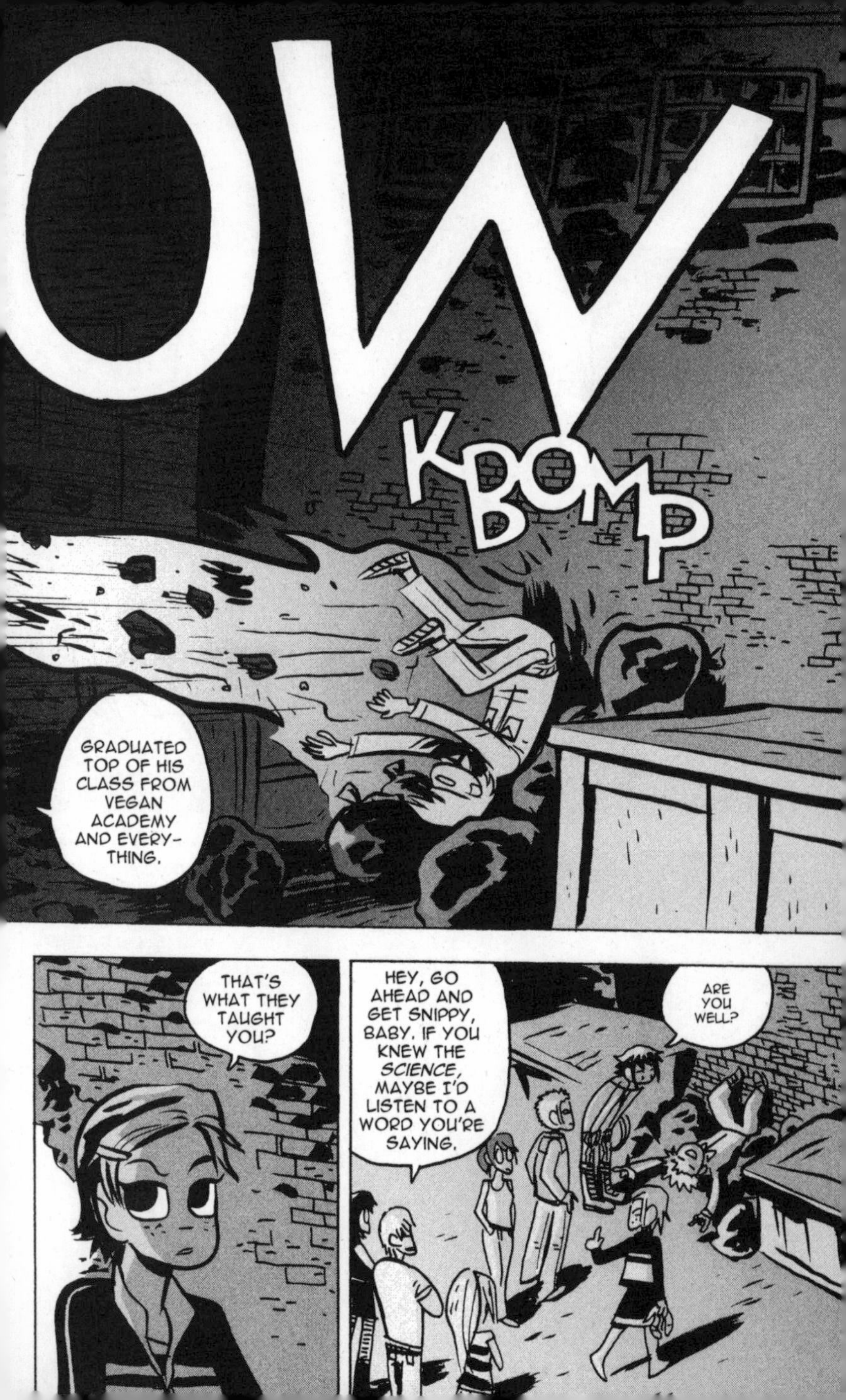
OW
KBOMP
GRADUATED TOP OF HIS CLASS FROM VEGAN ACADEMY AND EVERY-THING.
THAT'S WHAT THEY TAUGHT YOU?
HEY, GO AHEAD AND GET SNIPPY, BABY. IF YOU KNEW THE *SCIENCE*, MAYBE I'D LISTEN TO A WORD YOU'RE SAYING.
ARE YOU WELL?

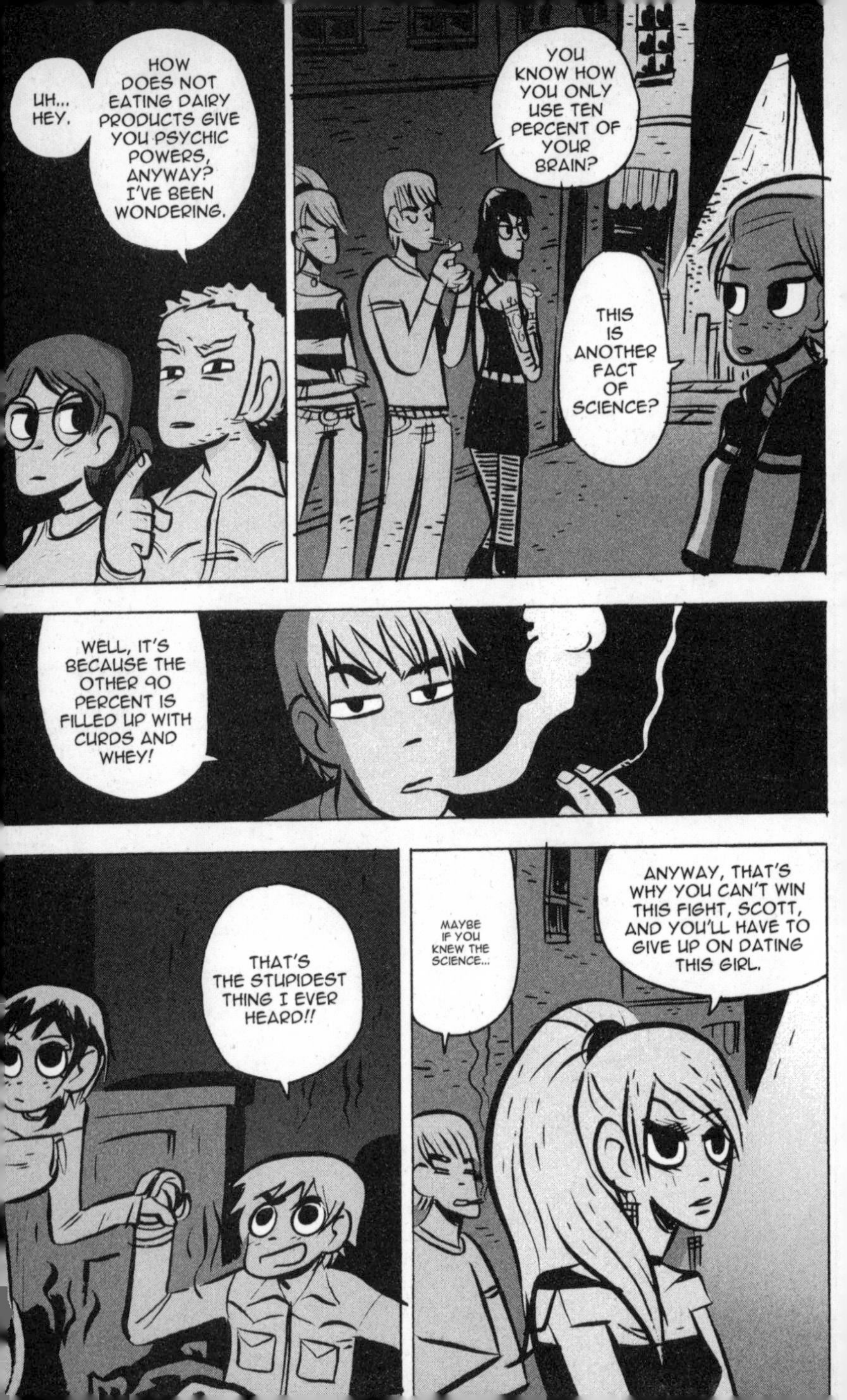
UH... HEY.
HOW DOES NOT EATING DAIRY PRODUCTS GIVE YOU PSYCHIC POWERS, ANYWAY? I'VE BEEN WONDERING.
YOU KNOW HOW YOU ONLY USE TEN PERCENT OF YOUR BRAIN?
THIS IS ANOTHER FACT OF SCIENCE?
WELL, IT'S BECAUSE THE OTHER 90 PERCENT IS FILLED UP WITH CURDS AND WHEY!
THAT'S THE STUPIDEST THING I EVER HEARD!!
MAYBE IF YOU KNEW THE SCIENCE...
ANYWAY, THAT'S WHY YOU CAN'T WIN THIS FIGHT, SCOTT, AND YOU'LL HAVE TO GIVE UP ON DATING THIS GIRL.

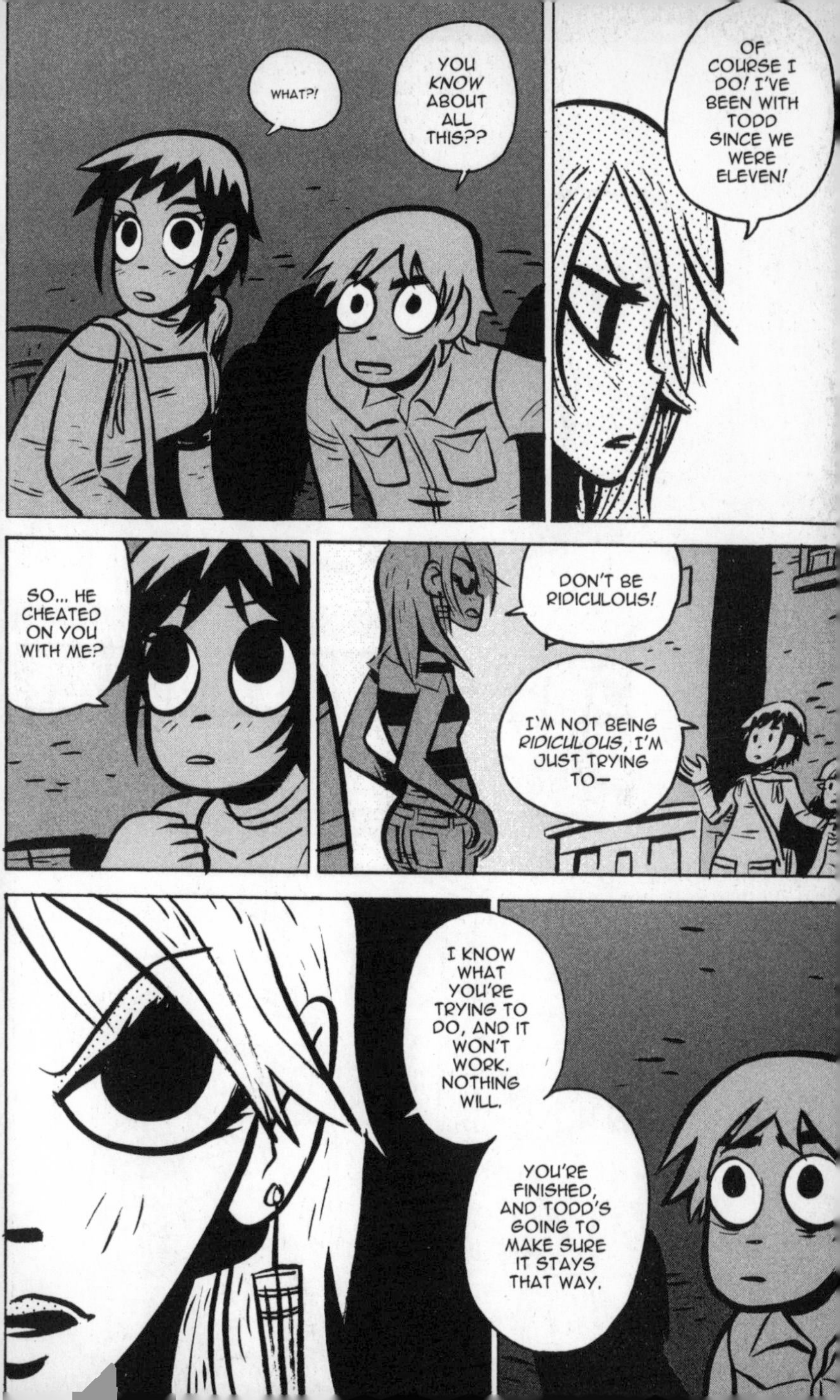
WHAT?!
YOU KNOW ABOUT ALL THIS??
OF COURSE I DO! I'VE BEEN WITH TODD SINCE WE WERE ELEVEN!
SO... HE CHEATED ON YOU WITH ME?
DON'T BE RIDICULOUS!
I'M NOT BEING RIDICULOUS, I'M JUST TRYING TO–
I KNOW WHAT YOU'RE TRYING TO DO, AND IT WON'T WORK. NOTHING WILL.
YOU'RE FINISHED, AND TODD'S GOING TO MAKE SURE IT STAYS THAT WAY.

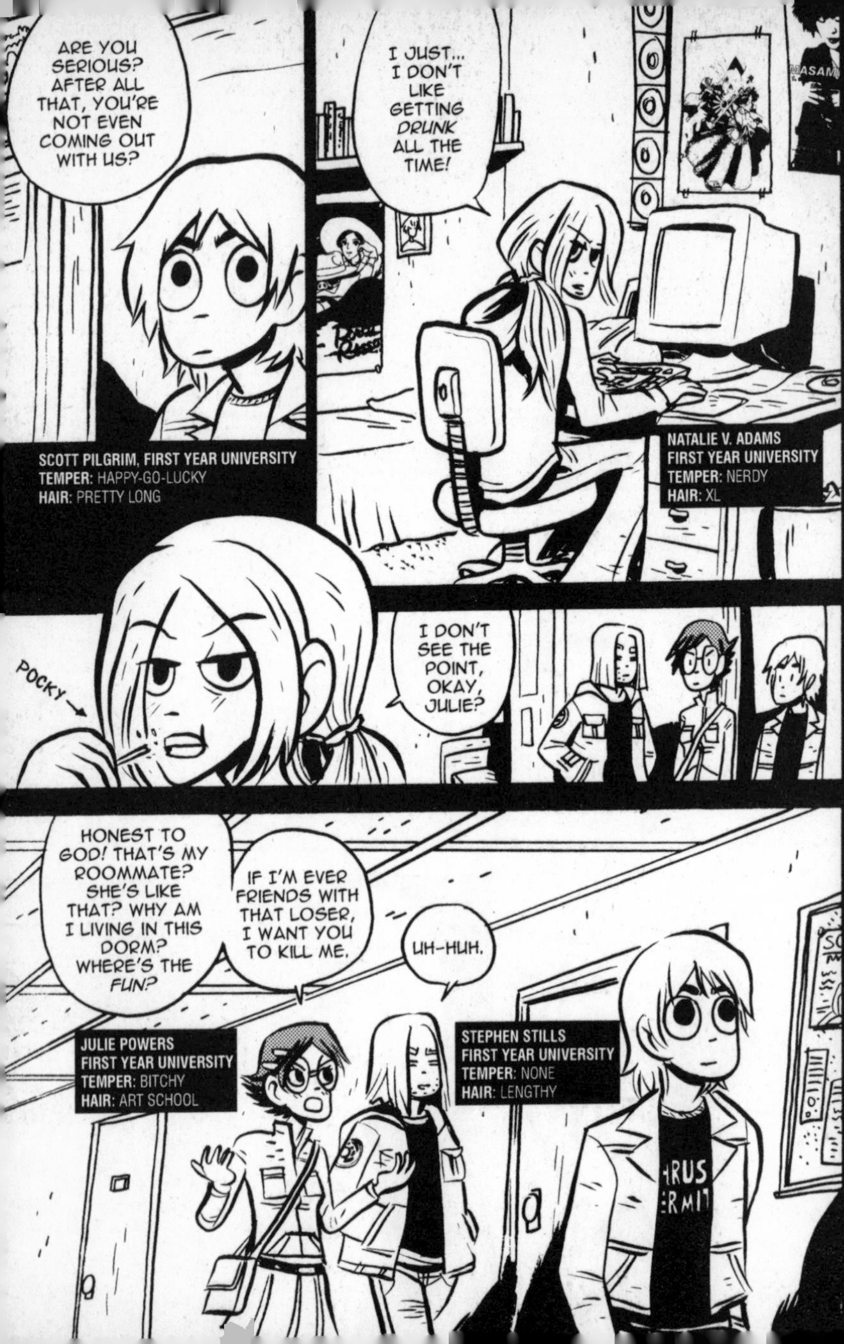
ARE YOU SERIOUS? AFTER ALL THAT, YOU'RE NOT EVEN COMING OUT WITH US?
SCOTT PILGRIM, FIRST YEAR UNIVERSITY
TEMPER: HAPPY-GO-LUCKY
HAIR: PRETTY LONG
I JUST... I DON'T LIKE GETTING DRUNK ALL THE TIME!
MASAMI
NATALIE V. ADAMS
FIRST YEAR UNIVERSITY
TEMPER: NERDY
HAIR: XL
POCKY
I DON'T SEE THE POINT, OKAY, JULIE?
HONEST TO GOD! THAT'S MY ROOMMATE? SHE'S LIKE THAT? WHY AM I LIVING IN THIS DORM? WHERE'S THE FUN?
IF I'M EVER FRIENDS WITH THAT LOSER, I WANT YOU TO KILL ME.
UH-HUH.
JULIE POWERS
FIRST YEAR UNIVERSITY
TEMPER: BITCHY
HAIR: ART SCHOOL
STEPHEN STILLS
FIRST YEAR UNIVERSITY
TEMPER: NONE
HAIR: LENGTHY

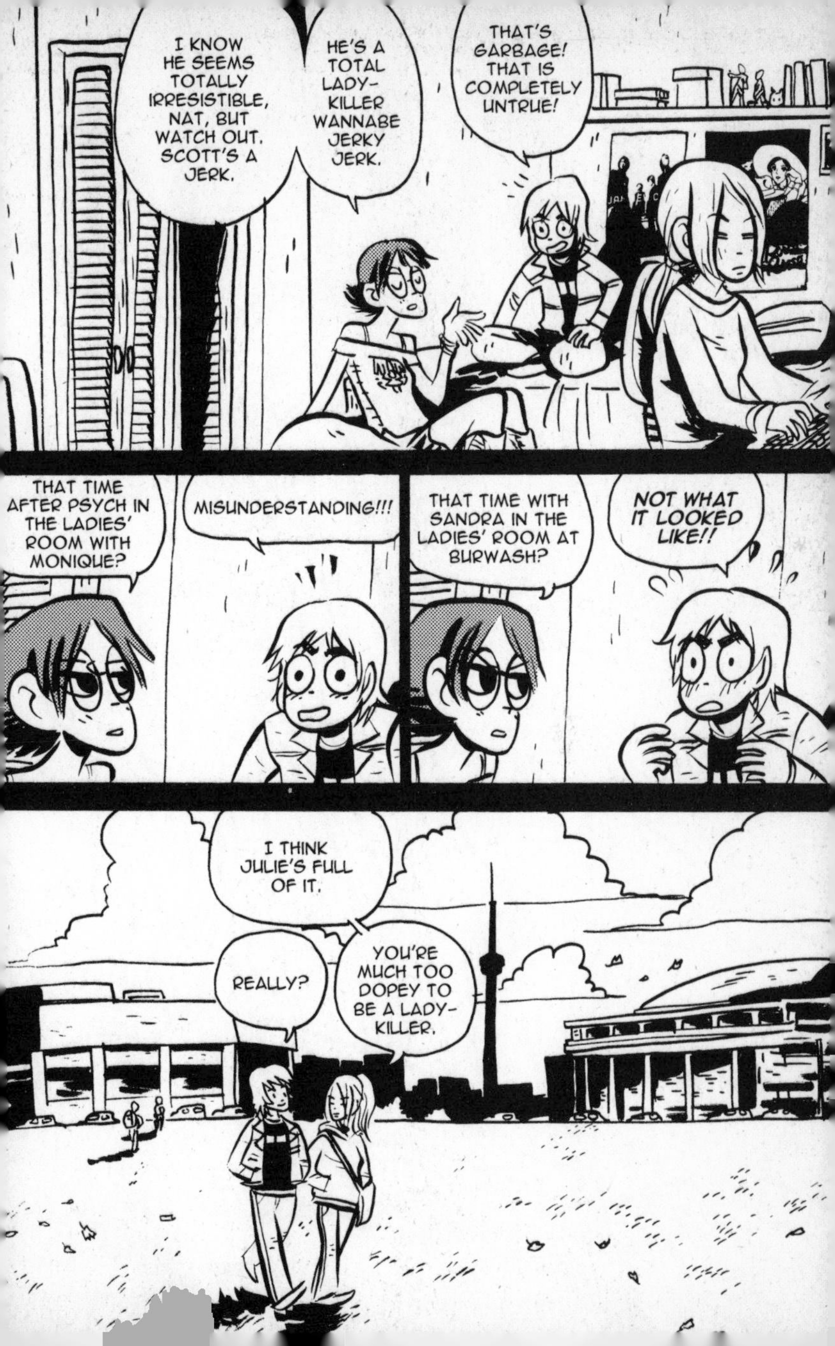
I KNOW HE SEEMS TOTALLY IRRESISTIBLE, NAT, BUT WATCH OUT. SCOTT'S A JERK.
HE'S A TOTAL LADY-KILLER WANNABE JERKY JERK.
THAT'S GARBAGE! THAT IS COMPLETELY UNTRUE!
THAT TIME AFTER PSYCH IN THE LADIES' ROOM WITH MONIQUE?
MISUNDERSTANDING!!!
THAT TIME WITH SANDRA IN THE LADIES' ROOM AT BURWASH?
NOT WHAT IT LOOKED LIKE!!
I THINK JULIE'S FULL OF IT.
REALLY?
YOU'RE MUCH TOO DOPEY TO BE A LADY-KILLER.

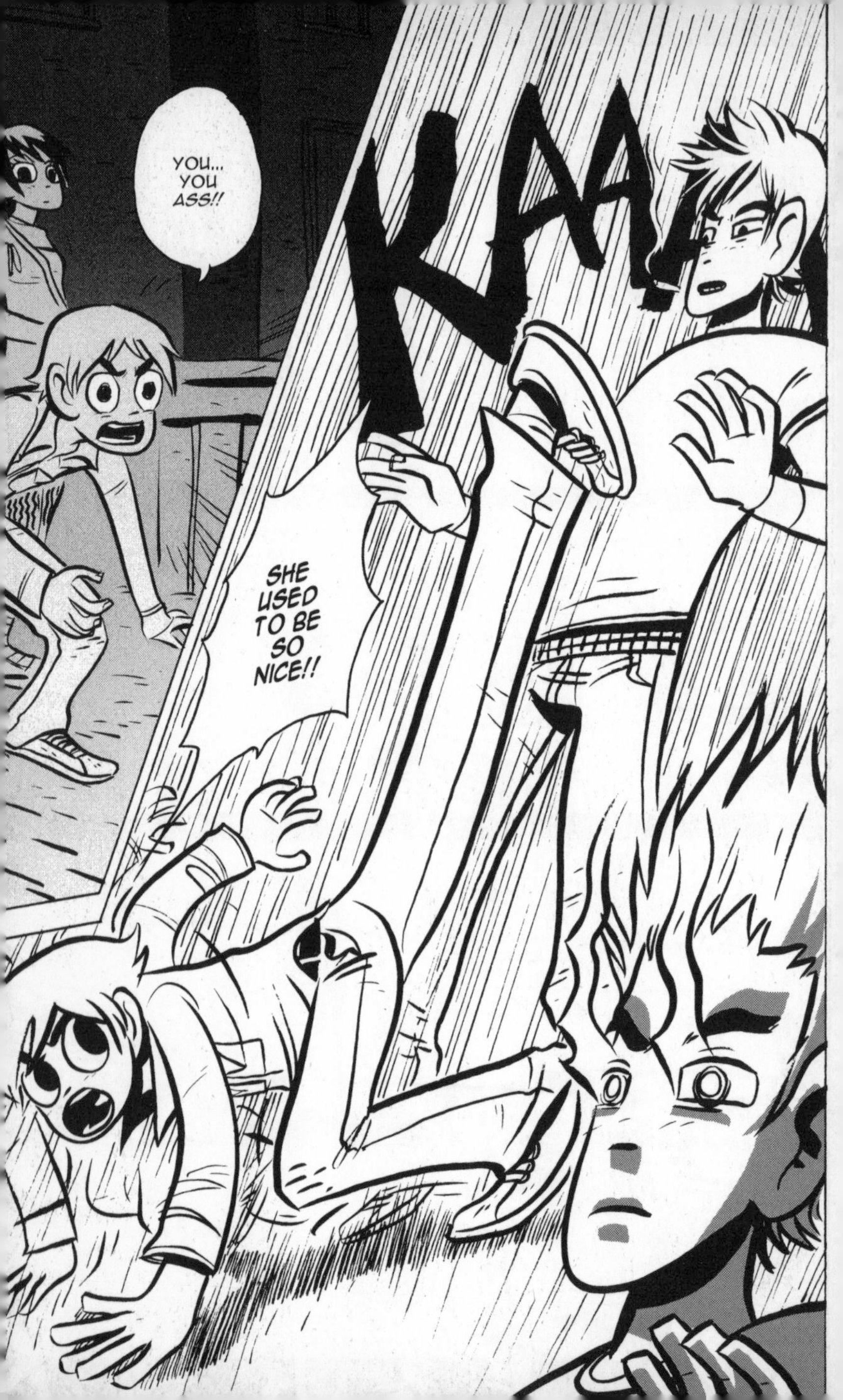
YOU... YOU ASS!!
KAA!
SHE USED TO BE SO NICE!!

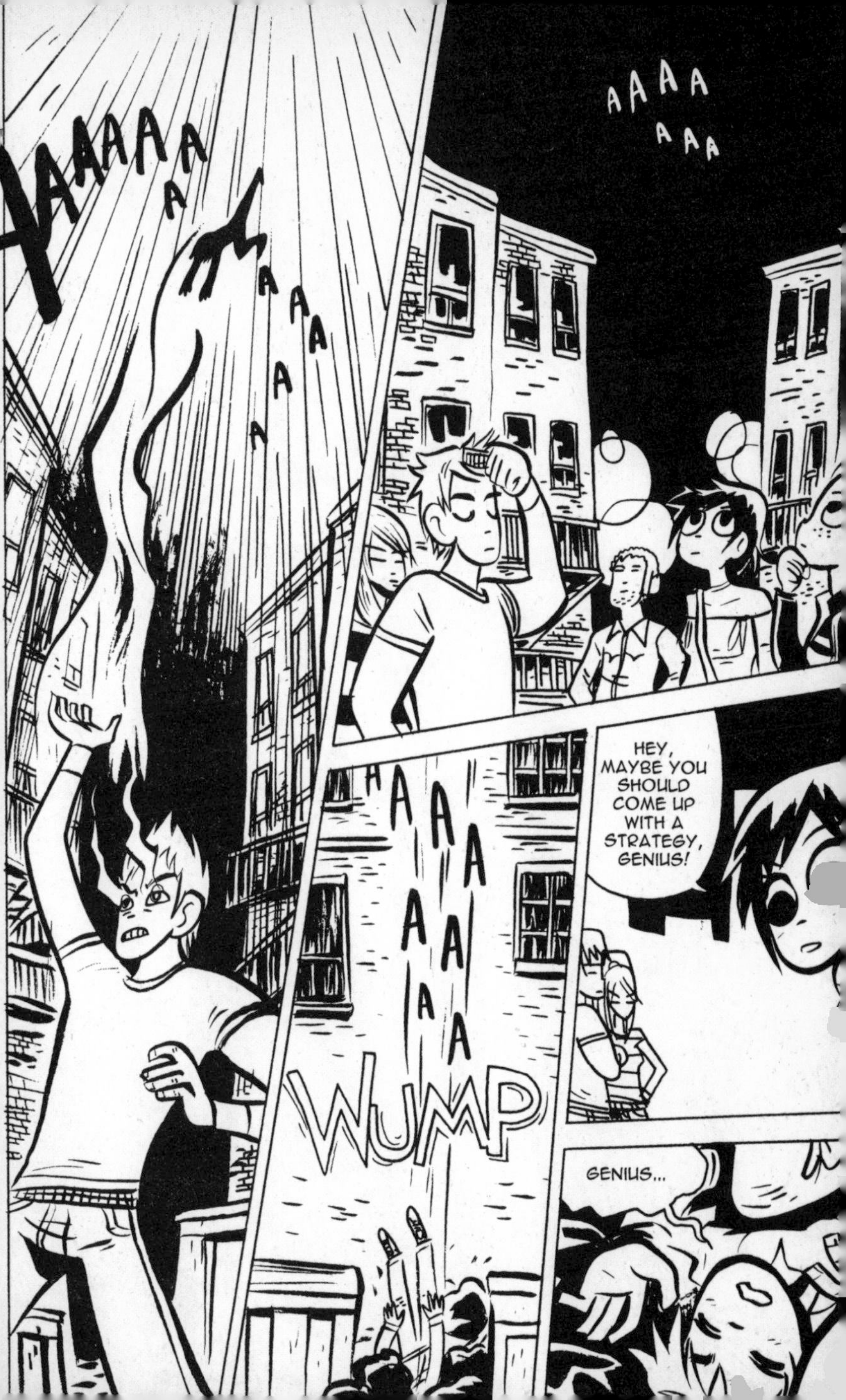

AAAAAAA
AAAA
AAAA
AAA
AAAAAAA
WUMP
HEY, MAYBE YOU SHOULD COME UP WITH A STRATEGY, GENIUS!
GENIUS...

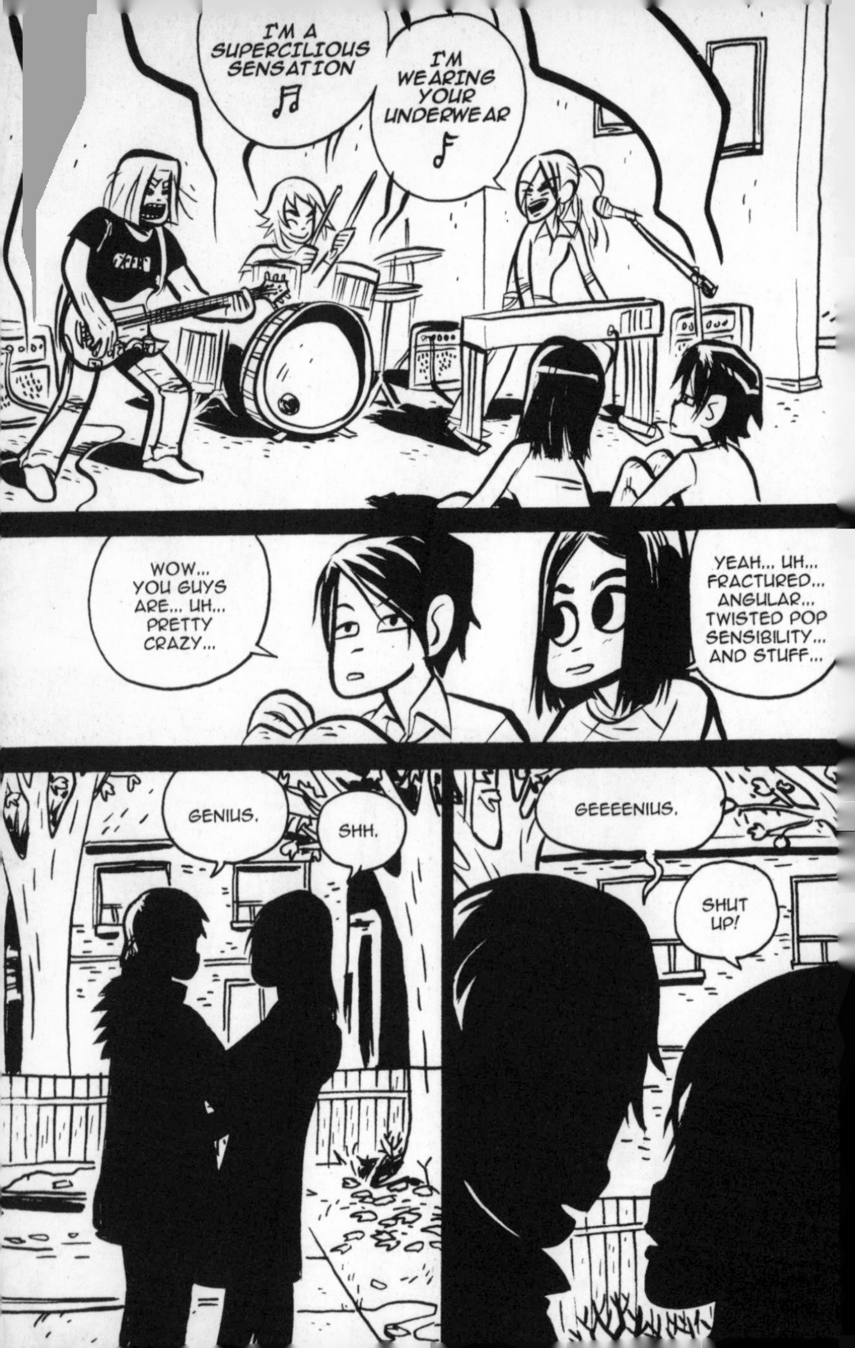
I'M A SUPERCILIOUS SENSATION
I'M WEARING YOUR UNDERWEAR
WOW... YOU GUYS ARE... UH... PRETTY CRAZY...
YEAH... UH... FRACTURED... ANGULAR... TWISTED POP SENSIBILITY... AND STUFF...
GENIUS.
SHH.
GEEEENIUS.
SHUT UP!

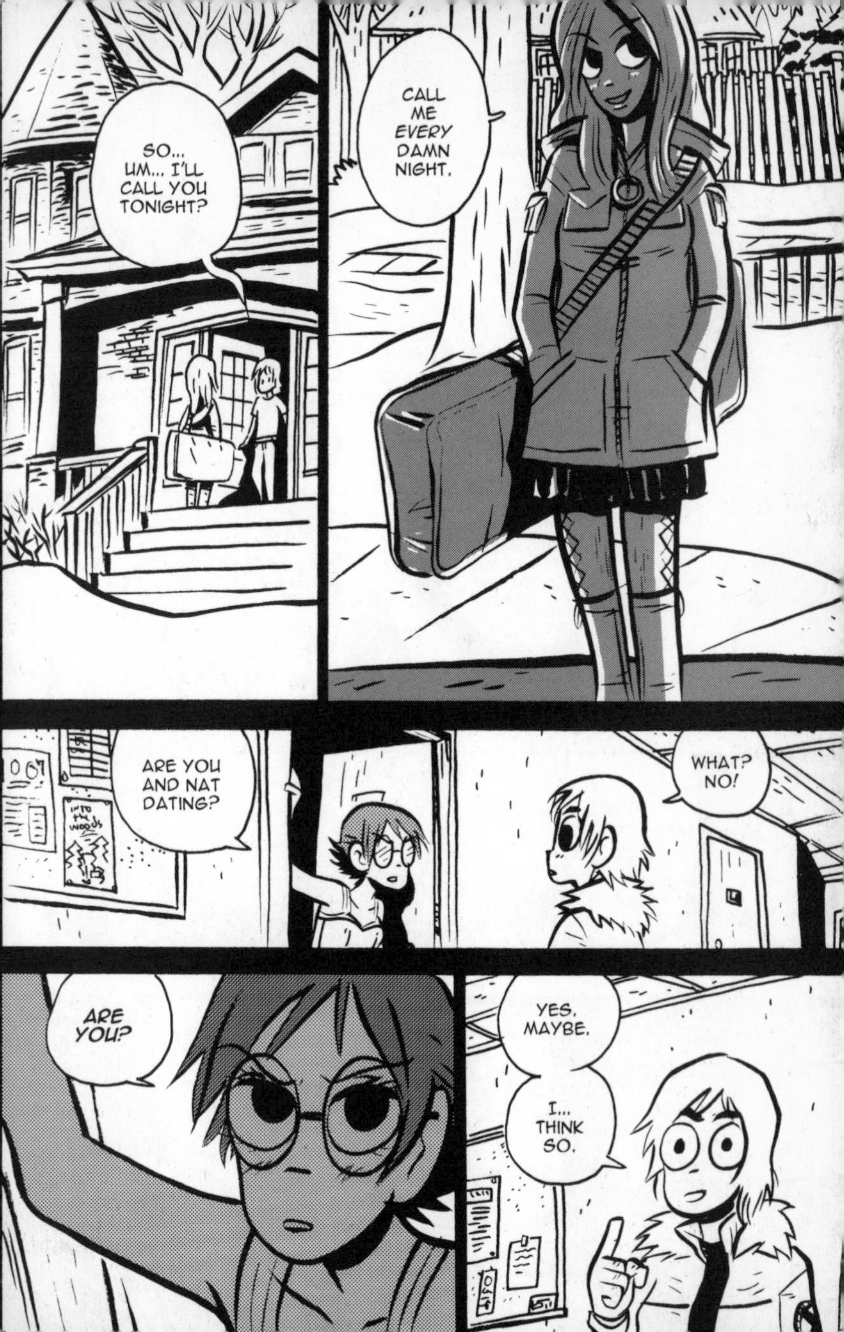
SO... UM... I'LL CALL YOU TONIGHT?
CALL ME EVERY DAMN NIGHT.
ARE YOU AND NAT DATING?
WHAT? NO!
ARE YOU?
YES. MAYBE.
I... THINK SO.

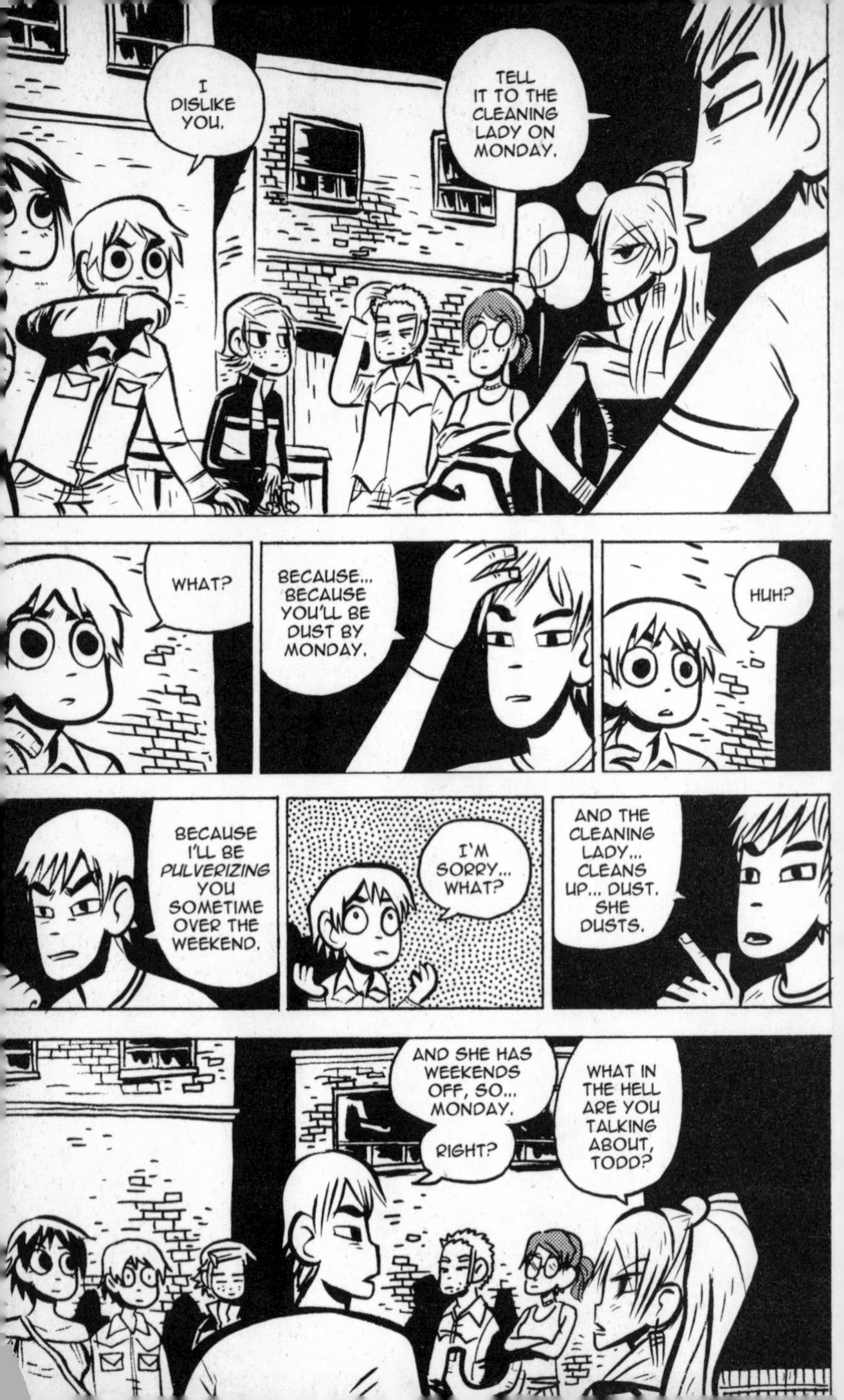
I DISLIKE YOU.
TELL IT TO THE CLEANING LADY ON MONDAY.
WHAT?
BECAUSE... BECAUSE YOU'LL BE DUST BY MONDAY.
HUH?
BECAUSE I'LL BE *PULVERIZING* YOU SOMETIME OVER THE WEEKEND.
I'M SORRY... WHAT?
AND THE CLEANING LADY... CLEANS UP... DUST. SHE DUSTS.
AND SHE HAS WEEKENDS OFF, SO... MONDAY.
RIGHT?
WHAT IN THE HELL ARE YOU TALKING ABOUT, TODD?

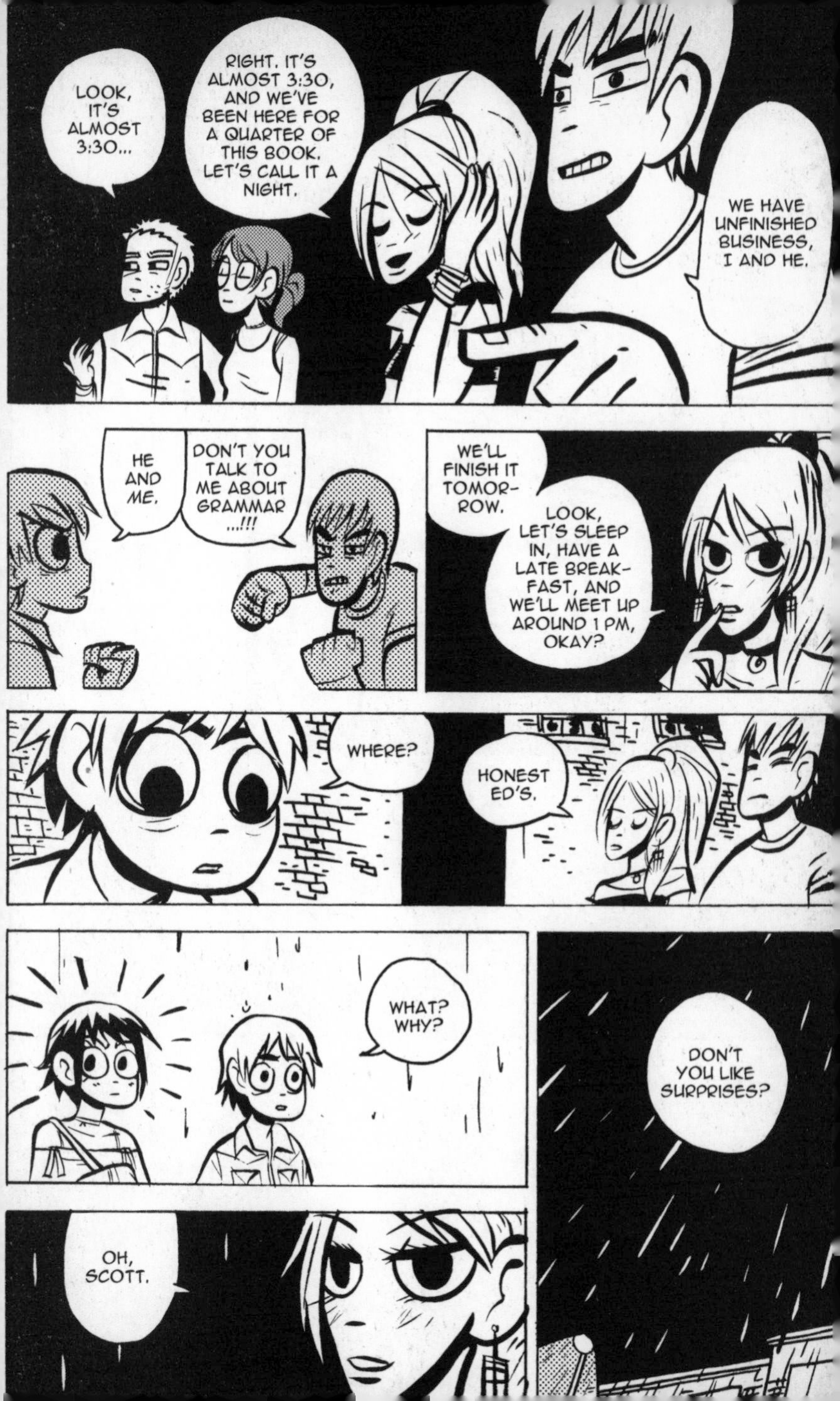
LOOK, IT'S ALMOST 3:30...
RIGHT. IT'S ALMOST 3:30, AND WE'VE BEEN HERE FOR A QUARTER OF THIS BOOK. LET'S CALL IT A NIGHT.
WE HAVE UNFINISHED BUSINESS, I AND HE.
HE AND ME.
DON'T YOU TALK TO ME ABOUT GRAMMAR ...!!!
WE'LL FINISH IT TOMOR-ROW.
LOOK, LET'S SLEEP IN, HAVE A LATE BREAK-FAST, AND WE'LL MEET UP AROUND 1 PM, OKAY?
WHERE?
HONEST ED'S.
WHAT? WHY?
DON'T YOU LIKE SURPRISES?
OH, SCOTT.

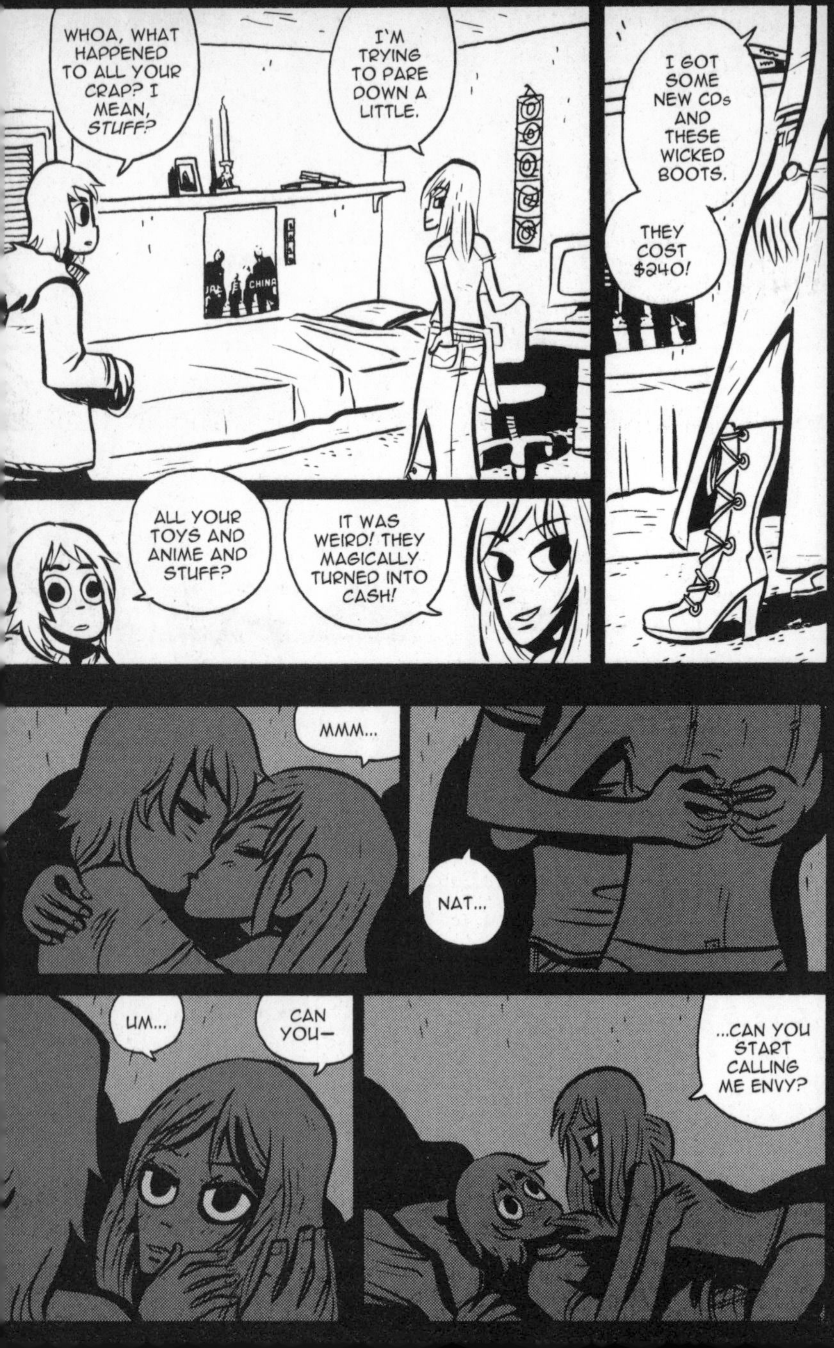
WHOA, WHAT HAPPENED TO ALL YOUR CRAP? I MEAN, STUFF?
I'M TRYING TO PARE DOWN A LITTLE.
I GOT SOME NEW CDs AND THESE WICKED BOOTS.
THEY COST $240!
ALL YOUR TOYS AND ANIME AND STUFF?
IT WAS WEIRD! THEY MAGICALLY TURNED INTO CASH!
MMM...
NAT...
UM...
CAN YOU—
...CAN YOU START CALLING ME ENVY?

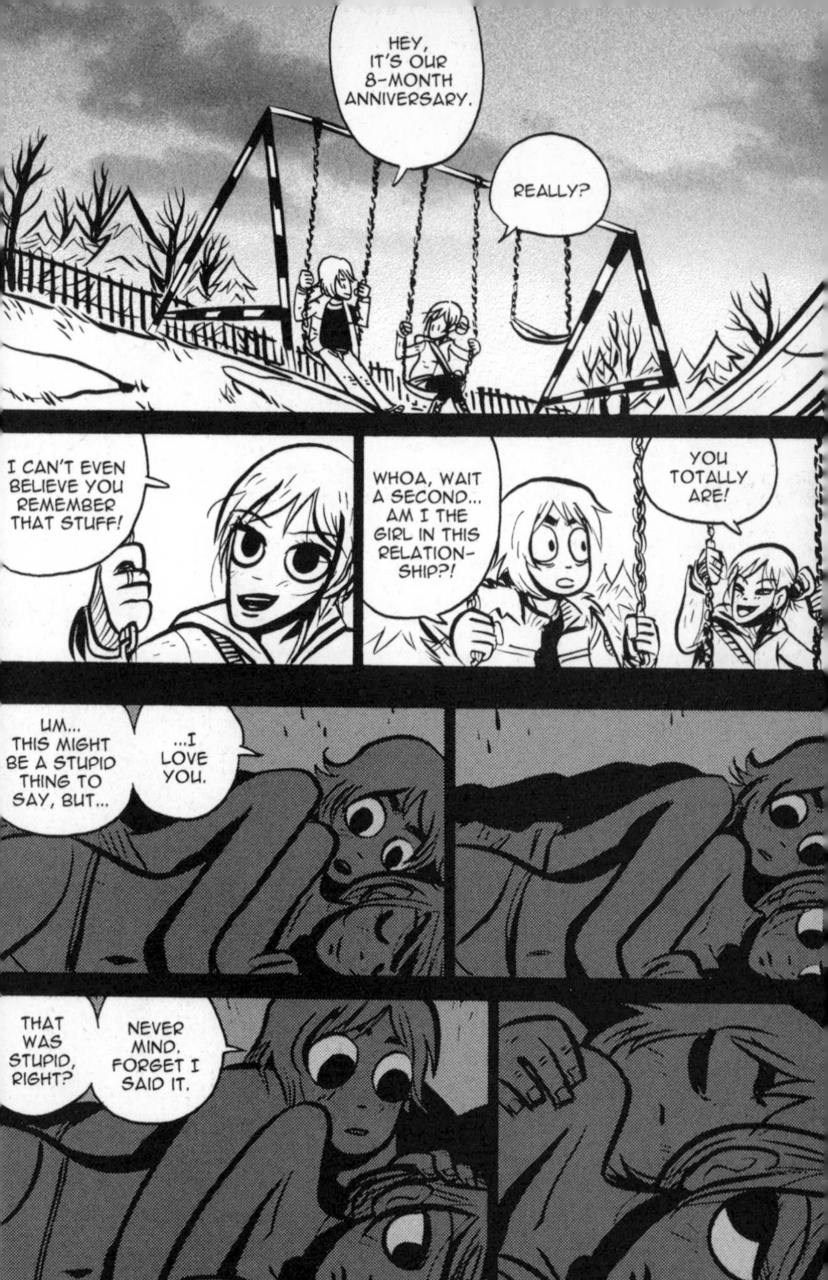
HEY, IT'S OUR 8-MONTH ANNIVERSARY.
REALLY?
I CAN'T EVEN BELIEVE YOU REMEMBER THAT STUFF!
WHOA, WAIT A SECOND... AM I THE GIRL IN THIS RELATION-SHIP?!
YOU TOTALLY ARE!
UM... THIS MIGHT BE A STUPID THING TO SAY, BUT...
...I LOVE YOU.
THAT WAS STUPID, RIGHT?
NEVER MIND. FORGET I SAID IT.

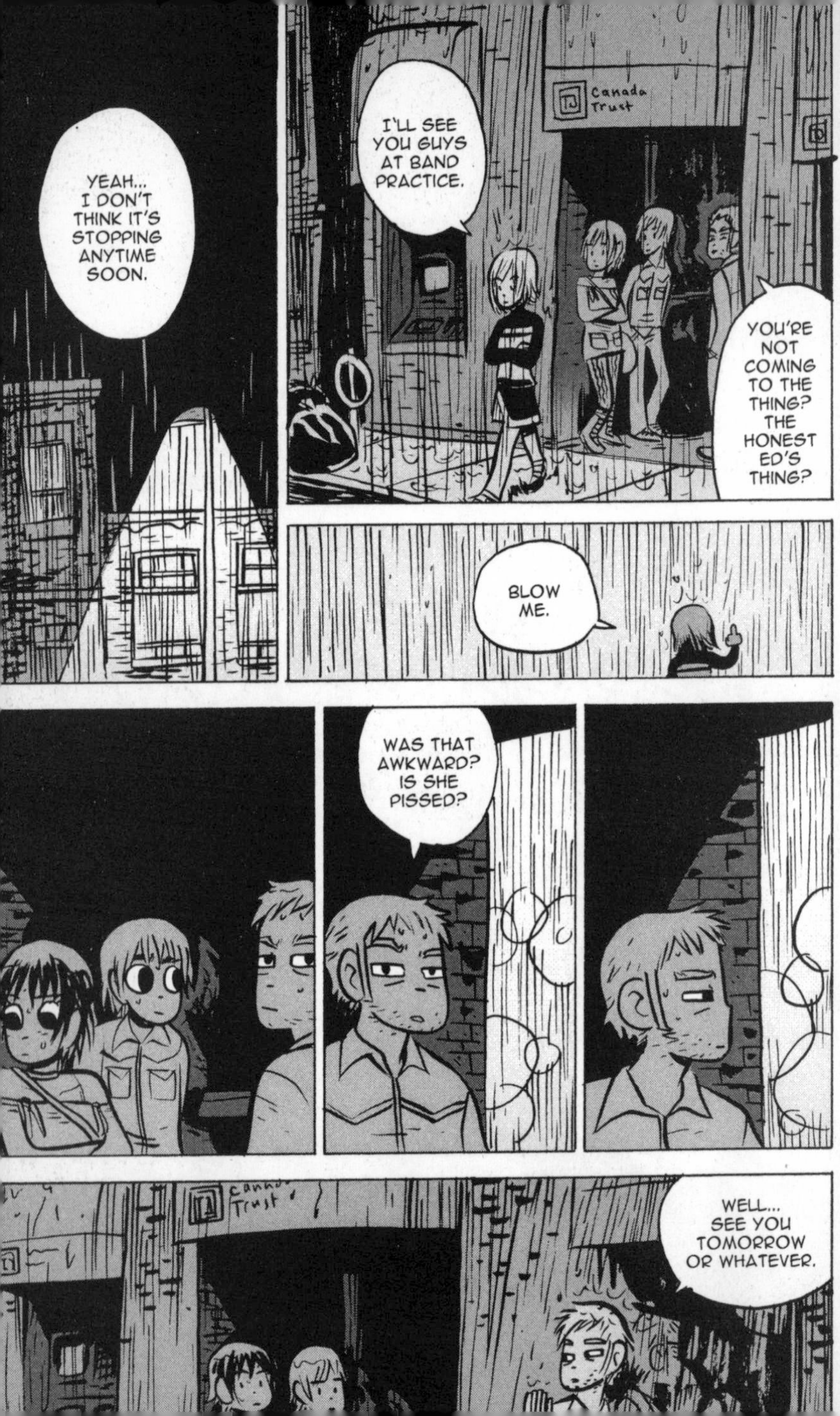
YEAH... I DON'T THINK IT'S STOPPING ANYTIME SOON.
I'LL SEE YOU GUYS AT BAND PRACTICE.
Canada Trust
YOU'RE NOT COMING TO THE THING? THE HONEST ED'S THING?
BLOW ME.
WAS THAT AWKWARD? IS SHE PISSED?
WELL... SEE YOU TOMORROW OR WHATEVER.

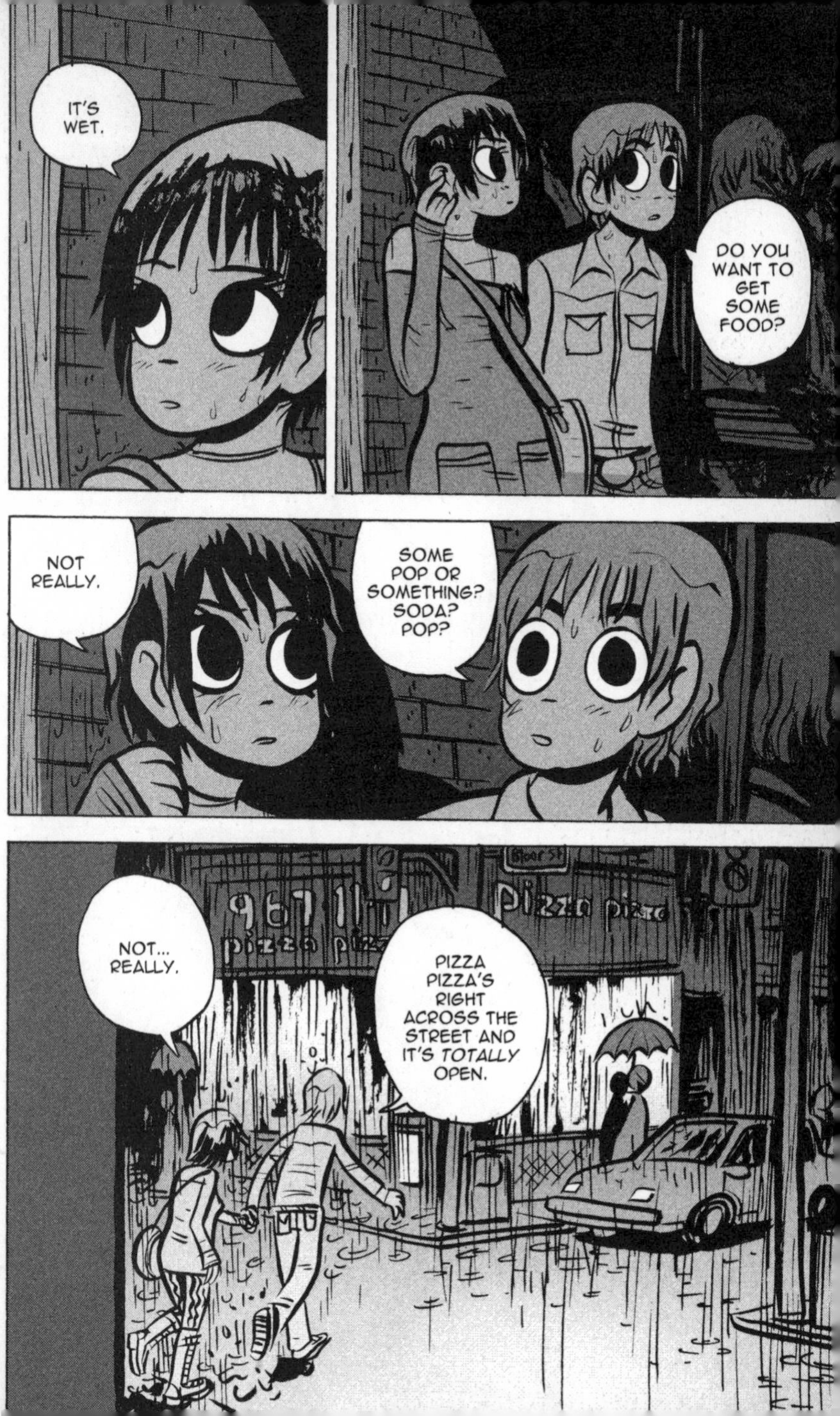
IT'S WET.
DO YOU WANT TO GET SOME FOOD?
NOT REALLY.
SOME POP OR SOMETHING? SODA? POP?
NOT... REALLY.
PIZZA PIZZA'S RIGHT ACROSS THE STREET AND IT'S *TOTALLY* OPEN.

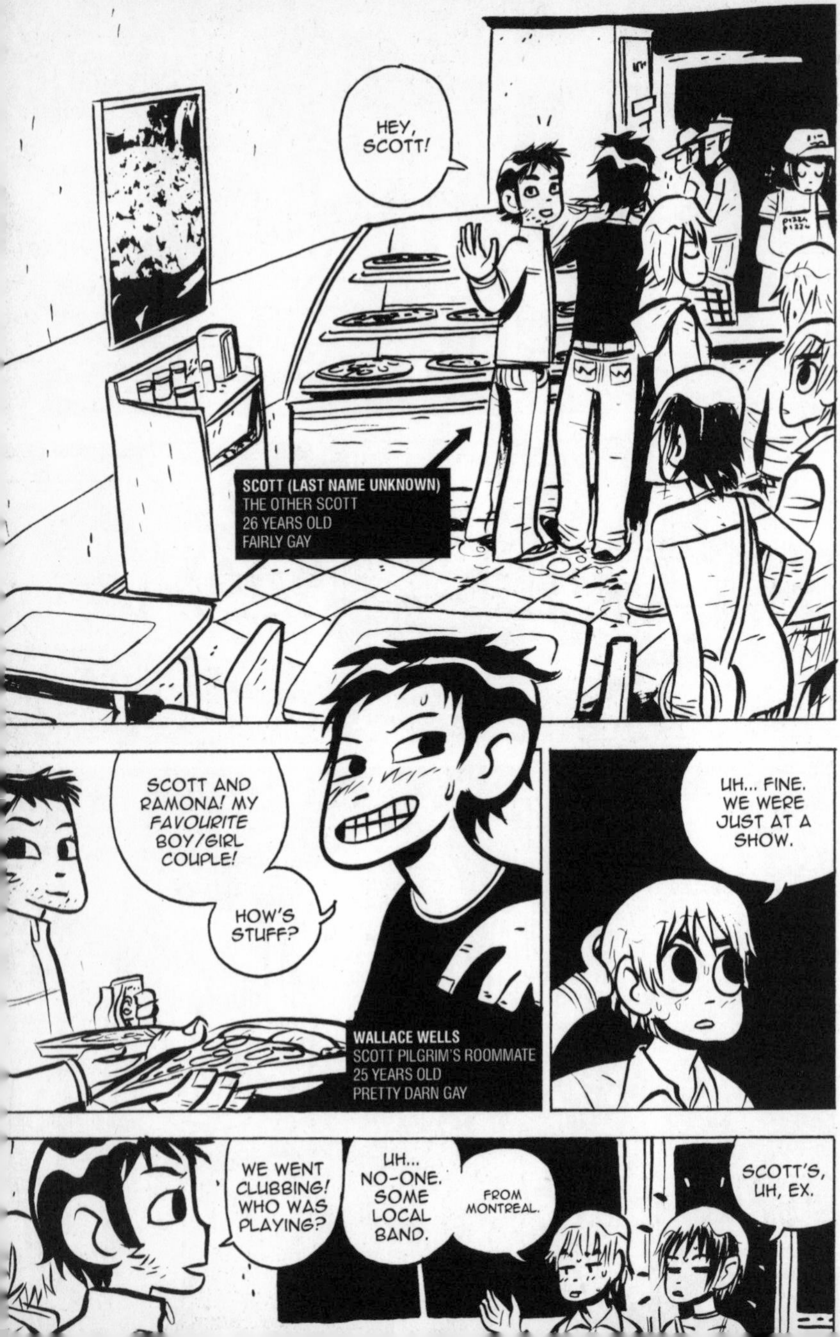
HEY, SCOTT!
SCOTT (LAST NAME UNKNOWN)
THE OTHER SCOTT
26 YEARS OLD
FAIRLY GAY
SCOTT AND RAMONA! MY FAVOURITE BOY/GIRL COUPLE!
HOW'S STUFF?
WALLACE WELLS
SCOTT PILGRIM'S ROOMMATE
25 YEARS OLD
PRETTY DARN GAY
UH... FINE. WE WERE JUST AT A SHOW.
WE WENT CLUBBING! WHO WAS PLAYING?
UH... NO-ONE. SOME LOCAL BAND.
FROM MONTREAL.
SCOTT'S, UH, EX.

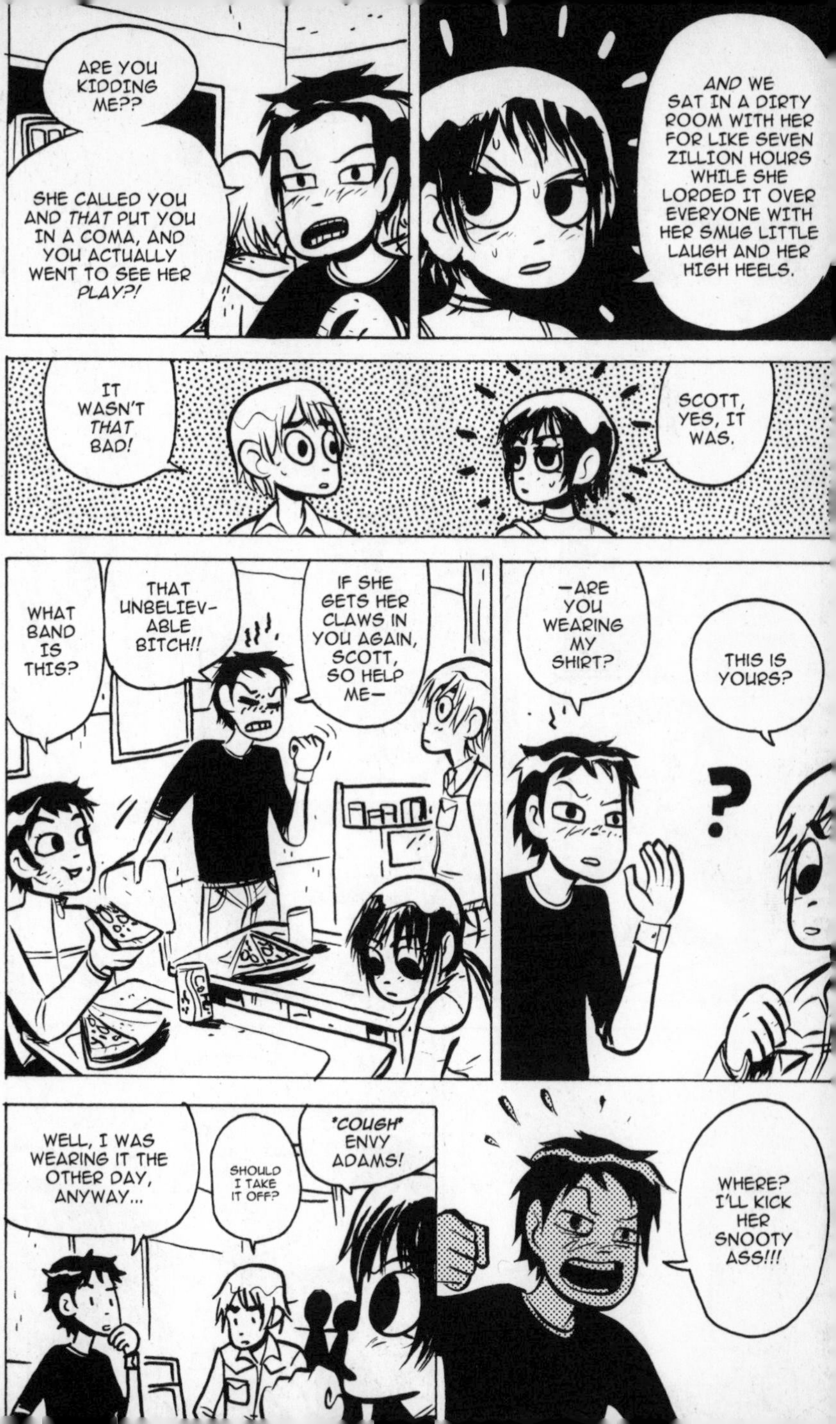
ARE YOU KIDDING ME??
SHE CALLED YOU AND THAT PUT YOU IN A COMA, AND YOU ACTUALLY WENT TO SEE HER PLAY?!
AND WE SAT IN A DIRTY ROOM WITH HER FOR LIKE SEVEN ZILLION HOURS WHILE SHE LORDED IT OVER EVERYONE WITH HER SMUG LITTLE LAUGH AND HER HIGH HEELS.
IT WASN'T THAT BAD!
SCOTT, YES, IT WAS.
WHAT BAND IS THIS?
THAT UNBELIEV-ABLE BITCH!!
IF SHE GETS HER CLAWS IN YOU AGAIN, SCOTT, SO HELP ME—
—ARE YOU WEARING MY SHIRT?
THIS IS YOURS?
?
WELL, I WAS WEARING IT THE OTHER DAY, ANYWAY...
SHOULD I TAKE IT OFF?
COUGH ENVY ADAMS!
WHERE? I'LL KICK HER SNOOTY ASS!!!

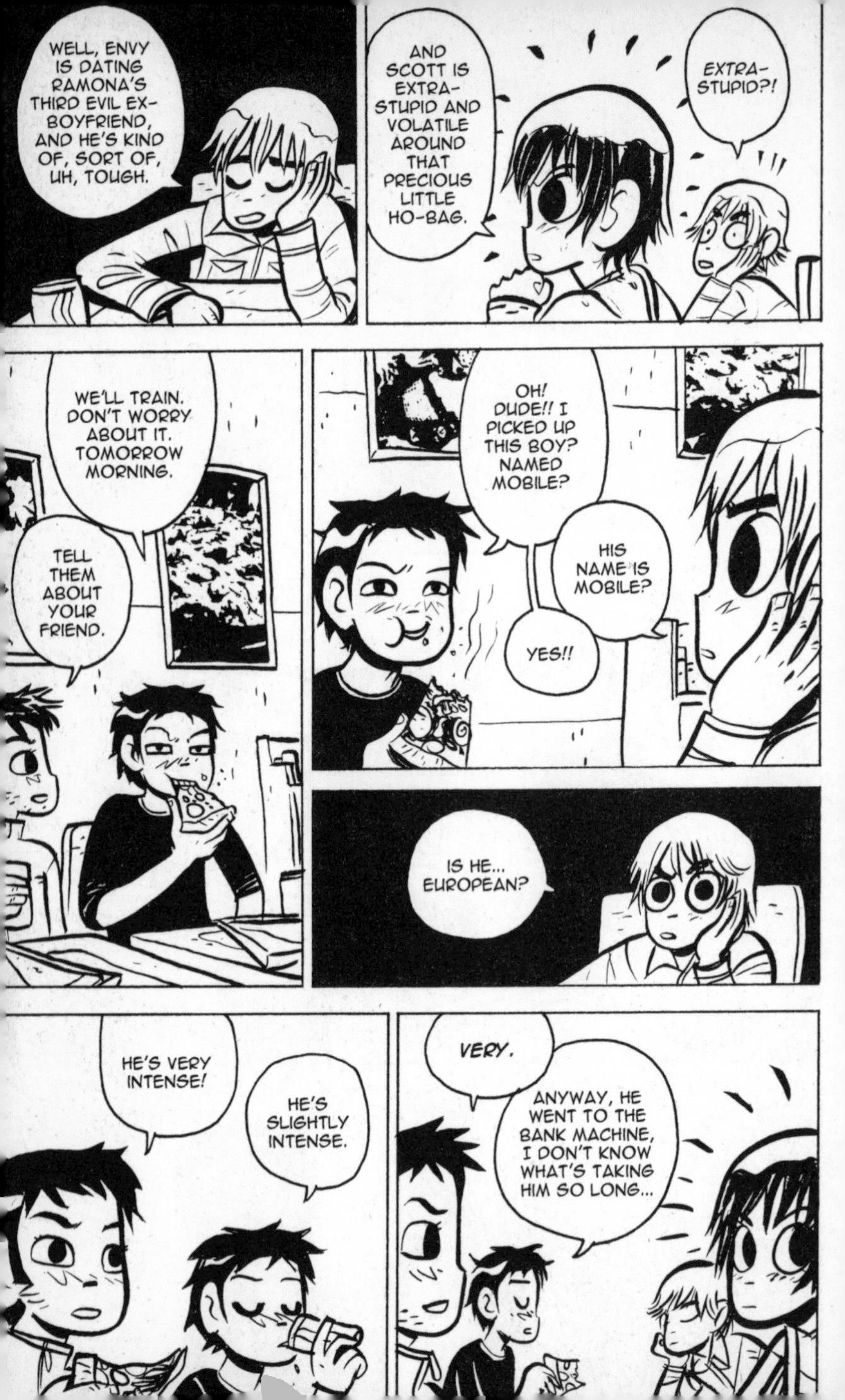
WELL, ENVY IS DATING RAMONA'S THIRD EVIL EX-BOYFRIEND, AND HE'S KIND OF, SORT OF, UH, TOUGH.
AND SCOTT IS EXTRA-STUPID AND VOLATILE AROUND THAT PRECIOUS LITTLE HO-BAG.
EXTRA-STUPID?!
WE'LL TRAIN. DON'T WORRY ABOUT IT. TOMORROW MORNING.
TELL THEM ABOUT YOUR FRIEND.
OH! DUDE!! I PICKED UP THIS BOY? NAMED MOBILE?
HIS NAME IS MOBILE?
YES!!
IS HE... EUROPEAN?
HE'S VERY INTENSE!
HE'S SLIGHTLY INTENSE.
VERY.
ANYWAY, HE WENT TO THE BANK MACHINE, I DON'T KNOW WHAT'S TAKING HIM SO LONG...

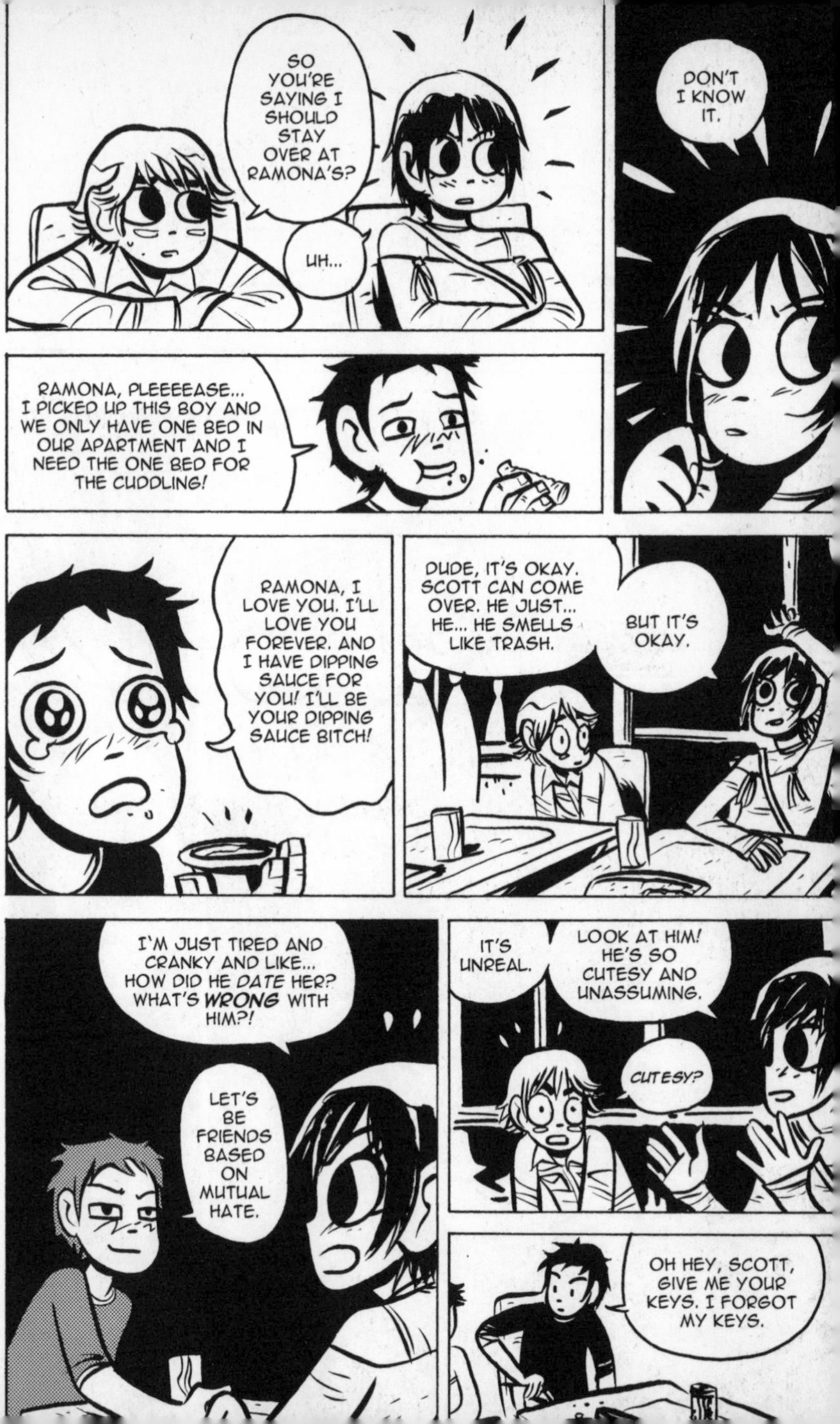
SO YOU'RE SAYING I SHOULD STAY OVER AT RAMONA'S?
UH...
DON'T I KNOW IT.
RAMONA, PLEEEEASE... I PICKED UP THIS BOY AND WE ONLY HAVE ONE BED IN OUR APARTMENT AND I NEED THE ONE BED FOR THE CUDDLING!
RAMONA, I LOVE YOU. I'LL LOVE YOU FOREVER. AND I HAVE DIPPING SAUCE FOR YOU! I'LL BE YOUR DIPPING SAUCE BITCH!
DUDE, IT'S OKAY. SCOTT CAN COME OVER. HE JUST... HE... HE SMELLS LIKE TRASH.
BUT IT'S OKAY.
I'M JUST TIRED AND CRANKY AND LIKE... HOW DID HE *DATE* HER? WHAT'S ***WRONG*** WITH HIM?!
LET'S BE FRIENDS BASED ON MUTUAL HATE.
IT'S UNREAL.
LOOK AT HIM! HE'S SO CUTESY AND UNASSUMING.
CUTESY?
OH HEY, SCOTT, GIVE ME YOUR KEYS. I FORGOT MY KEYS.

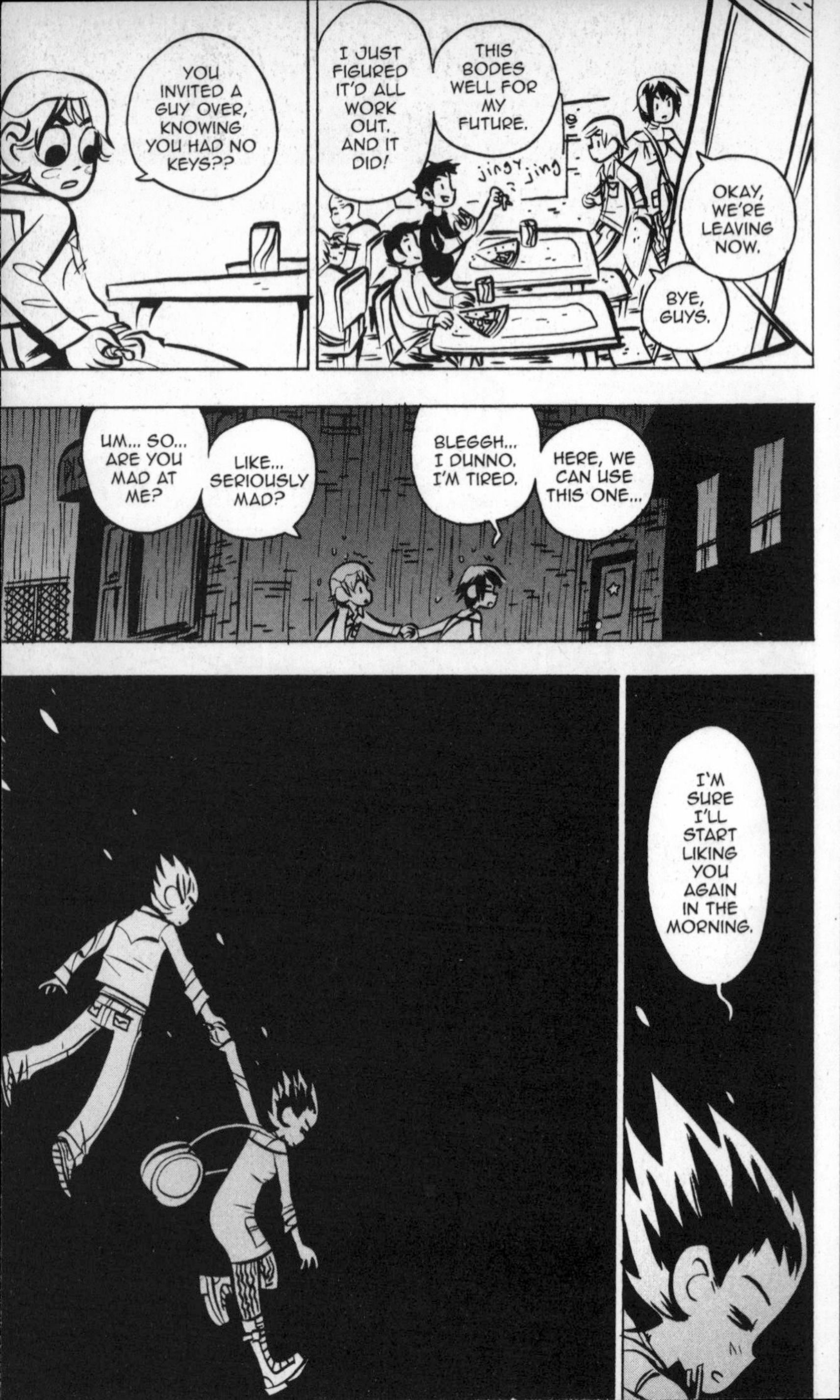
YOU INVITED A GUY OVER, KNOWING YOU HAD NO KEYS??
I JUST FIGURED IT'D ALL WORK OUT. AND IT DID!
THIS BODES WELL FOR MY FUTURE.
jingy jing
OKAY, WE'RE LEAVING NOW.
BYE, GUYS.
UM... SO... ARE YOU MAD AT ME?
LIKE... SERIOUSLY MAD?
BLEGGH... I DUNNO. I'M TIRED.
HERE, WE CAN USE THIS ONE...
I'M SURE I'LL START LIKING YOU AGAIN IN THE MORNING.

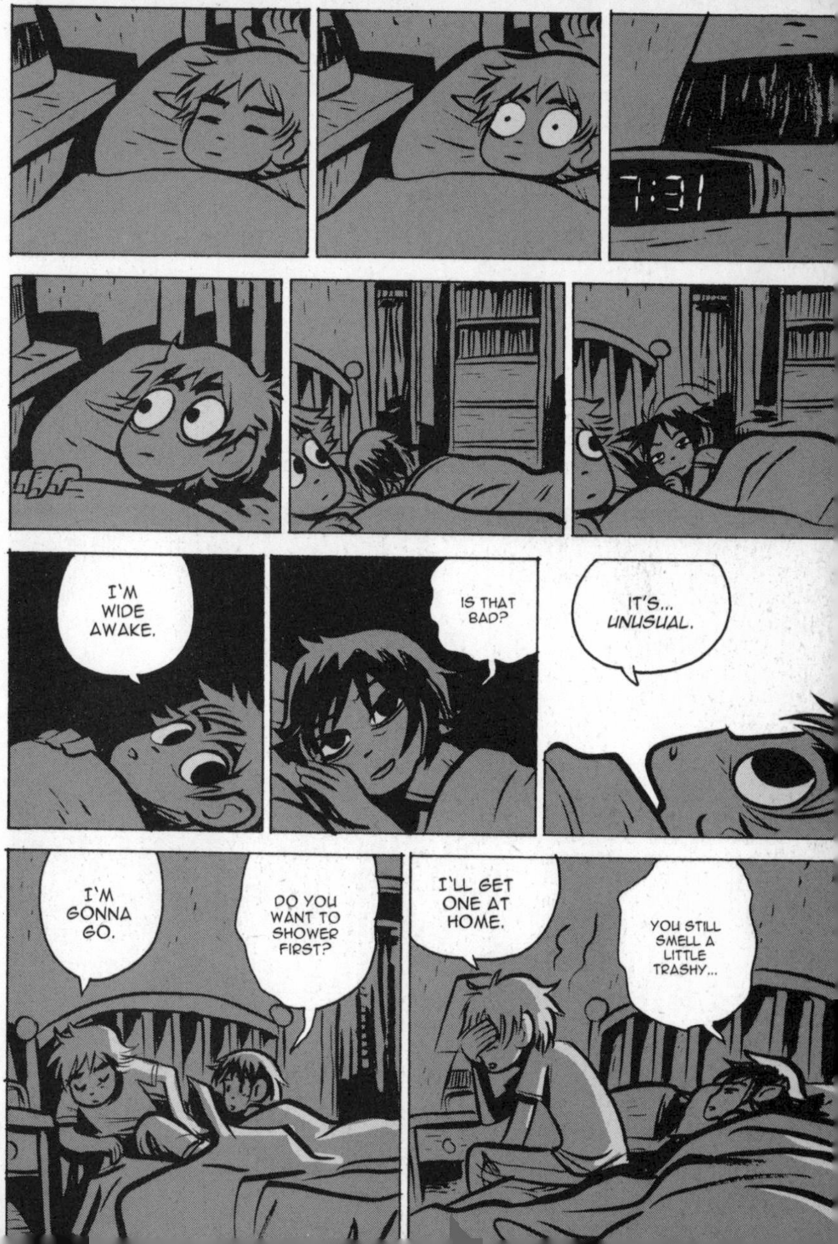
7:31
I'M WIDE AWAKE.
IS THAT BAD?
IT'S... UNUSUAL.
I'M GONNA GO.
DO YOU WANT TO SHOWER FIRST?
I'LL GET ONE AT HOME.
YOU STILL SMELL A LITTLE TRASHY...

14

about to e-x-p-l-o-d-e

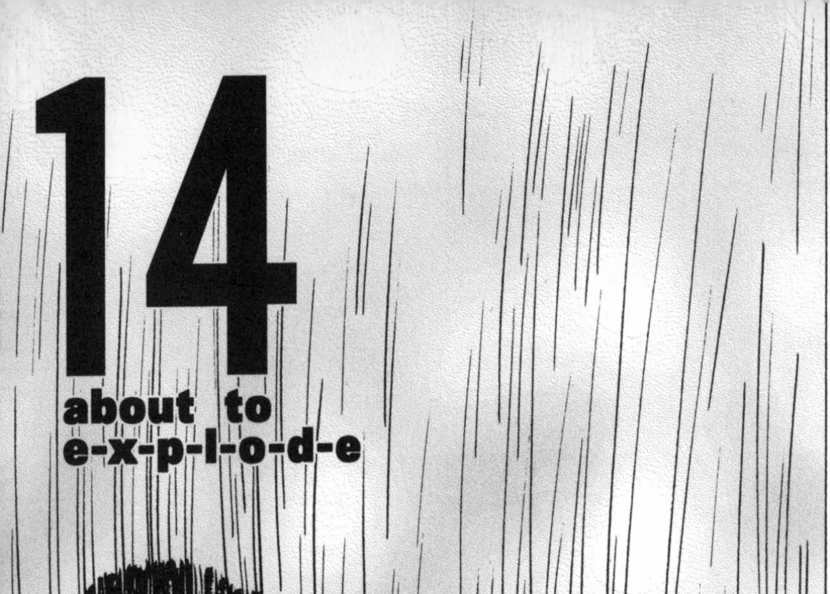

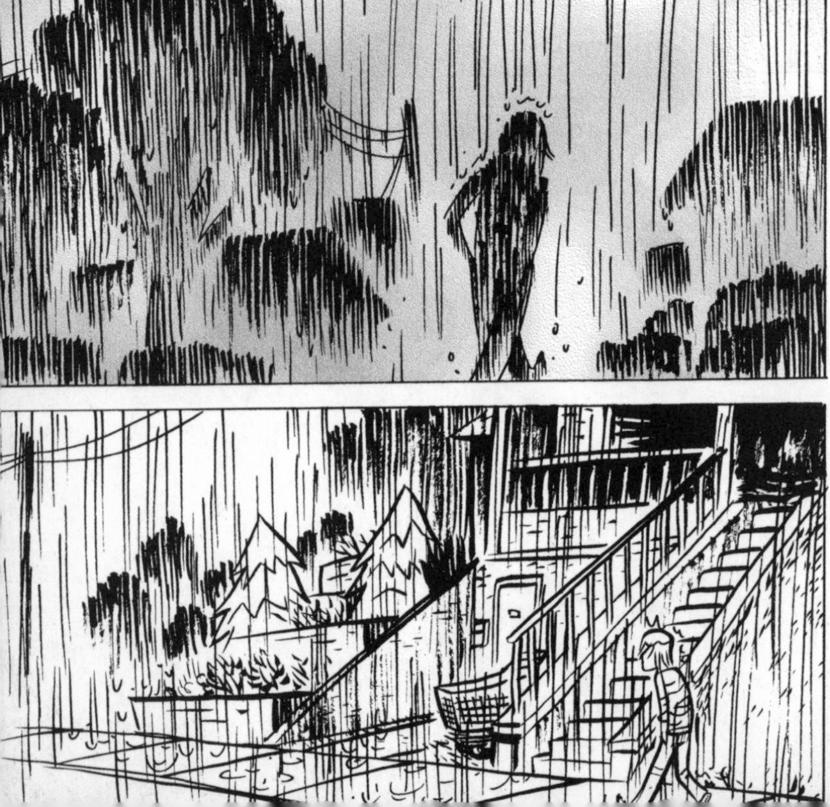

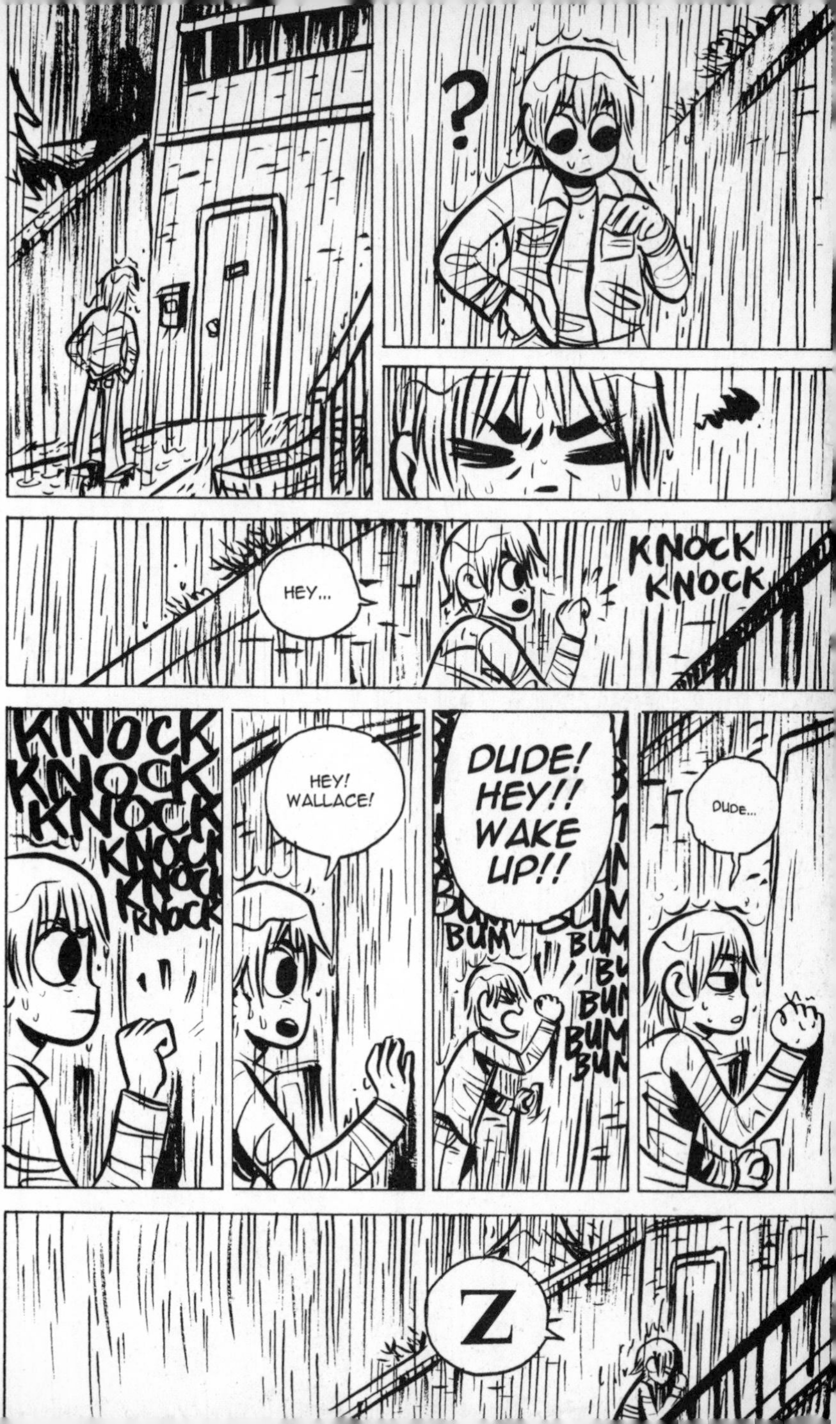
?
HEY...
KNOCK KNOCK
KNOCK KNOCK KNOCK
HEY! WALLACE!
DUDE! HEY!! WAKE UP!!
BUM BUM BUM BUM BUM
DUDE...
Z

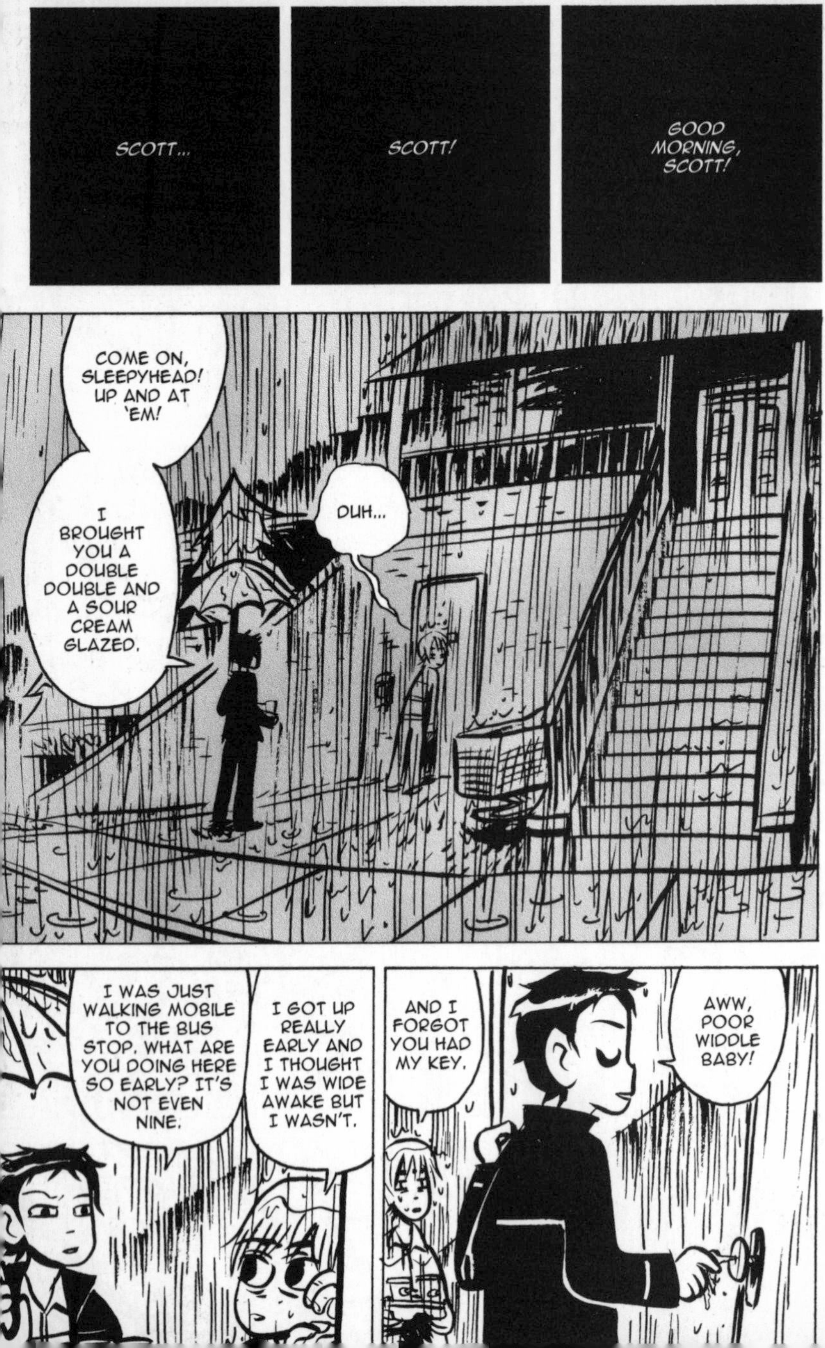
SCOTT...
SCOTT!
GOOD MORNING, SCOTT!
COME ON, SLEEPYHEAD! UP AND AT 'EM!
I BROUGHT YOU A DOUBLE DOUBLE AND A SOUR CREAM GLAZED.
DUH...
I WAS JUST WALKING MOBILE TO THE BUS STOP. WHAT ARE YOU DOING HERE SO EARLY? IT'S NOT EVEN NINE.
I GOT UP REALLY EARLY AND I THOUGHT I WAS WIDE AWAKE BUT I WASN'T.
AND I FORGOT YOU HAD MY KEY.
AWW, POOR WIDDLE BABY!

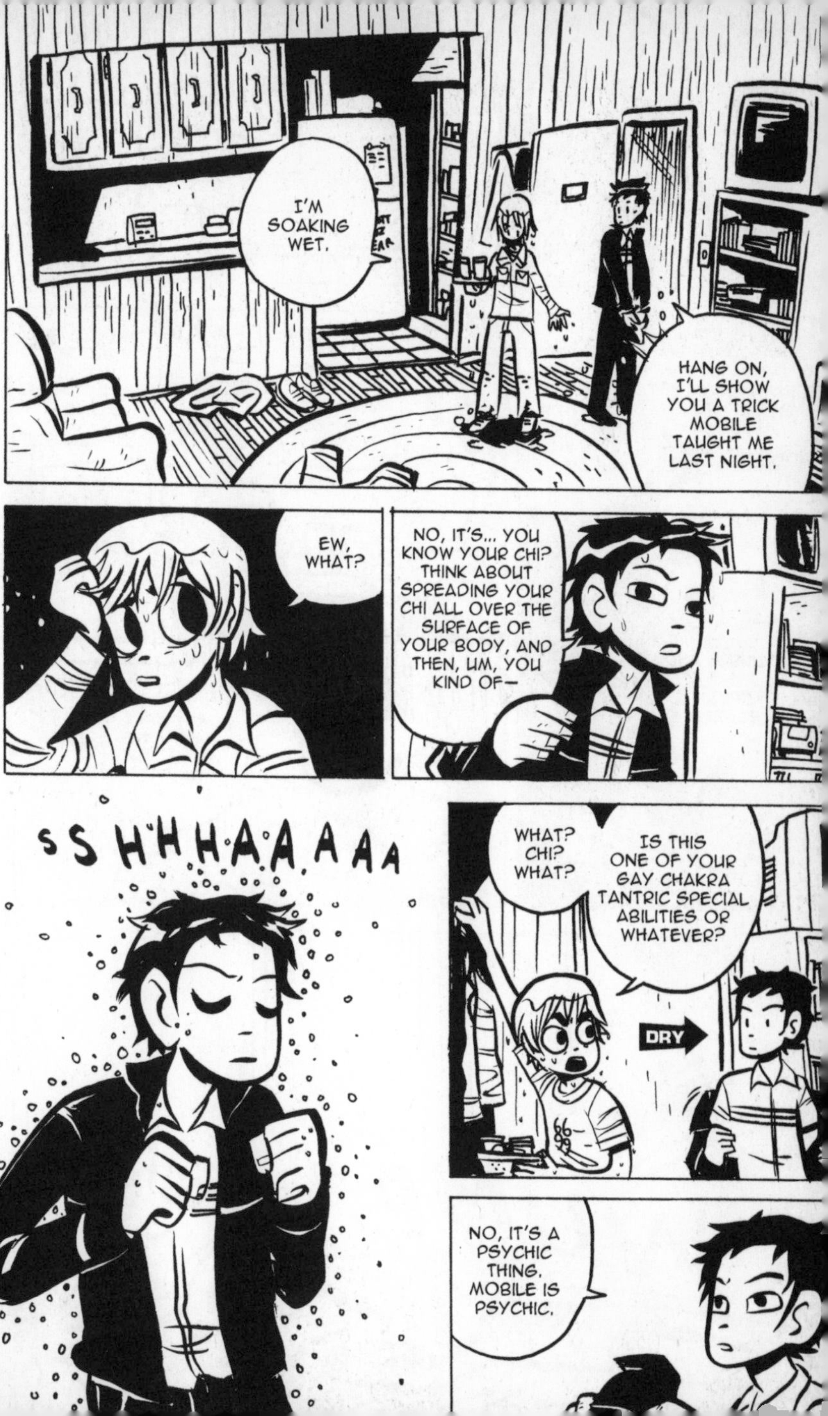
I'M SOAKING WET.
HANG ON, I'LL SHOW YOU A TRICK MOBILE TAUGHT ME LAST NIGHT.
EW, WHAT?
NO, IT'S... YOU KNOW YOUR CHI? THINK ABOUT SPREADING YOUR CHI ALL OVER THE SURFACE OF YOUR BODY, AND THEN, UM, YOU KIND OF—
SSHHHAAAAA
WHAT? CHI? WHAT?
IS THIS ONE OF YOUR GAY CHAKRA TANTRIC SPECIAL ABILITIES OR WHATEVER?
DRY
NO, IT'S A PSYCHIC THING. MOBILE IS PSYCHIC.

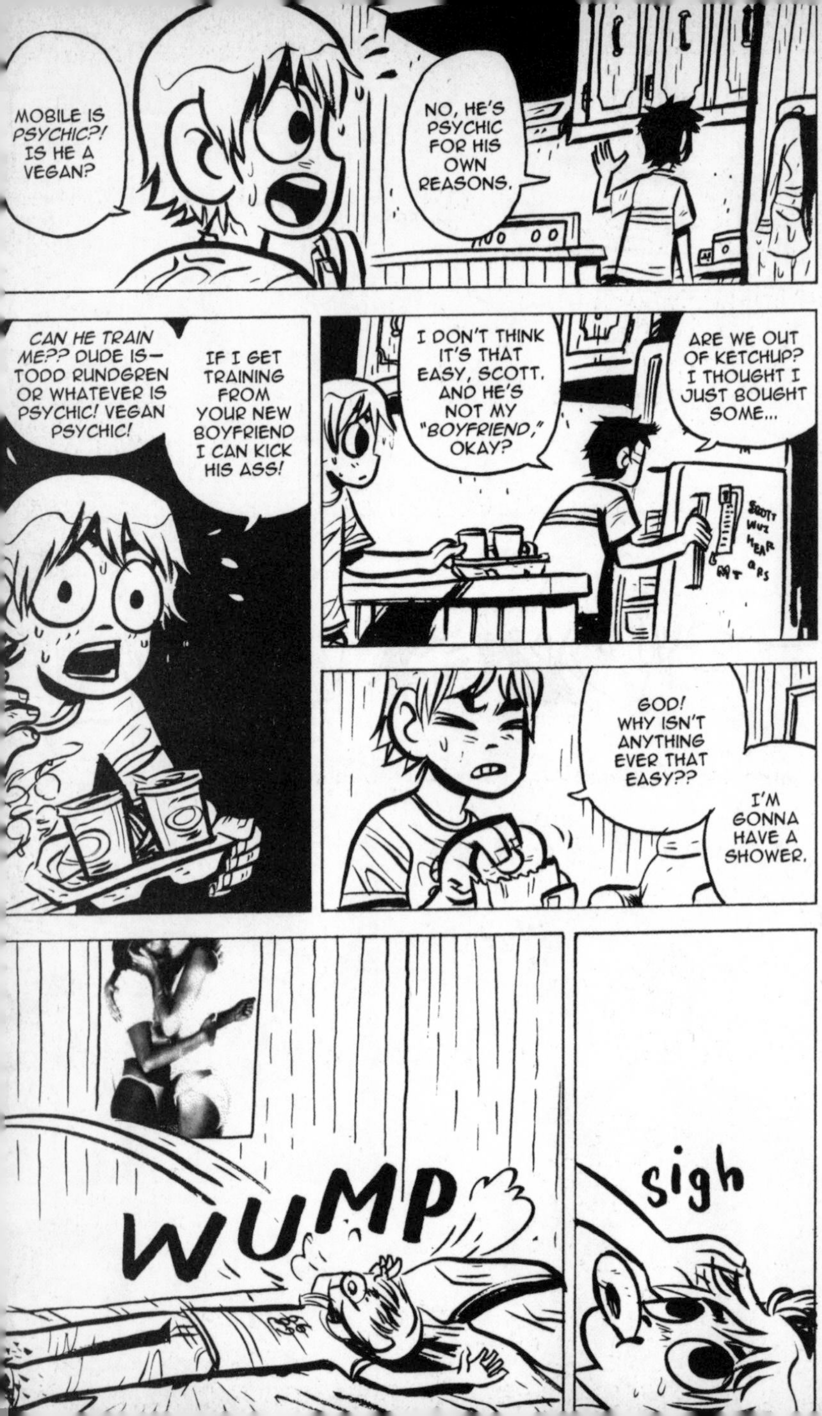
MOBILE IS PSYCHIC?! IS HE A VEGAN?
NO, HE'S PSYCHIC FOR HIS OWN REASONS.
CAN HE TRAIN ME?? DUDE IS— TODD RUNDGREN OR WHATEVER IS PSYCHIC! VEGAN PSYCHIC!
IF I GET TRAINING FROM YOUR NEW BOYFRIEND I CAN KICK HIS ASS!
I DON'T THINK IT'S THAT EASY, SCOTT. AND HE'S NOT MY "BOYFRIEND," OKAY?
ARE WE OUT OF KETCHUP? I THOUGHT I JUST BOUGHT SOME...
GOD! WHY ISN'T ANYTHING EVER THAT EASY??
I'M GONNA HAVE A SHOWER.
WUMP
sigh

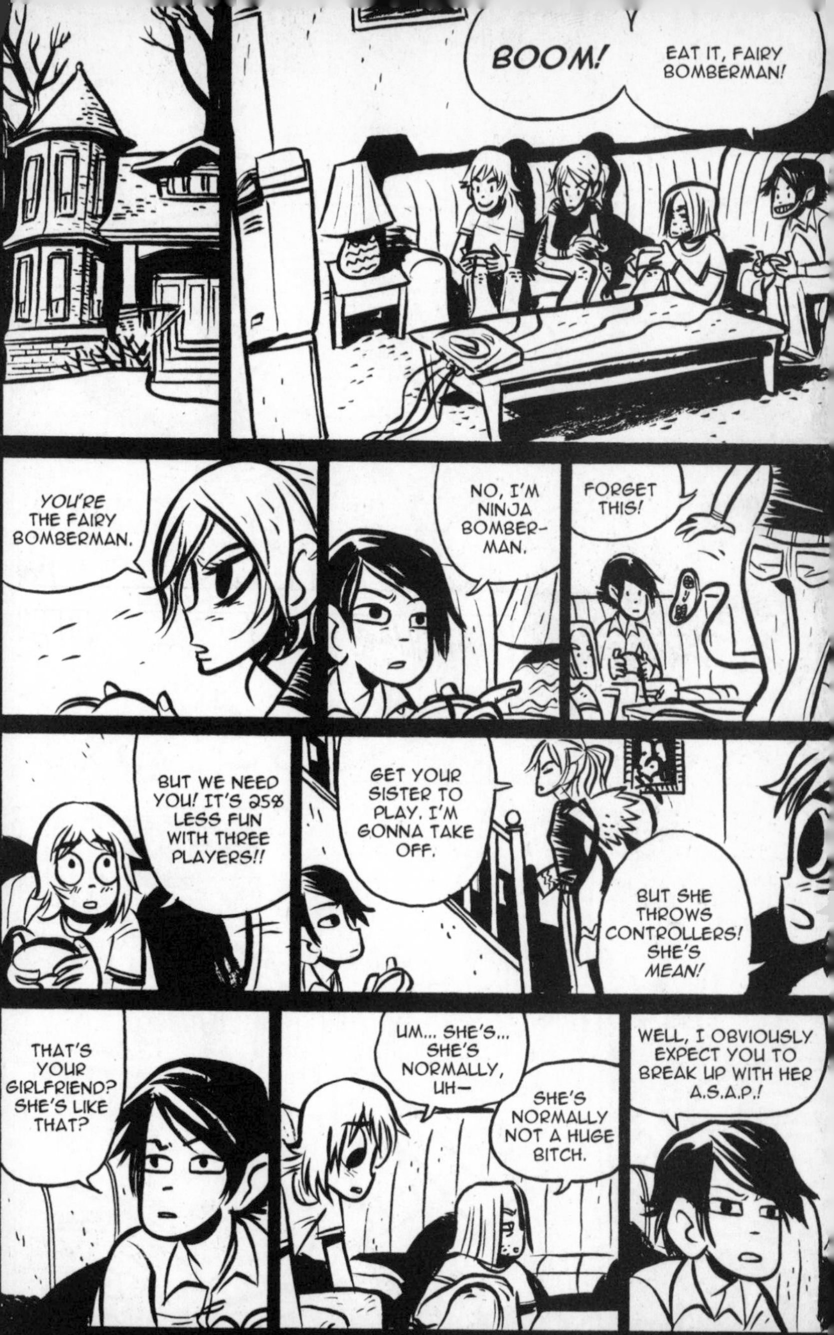
BOOM!
EAT IT, FAIRY BOMBERMAN!
YOU'RE THE FAIRY BOMBERMAN.
NO, I'M NINJA BOMBERMAN.
FORGET THIS!
BUT WE NEED YOU! IT'S 25% LESS FUN WITH THREE PLAYERS!!
GET YOUR SISTER TO PLAY. I'M GONNA TAKE OFF.
BUT SHE THROWS CONTROLLERS! SHE'S MEAN!
THAT'S YOUR GIRLFRIEND? SHE'S LIKE THAT?
UM... SHE'S... SHE'S NORMALLY, UH—
SHE'S NORMALLY NOT A HUGE BITCH.
WELL, I OBVIOUSLY EXPECT YOU TO BREAK UP WITH HER A.S.A.P.!

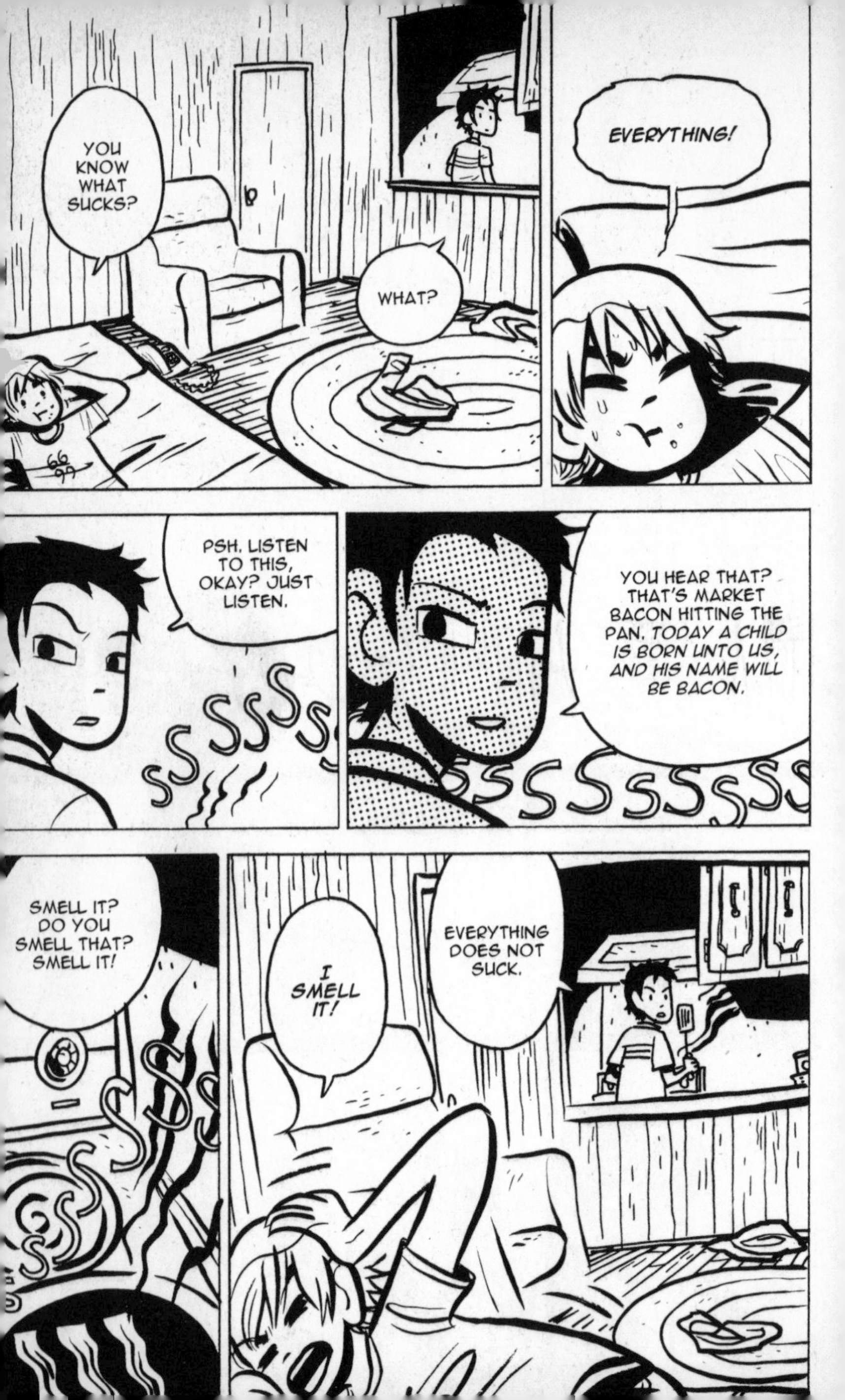
YOU KNOW WHAT SUCKS?
WHAT?
EVERYTHING!
PSH. LISTEN TO THIS, OKAY? JUST LISTEN.
YOU HEAR THAT? THAT'S MARKET BACON HITTING THE PAN. TODAY A CHILD IS BORN UNTO US, AND HIS NAME WILL BE BACON.
SMELL IT? DO YOU SMELL THAT? SMELL IT!
EVERYTHING DOES NOT SUCK.
I SMELL IT!

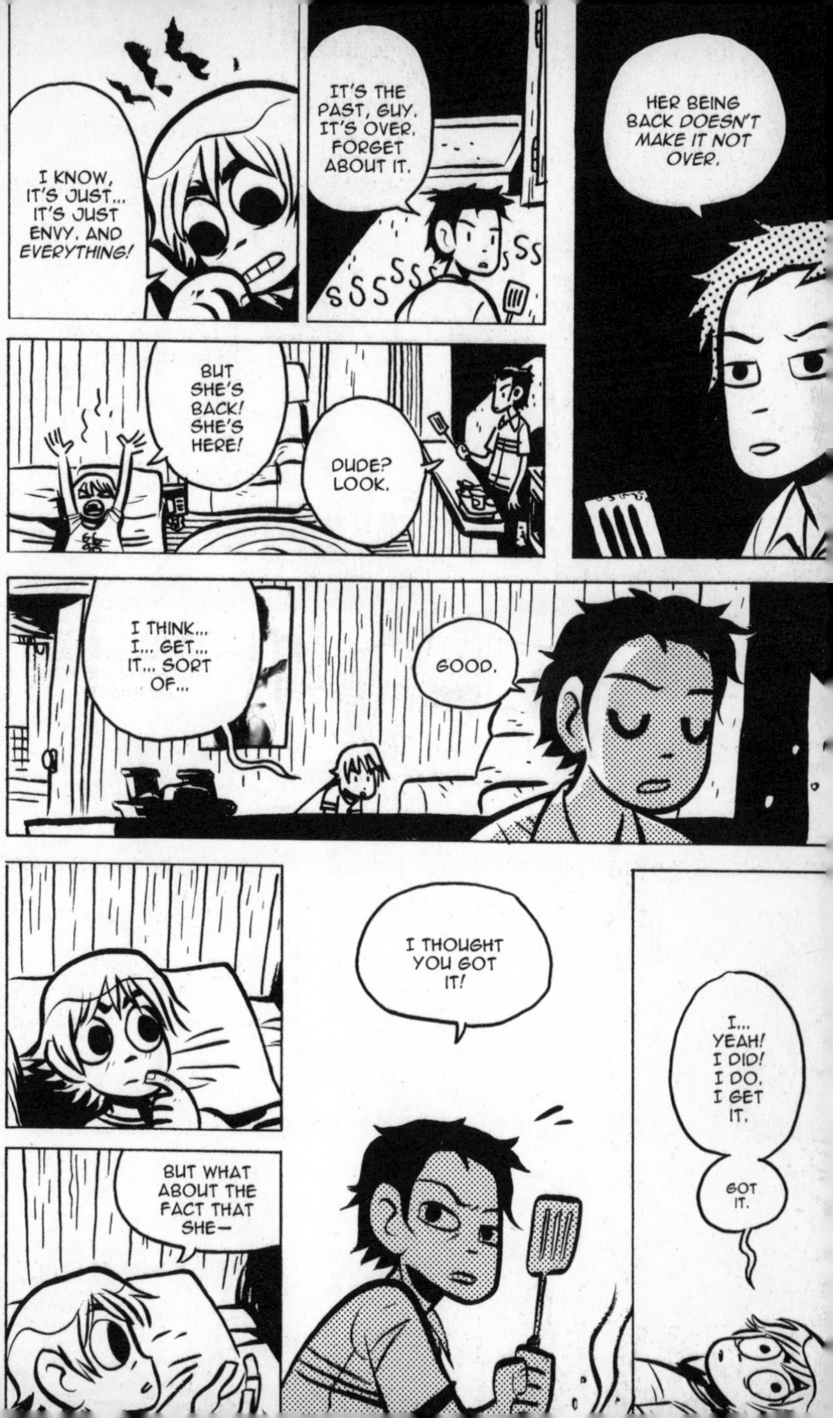
I KNOW, IT'S JUST... IT'S JUST ENVY. AND EVERYTHING!
IT'S THE PAST, GUY. IT'S OVER. FORGET ABOUT IT.
SSSSSSSSS
HER BEING BACK DOESN'T MAKE IT NOT OVER.
BUT SHE'S BACK! SHE'S HERE!
DUDE? LOOK.
I THINK... I... GET... IT... SORT OF...
GOOD.
I THOUGHT YOU GOT IT!
BUT WHAT ABOUT THE FACT THAT SHE—
I... YEAH! I DID! I DO. I GET IT.
GOT IT.

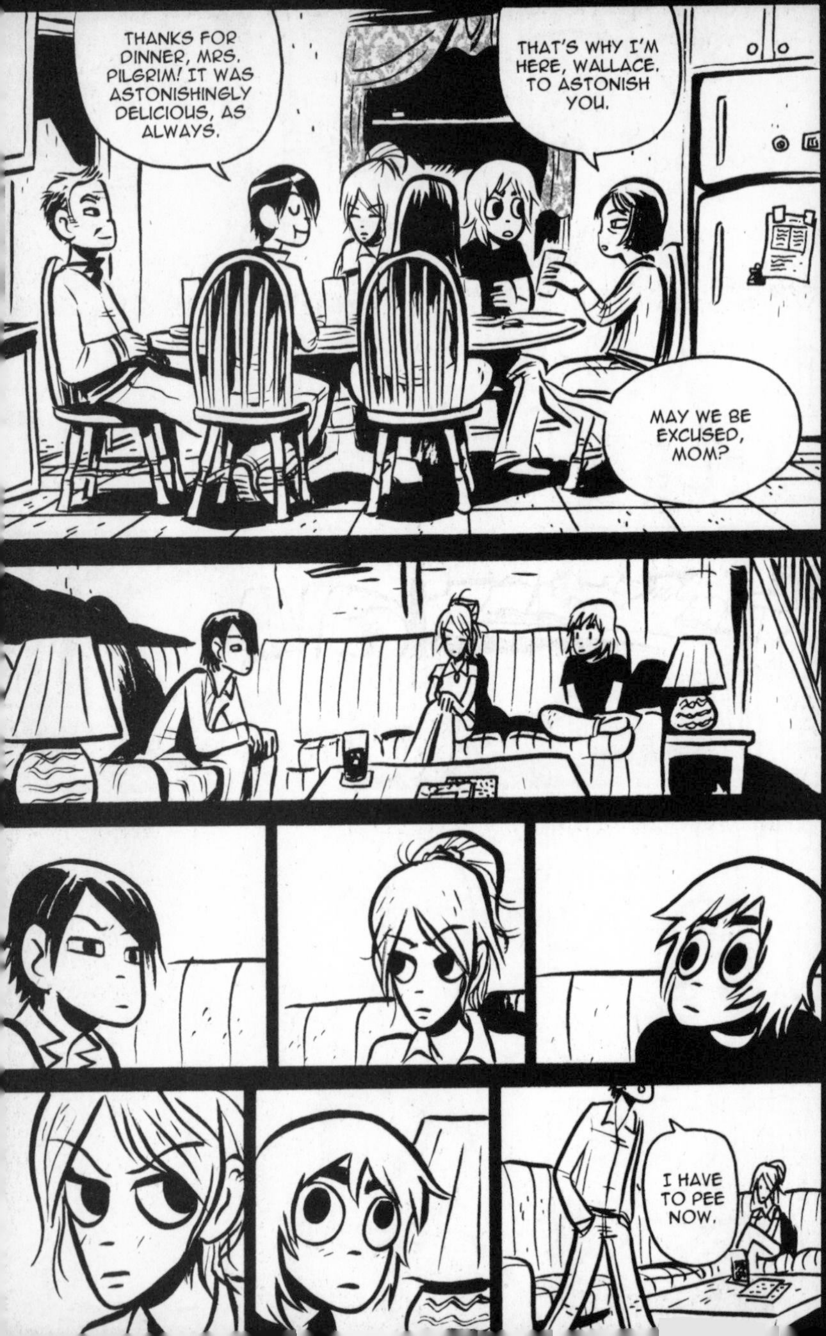
THANKS FOR DINNER, MRS. PILGRIM! IT WAS ASTONISHINGLY DELICIOUS, AS ALWAYS.
THAT'S WHY I'M HERE, WALLACE. TO ASTONISH YOU.
MAY WE BE EXCUSED, MOM?
I HAVE TO PEE NOW.

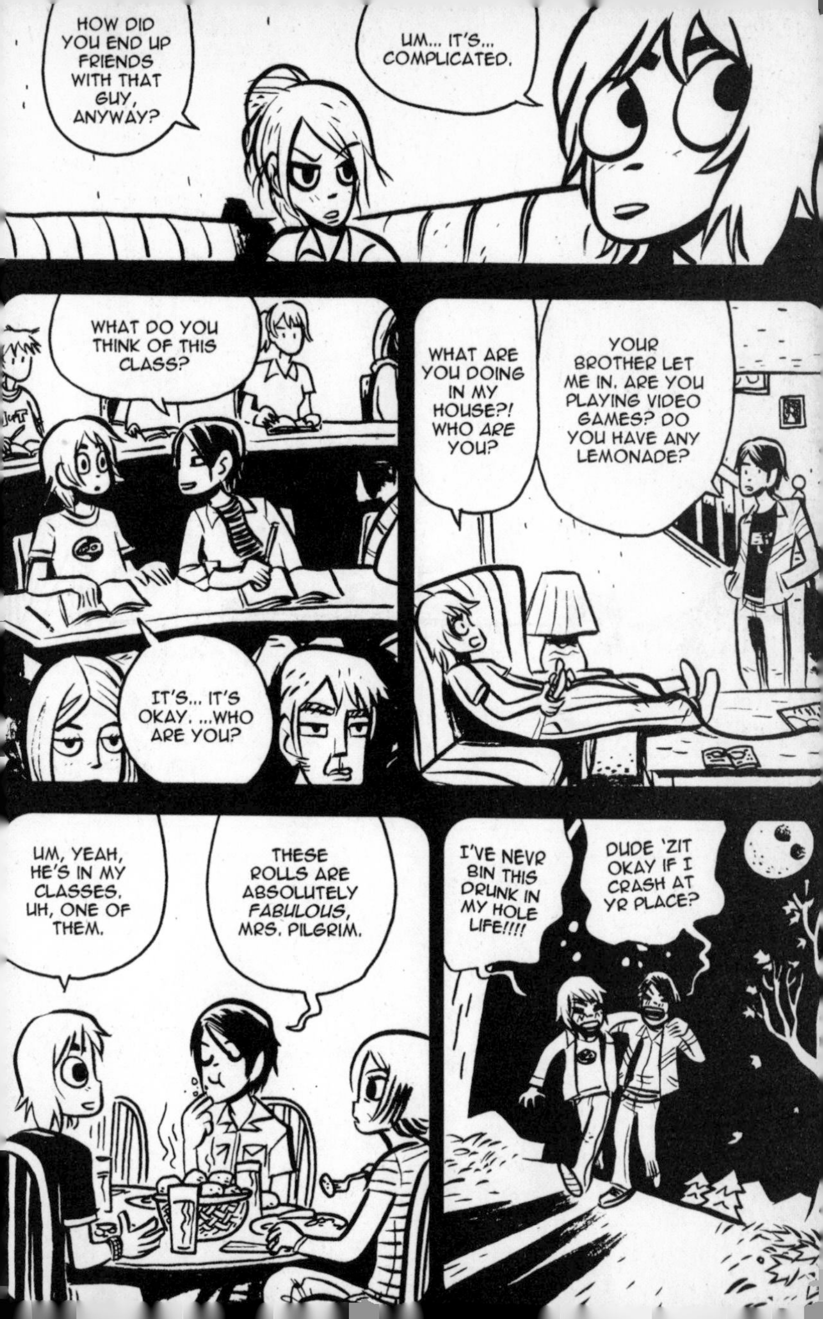
HOW DID YOU END UP FRIENDS WITH THAT GUY, ANYWAY?
UM... IT'S... COMPLICATED.
WHAT DO YOU THINK OF THIS CLASS?
IT'S... IT'S OKAY. ...WHO ARE YOU?
WHAT ARE YOU DOING IN MY HOUSE?! WHO ARE YOU?
YOUR BROTHER LET ME IN. ARE YOU PLAYING VIDEO GAMES? DO YOU HAVE ANY LEMONADE?
UM, YEAH, HE'S IN MY CLASSES. UH, ONE OF THEM.
THESE ROLLS ARE ABSOLUTELY FABULOUS, MRS. PILGRIM.
I'VE NEVR BIN THIS DRUNK IN MY HOLE LIFE!!!!
DUDE 'ZIT OKAY IF I CRASH AT YR PLACE?

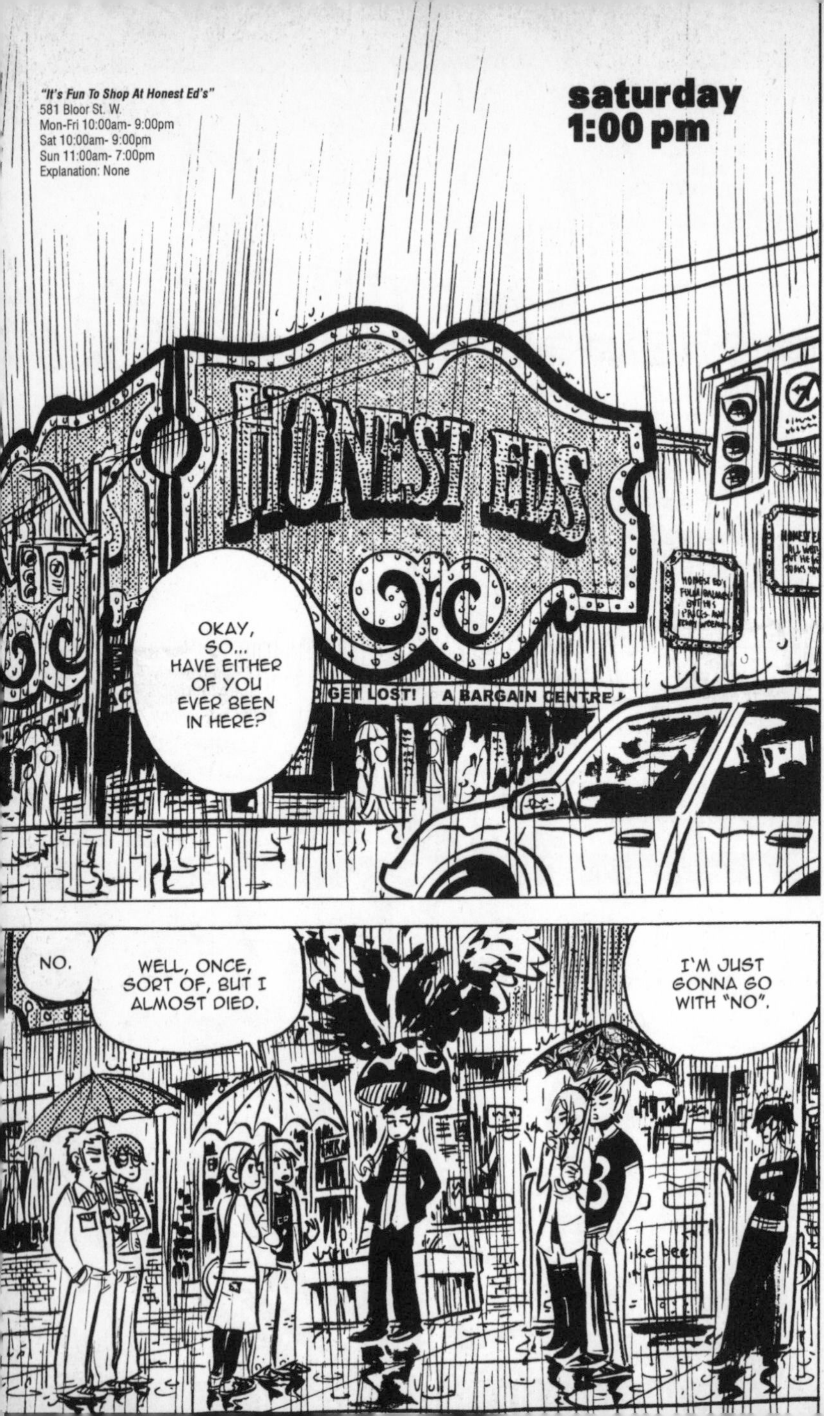

"It's Fun To Shop At Honest Ed's"
581 Bloor St. W.
Mon-Fri 10:00am- 9:00pm
Sat 10:00am- 9:00pm
Sun 11:00am- 7:00pm
Explanation: None
saturday
1:00 pm
HONEST EDS
GET LOST!
A BARGAIN CENTRE
OKAY, SO... HAVE EITHER OF YOU EVER BEEN IN HERE?
NO.
WELL, ONCE, SORT OF, BUT I ALMOST DIED.
I'M JUST GONNA GO WITH "NO".

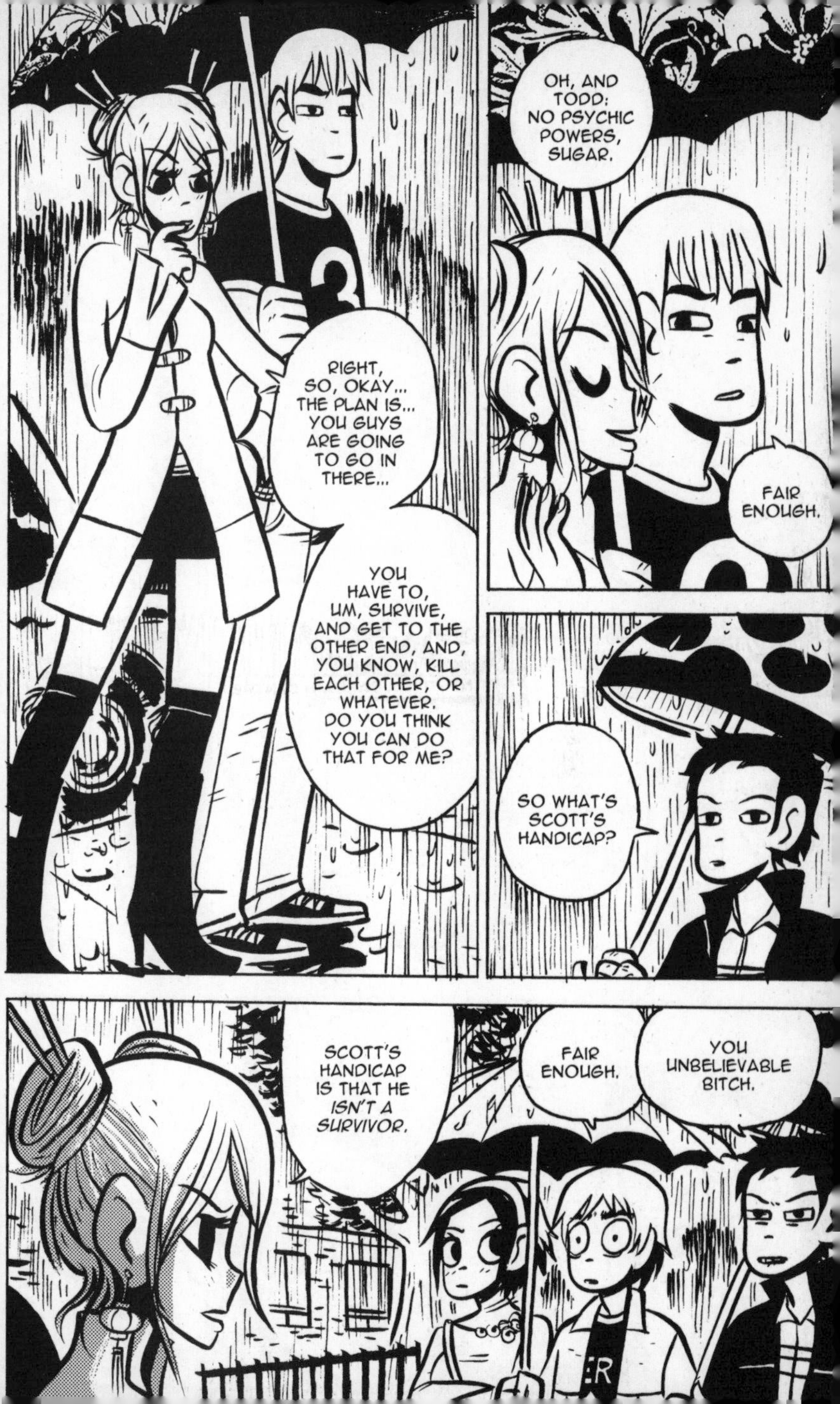
RIGHT, SO, OKAY... THE PLAN IS... YOU GUYS ARE GOING TO GO IN THERE...
YOU HAVE TO, UM, SURVIVE, AND GET TO THE OTHER END, AND, YOU KNOW, KILL EACH OTHER, OR WHATEVER. DO YOU THINK YOU CAN DO THAT FOR ME?
OH, AND TODD: NO PSYCHIC POWERS, SUGAR.
FAIR ENOUGH.
SO WHAT'S SCOTT'S HANDICAP?
SCOTT'S HANDICAP IS THAT HE *ISN'T A SURVIVOR.*
FAIR ENOUGH.
YOU UNBELIEVABLE BITCH.

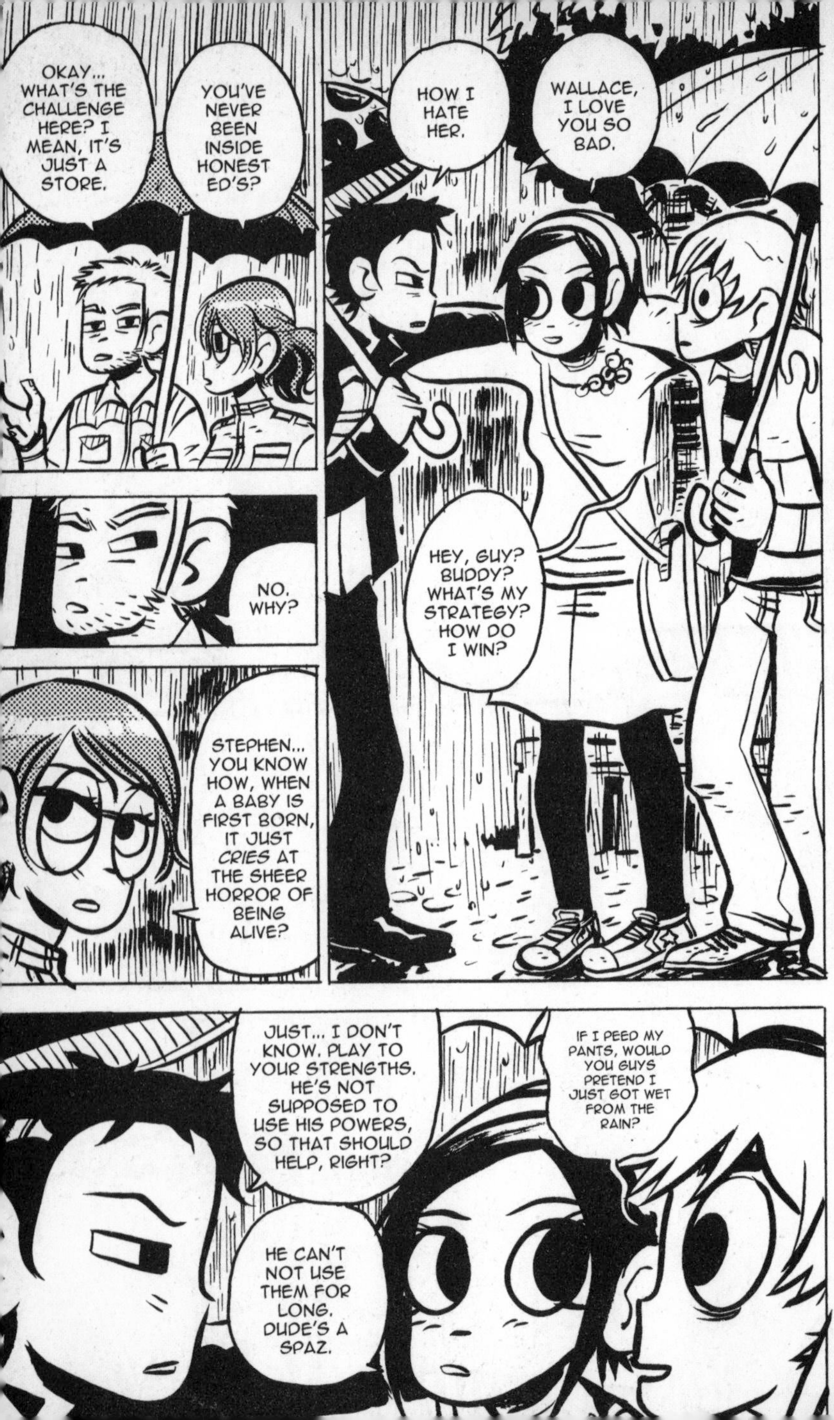
OKAY... WHAT'S THE CHALLENGE HERE? I MEAN, IT'S JUST A STORE.
YOU'VE NEVER BEEN INSIDE HONEST ED'S?
HOW I HATE HER.
WALLACE, I LOVE YOU SO BAD.
NO. WHY?
STEPHEN... YOU KNOW HOW, WHEN A BABY IS FIRST BORN, IT JUST *CRIES* AT THE SHEER HORROR OF BEING ALIVE?
HEY, GUY? BUDDY? WHAT'S MY STRATEGY? HOW DO I WIN?
JUST... I DON'T KNOW. PLAY TO YOUR STRENGTHS. HE'S NOT SUPPOSED TO USE HIS POWERS, SO THAT SHOULD HELP, RIGHT?
IF I PEED MY PANTS, WOULD YOU GUYS PRETEND I JUST GOT WET FROM THE RAIN?
HE CAN'T NOT USE THEM FOR LONG. DUDE'S A SPAZ.

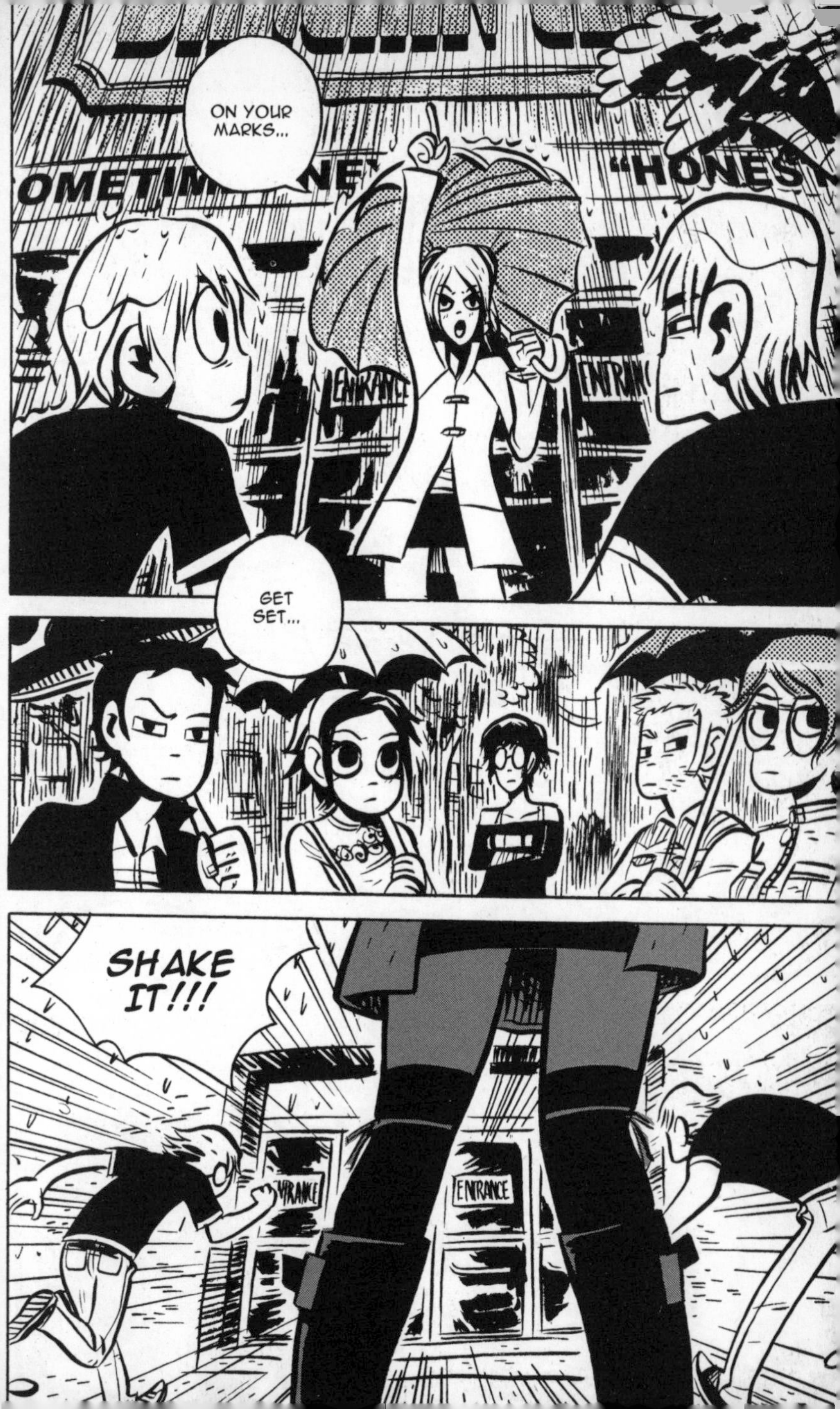
ON YOUR MARKS...
GET SET...
SHAKE IT!!!
ENTRANCE

THE STARK EXISTENTIAL HORROR OF HONEST ED'S

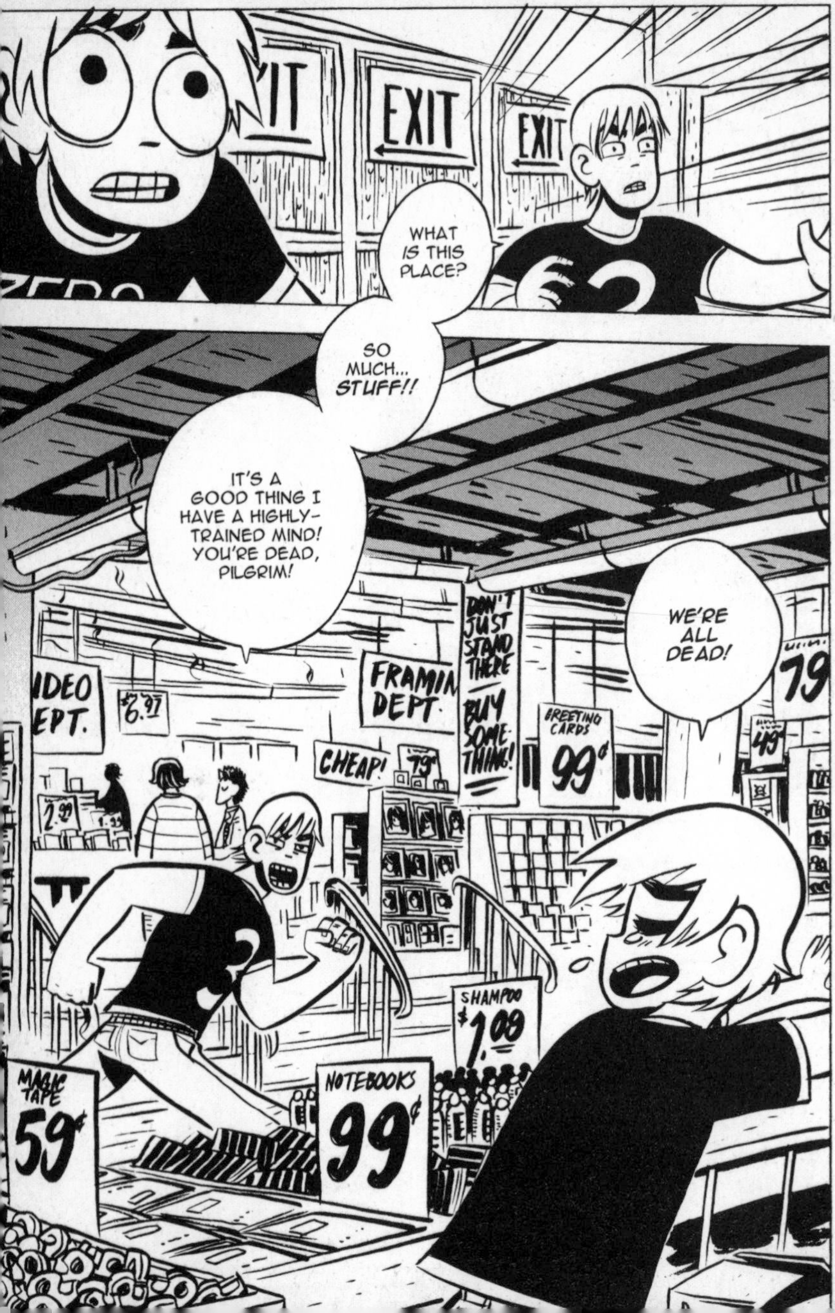
EXIT
EXIT
WHAT IS THIS PLACE?
SO MUCH... STUFF!!
IT'S A GOOD THING I HAVE A HIGHLY-TRAINED MIND! YOU'RE DEAD, PILGRIM!
WE'RE ALL DEAD!
CHEAP!
DON'T JUST STAND THERE BUY SOMETHING!
GREETING CARDS 99¢
NOTEBOOKS 99¢
MAGIC TAPE 59¢

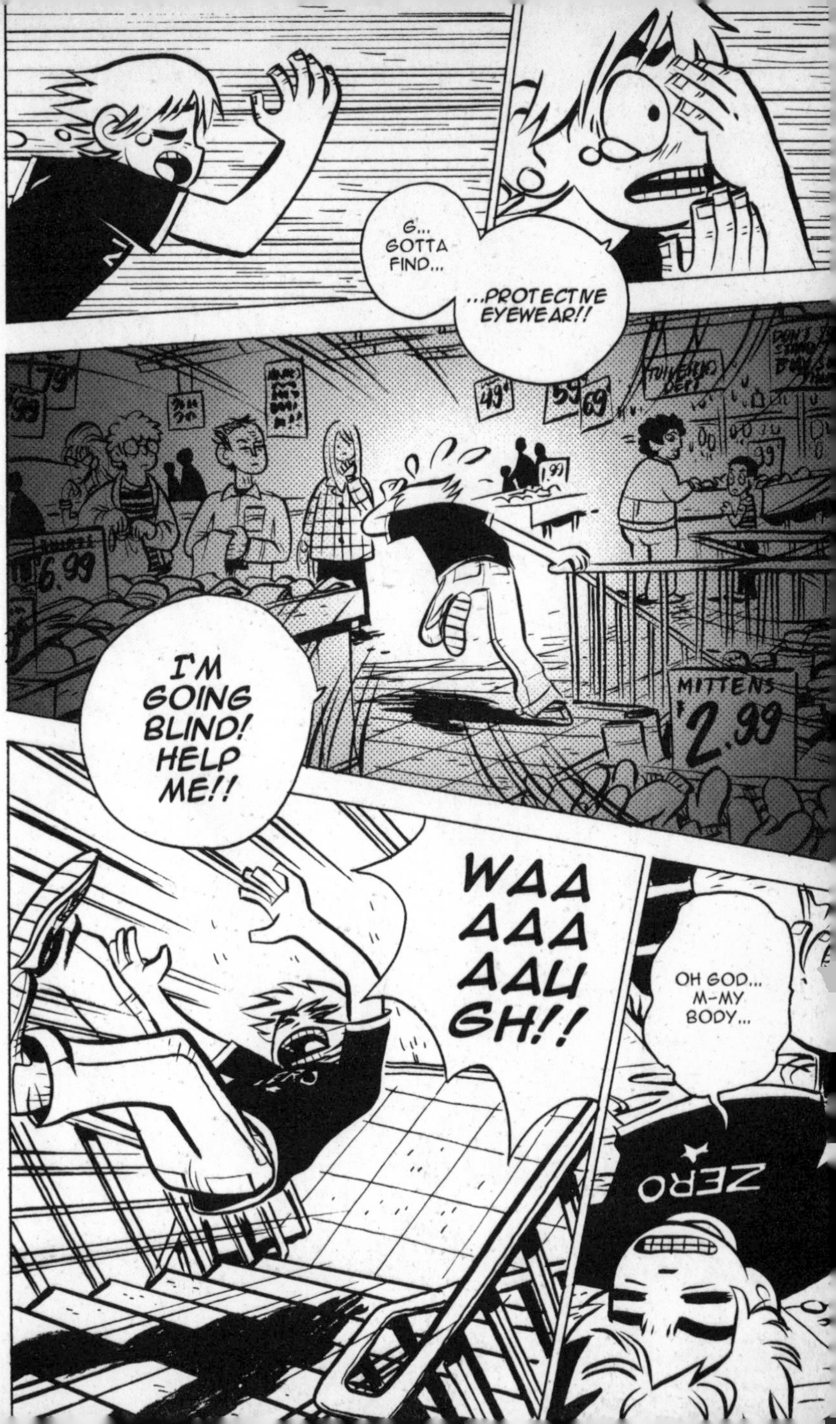
G... GOTTA FIND...
...PROTECTIVE EYEWEAR!!
I'M GOING BLIND! HELP ME!!
MITTENS $2.99
WAA AAA AAU GH!!
OH GOD... M-MY BODY...
ZERO

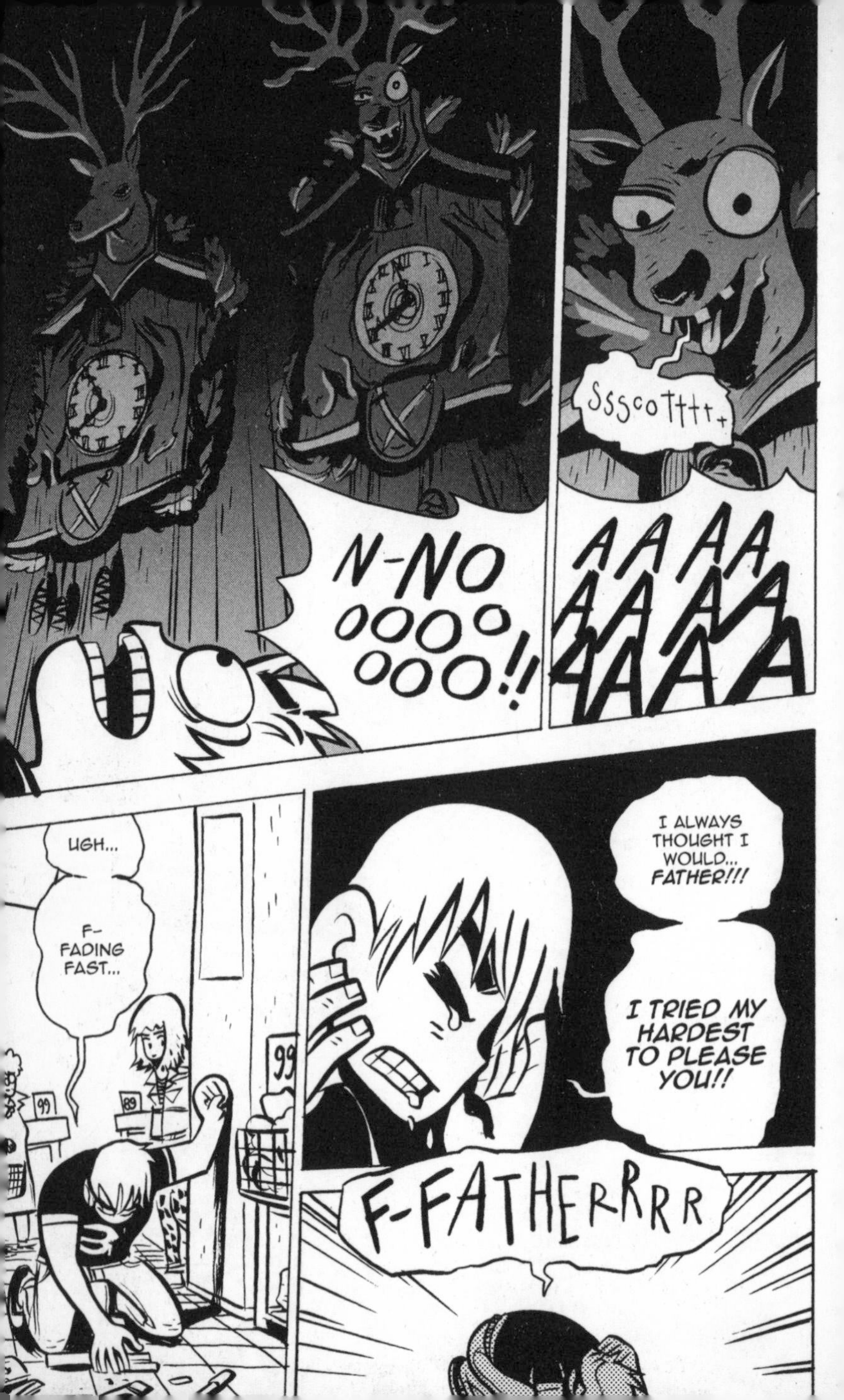
Sssco††††
N-NOOOOOOOO!!
AAAAAAAAAAAA
UGH...
F- FADING FAST...
I ALWAYS THOUGHT I WOULD... FATHER!!!
I TRIED MY HARDEST TO PLEASE YOU!!
F-FATHERRRR

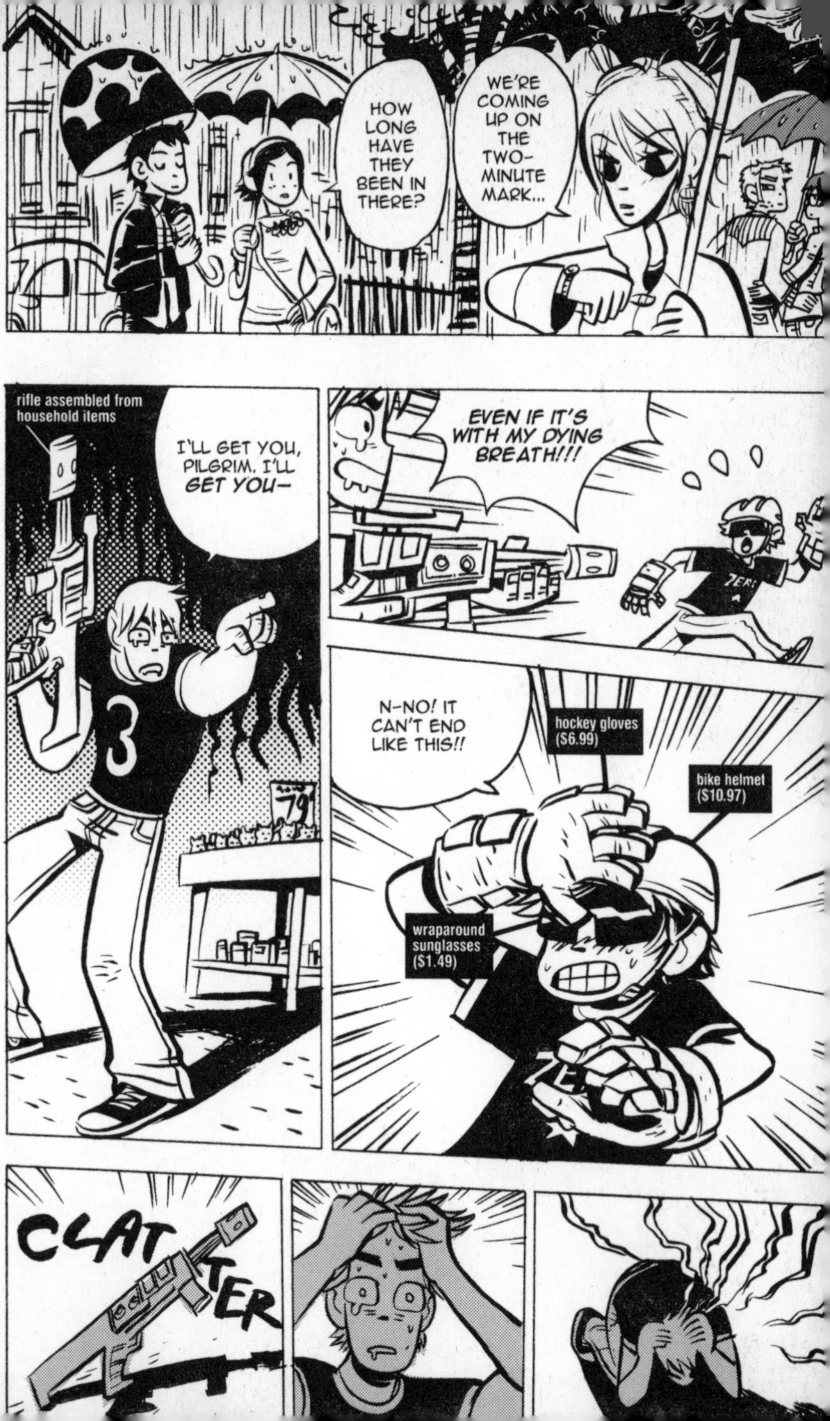
HOW LONG HAVE THEY BEEN IN THERE?
WE'RE COMING UP ON THE TWO-MINUTE MARK...
rifle assembled from household items
I'LL GET YOU, PILGRIM. I'LL GET YOU–
EVEN IF IT'S WITH MY DYING BREATH!!!
N-NO! IT CAN'T END LIKE THIS!!
hockey gloves ($6.99)
bike helmet ($10.97)
wraparound sunglasses ($1.49)
CLATTER

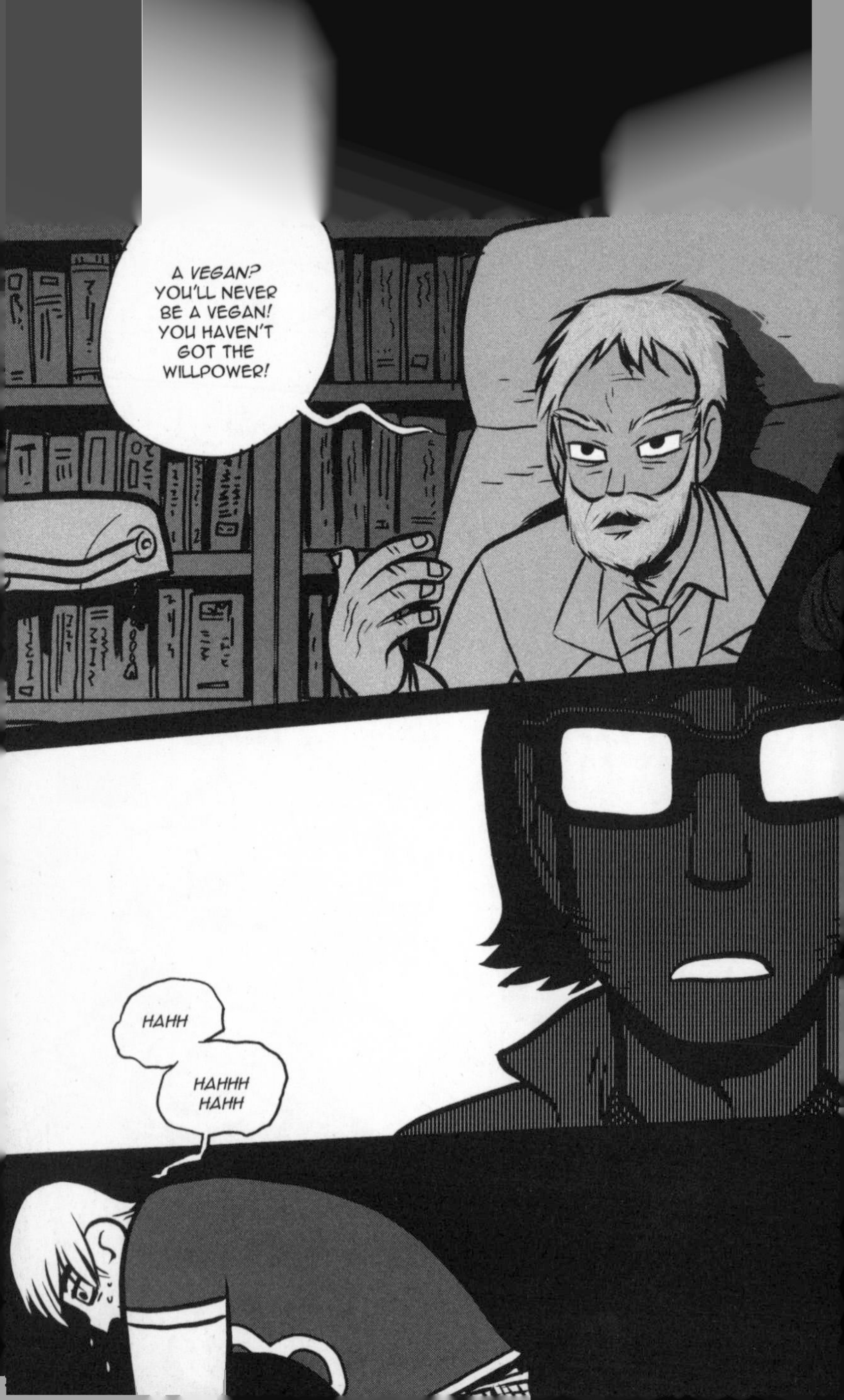
A VEGAN? YOU'LL NEVER BE A VEGAN! YOU HAVEN'T GOT THE WILLPOWER!
HAHH
HAHHH HAHH

COME ON. SHE'LL NEVER KNOW, TODD. I'M YOURS FOR THE TAKING.
JUST USE YOUR VEGAN POWERS OR WHATEVER.
HE'LL NEVER KNOW WHAT HIT HIM, RIGHT?
HAHHH
HGGGH
HAAGGHH

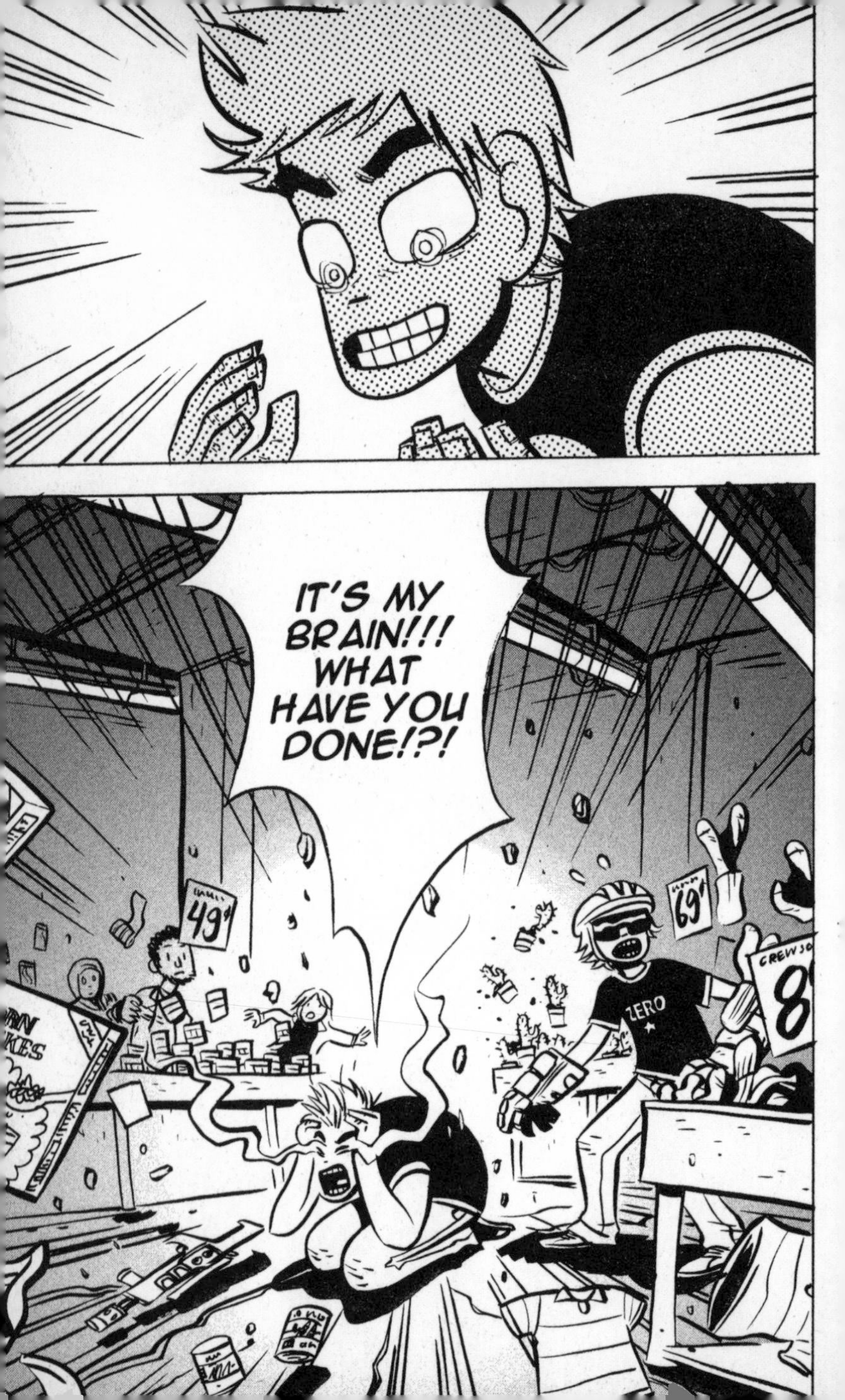
IT'S MY BRAIN!!! WHAT HAVE YOU DONE!?!
49¢
69¢
ZERO

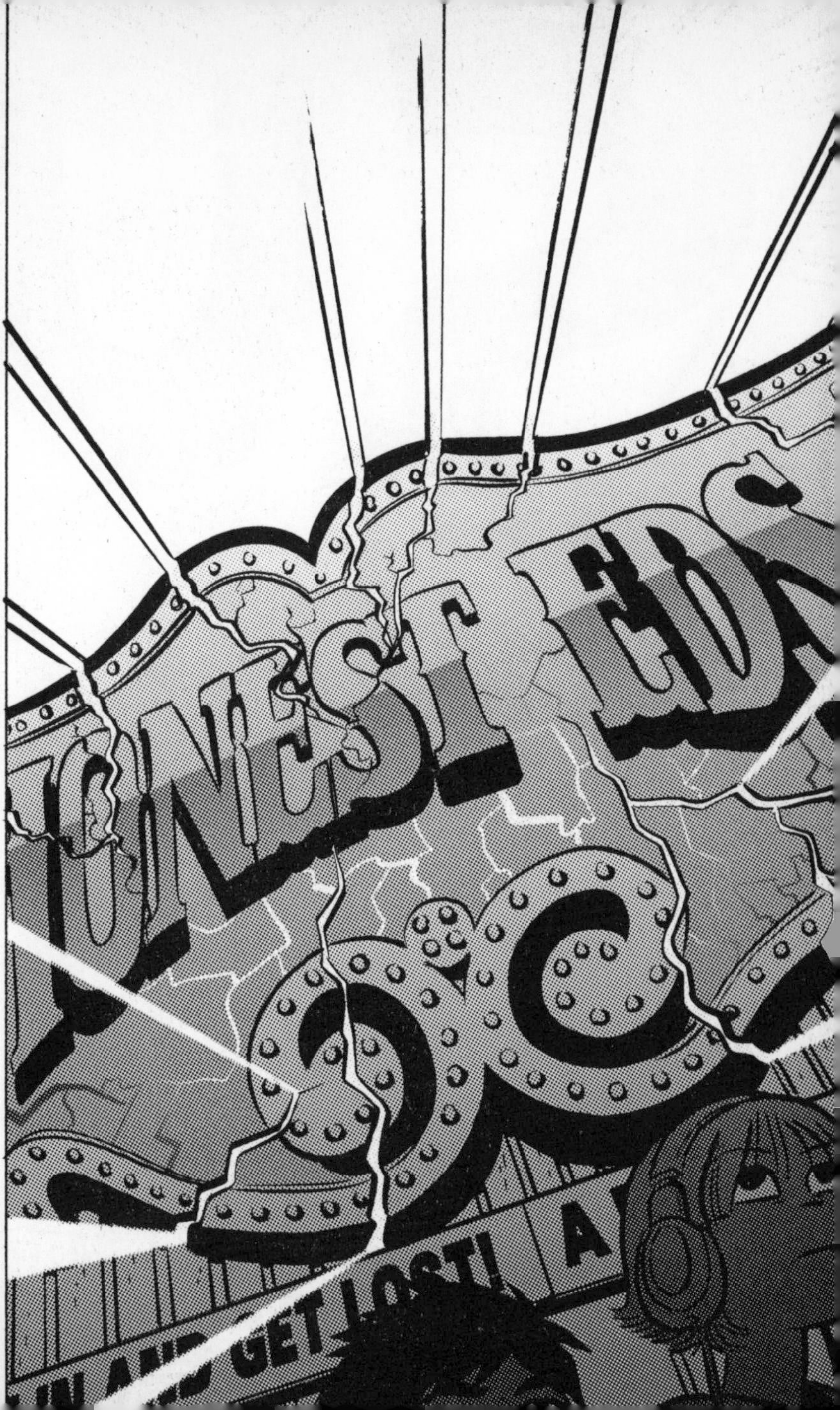
AND GET LOST!

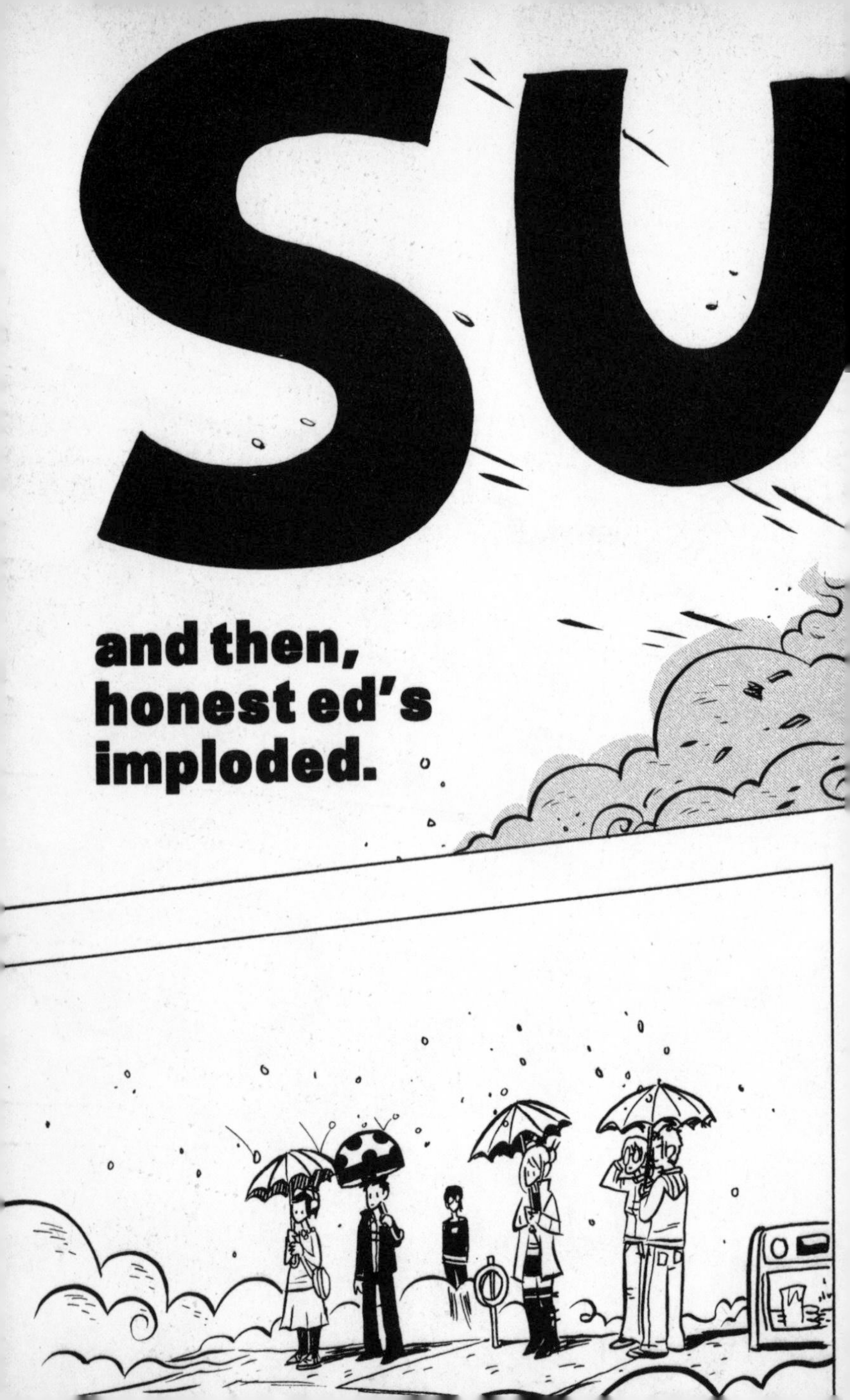
SU
and then, honest ed's imploded.

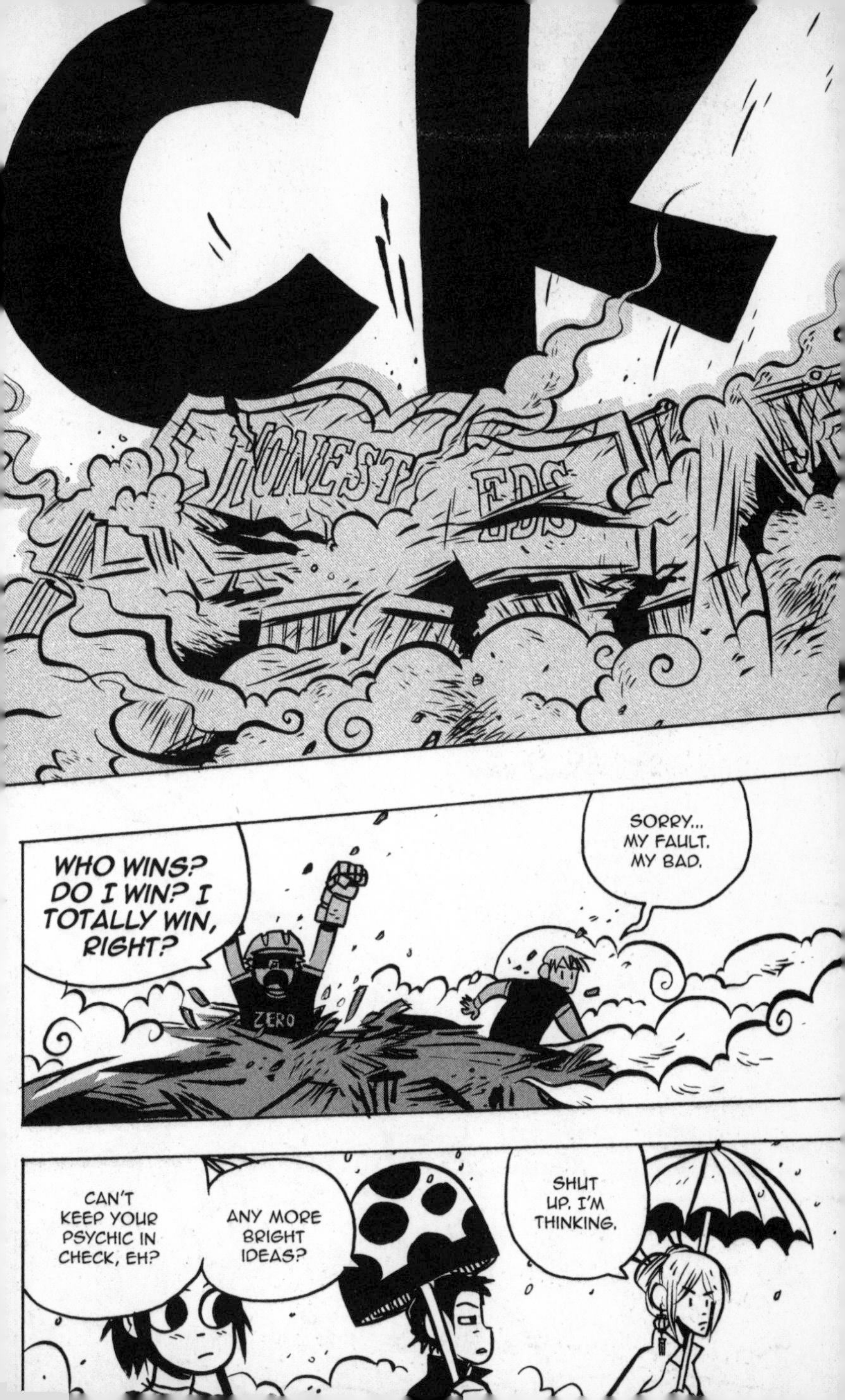
CK
HONEST EDS
WHO WINS? DO I WIN? I TOTALLY WIN, RIGHT?
SORRY... MY FAULT. MY BAD.
ZERO
CAN'T KEEP YOUR PSYCHIC IN CHECK, EH?
ANY MORE BRIGHT IDEAS?
SHUT UP. I'M THINKING.

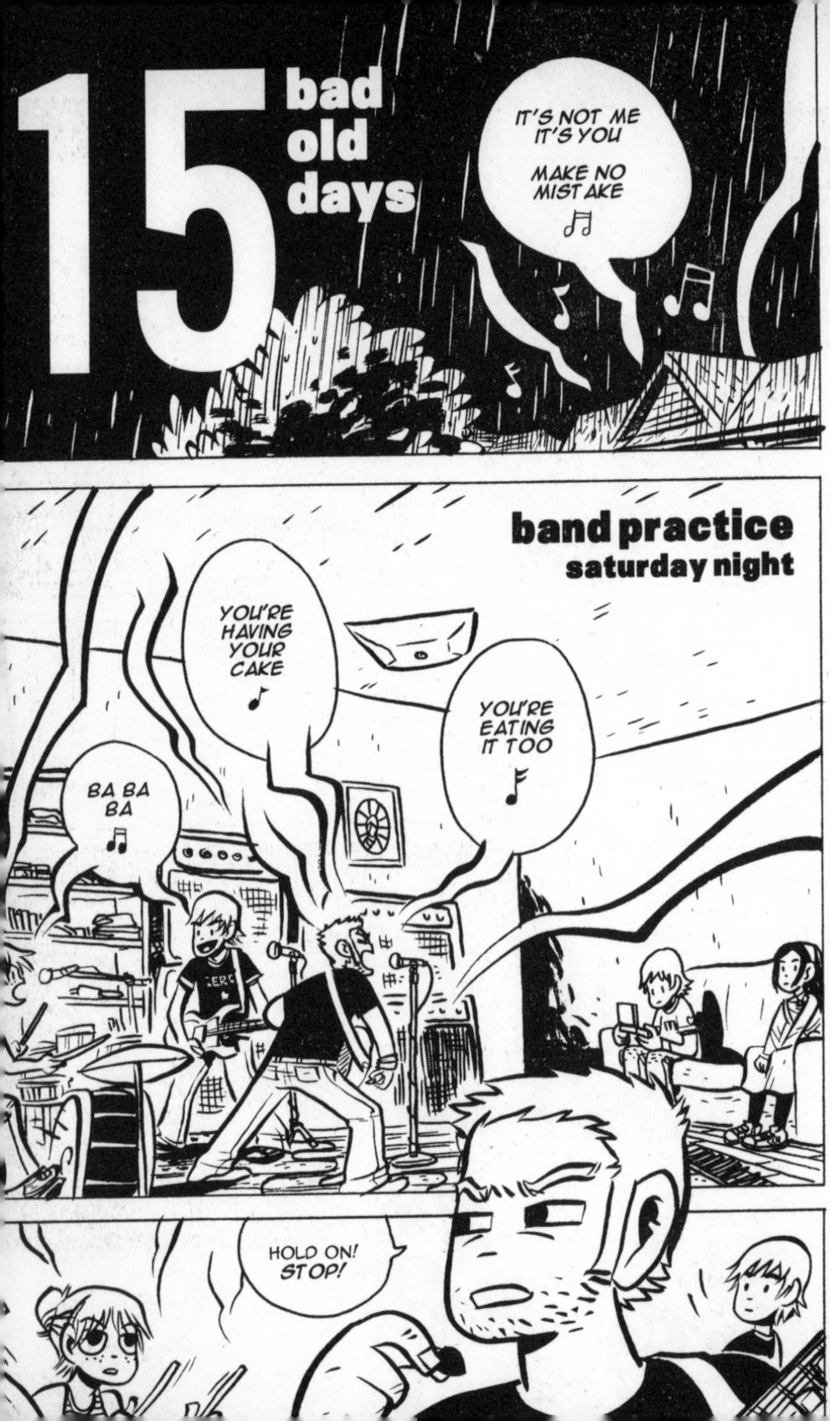

15
bad old days
IT'S NOT ME
IT'S YOU
MAKE NO MISTAKE
band practice
saturday night
YOU'RE HAVING YOUR CAKE
YOU'RE EATING IT TOO
BA BA BA
ZERO
HOLD ON! STOP!

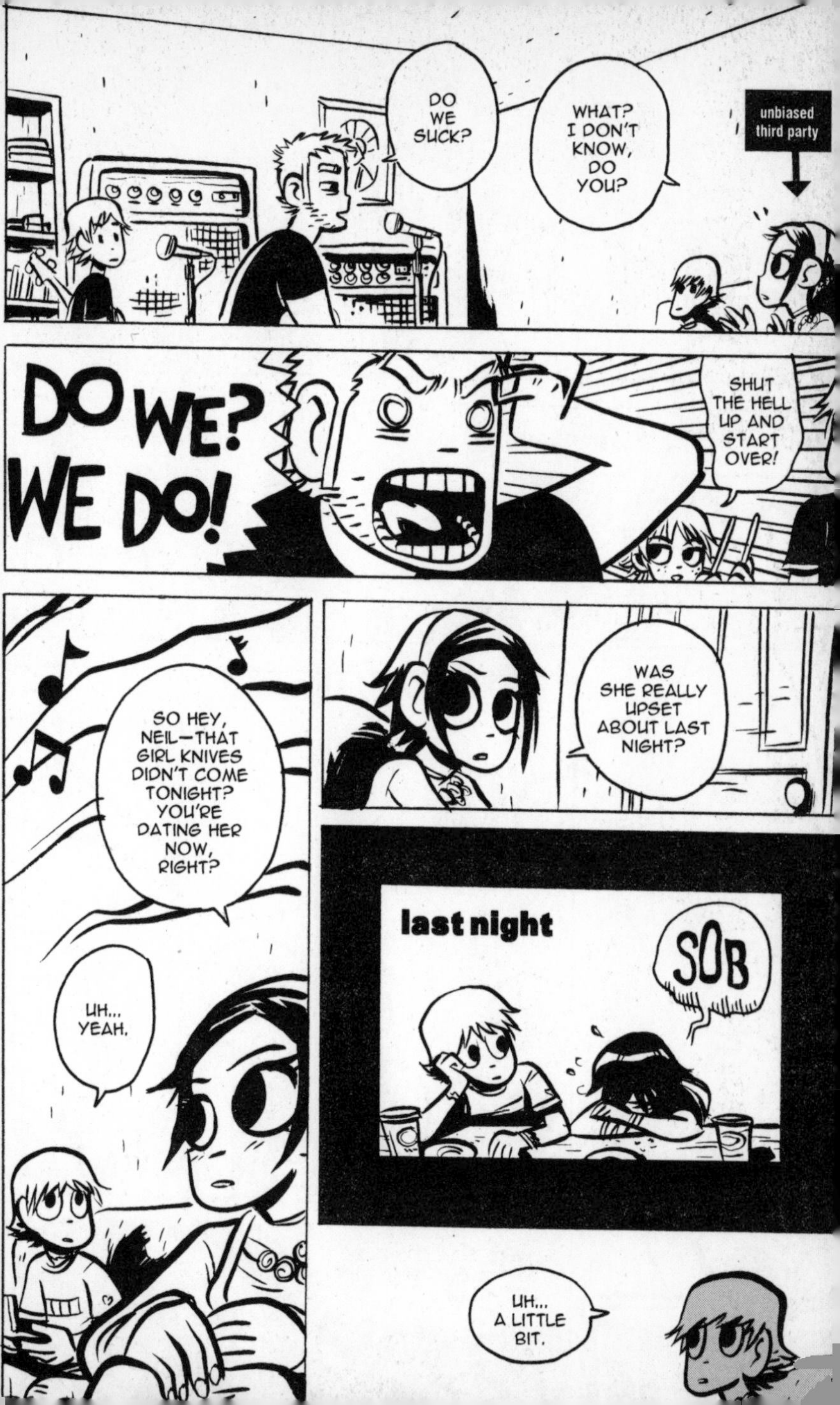
DO WE SUCK?
WHAT? I DON'T KNOW, DO YOU?
unbiased third party
DO WE? WE DO!
SHUT THE HELL UP AND START OVER!
SO HEY, NEIL—THAT GIRL KNIVES DIDN'T COME TONIGHT? YOU'RE DATING HER NOW, RIGHT?
UH... YEAH.
WAS SHE REALLY UPSET ABOUT LAST NIGHT?
last night
SOB
UH... A LITTLE BIT.

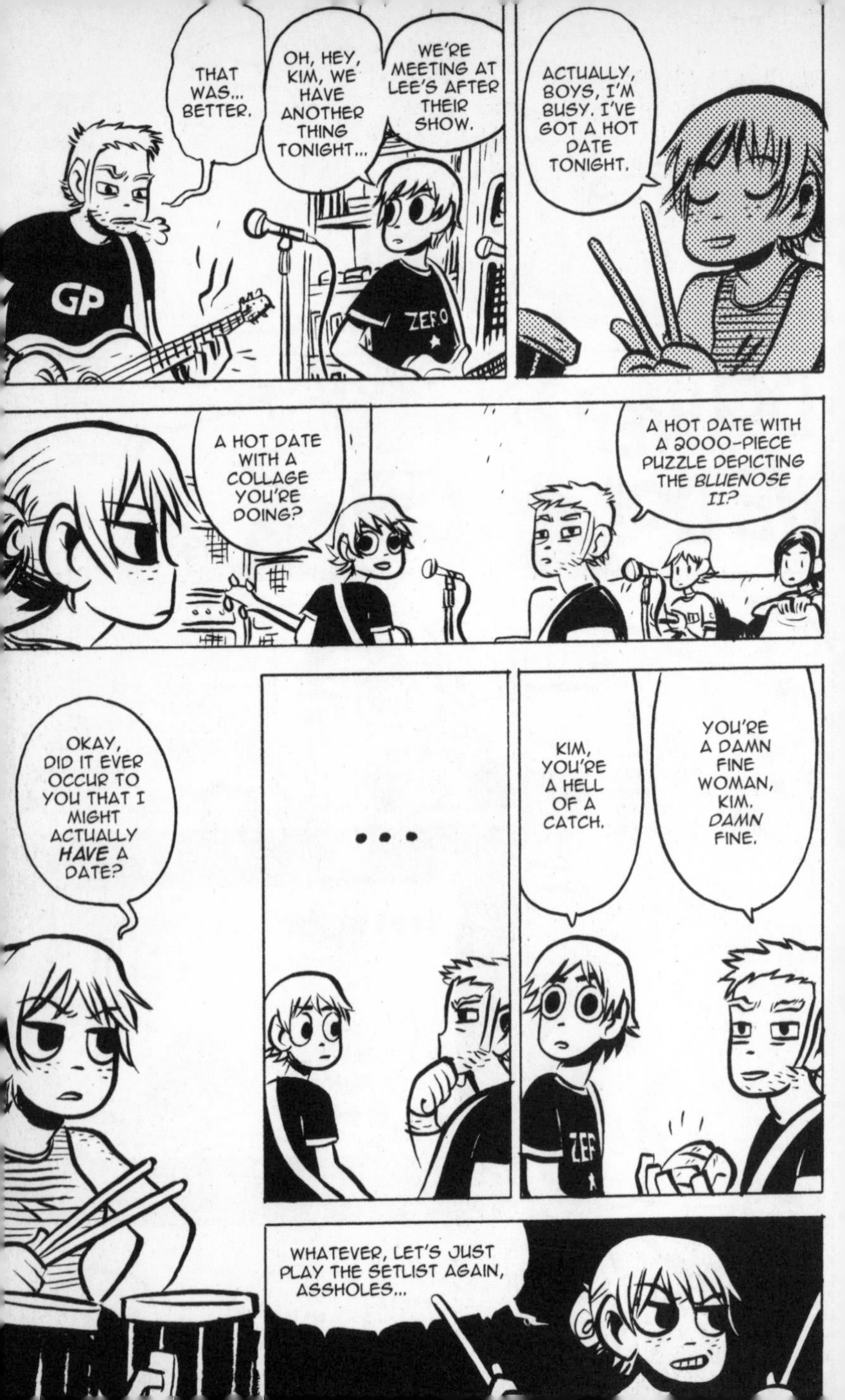
THAT WAS... BETTER.
OH, HEY, KIM, WE HAVE ANOTHER THING TONIGHT...
WE'RE MEETING AT LEE'S AFTER THEIR SHOW.
GP
ZERO
ACTUALLY, BOYS, I'M BUSY. I'VE GOT A HOT DATE TONIGHT.
A HOT DATE WITH A COLLAGE YOU'RE DOING?
A HOT DATE WITH A 2000-PIECE PUZZLE DEPICTING THE *BLUENOSE II*?
OKAY, DID IT EVER OCCUR TO YOU THAT I MIGHT ACTUALLY *HAVE* A DATE?
...
KIM, YOU'RE A HELL OF A CATCH.
YOU'RE A DAMN FINE WOMAN, KIM. *DAMN* FINE.
WHATEVER, LET'S JUST PLAY THE SETLIST AGAIN, ASSHOLES...

saturday night (later)

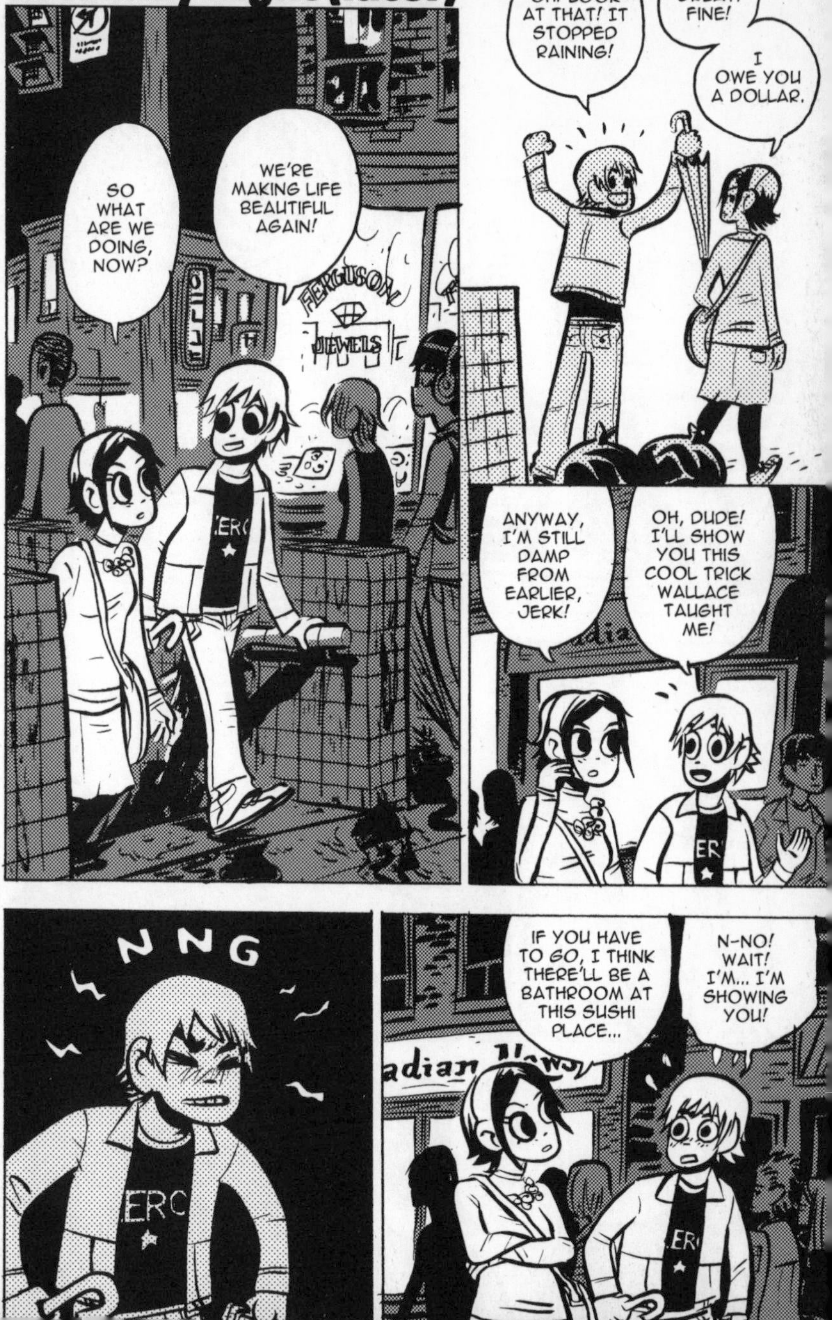
SO WHAT ARE WE DOING, NOW?
WE'RE MAKING LIFE BEAUTIFUL AGAIN!
FERGUSON
JEWELS
OH! LOOK AT THAT! IT STOPPED RAINING!
GREAT. FINE!
I OWE YOU A DOLLAR.
ANYWAY, I'M STILL DAMP FROM EARLIER, JERK!
OH, DUDE! I'LL SHOW YOU THIS COOL TRICK WALLACE TAUGHT ME!
NNG
IF YOU HAVE TO *GO*, I THINK THERE'LL BE A BATHROOM AT THIS SUSHI PLACE...
N-NO! WAIT! I'M... I'M SHOWING YOU!

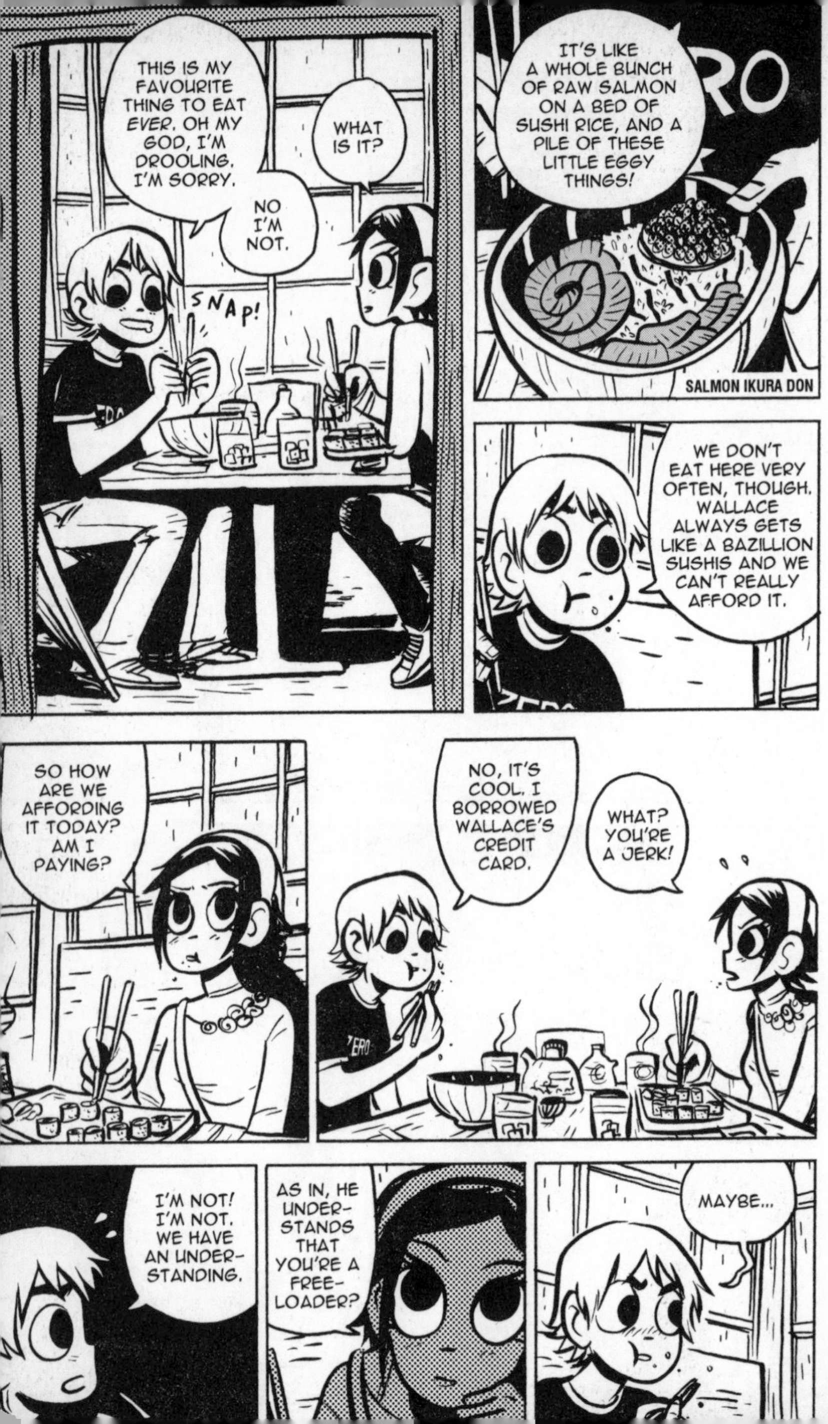
THIS IS MY FAVOURITE THING TO EAT EVER. OH MY GOD, I'M DROOLING. I'M SORRY.
WHAT IS IT?
NO I'M NOT.
SNAP!
IT'S LIKE A WHOLE BUNCH OF RAW SALMON ON A BED OF SUSHI RICE, AND A PILE OF THESE LITTLE EGGY THINGS!
SALMON IKURA DON
WE DON'T EAT HERE VERY OFTEN, THOUGH. WALLACE ALWAYS GETS LIKE A BAZILLION SUSHIS AND WE CAN'T REALLY AFFORD IT.
SO HOW ARE WE AFFORDING IT TODAY? AM I PAYING?
NO, IT'S COOL. I BORROWED WALLACE'S CREDIT CARD.
WHAT? YOU'RE A JERK!
I'M NOT! I'M NOT. WE HAVE AN UNDER-STANDING.
AS IN, HE UNDER-STANDS THAT YOU'RE A FREE-LOADER?
MAYBE...

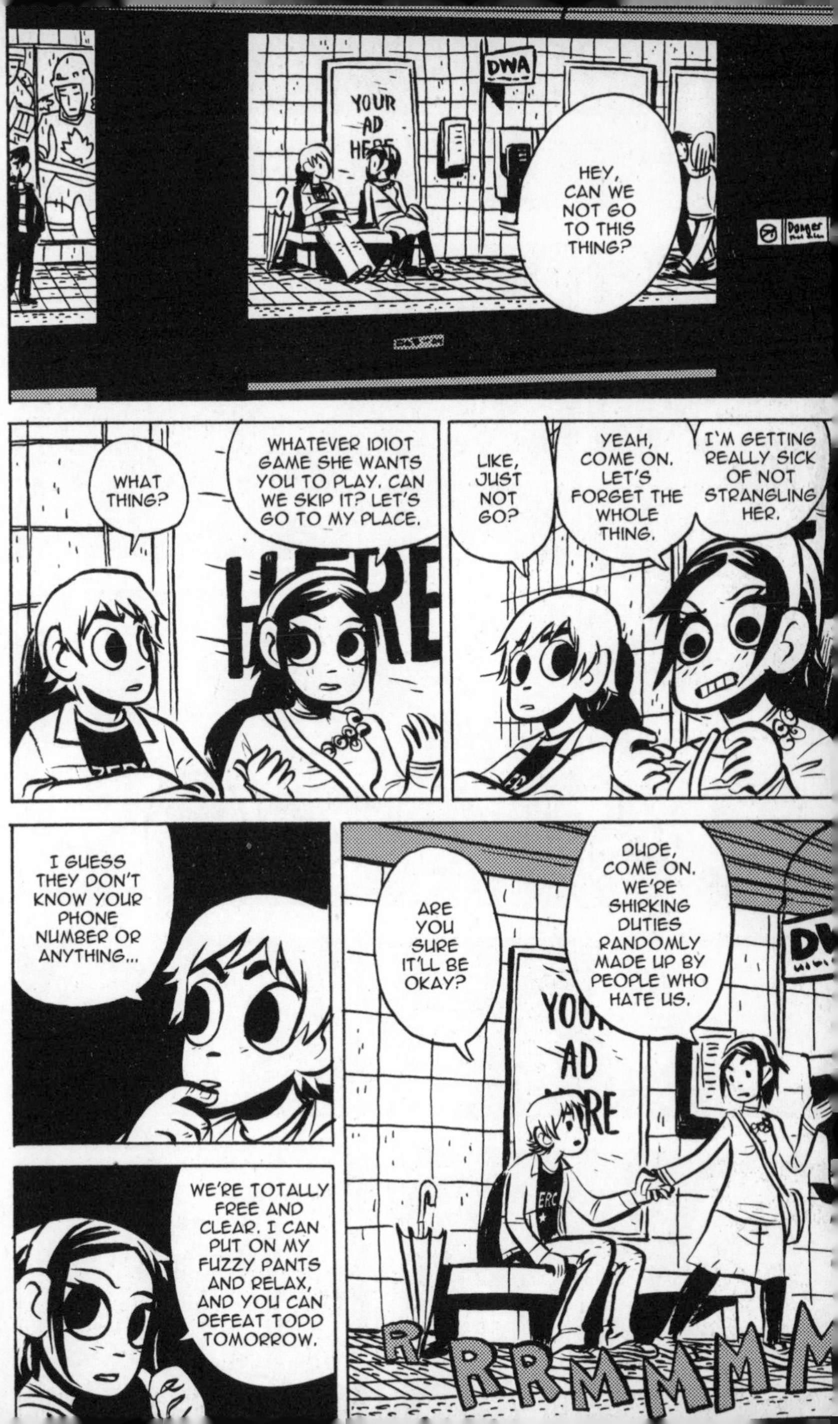
YOUR AD HERE
DWA
HEY, CAN WE NOT GO TO THIS THING?
WHAT THING?
WHATEVER IDIOT GAME SHE WANTS YOU TO PLAY. CAN WE SKIP IT? LET'S GO TO MY PLACE.
HERE
LIKE, JUST NOT GO?
YEAH, COME ON. LET'S FORGET THE WHOLE THING.
I'M GETTING REALLY SICK OF NOT STRANGLING HER.
I GUESS THEY DON'T KNOW YOUR PHONE NUMBER OR ANYTHING...
WE'RE TOTALLY FREE AND CLEAR. I CAN PUT ON MY FUZZY PANTS AND RELAX, AND YOU CAN DEFEAT TODD TOMORROW.
ARE YOU SURE IT'LL BE OKAY?
DUDE, COME ON. WE'RE SHIRKING DUTIES RANDOMLY MADE UP BY PEOPLE WHO HATE US.
RRRMMMMM

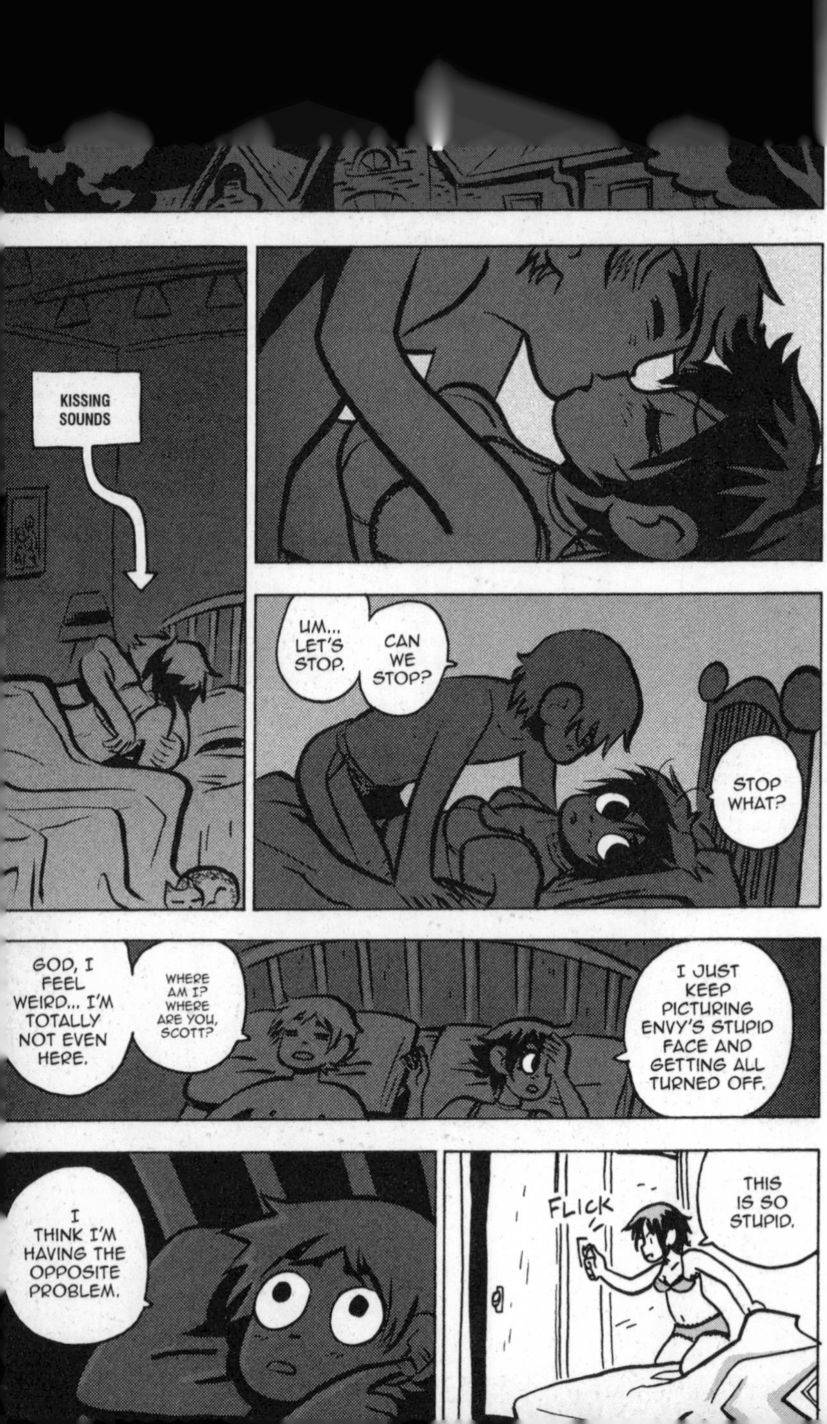
KISSING SOUNDS
UM... LET'S STOP.
CAN WE STOP?
STOP WHAT?
GOD, I FEEL WEIRD... I'M TOTALLY NOT EVEN HERE.
WHERE AM I? WHERE ARE YOU, SCOTT?
I JUST KEEP PICTURING ENVY'S STUPID FACE AND GETTING ALL TURNED OFF.
I THINK I'M HAVING THE OPPOSITE PROBLEM.
FLICK
THIS IS SO STUPID.

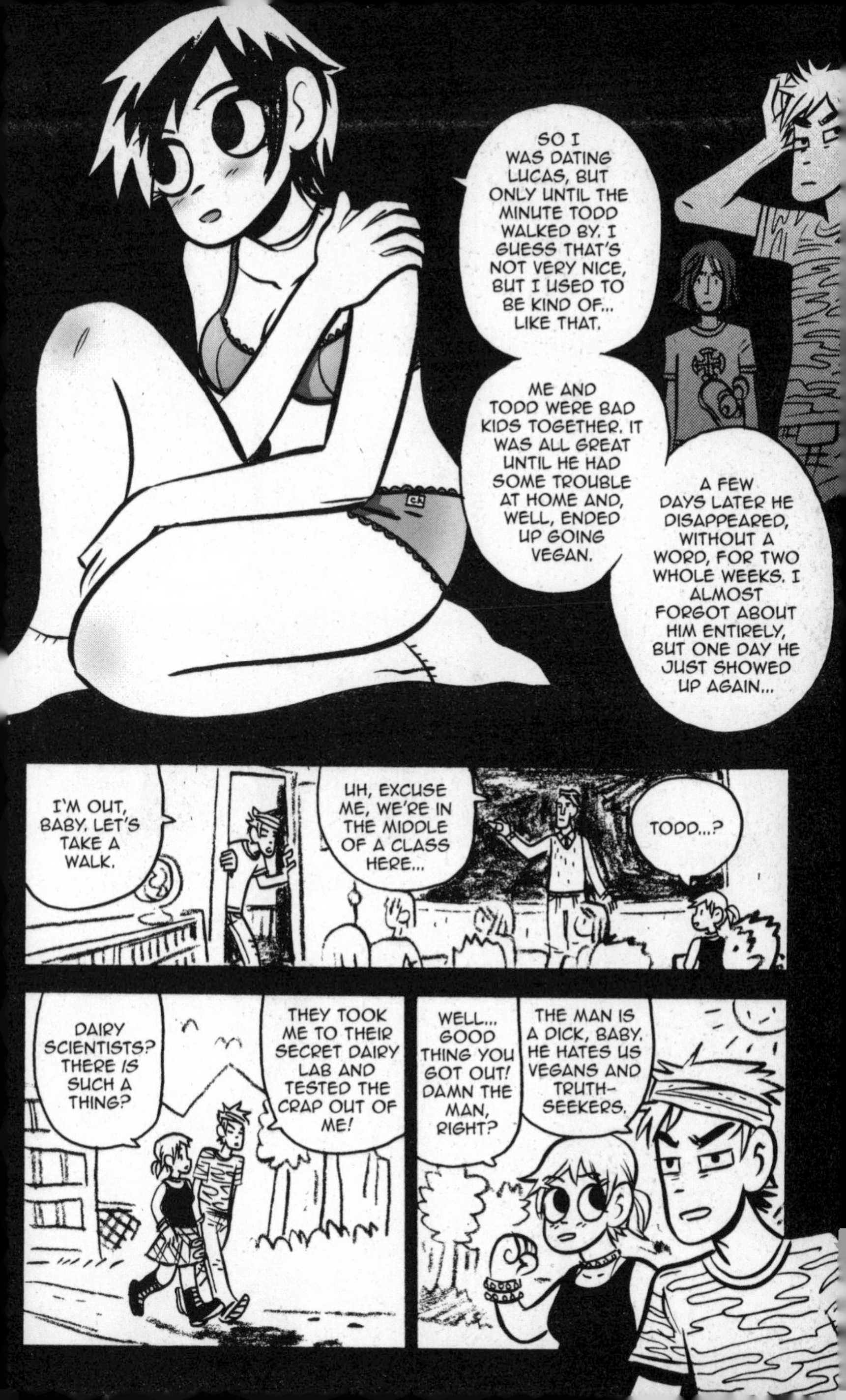
SO I WAS DATING LUCAS, BUT ONLY UNTIL THE MINUTE TODD WALKED BY. I GUESS THAT'S NOT VERY NICE, BUT I USED TO BE KIND OF... LIKE THAT.
ME AND TODD WERE BAD KIDS TOGETHER. IT WAS ALL GREAT UNTIL HE HAD SOME TROUBLE AT HOME AND, WELL, ENDED UP GOING VEGAN.
A FEW DAYS LATER HE DISAPPEARED, WITHOUT A WORD, FOR TWO WHOLE WEEKS. I ALMOST FORGOT ABOUT HIM ENTIRELY, BUT ONE DAY HE JUST SHOWED UP AGAIN...
I'M OUT, BABY. LET'S TAKE A WALK.
UH, EXCUSE ME, WE'RE IN THE MIDDLE OF A CLASS HERE...
TODD...?
DAIRY SCIENTISTS? THERE *IS* SUCH A THING?
THEY TOOK ME TO THEIR SECRET DAIRY LAB AND TESTED THE CRAP OUT OF ME!
WELL... GOOD THING YOU GOT OUT! DAMN THE MAN, RIGHT?
THE MAN IS A DICK, BABY. HE HATES US VEGANS AND TRUTH-SEEKERS.

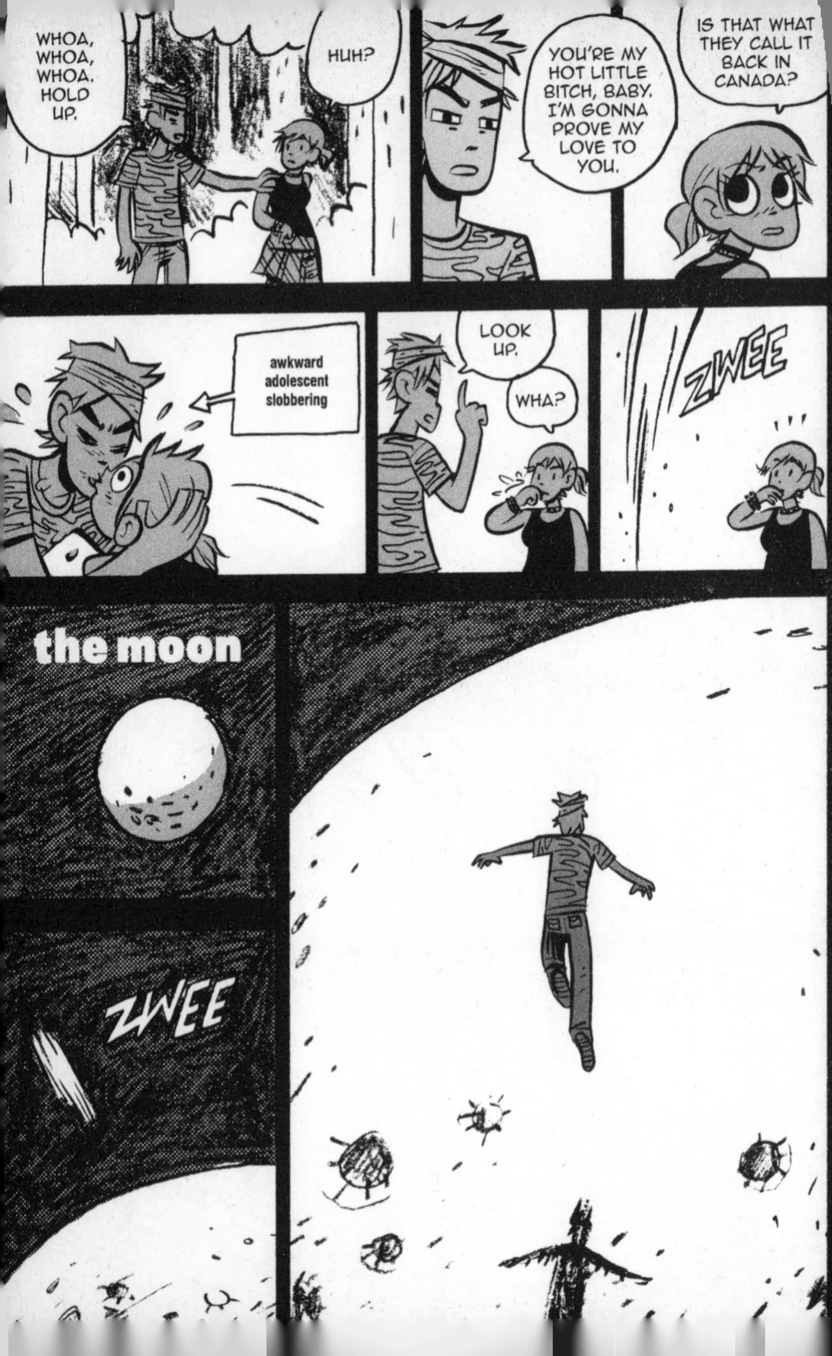
WHOA, WHOA, WHOA. HOLD UP.
HUH?
YOU'RE MY HOT LITTLE BITCH, BABY. I'M GONNA PROVE MY LOVE TO YOU.
IS THAT WHAT THEY CALL IT BACK IN CANADA?
awkward adolescent slobbering
LOOK UP.
WHA?
ZWEE
the moon
ZWEE

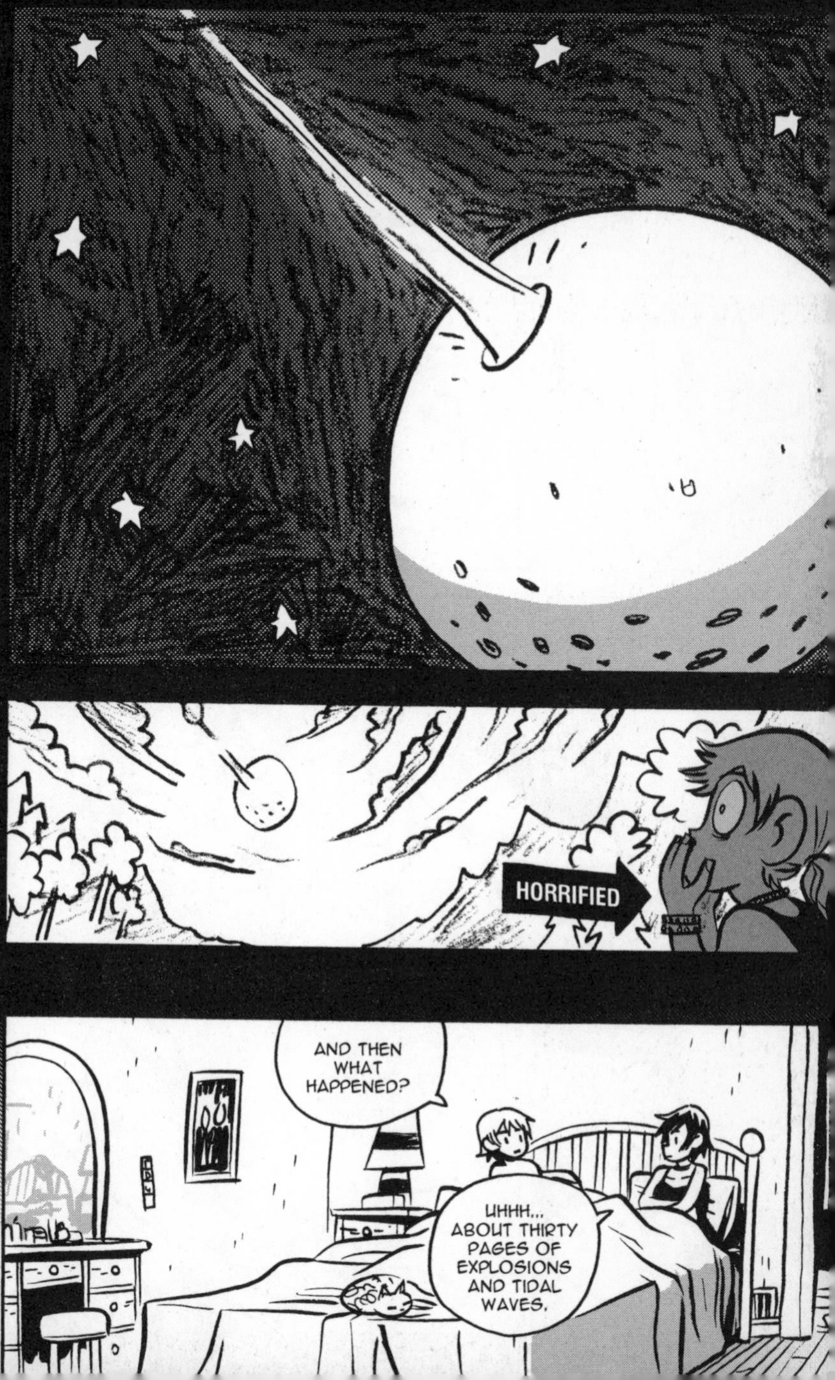
HORRIFIED
AND THEN WHAT HAPPENED?
UHHH... ABOUT THIRTY PAGES OF EXPLOSIONS AND TIDAL WAVES.

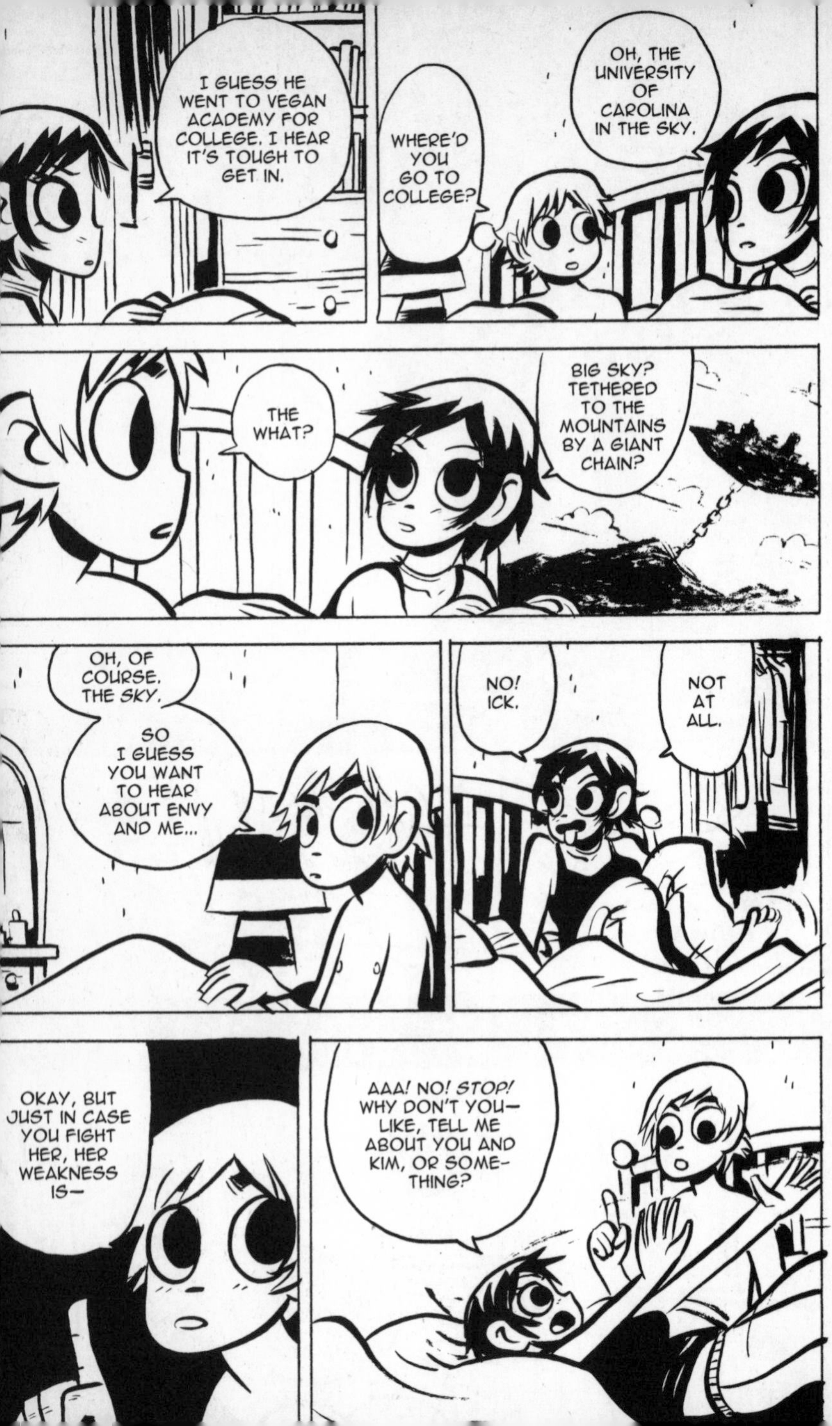
I GUESS HE WENT TO VEGAN ACADEMY FOR COLLEGE. I HEAR IT'S TOUGH TO GET IN.
WHERE'D YOU GO TO COLLEGE?
OH, THE UNIVERSITY OF CAROLINA IN THE SKY.
THE WHAT?
BIG SKY? TETHERED TO THE MOUNTAINS BY A GIANT CHAIN?
OH, OF COURSE. THE *SKY*.
SO I GUESS YOU WANT TO HEAR ABOUT ENVY AND ME...
NO! ICK.
NOT AT ALL.
OKAY, BUT JUST IN CASE YOU FIGHT HER, HER WEAKNESS IS—
AAA! NO! *STOP!* WHY DON'T YOU— LIKE, TELL ME ABOUT YOU AND KIM, OR SOME-THING?

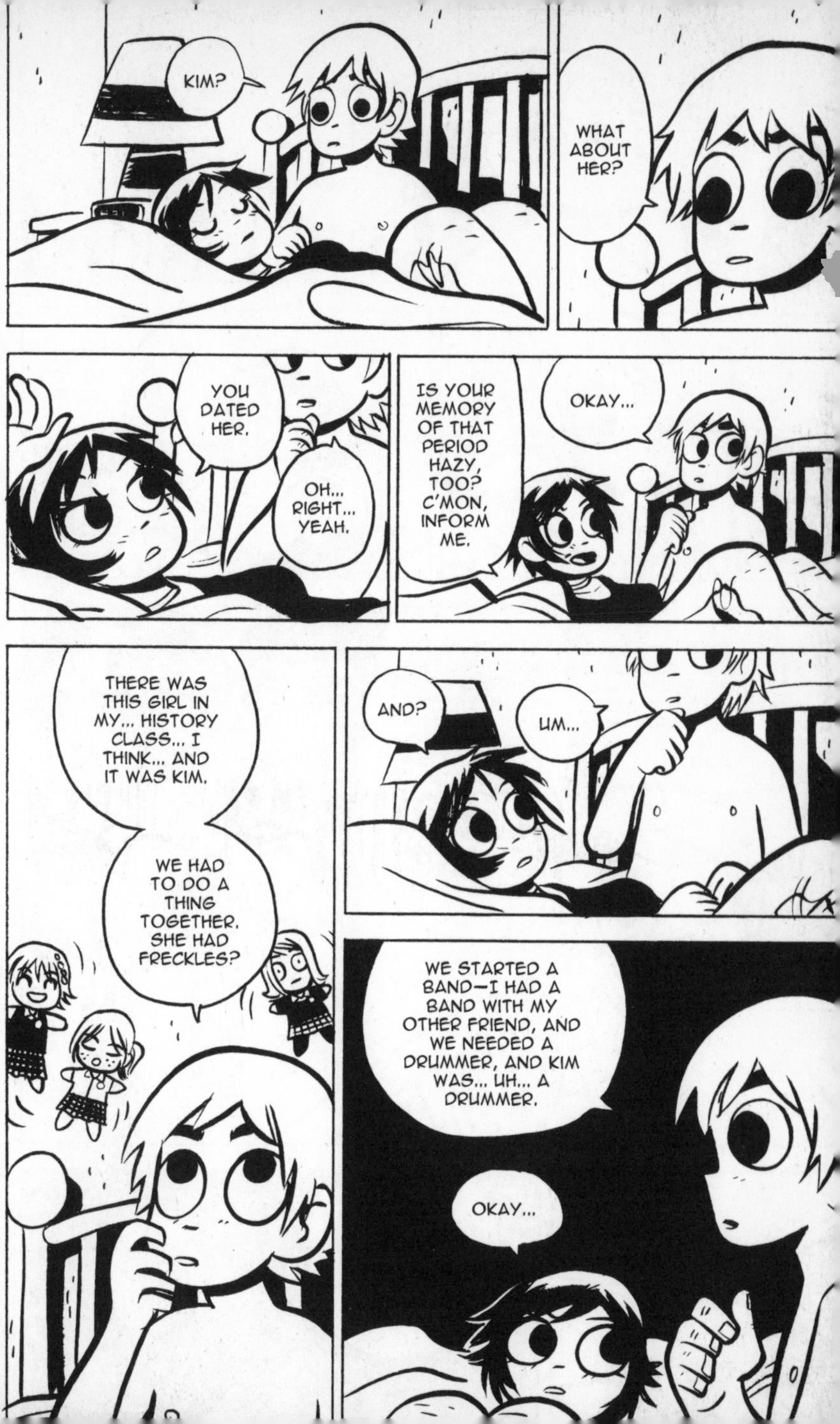
KIM?
WHAT ABOUT HER?
YOU DATED HER.
OH... RIGHT... YEAH.
IS YOUR MEMORY OF THAT PERIOD HAZY, TOO? C'MON, INFORM ME.
OKAY...
THERE WAS THIS GIRL IN MY... HISTORY CLASS... I THINK... AND IT WAS KIM.
WE HAD TO DO A THING TOGETHER. SHE HAD FRECKLES?
AND?
UM...
WE STARTED A BAND—I HAD A BAND WITH MY OTHER FRIEND, AND WE NEEDED A DRUMMER, AND KIM WAS... UH... A DRUMMER.
OKAY...

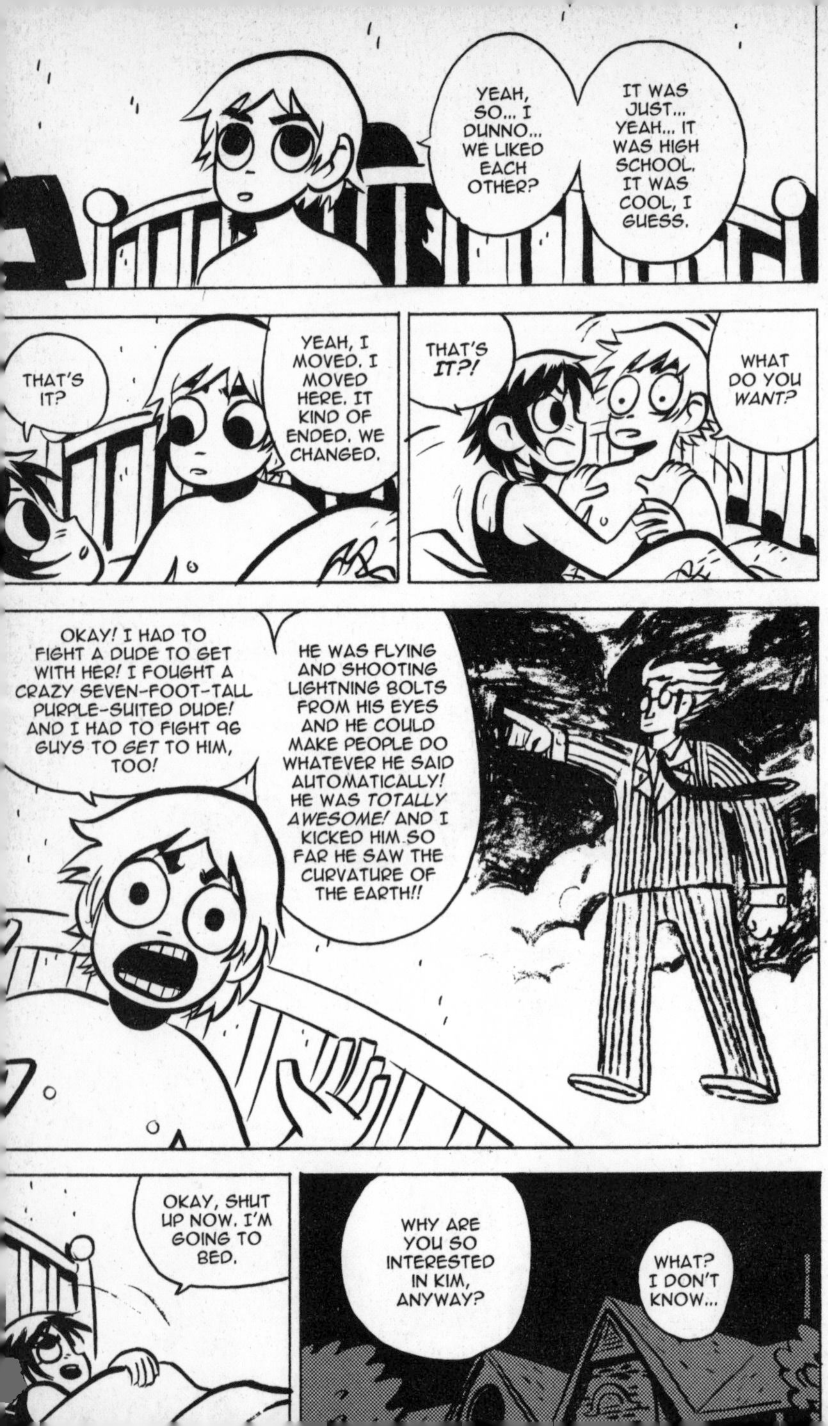
YEAH, SO... I DUNNO... WE LIKED EACH OTHER?
IT WAS JUST... YEAH... IT WAS HIGH SCHOOL. IT WAS COOL, I GUESS.
THAT'S IT?
YEAH, I MOVED. I MOVED HERE. IT KIND OF ENDED. WE CHANGED.
THAT'S *IT?!*
WHAT DO YOU *WANT?*
OKAY! I HAD TO FIGHT A DUDE TO GET WITH HER! I FOUGHT A CRAZY SEVEN-FOOT-TALL PURPLE-SUITED DUDE! AND I HAD TO FIGHT 96 GUYS TO *GET* TO HIM, TOO!
HE WAS FLYING AND SHOOTING LIGHTNING BOLTS FROM HIS EYES AND HE COULD MAKE PEOPLE DO WHATEVER HE SAID AUTOMATICALLY! HE WAS *TOTALLY AWESOME!* AND I KICKED HIM SO FAR HE SAW THE CURVATURE OF THE EARTH!!
OKAY, SHUT UP NOW. I'M GOING TO BED.
WHY ARE YOU SO INTERESTED IN KIM, ANYWAY?
WHAT? I DON'T KNOW...

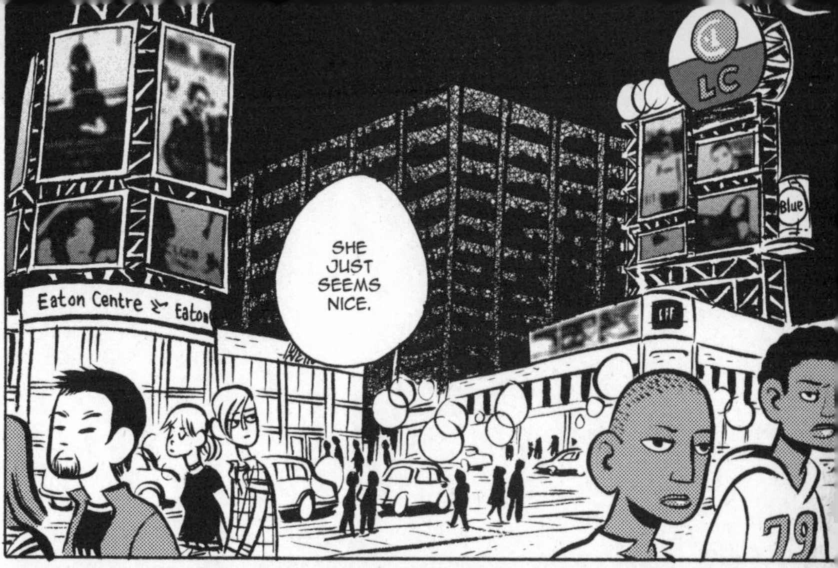

Eaton Centre
Eaton
LC
Blue
SHE JUST SEEMS NICE.
79

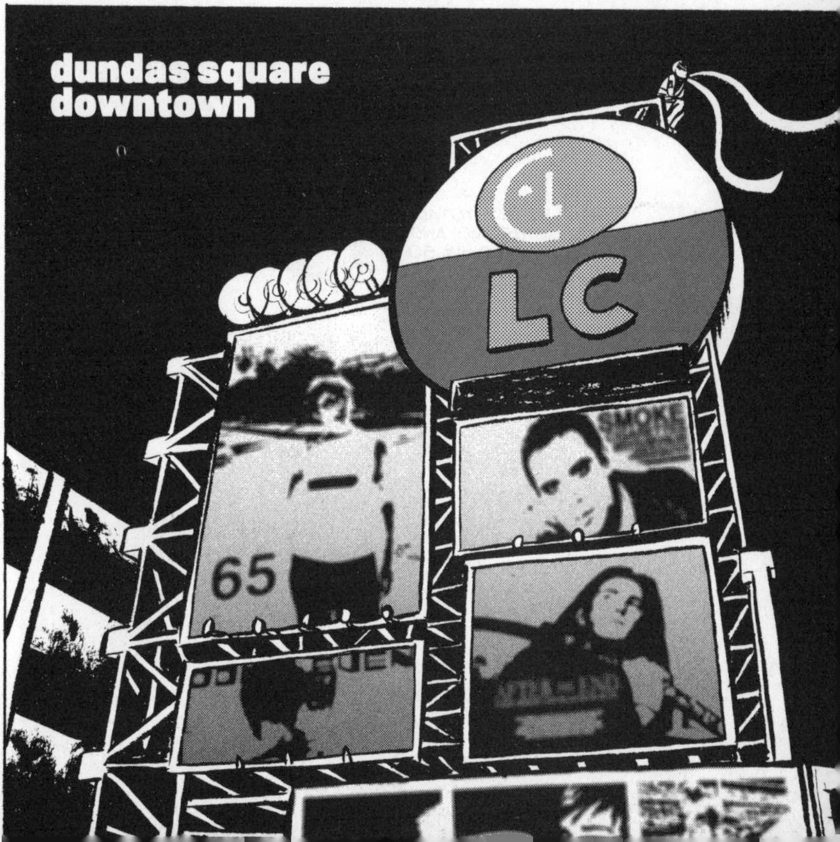

dundas square
downtown
LC
SMOKE
65

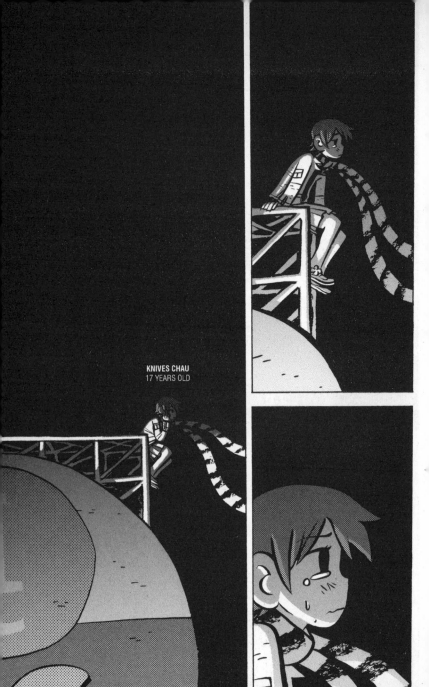

KNIVES CHAU
17 YEARS OLD

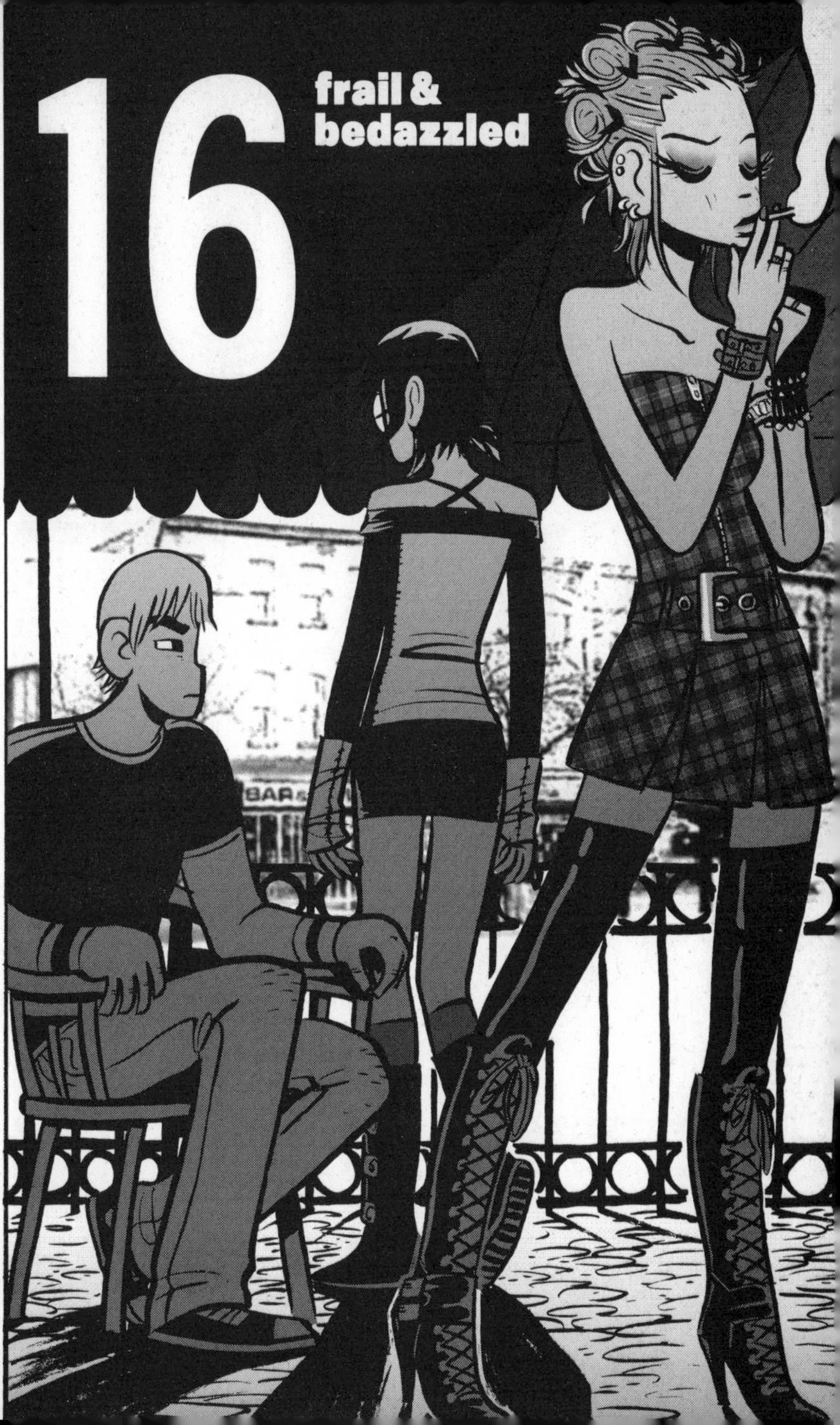
16
frail &
bedazzled
BAR

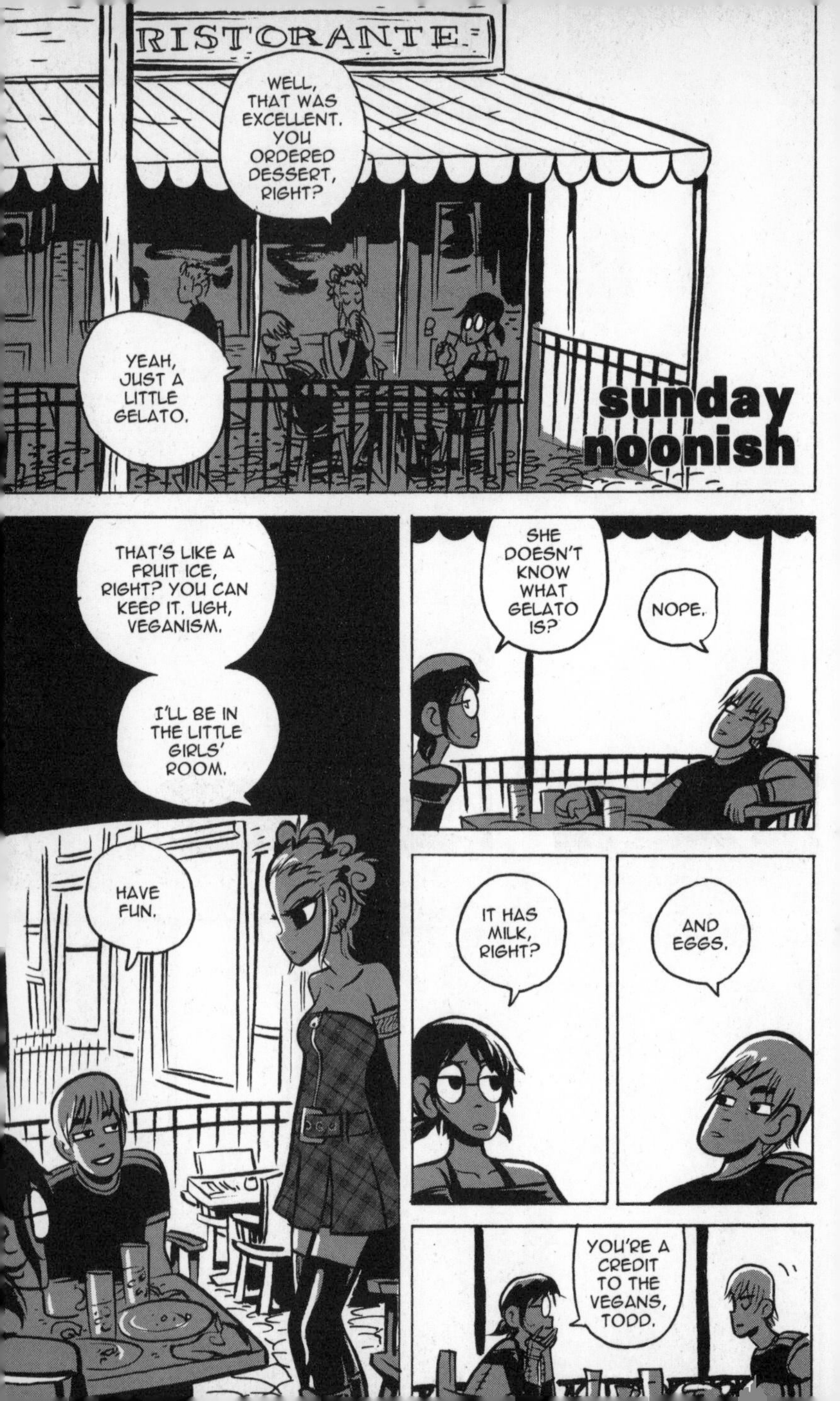
RISTORANTE
WELL, THAT WAS EXCELLENT. YOU ORDERED DESSERT, RIGHT?
YEAH, JUST A LITTLE GELATO.
sunday noonish
THAT'S LIKE A FRUIT ICE, RIGHT? YOU CAN KEEP IT. UGH, VEGANISM.
I'LL BE IN THE LITTLE GIRLS' ROOM.
SHE DOESN'T KNOW WHAT GELATO IS?
NOPE.
HAVE FUN.
IT HAS MILK, RIGHT?
AND EGGS.
YOU'RE A CREDIT TO THE VEGANS, TODD.

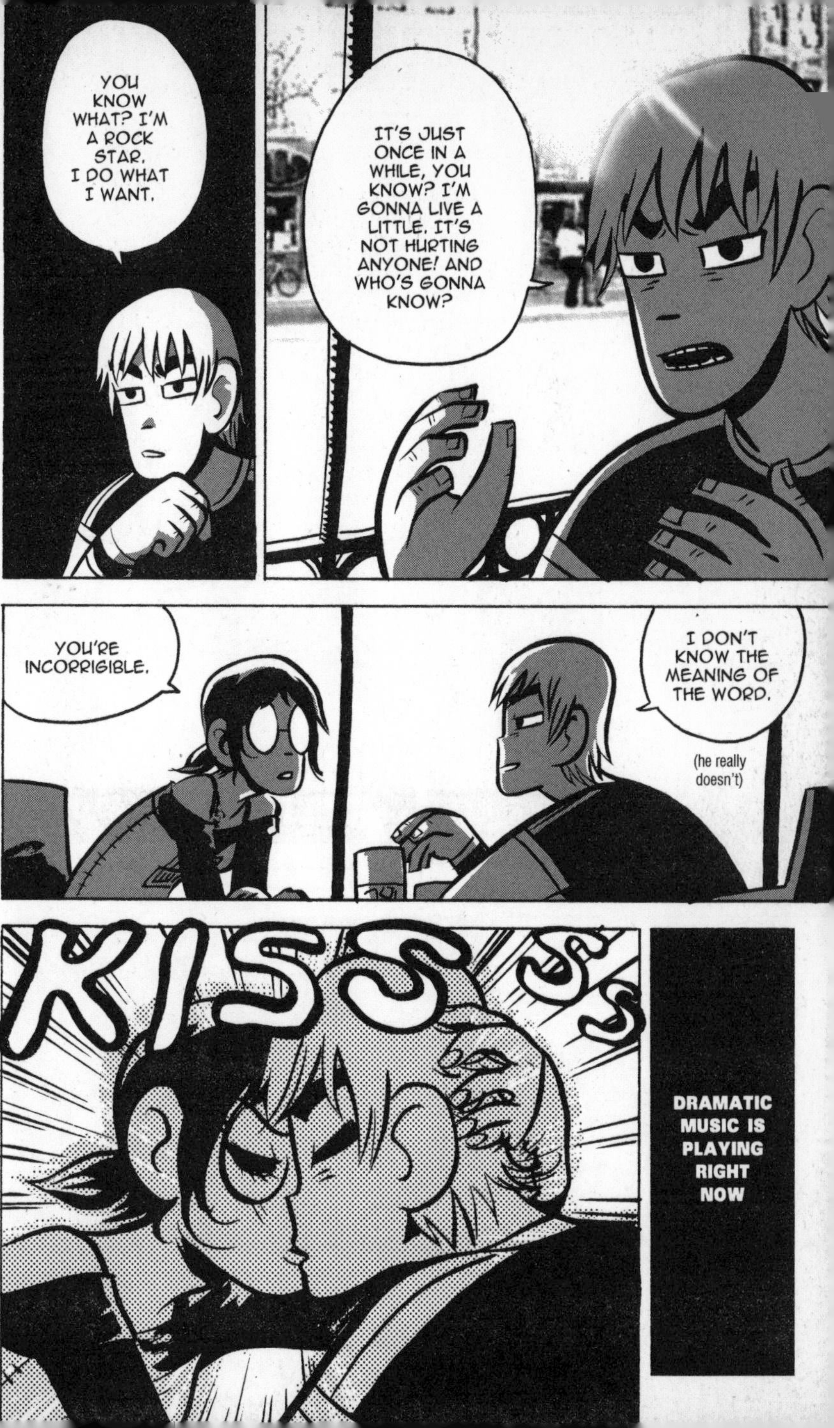

YOU KNOW WHAT? I'M A ROCK STAR. I DO WHAT I WANT.
IT'S JUST ONCE IN A WHILE, YOU KNOW? I'M GONNA LIVE A LITTLE. IT'S NOT HURTING ANYONE! AND WHO'S GONNA KNOW?
YOU'RE INCORRIGIBLE.
I DON'T KNOW THE MEANING OF THE WORD.
(he really doesn't)
KISSSS
DRAMATIC MUSIC IS PLAYING RIGHT NOW

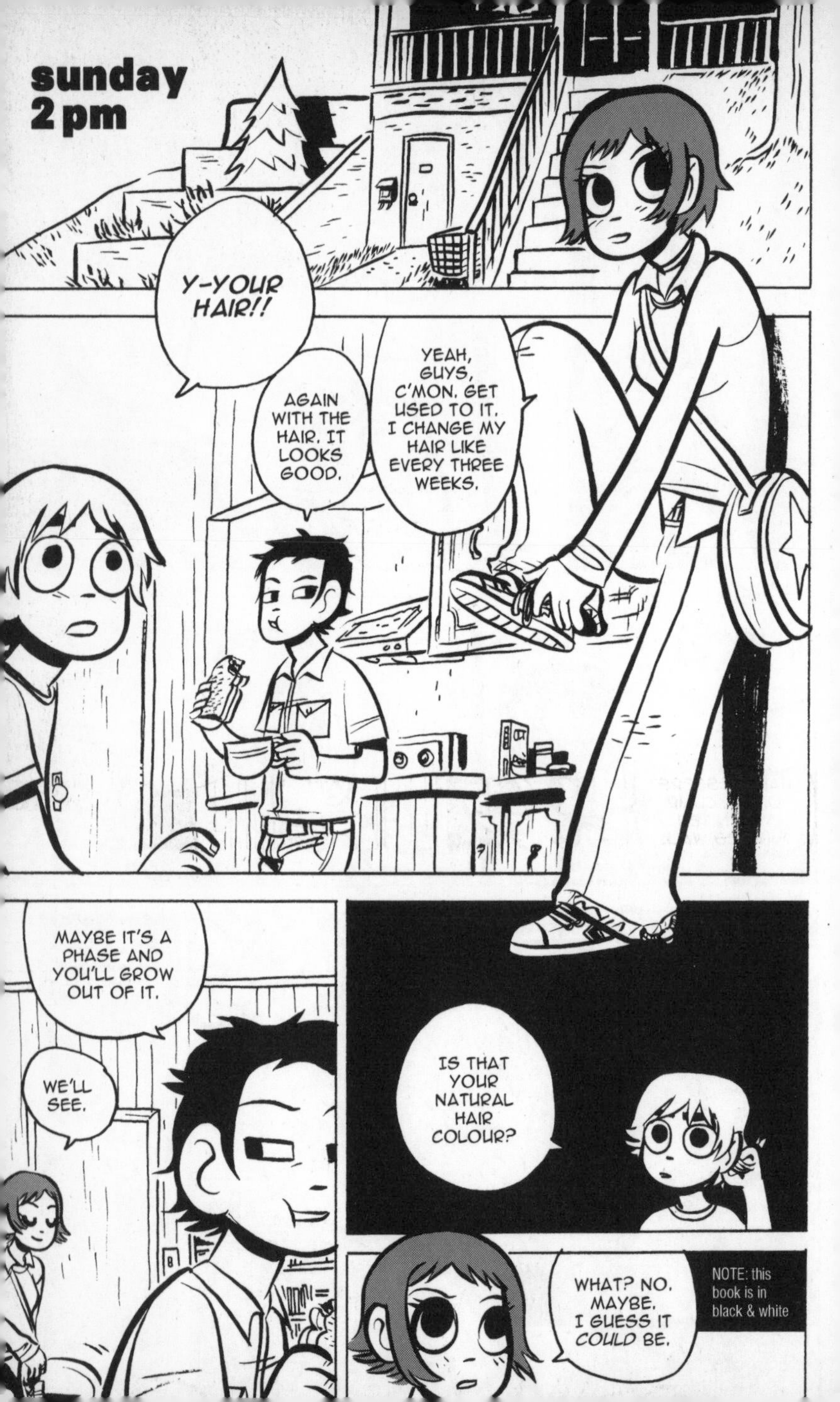
sunday
2 pm
Y-YOUR HAIR!!
AGAIN WITH THE HAIR. IT LOOKS GOOD.
YEAH, GUYS, C'MON. GET USED TO IT. I CHANGE MY HAIR LIKE EVERY THREE WEEKS.
MAYBE IT'S A PHASE AND YOU'LL GROW OUT OF IT.
WE'LL SEE.
IS THAT YOUR NATURAL HAIR COLOUR?
WHAT? NO. MAYBE. I GUESS IT COULD BE.
NOTE: this book is in black & white

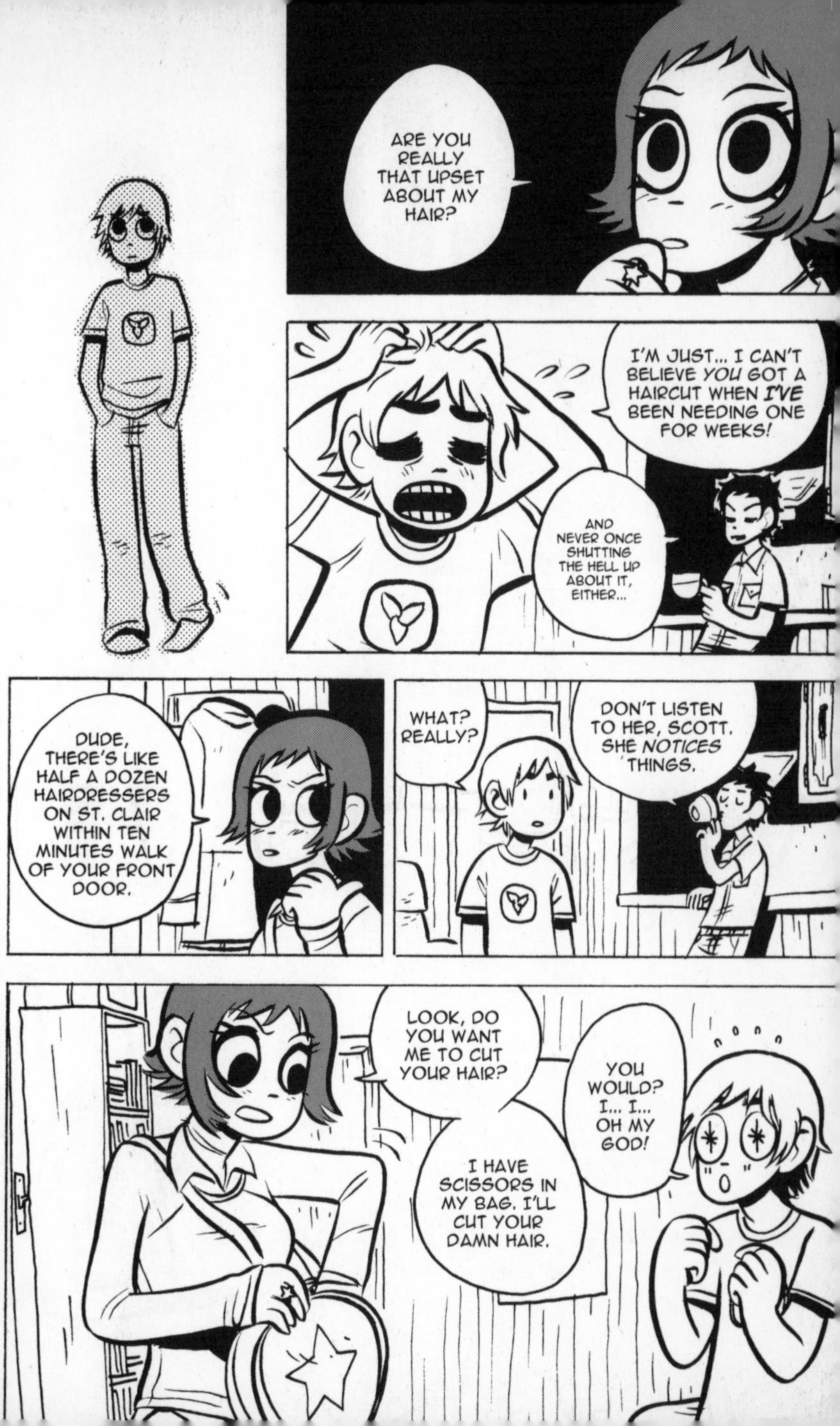
ARE YOU REALLY THAT UPSET ABOUT MY HAIR?
I'M JUST... I CAN'T BELIEVE *YOU* GOT A HAIRCUT WHEN *I'VE* BEEN NEEDING ONE FOR WEEKS!
AND NEVER ONCE SHUTTING THE HELL UP ABOUT IT, EITHER...
DUDE, THERE'S LIKE HALF A DOZEN HAIRDRESSERS ON ST. CLAIR WITHIN TEN MINUTES WALK OF YOUR FRONT DOOR.
WHAT? REALLY?
DON'T LISTEN TO HER, SCOTT. SHE *NOTICES* THINGS.
LOOK, DO YOU WANT ME TO CUT YOUR HAIR?
I HAVE SCISSORS IN MY BAG. I'LL CUT YOUR DAMN HAIR.
YOU WOULD? I... I... OH MY GOD!

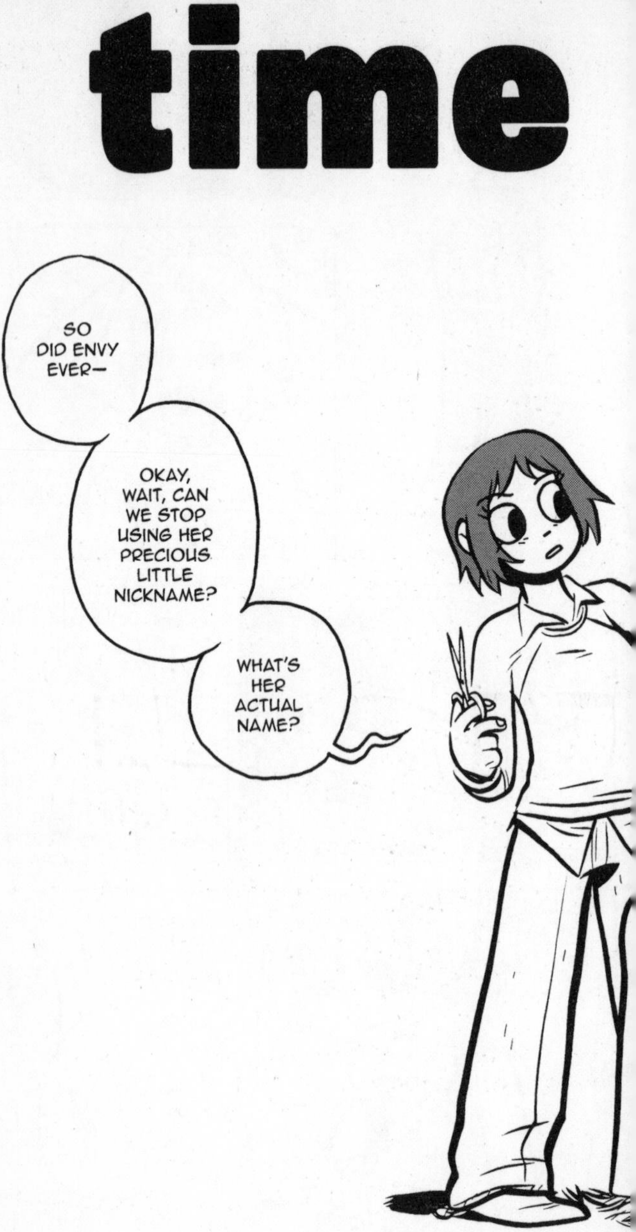
time
SO DID ENVY EVER—
OKAY, WAIT, CAN WE STOP USING HER PRECIOUS LITTLE NICKNAME?
WHAT'S HER ACTUAL NAME?

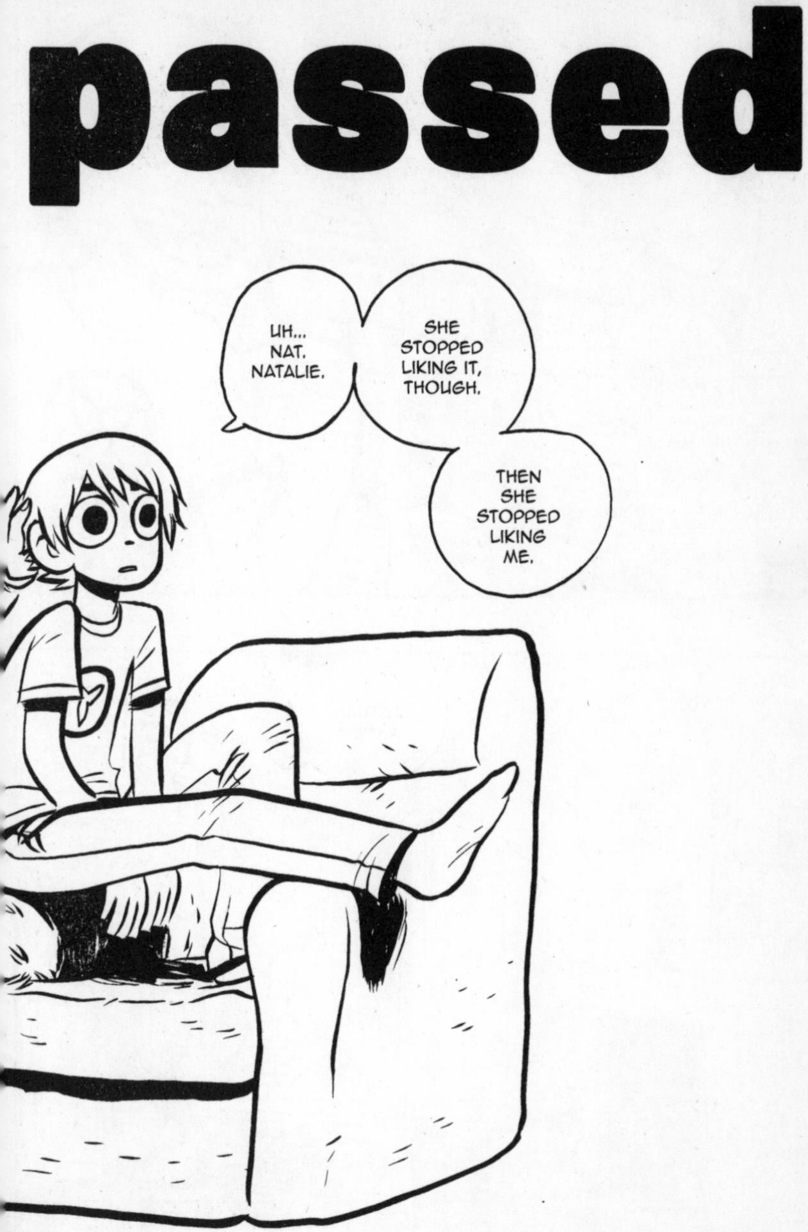
passed
UH... NAT. NATALIE.
SHE STOPPED LIKING IT, THOUGH.
THEN SHE STOPPED LIKING ME.

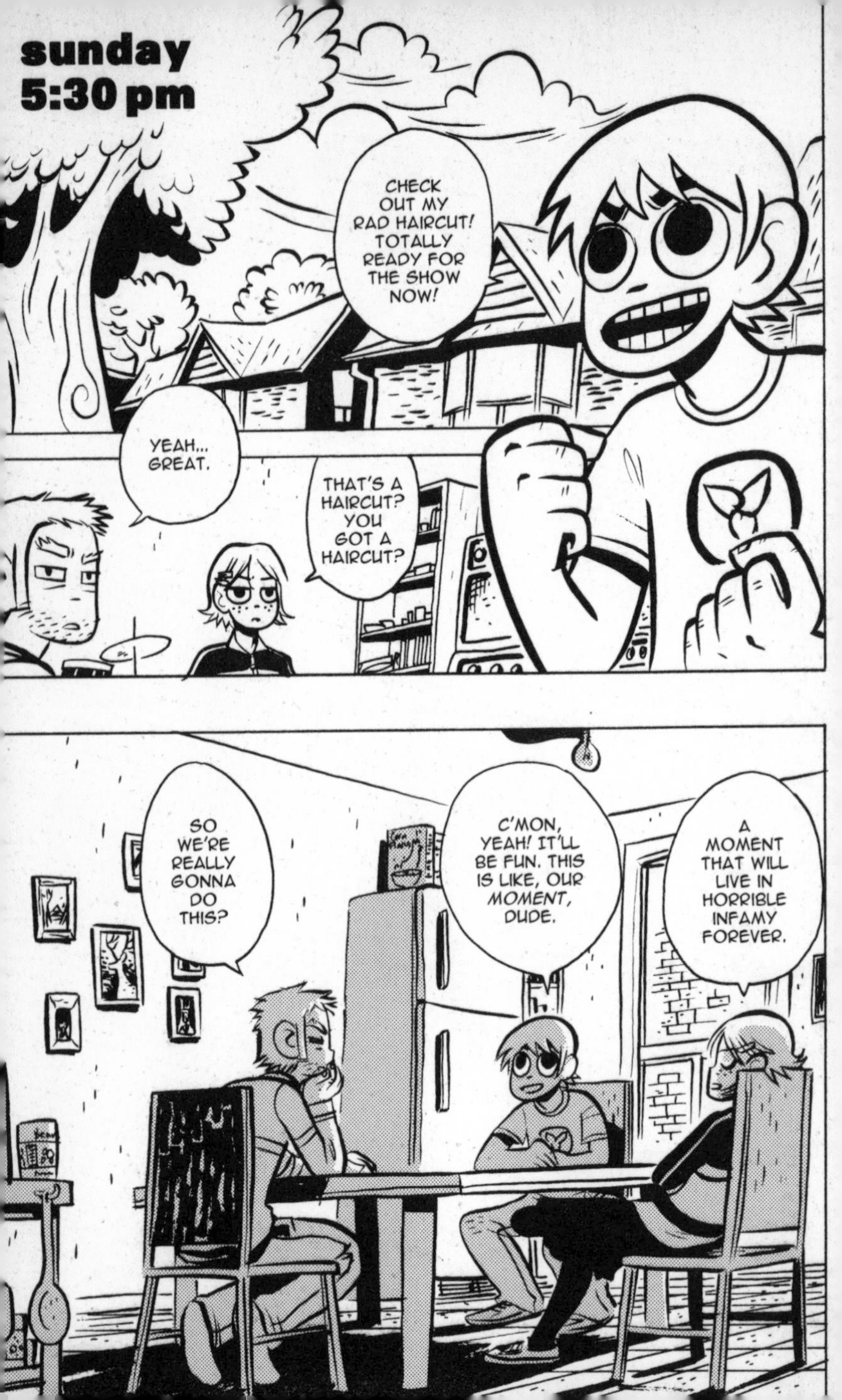
sunday
5:30 pm
CHECK OUT MY RAD HAIRCUT! TOTALLY READY FOR THE SHOW NOW!
YEAH... GREAT.
THAT'S A HAIRCUT? YOU GOT A HAIRCUT?
SO WE'RE REALLY GONNA DO THIS?
C'MON, YEAH! IT'LL BE FUN. THIS IS LIKE, OUR *MOMENT*, DUDE.
A MOMENT THAT WILL LIVE IN HORRIBLE INFAMY FOREVER.

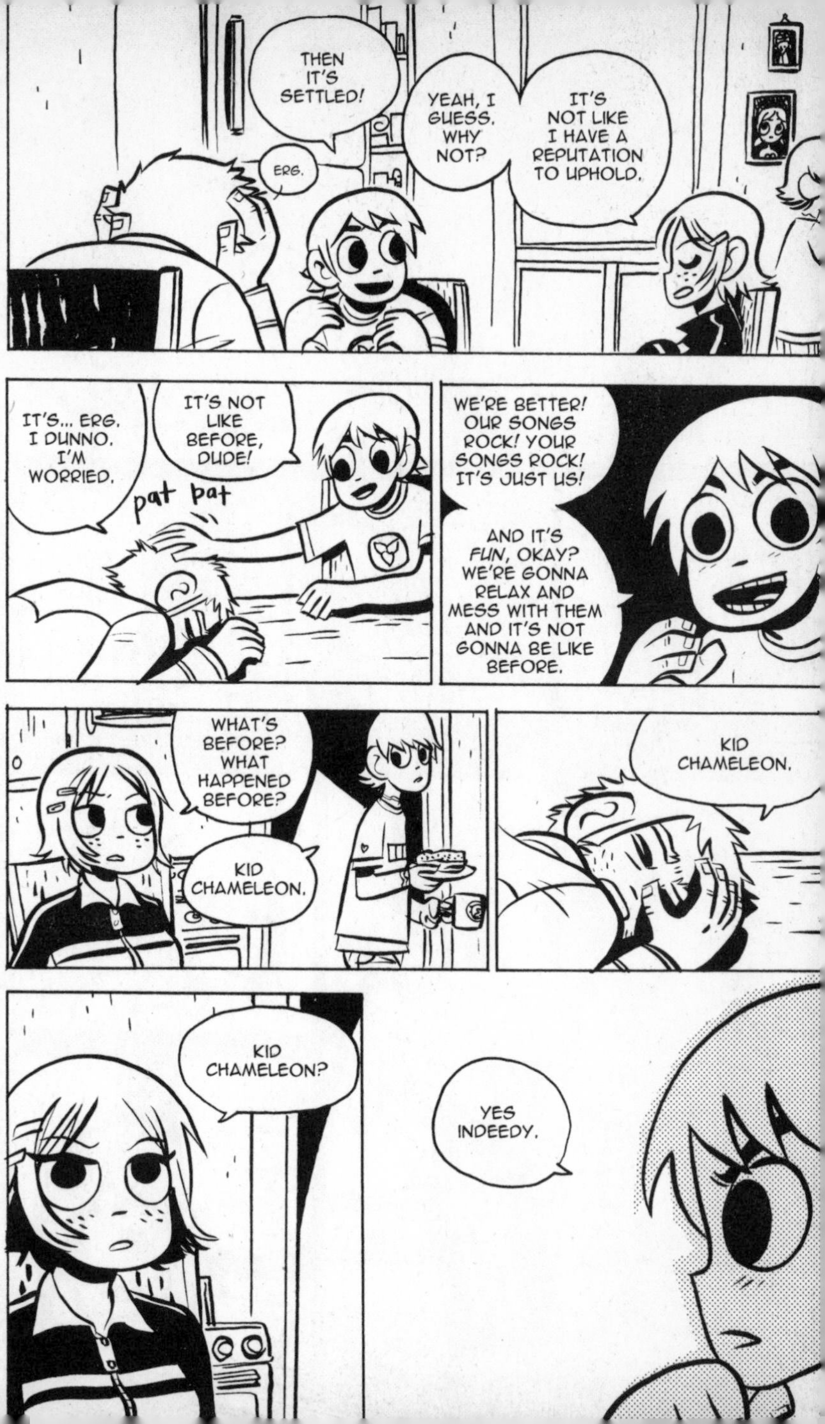
THEN IT'S SETTLED!
ERG.
YEAH, I GUESS. WHY NOT?
IT'S NOT LIKE I HAVE A REPUTATION TO UPHOLD.
IT'S... ERG. I DUNNO. I'M WORRIED.
IT'S NOT LIKE BEFORE, DUDE!
pat pat
WE'RE BETTER! OUR SONGS ROCK! YOUR SONGS ROCK! IT'S JUST US!
AND IT'S FUN, OKAY? WE'RE GONNA RELAX AND MESS WITH THEM AND IT'S NOT GONNA BE LIKE BEFORE.
WHAT'S BEFORE? WHAT HAPPENED BEFORE?
KID CHAMELEON.
KID CHAMELEON.
KID CHAMELEON?
YES INDEEDY.

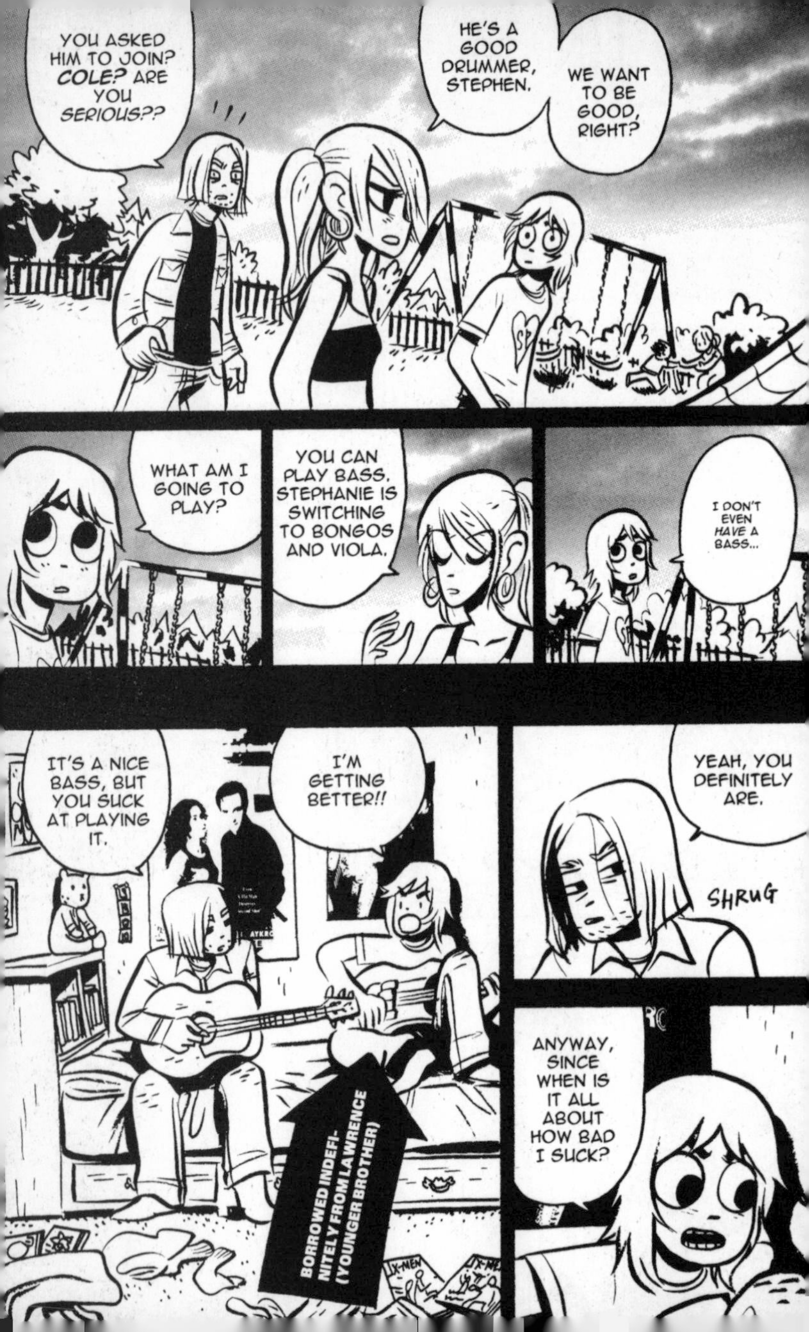

YOU ASKED HIM TO JOIN? COLE? ARE YOU SERIOUS??
HE'S A GOOD DRUMMER, STEPHEN.
WE WANT TO BE GOOD, RIGHT?
WHAT AM I GOING TO PLAY?
YOU CAN PLAY BASS. STEPHANIE IS SWITCHING TO BONGOS AND VIOLA.
I DON'T EVEN HAVE A BASS...
IT'S A NICE BASS, BUT YOU SUCK AT PLAYING IT.
I'M GETTING BETTER!!
BORROWED INDEFINITELY FROM LAWRENCE (YOUNGER BROTHER)
YEAH, YOU DEFINITELY ARE.
SHRUG
ANYWAY, SINCE WHEN IS IT ALL ABOUT HOW BAD I SUCK?

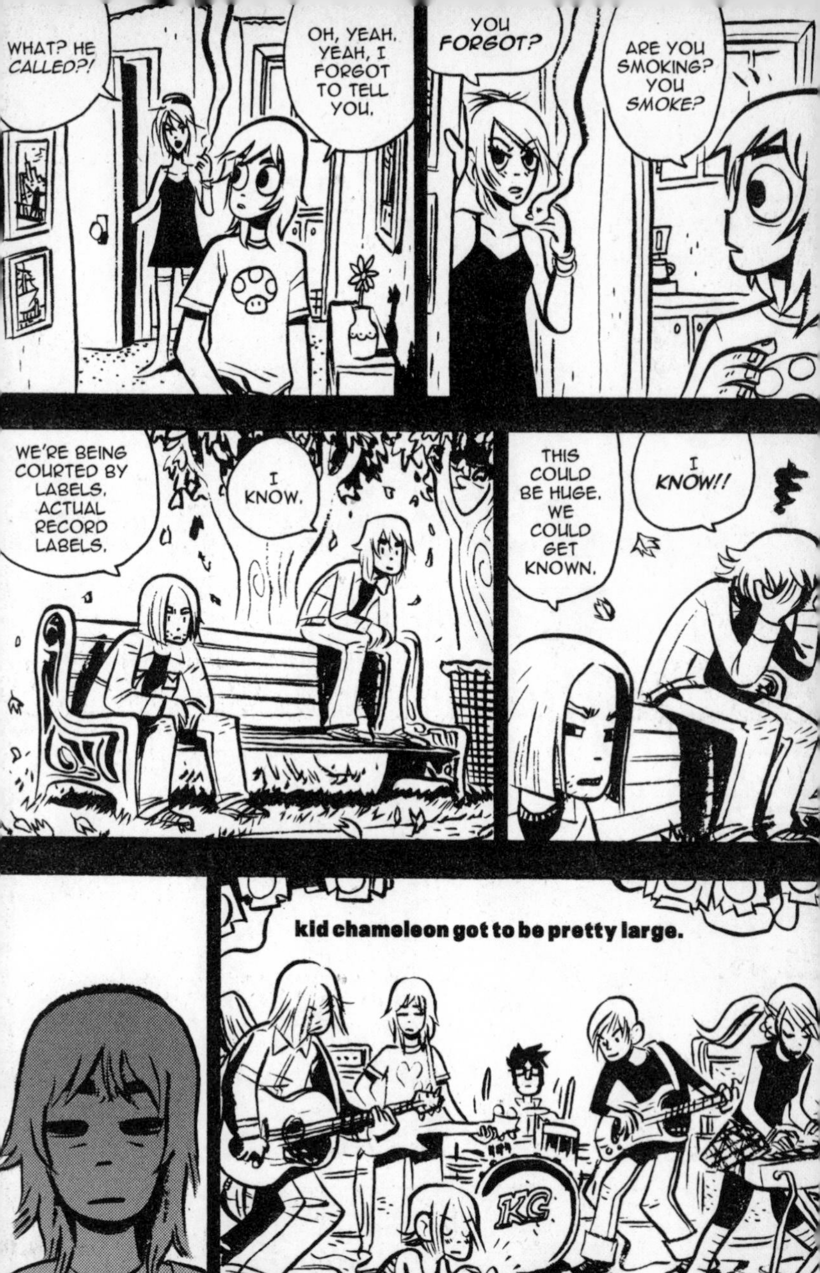

WHAT? HE CALLED?!
OH, YEAH. YEAH, I FORGOT TO TELL YOU.
YOU FORGOT?
ARE YOU SMOKING? YOU SMOKE?
WE'RE BEING COURTED BY LABELS. ACTUAL RECORD LABELS.
I KNOW.
THIS COULD BE HUGE. WE COULD GET KNOWN.
I KNOW!!
kid chameleon got to be pretty large.
KC

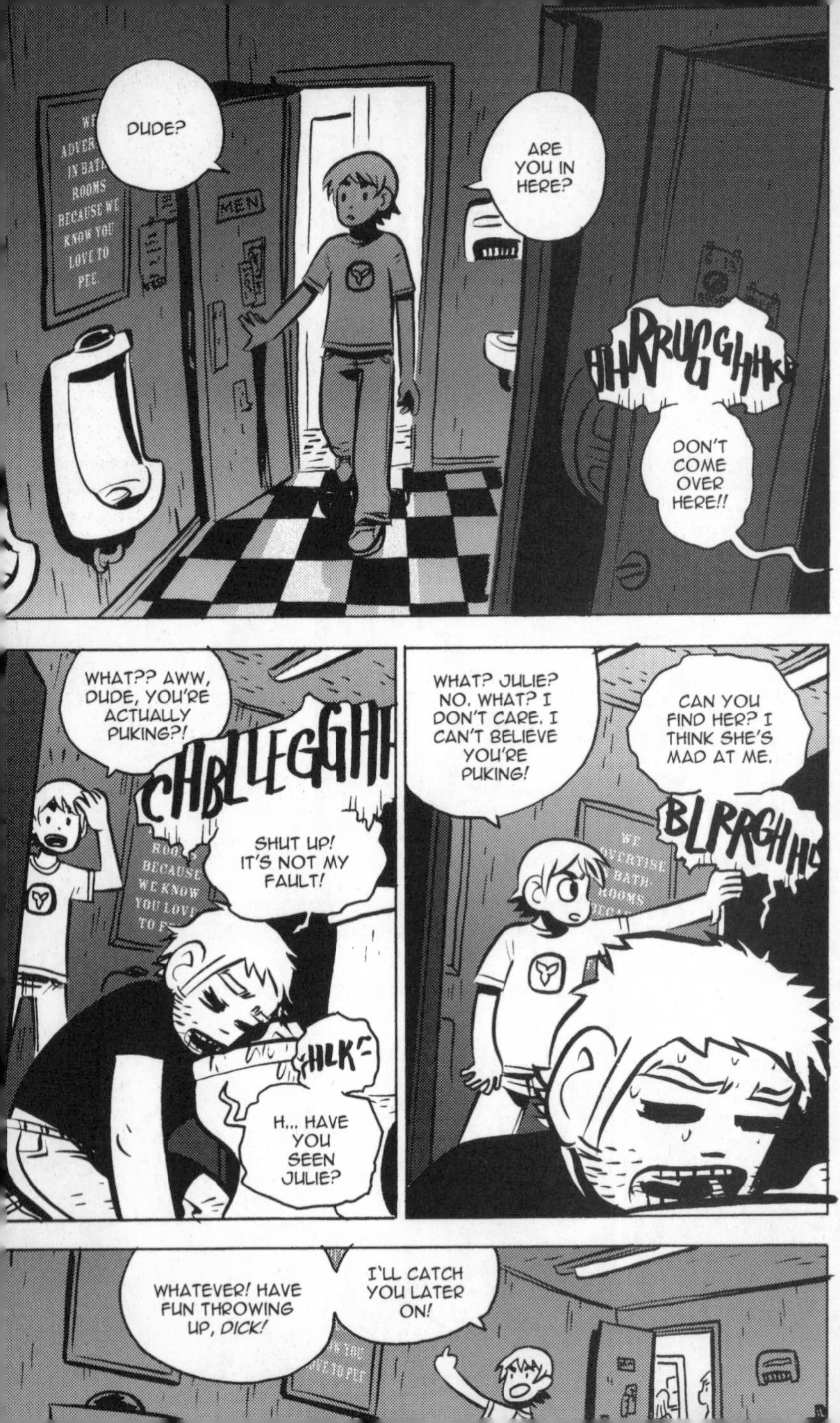
WE ADVERTISE IN BATHROOMS BECAUSE WE KNOW YOU LOVE TO PEE
DUDE?
MEN
ARE YOU IN HERE?
HHRRUGGHHK
DON'T COME OVER HERE!!
WHAT?? AWW, DUDE, YOU'RE ACTUALLY PUKING?!
CHBLLEGGHH
SHUT UP! IT'S NOT MY FAULT!
HLK
H... HAVE YOU SEEN JULIE?
WHAT? JULIE? NO. WHAT? I DON'T CARE. I CAN'T BELIEVE YOU'RE PUKING!
CAN YOU FIND HER? I THINK SHE'S MAD AT ME.
BLRRGHH
WHATEVER! HAVE FUN THROWING UP, DICK!
I'LL CATCH YOU LATER ON!

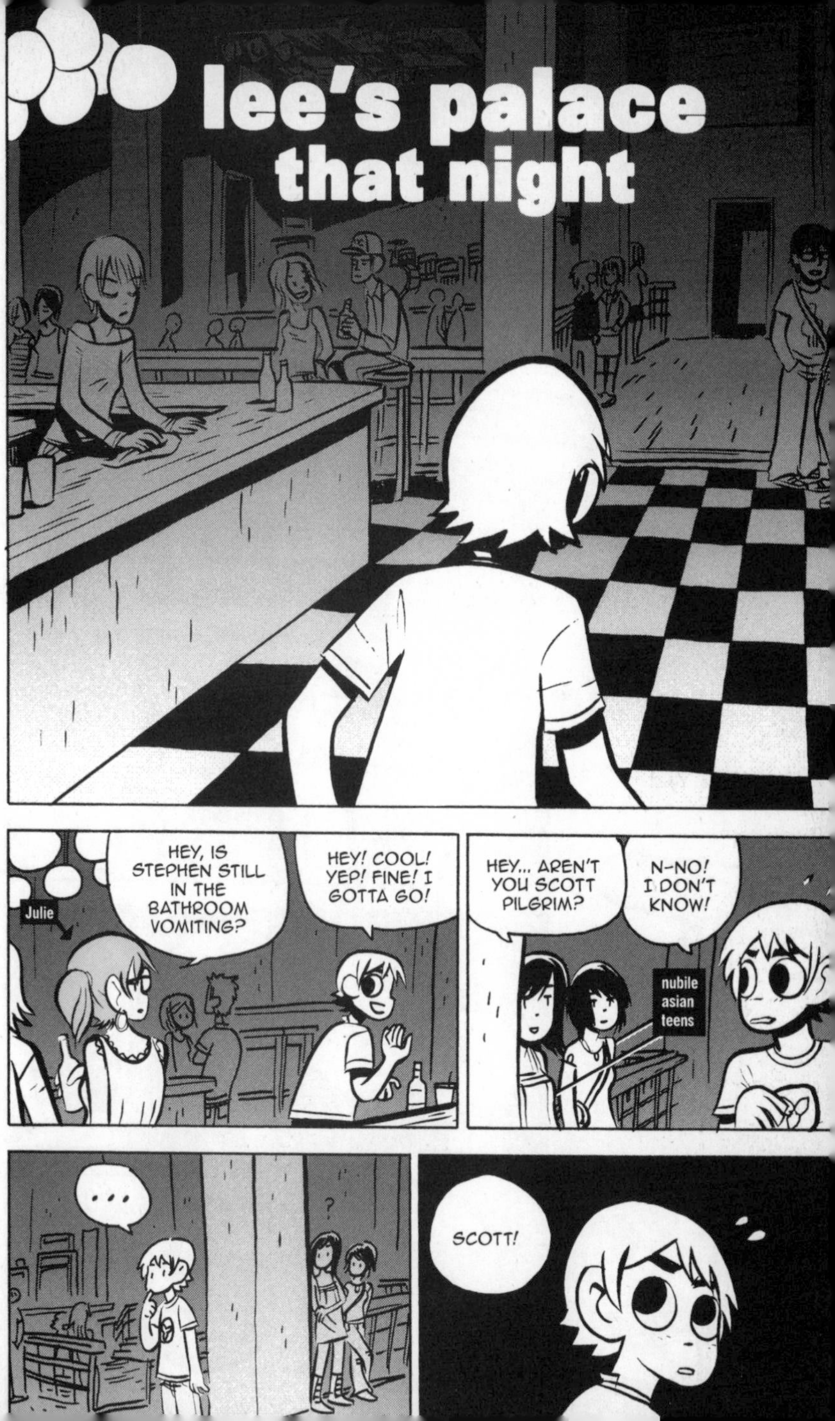
lee's palace
that night
HEY, IS STEPHEN STILL IN THE BATHROOM VOMITING?
Julie
HEY! COOL! YEP! FINE! I GOTTA GO!
HEY... AREN'T YOU SCOTT PILGRIM?
N-NO! I DON'T KNOW!
nubile asian teens
...
?
SCOTT!

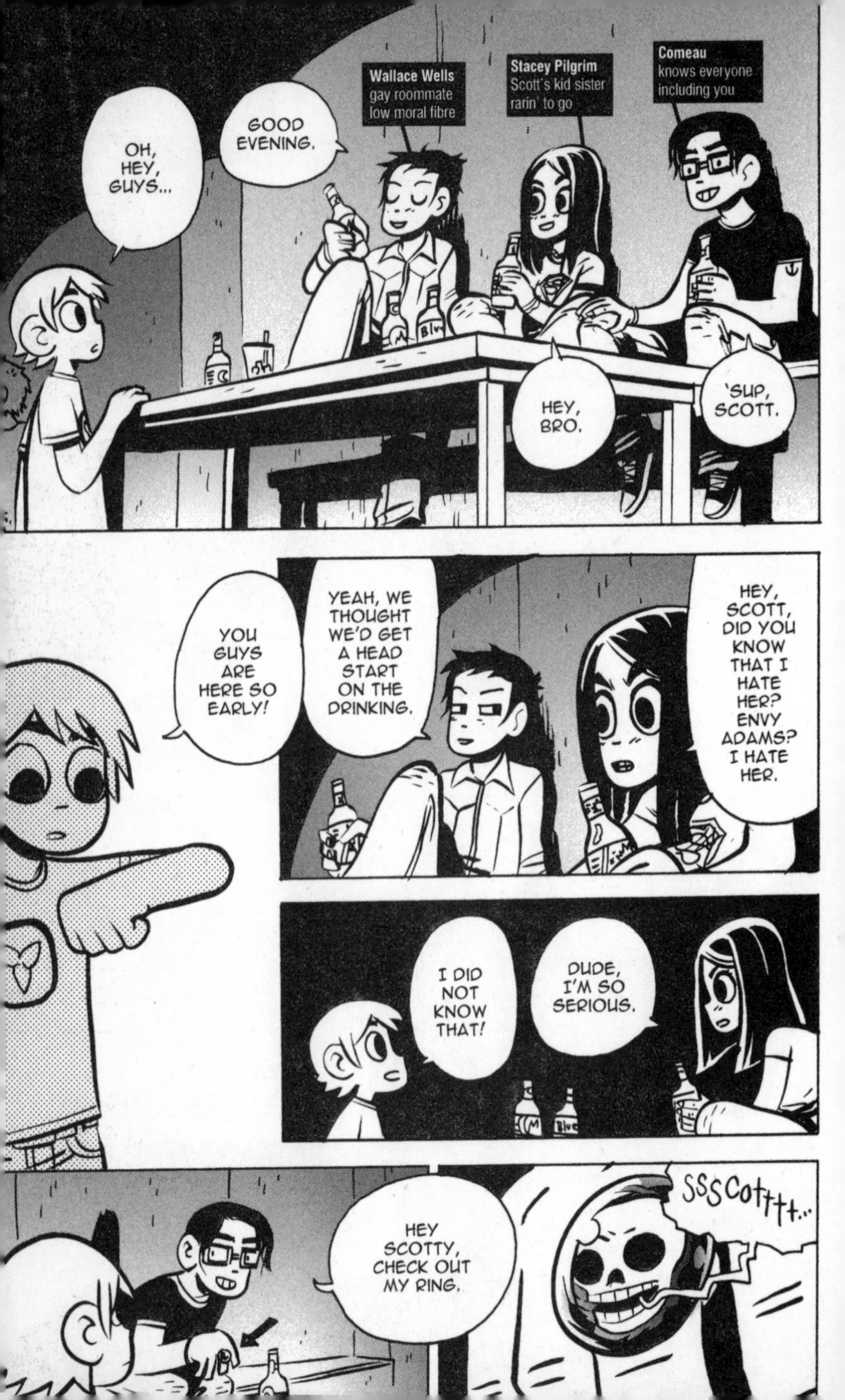
Wallace Wells
gay roommate
low moral fibre
Stacey Pilgrim
Scott's kid sister
rarin' to go
Comeau
knows everyone
including you
OH, HEY, GUYS...
GOOD EVENING.
HEY, BRO.
'SUP, SCOTT.
YOU GUYS ARE HERE SO EARLY!
YEAH, WE THOUGHT WE'D GET A HEAD START ON THE DRINKING.
HEY, SCOTT, DID YOU KNOW THAT I HATE HER? ENVY ADAMS? I HATE HER.
I DID NOT KNOW THAT!
DUDE, I'M SO SERIOUS.
HEY SCOTTY, CHECK OUT MY RING.
SSSCOTTTT...

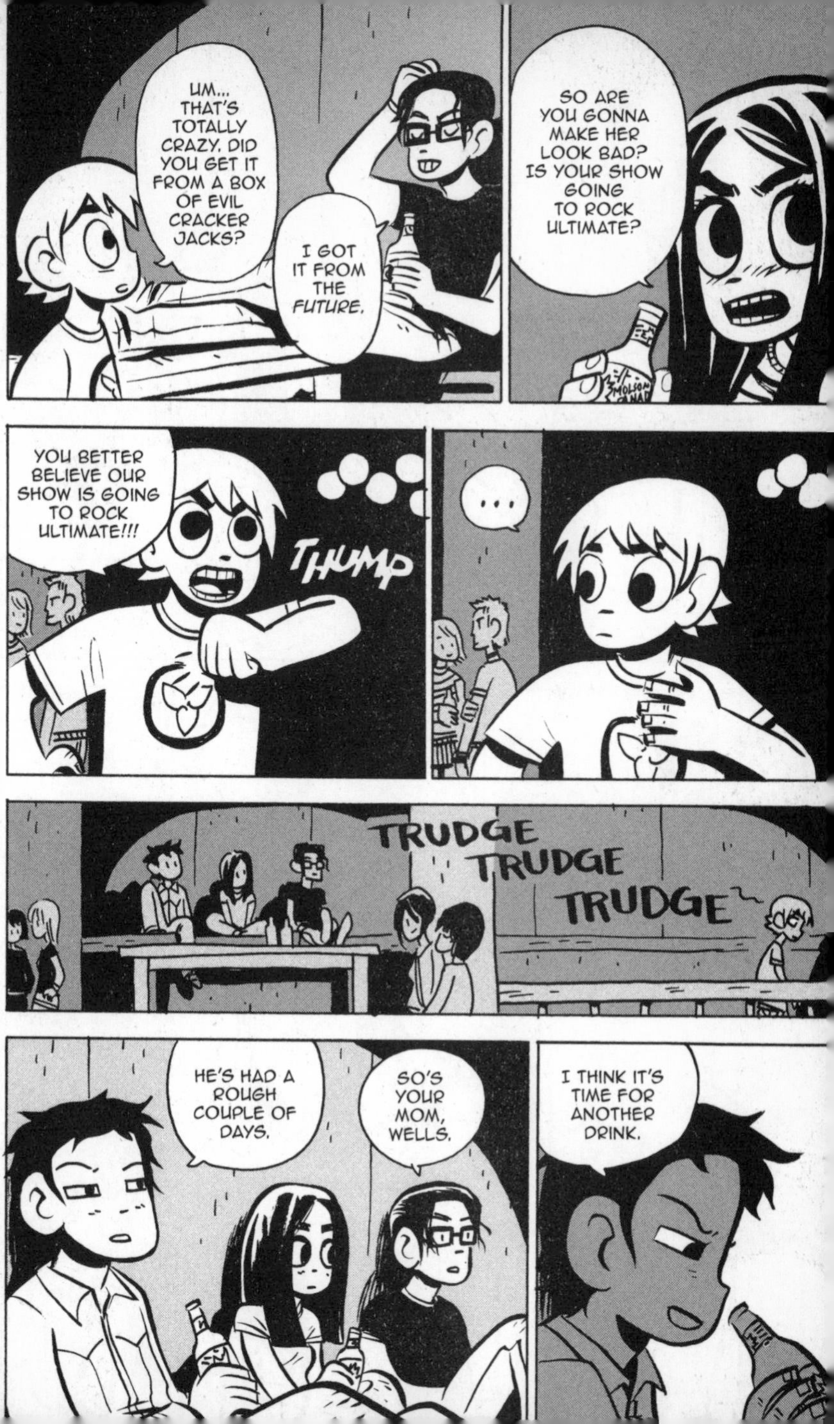
UM... THAT'S TOTALLY CRAZY. DID YOU GET IT FROM A BOX OF EVIL CRACKER JACKS?
I GOT IT FROM THE FUTURE.
SO ARE YOU GONNA MAKE HER LOOK BAD? IS YOUR SHOW GOING TO ROCK ULTIMATE?
YOU BETTER BELIEVE OUR SHOW IS GOING TO ROCK ULTIMATE!!!
THUMP
...
TRUDGE
TRUDGE
TRUDGE
HE'S HAD A ROUGH COUPLE OF DAYS.
SO'S YOUR MOM, WELLS.
I THINK IT'S TIME FOR ANOTHER DRINK.

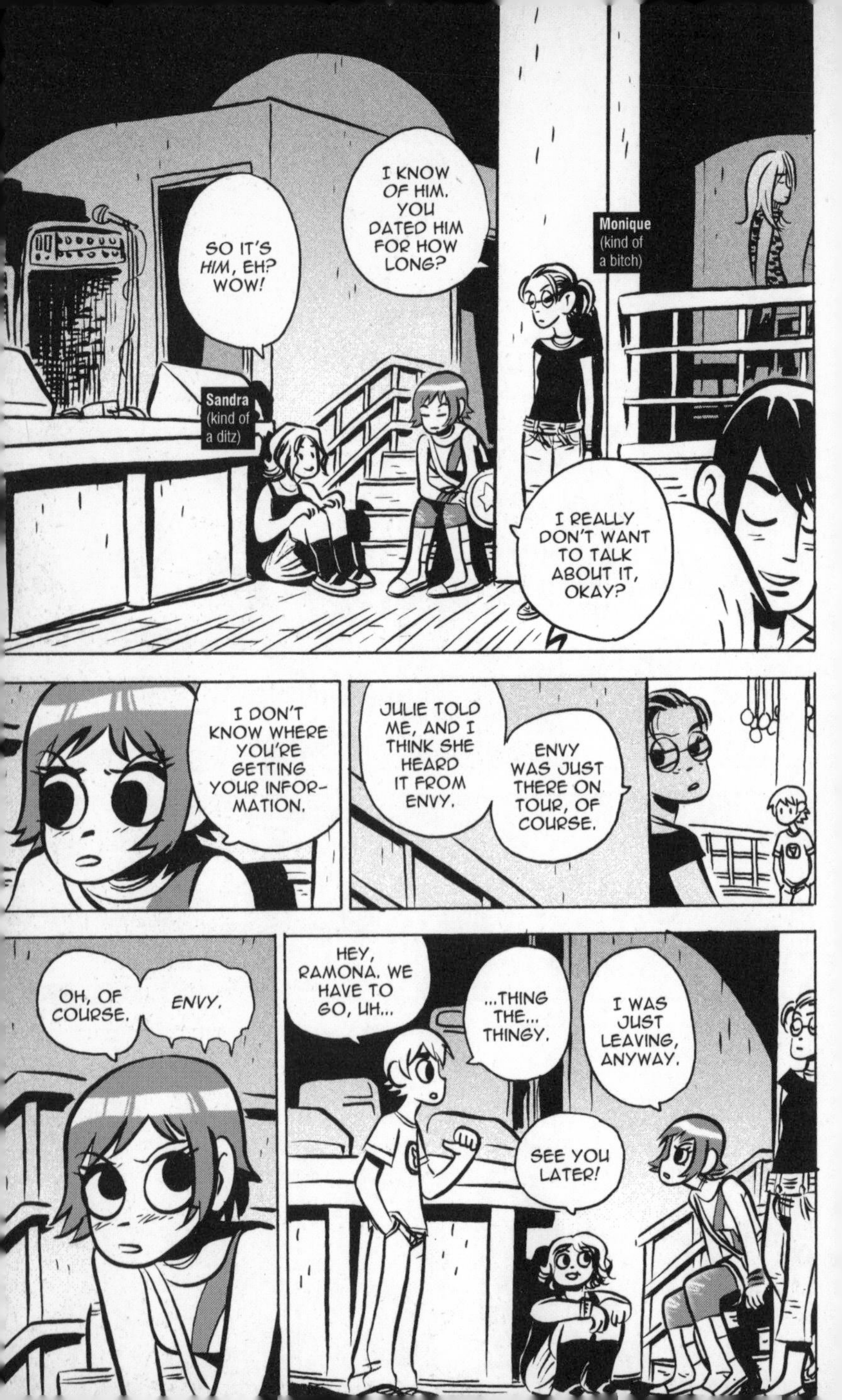
SO IT'S *HIM*, EH? WOW!
I KNOW *OF* HIM. YOU DATED HIM FOR HOW LONG?
Monique (kind of a bitch)
Sandra (kind of a ditz)
I REALLY DON'T WANT TO TALK ABOUT IT, OKAY?
I DON'T KNOW WHERE YOU'RE GETTING YOUR INFORMATION.
JULIE TOLD ME, AND I THINK SHE HEARD IT FROM ENVY.
ENVY WAS JUST THERE ON TOUR, OF COURSE.
OH, OF COURSE.
ENVY.
HEY, RAMONA. WE HAVE TO GO, UH...
...THING THE... THINGY.
I WAS JUST LEAVING, ANYWAY.
SEE YOU LATER!

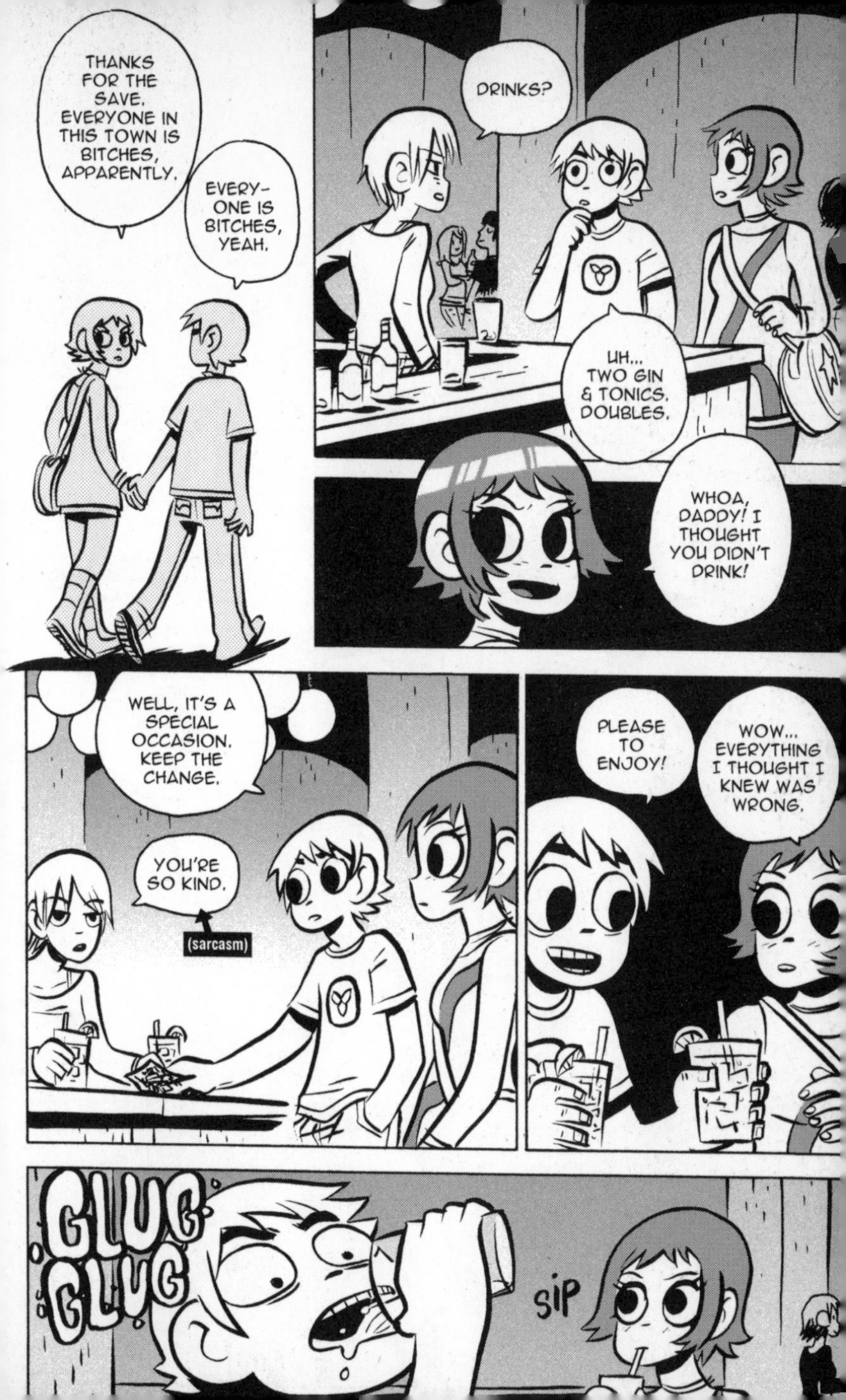
THANKS FOR THE SAVE. EVERYONE IN THIS TOWN IS BITCHES, APPARENTLY.
EVERY-ONE IS BITCHES, YEAH.
DRINKS?
UH... TWO GIN & TONICS. DOUBLES.
WHOA, DADDY! I THOUGHT YOU DIDN'T DRINK!
WELL, IT'S A SPECIAL OCCASION. KEEP THE CHANGE.
YOU'RE SO KIND.
(sarcasm)
PLEASE TO ENJOY!
WOW... EVERYTHING I THOUGHT I KNEW WAS WRONG.
GLUG GLUG
SIP

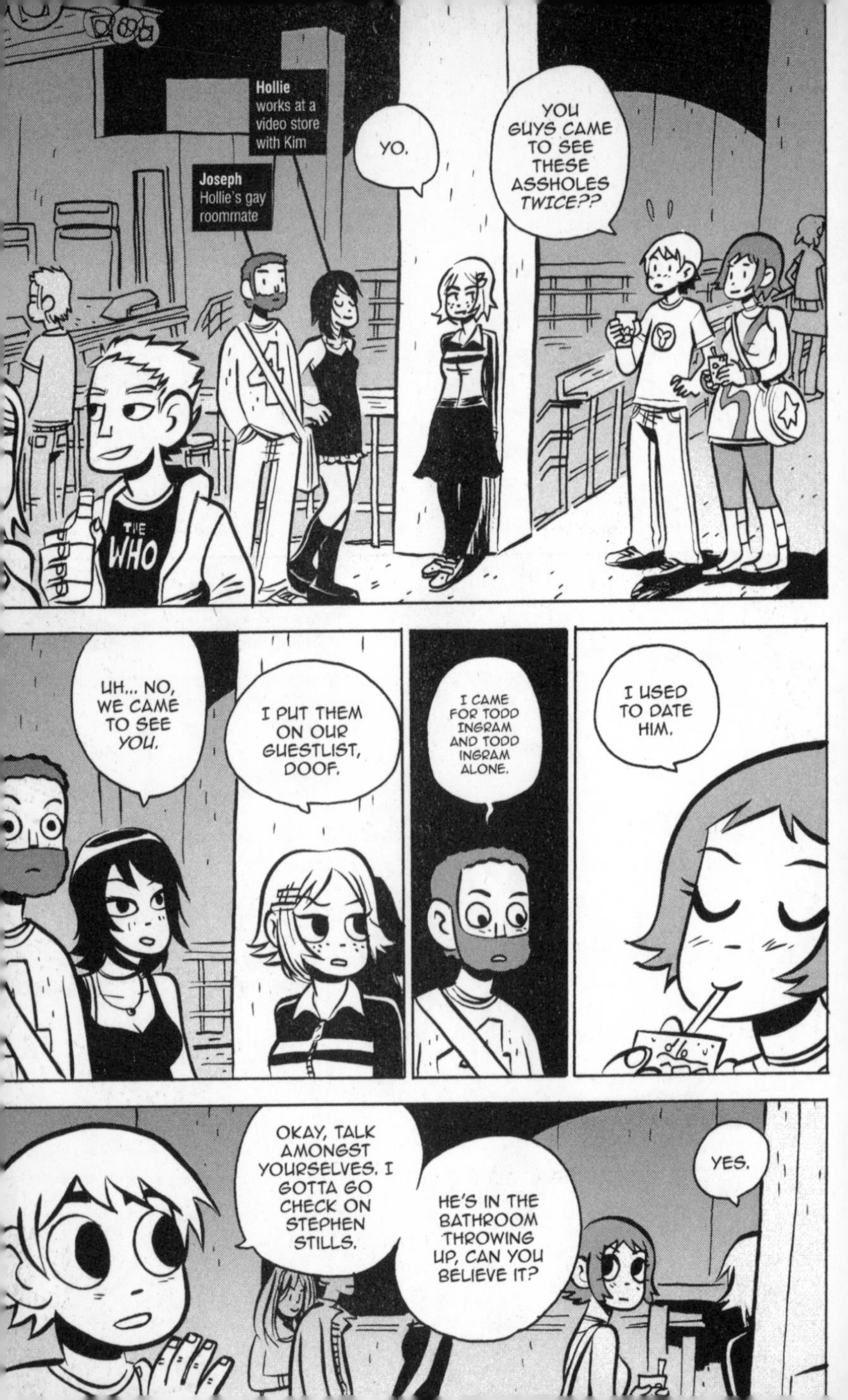
Hollie
works at a video store with Kim
Joseph
Hollie's gay roommate
YO.
YOU GUYS CAME TO SEE THESE ASSHOLES TWICE??
THE WHO
UH... NO, WE CAME TO SEE YOU.
I PUT THEM ON OUR GUESTLIST, DOOF.
I CAME FOR TODD INGRAM AND TODD INGRAM ALONE.
I USED TO DATE HIM.
OKAY, TALK AMONGST YOURSELVES. I GOTTA GO CHECK ON STEPHEN STILLS.
HE'S IN THE BATHROOM THROWING UP, CAN YOU BELIEVE IT?
YES.

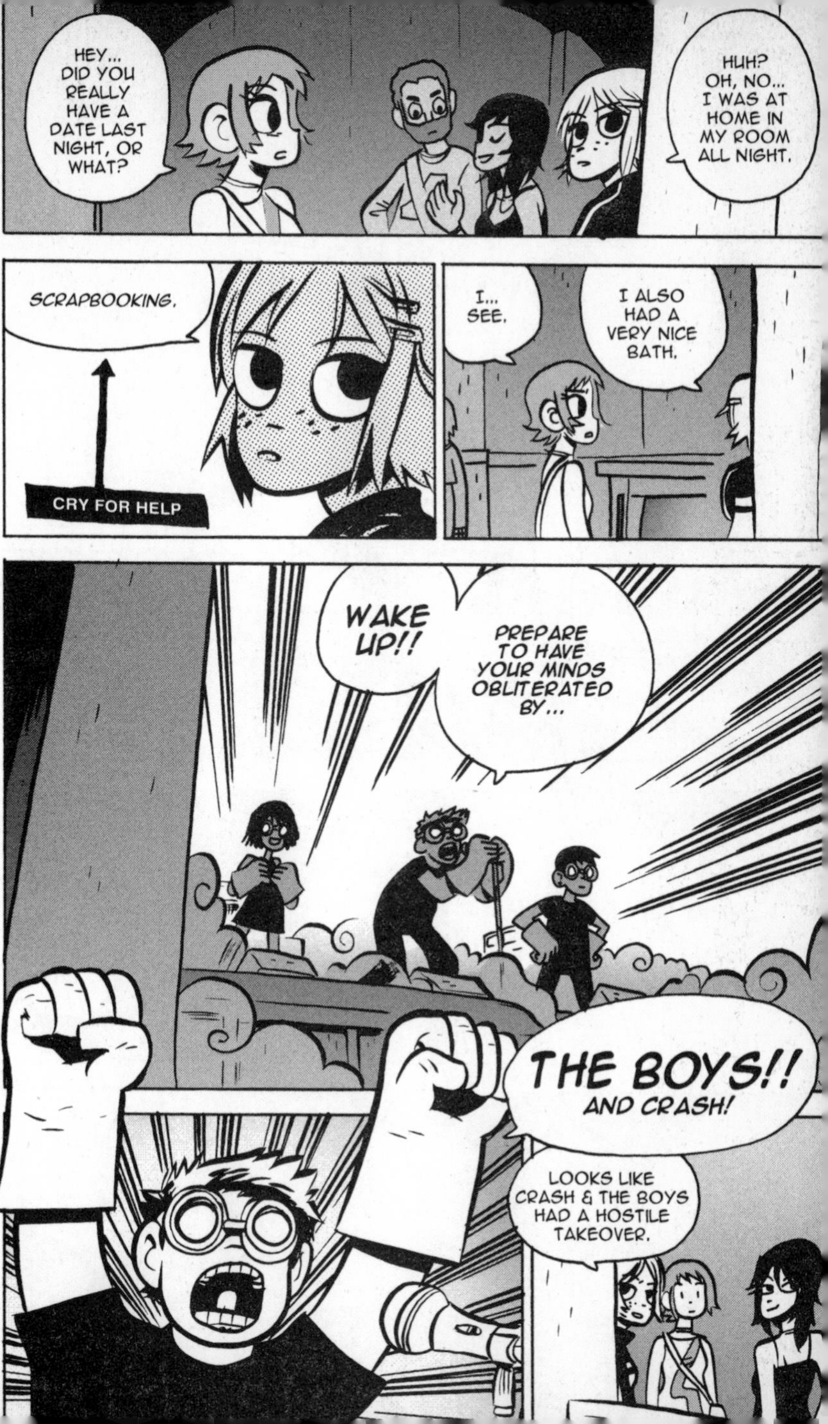
HEY... DID YOU REALLY HAVE A DATE LAST NIGHT, OR WHAT?
HUH? OH, NO... I WAS AT HOME IN MY ROOM ALL NIGHT.
SCRAPBOOKING.
CRY FOR HELP
I... SEE.
I ALSO HAD A VERY NICE BATH.
WAKE UP!!
PREPARE TO HAVE YOUR MINDS OBLITERATED BY...
THE BOYS!!
AND CRASH!
LOOKS LIKE CRASH & THE BOYS HAD A HOSTILE TAKEOVER.

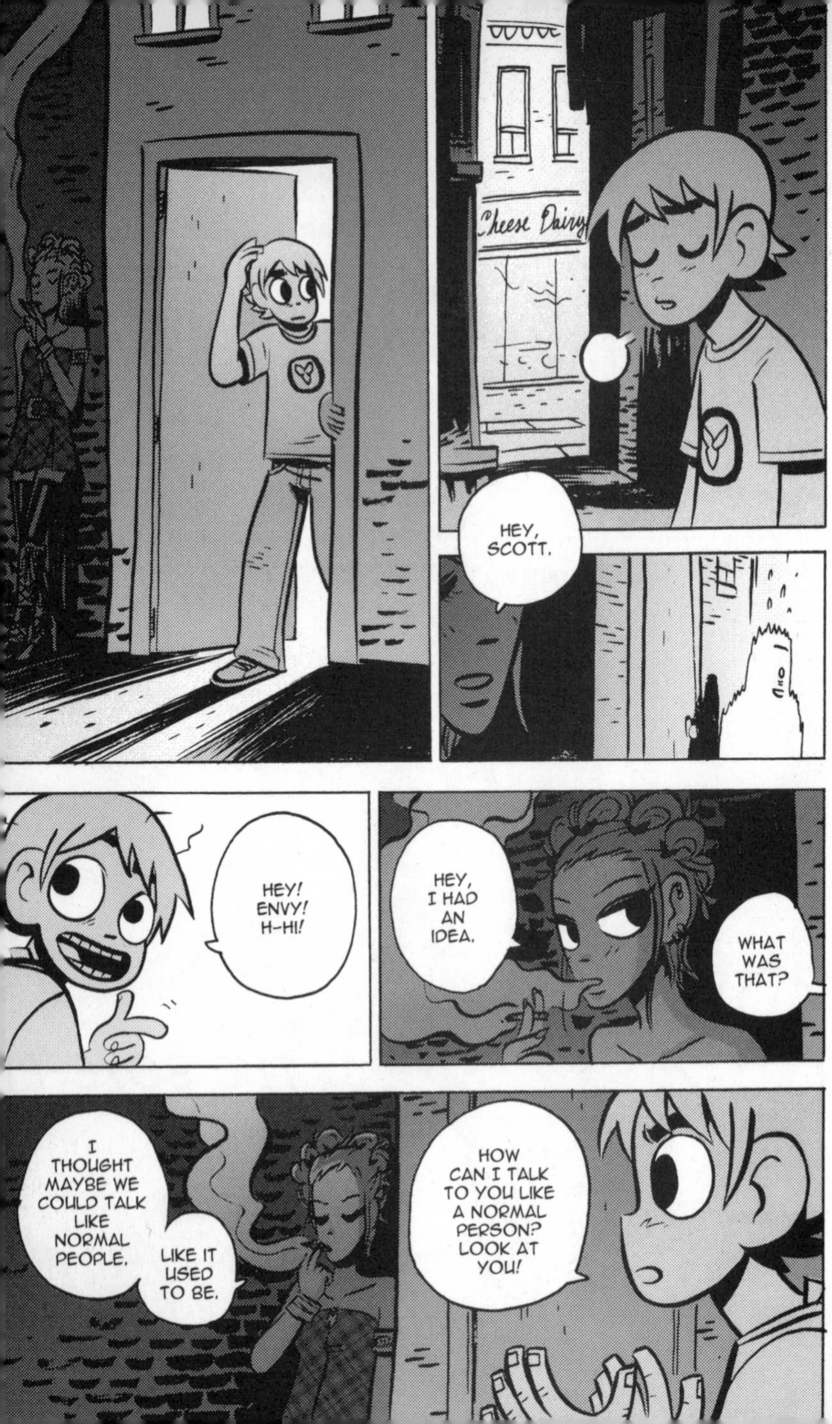
Cheese Dairy
HEY, SCOTT.
HEY! ENVY! H-HI!
HEY, I HAD AN IDEA.
WHAT WAS THAT?
I THOUGHT MAYBE WE COULD TALK LIKE NORMAL PEOPLE.
LIKE IT USED TO BE.
HOW CAN I TALK TO YOU LIKE A NORMAL PERSON? LOOK AT YOU!

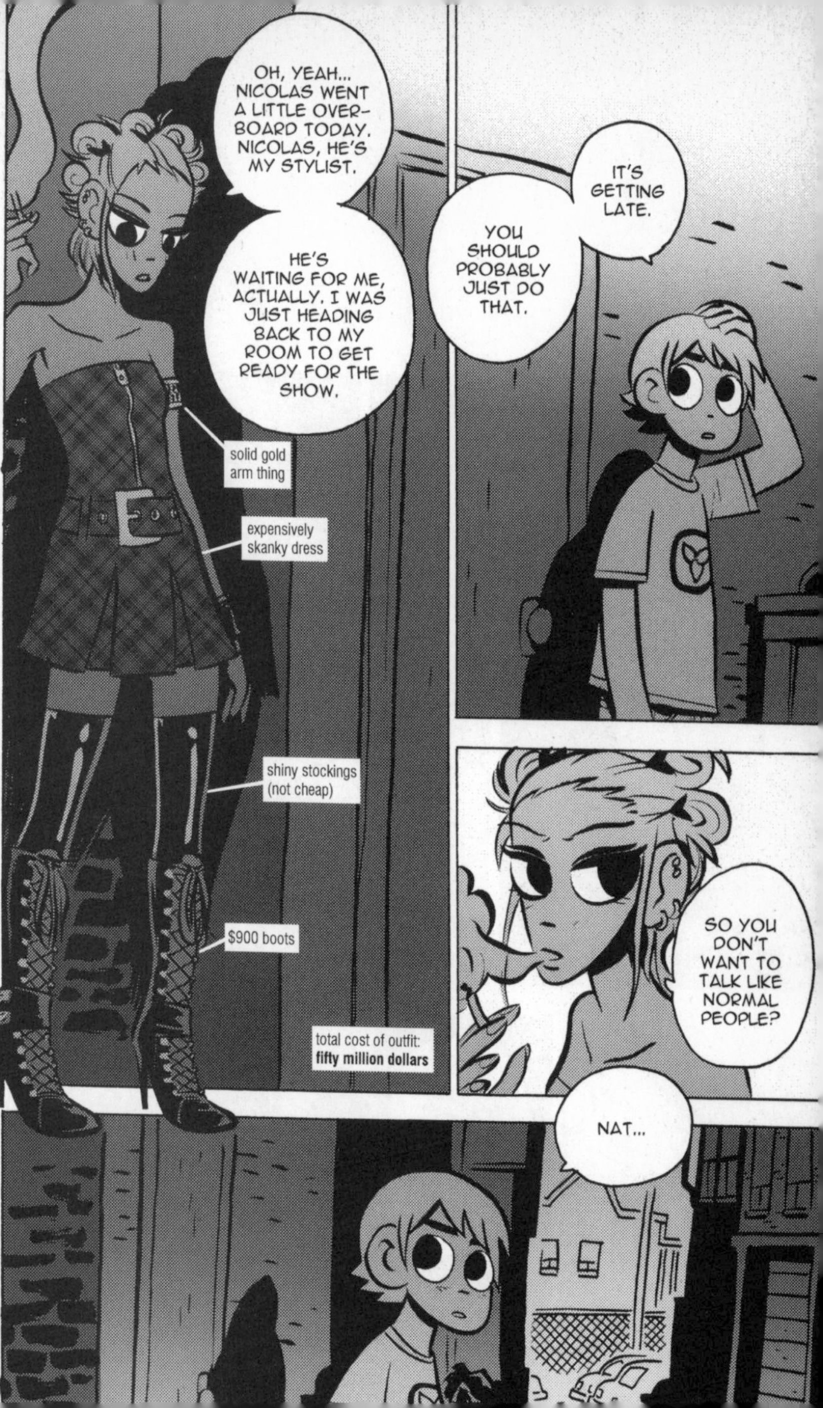
OH, YEAH... NICOLAS WENT A LITTLE OVER-BOARD TODAY. NICOLAS, HE'S MY STYLIST.
HE'S WAITING FOR ME, ACTUALLY. I WAS JUST HEADING BACK TO MY ROOM TO GET READY FOR THE SHOW.
solid gold arm thing
expensively skanky dress
shiny stockings (not cheap)
$900 boots
total cost of outfit:
fifty million dollars
IT'S GETTING LATE.
YOU SHOULD PROBABLY JUST DO THAT.
SO YOU DON'T WANT TO TALK LIKE NORMAL PEOPLE?
NAT...

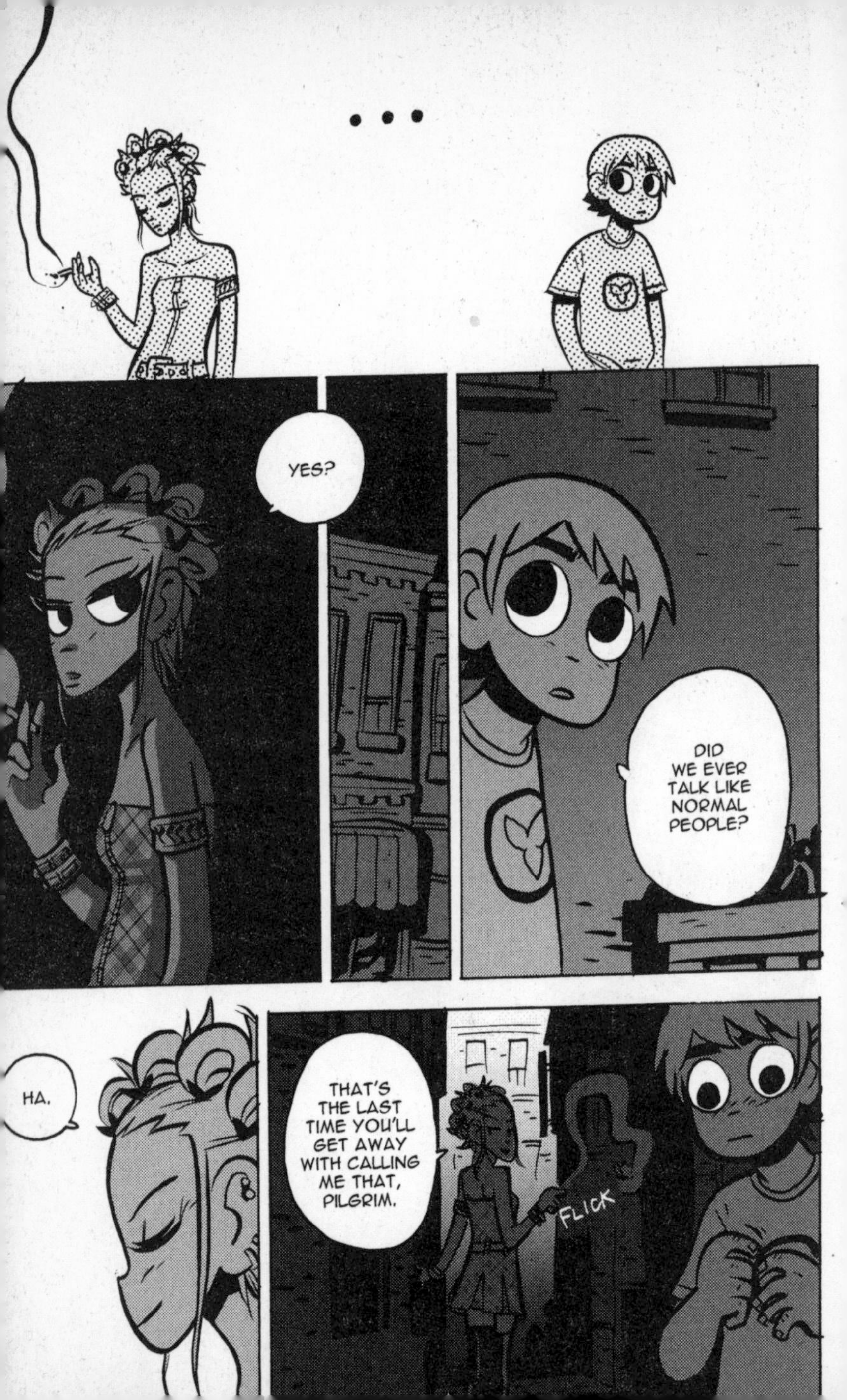
...
YES?
DID WE EVER TALK LIKE NORMAL PEOPLE?
HA.
THAT'S THE LAST TIME YOU'LL GET AWAY WITH CALLING ME THAT, PILGRIM.
FLICK

Cheese Dairy

H MY
OD,
NVY
AMS!

ENVY!

ENVY,
TALK
TO ME!

YOU
IGN
CD?

ENVY
ADAMS IS
RIGHT
THERE!

SO
HOT!

BIGGEST
AN!

ENVY!
NVY!!

ELIEVE
SHE'S
HERE!

GOD!
BY
HEART!

HER

T
HERE!

I LOVE
YOU!

YOU
RO

KNIVES CHAU
17 YEARS OLD

ENVY
AMS!

SKRCH
SKRCH

UM...
HEY,
KNIVES.

SCOTT!

QUAY
CUR

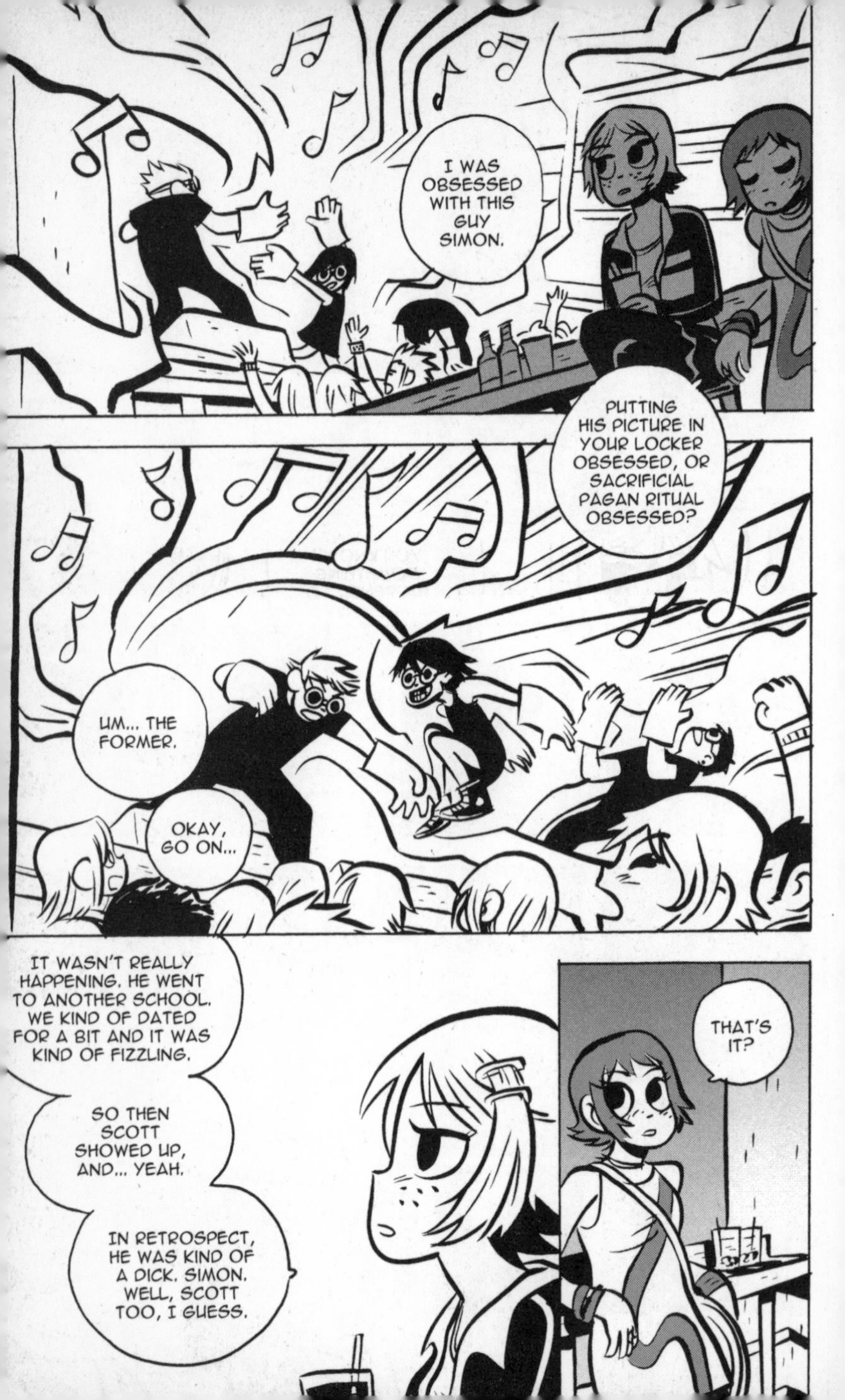
I WAS OBSESSED WITH THIS GUY SIMON.
PUTTING HIS PICTURE IN YOUR LOCKER OBSESSED, OR SACRIFICIAL PAGAN RITUAL OBSESSED?
UM... THE FORMER.
OKAY, GO ON...
IT WASN'T REALLY HAPPENING. HE WENT TO ANOTHER SCHOOL. WE KIND OF DATED FOR A BIT AND IT WAS KIND OF FIZZLING.
SO THEN SCOTT SHOWED UP, AND... YEAH.
IN RETROSPECT, HE WAS KIND OF A DICK. SIMON. WELL, SCOTT TOO, I GUESS.
THAT'S IT?

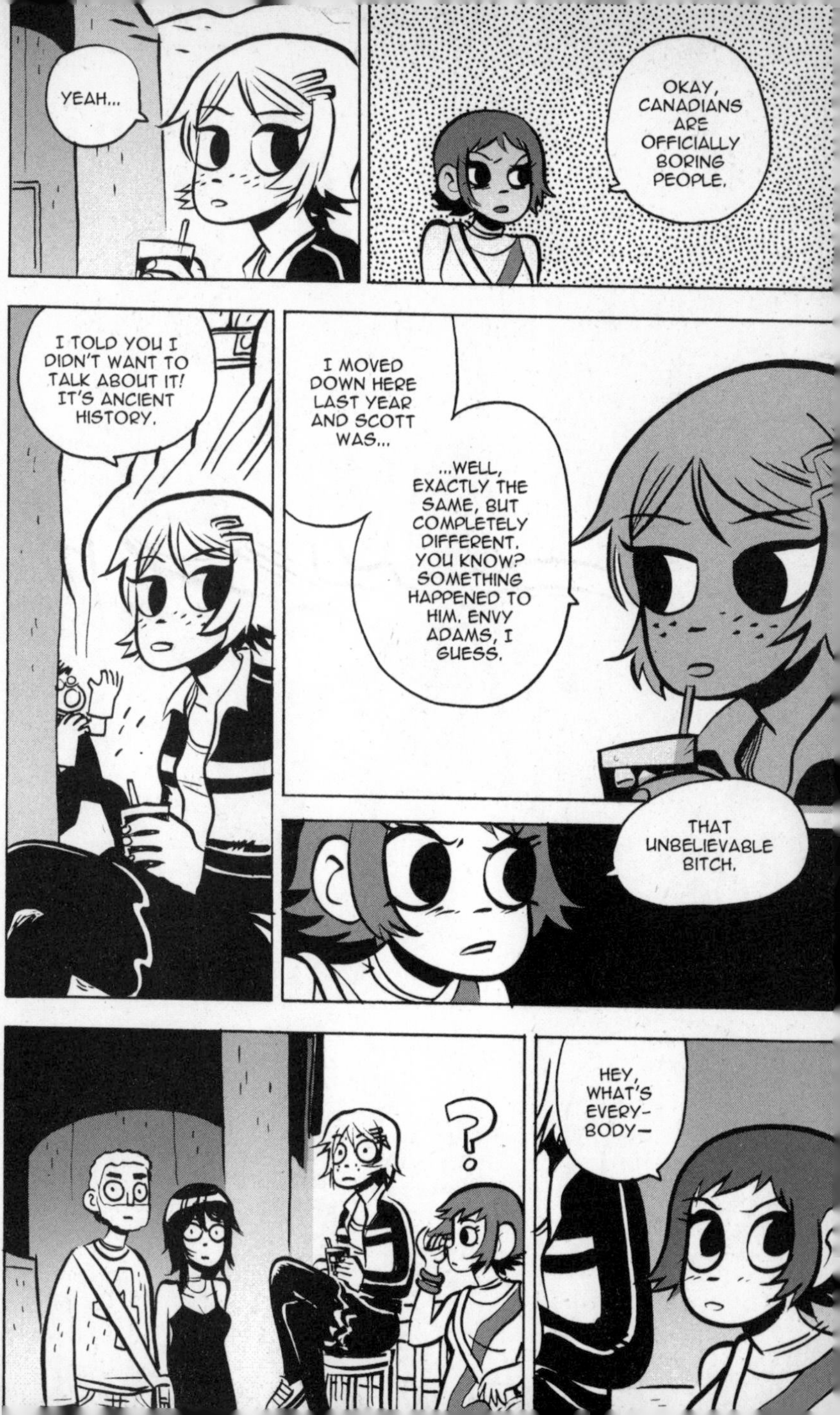
YEAH...
OKAY, CANADIANS ARE OFFICIALLY BORING PEOPLE.
I TOLD YOU I DIDN'T WANT TO TALK ABOUT IT! IT'S ANCIENT HISTORY.
I MOVED DOWN HERE LAST YEAR AND SCOTT WAS...
...WELL, EXACTLY THE SAME, BUT COMPLETELY DIFFERENT. YOU KNOW? SOMETHING HAPPENED TO HIM. ENVY ADAMS, I GUESS.
THAT UNBELIEVABLE BITCH.
?
HEY, WHAT'S EVERY-BODY—

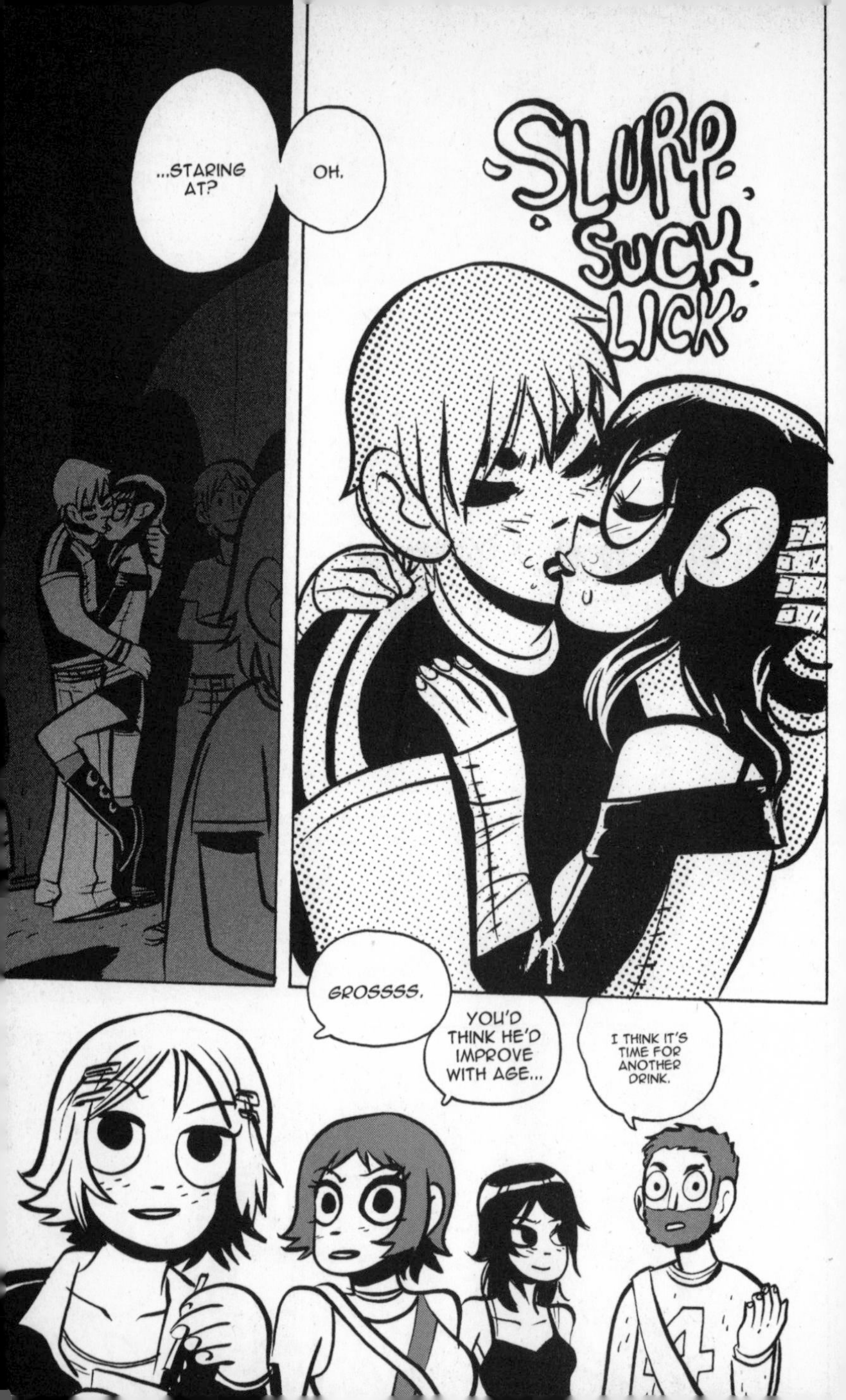
...STARING AT?
OH.
SLURP SUCK LICK
GROSSSS.
YOU'D THINK HE'D IMPROVE WITH AGE...
I THINK IT'S TIME FOR ANOTHER DRINK.

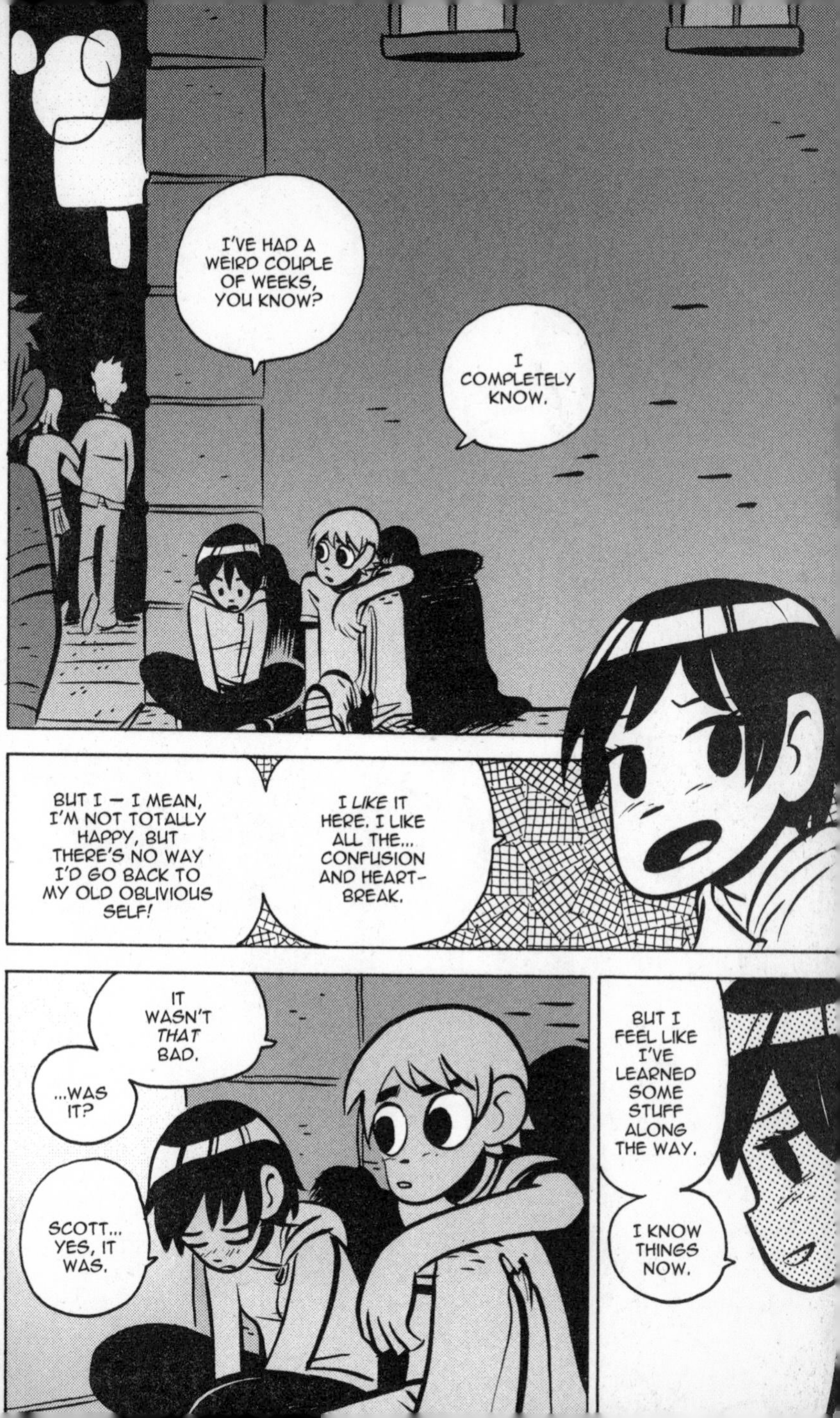
I'VE HAD A WEIRD COUPLE OF WEEKS, YOU KNOW?
I COMPLETELY KNOW.
BUT I — I MEAN, I'M NOT TOTALLY HAPPY, BUT THERE'S NO WAY I'D GO BACK TO MY OLD OBLIVIOUS SELF!
I *LIKE* IT HERE. I LIKE ALL THE... CONFUSION AND HEART-BREAK.
IT WASN'T *THAT* BAD.
...WAS IT?
SCOTT... YES, IT WAS.
BUT I FEEL LIKE I'VE LEARNED SOME STUFF ALONG THE WAY.
I KNOW THINGS NOW.

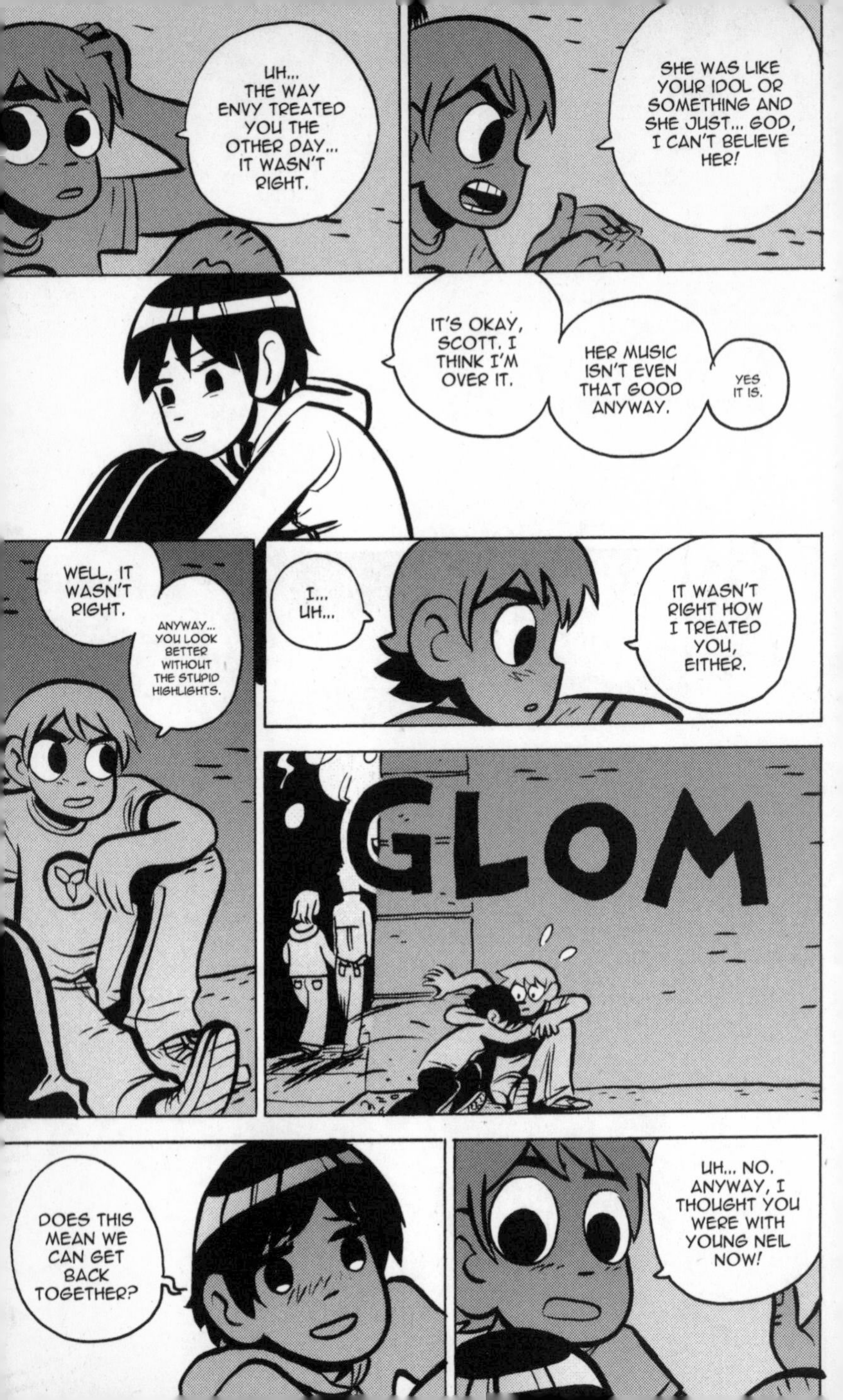
UH... THE WAY ENVY TREATED YOU THE OTHER DAY... IT WASN'T RIGHT.
SHE WAS LIKE YOUR IDOL OR SOMETHING AND SHE JUST... GOD, I CAN'T BELIEVE HER!
IT'S OKAY, SCOTT. I THINK I'M OVER IT.
HER MUSIC ISN'T EVEN THAT GOOD ANYWAY.
YES IT IS.
WELL, IT WASN'T RIGHT.
ANYWAY... YOU LOOK BETTER WITHOUT THE STUPID HIGHLIGHTS.
I... UH...
IT WASN'T RIGHT HOW I TREATED YOU, EITHER.
GLOM
DOES THIS MEAN WE CAN GET BACK TOGETHER?
UH... NO. ANYWAY, I THOUGHT YOU WERE WITH YOUNG NEIL NOW!

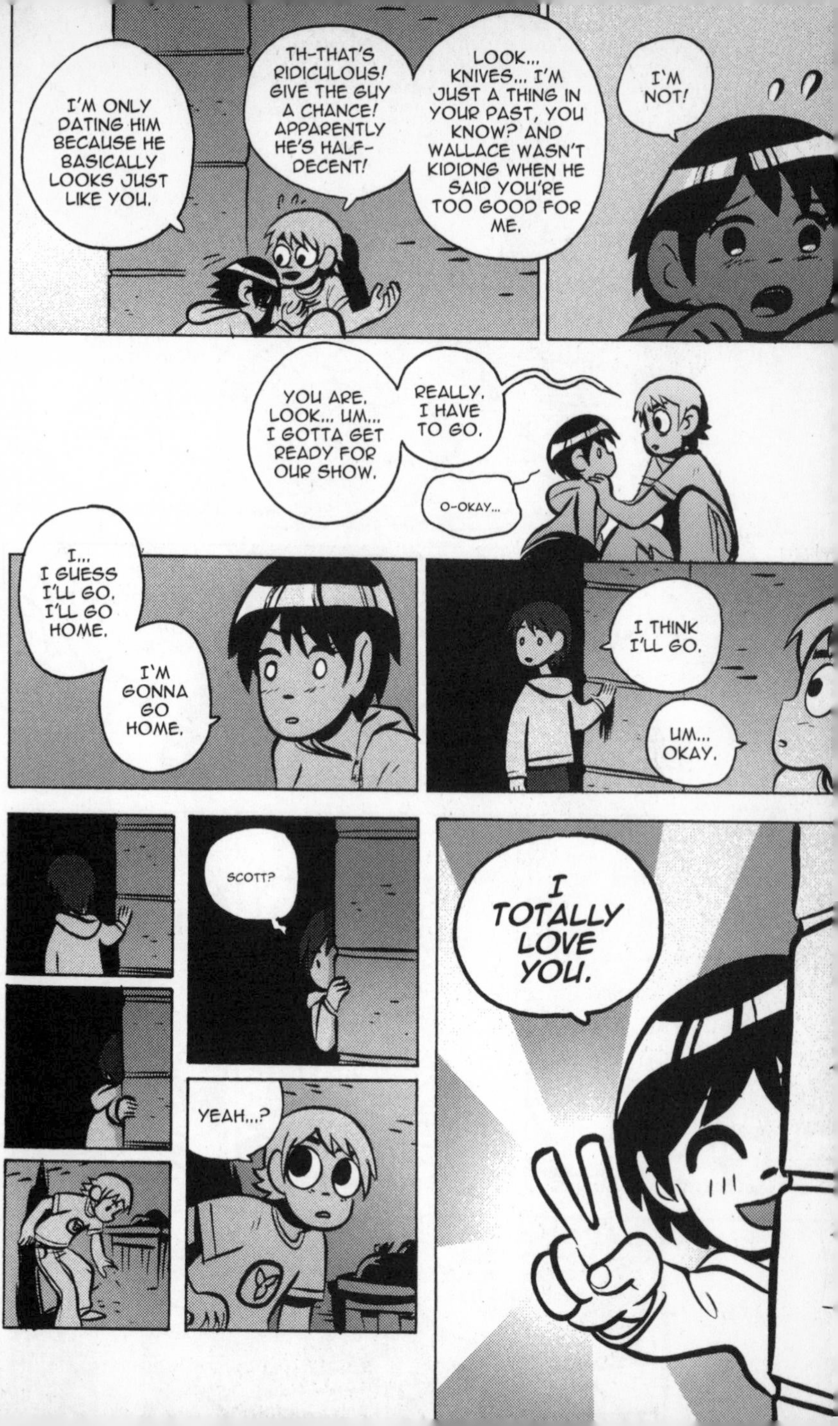
I'M ONLY DATING HIM BECAUSE HE BASICALLY LOOKS JUST LIKE YOU.
TH-THAT'S RIDICULOUS! GIVE THE GUY A CHANCE! APPARENTLY HE'S HALF-DECENT!
LOOK... KNIVES... I'M JUST A THING IN YOUR PAST, YOU KNOW? AND WALLACE WASN'T KIDIDNG WHEN HE SAID YOU'RE TOO GOOD FOR ME.
I'M NOT!
YOU ARE. LOOK... UM... I GOTTA GET READY FOR OUR SHOW.
REALLY. I HAVE TO GO.
O-OKAY...
I... I GUESS I'LL GO. I'LL GO HOME.
I'M GONNA GO HOME.
I THINK I'LL GO.
UM... OKAY.
SCOTT?
YEAH...?
I TOTALLY LOVE YOU.

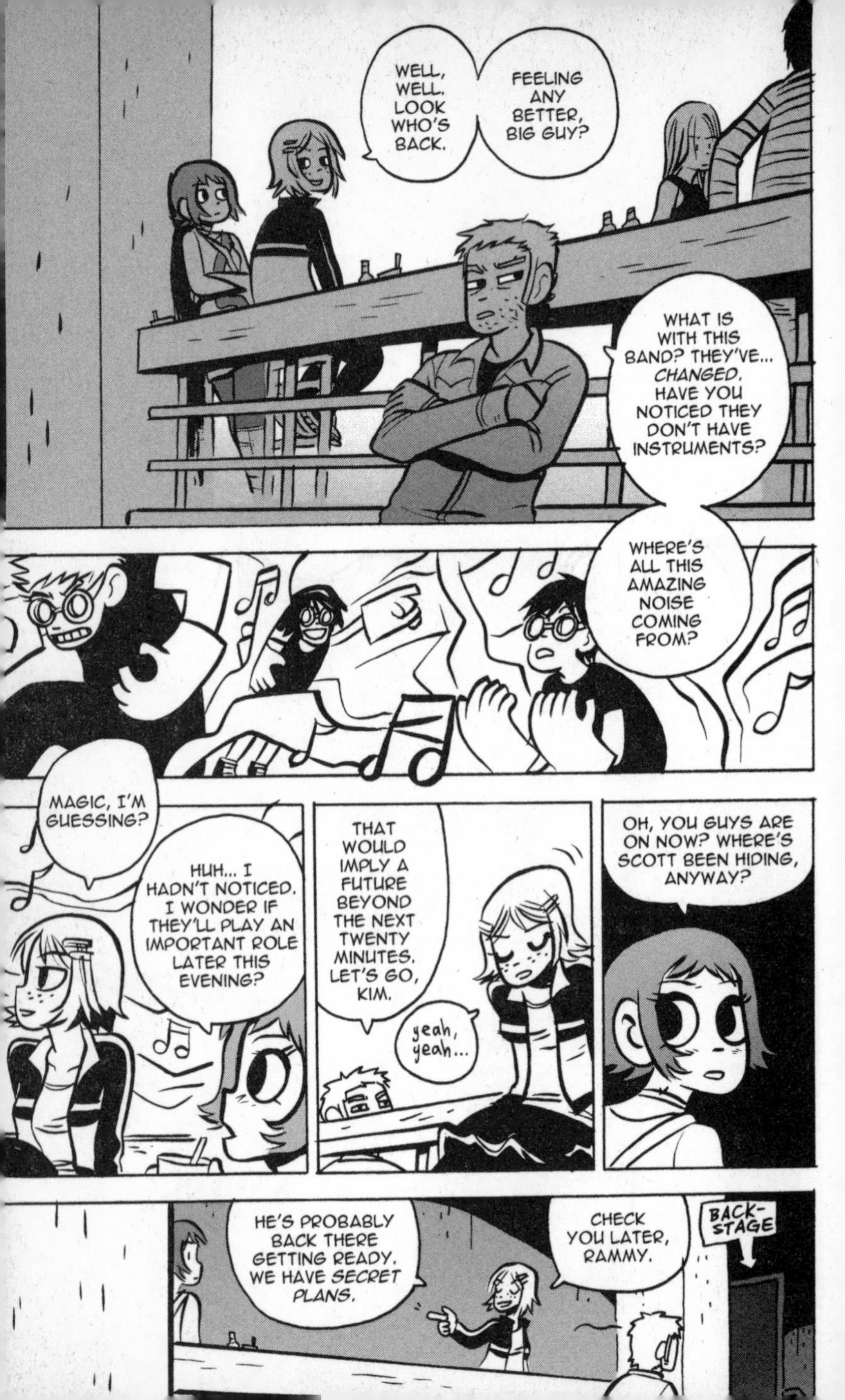

WELL, WELL. LOOK WHO'S BACK.
FEELING ANY BETTER, BIG GUY?
WHAT IS WITH THIS BAND? THEY'VE... CHANGED. HAVE YOU NOTICED THEY DON'T HAVE INSTRUMENTS?
WHERE'S ALL THIS AMAZING NOISE COMING FROM?
MAGIC, I'M GUESSING?
HUH... I HADN'T NOTICED. I WONDER IF THEY'LL PLAY AN IMPORTANT ROLE LATER THIS EVENING?
THAT WOULD IMPLY A FUTURE BEYOND THE NEXT TWENTY MINUTES. LET'S GO, KIM.
yeah, yeah...
OH, YOU GUYS ARE ON NOW? WHERE'S SCOTT BEEN HIDING, ANYWAY?
HE'S PROBABLY BACK THERE GETTING READY. WE HAVE SECRET PLANS.
CHECK YOU LATER, RAMMY.
BACK-STAGE

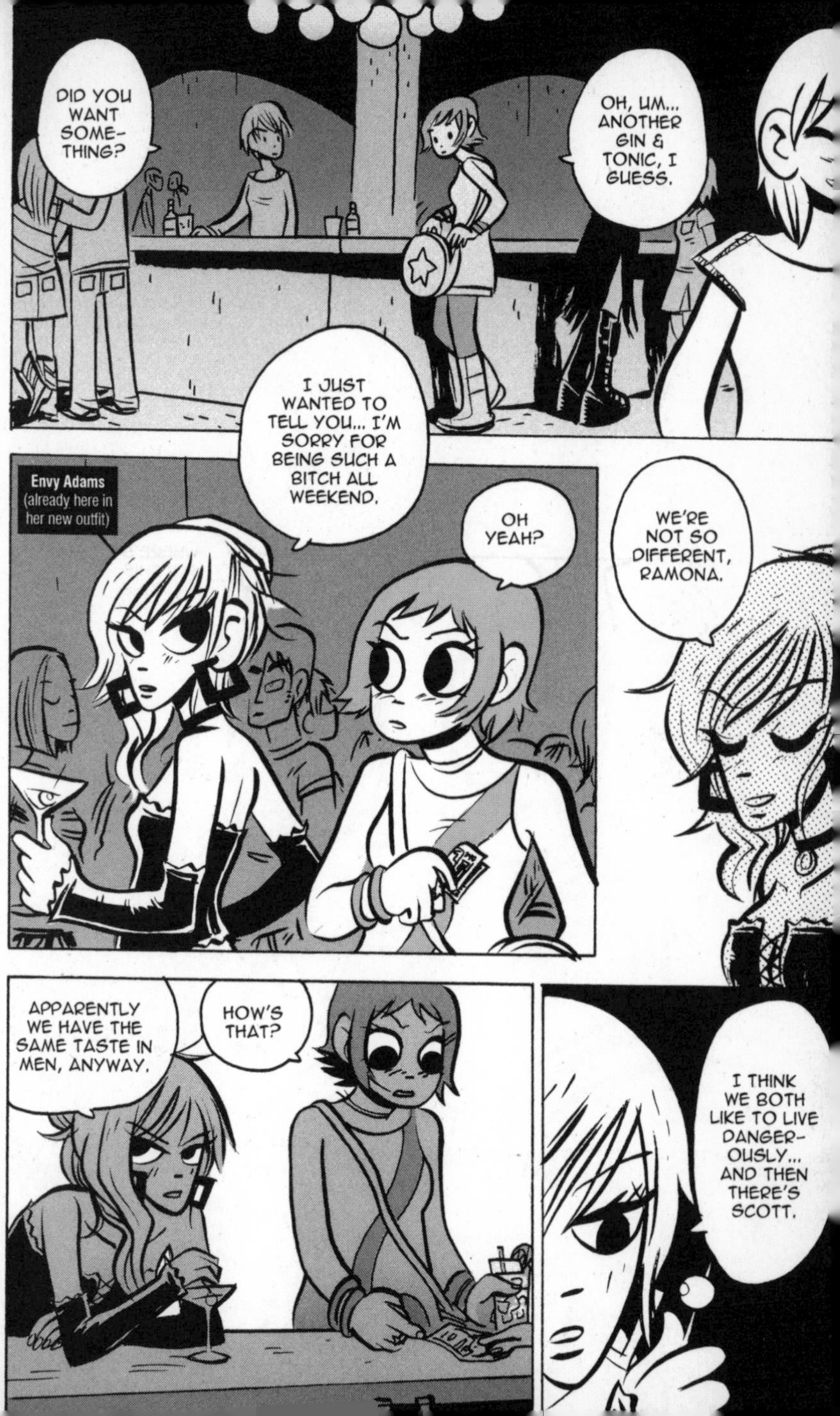
DID YOU WANT SOME-THING?
OH, UM... ANOTHER GIN & TONIC, I GUESS.
I JUST WANTED TO TELL YOU... I'M SORRY FOR BEING SUCH A BITCH ALL WEEKEND.
Envy Adams (already here in her new outfit)
OH YEAH?
WE'RE NOT SO DIFFERENT, RAMONA.
APPARENTLY WE HAVE THE SAME TASTE IN MEN, ANYWAY.
HOW'S THAT?
I THINK WE BOTH LIKE TO LIVE DANGER-OUSLY... AND THEN THERE'S SCOTT.

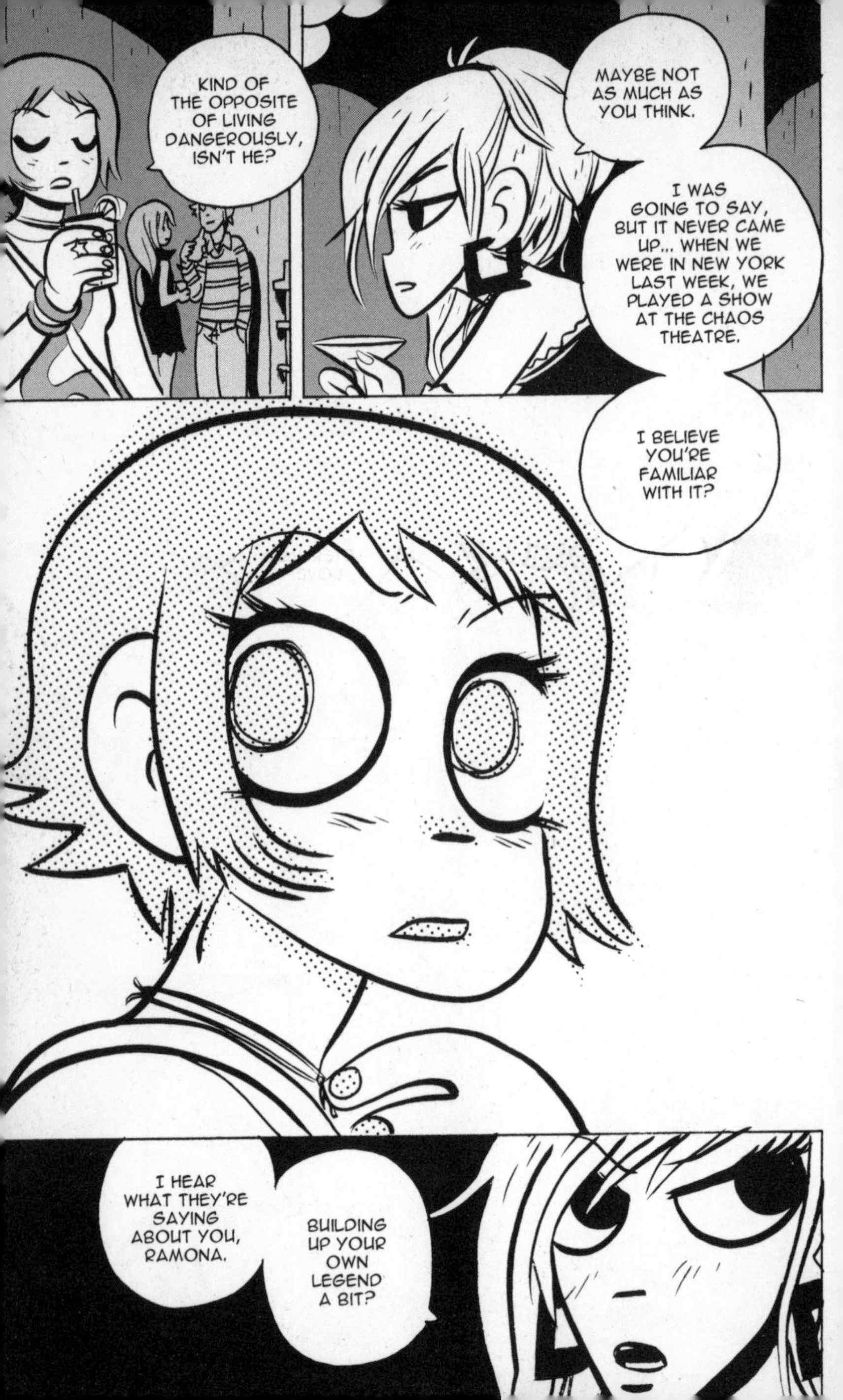
KIND OF THE OPPOSITE OF LIVING DANGEROUSLY, ISN'T HE?
MAYBE NOT AS MUCH AS YOU THINK.
I WAS GOING TO SAY, BUT IT NEVER CAME UP... WHEN WE WERE IN NEW YORK LAST WEEK, WE PLAYED A SHOW AT THE CHAOS THEATRE.
I BELIEVE YOU'RE FAMILIAR WITH IT?
I HEAR WHAT THEY'RE SAYING ABOUT YOU, RAMONA.
BUILDING UP YOUR OWN LEGEND A BIT?

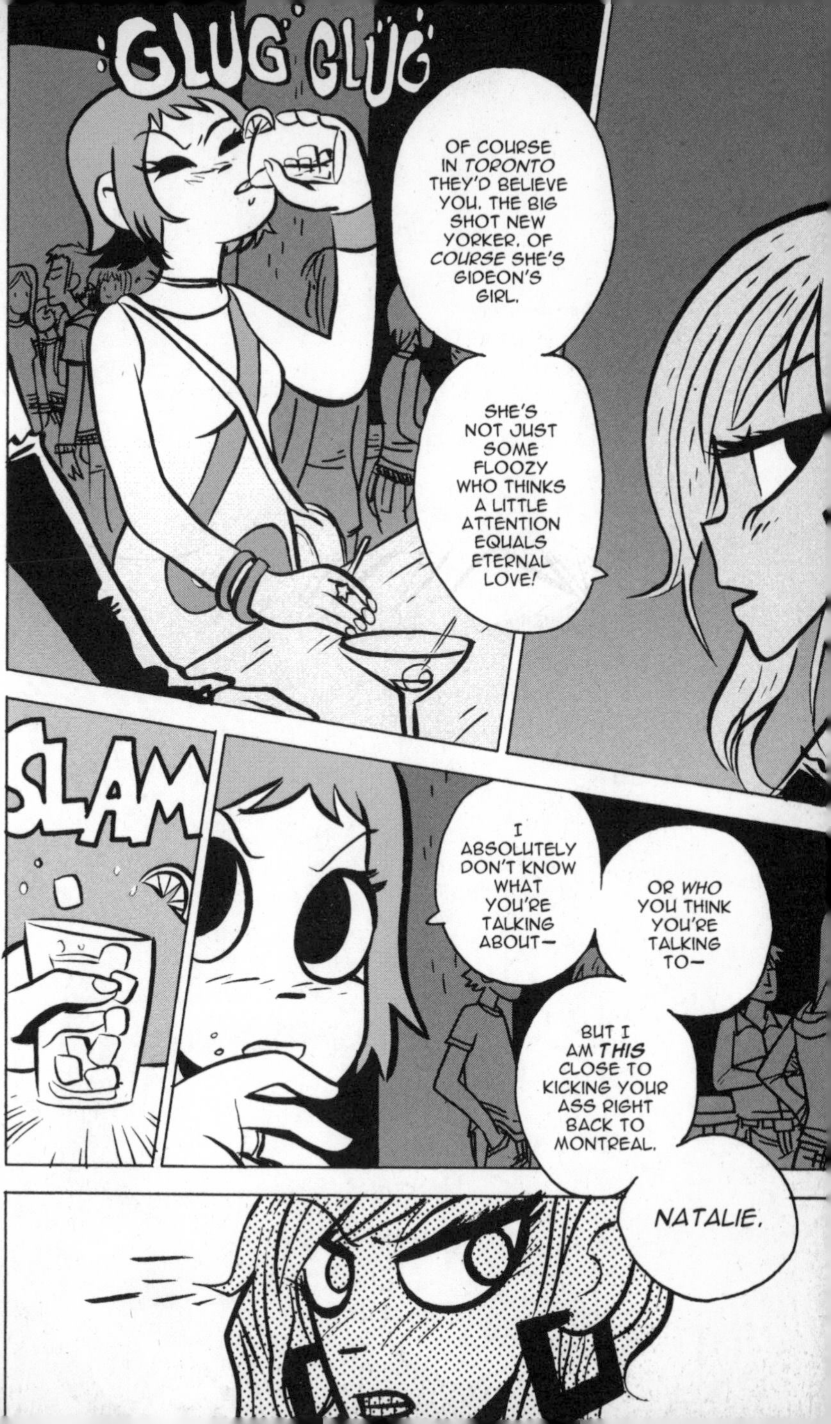
GLUG GLUG
OF COURSE IN TORONTO THEY'D BELIEVE YOU. THE BIG SHOT NEW YORKER. OF COURSE SHE'S GIDEON'S GIRL.
SHE'S NOT JUST SOME FLOOZY WHO THINKS A LITTLE ATTENTION EQUALS ETERNAL LOVE!
SLAM
I ABSOLUTELY DON'T KNOW WHAT YOU'RE TALKING ABOUT—
OR WHO YOU THINK YOU'RE TALKING TO—
BUT I AM THIS CLOSE TO KICKING YOUR ASS RIGHT BACK TO MONTREAL.
NATALIE.

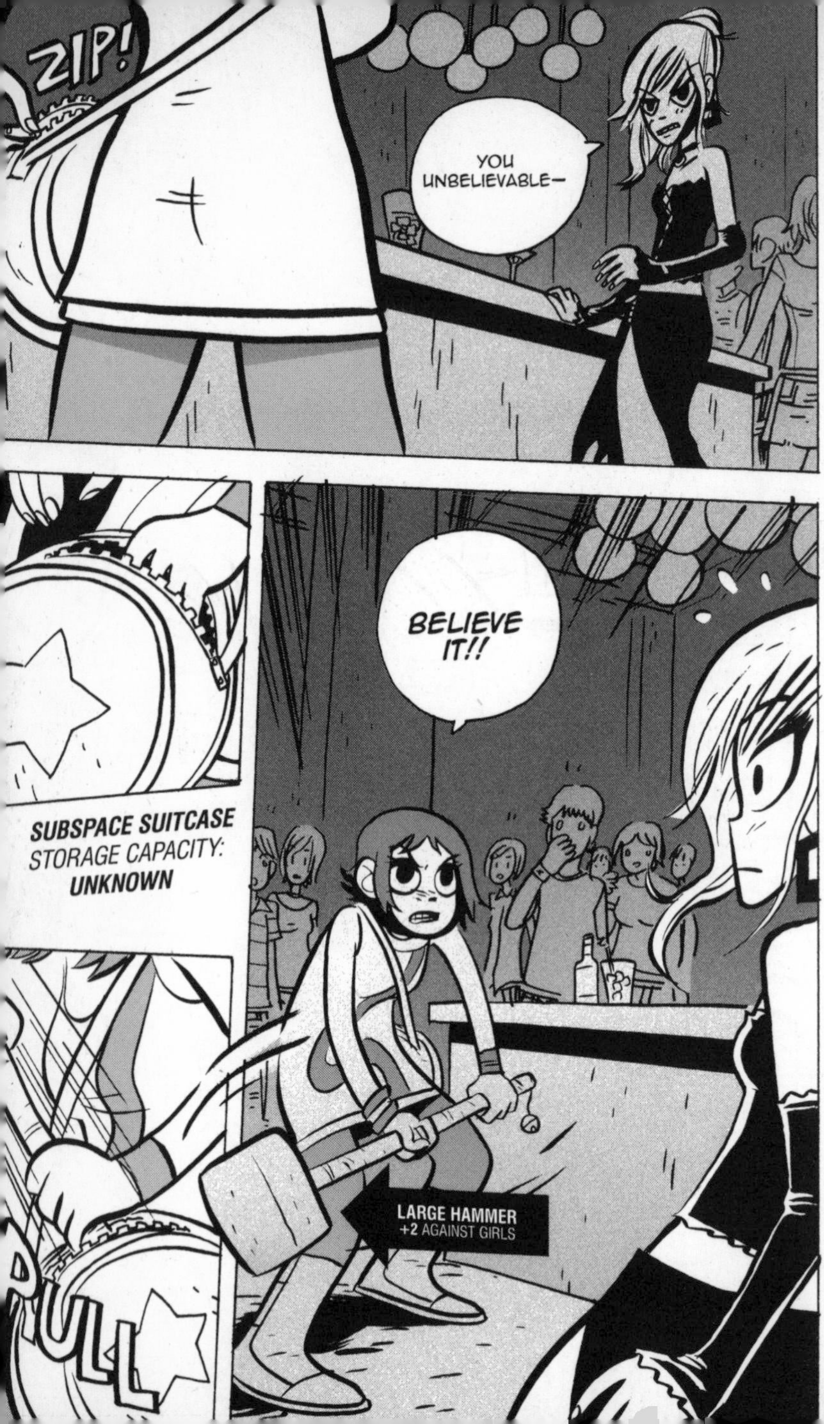
ZIP!
YOU UNBELIEVABLE—
BELIEVE IT!!
SUBSPACE SUITCASE
STORAGE CAPACITY:
UNKNOWN
LARGE HAMMER
+2 AGAINST GIRLS
PULL

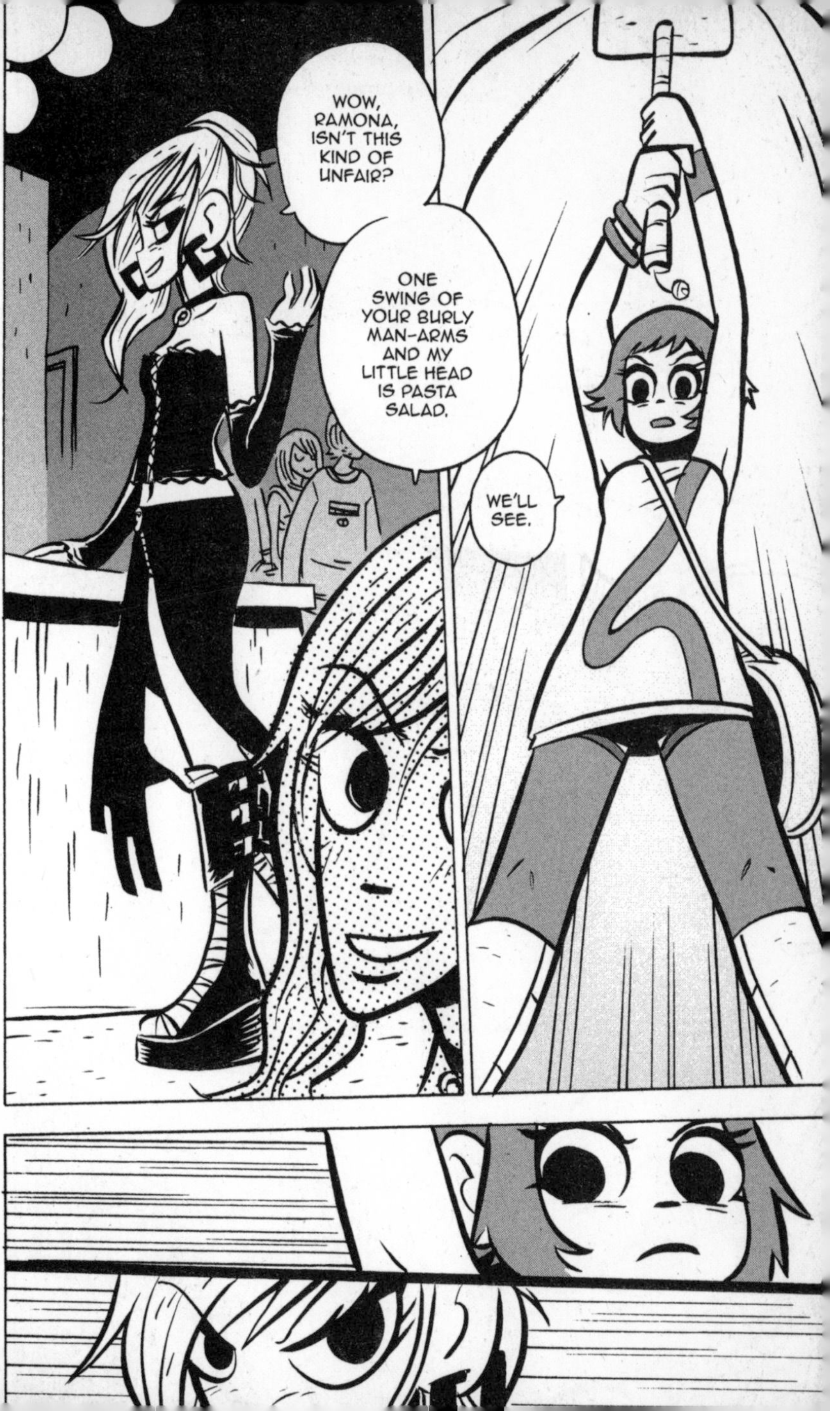
WOW, RAMONA, ISN'T THIS KIND OF UNFAIR?
ONE SWING OF YOUR BURLY MAN-ARMS AND MY LITTLE HEAD IS PASTA SALAD.
WE'LL SEE.

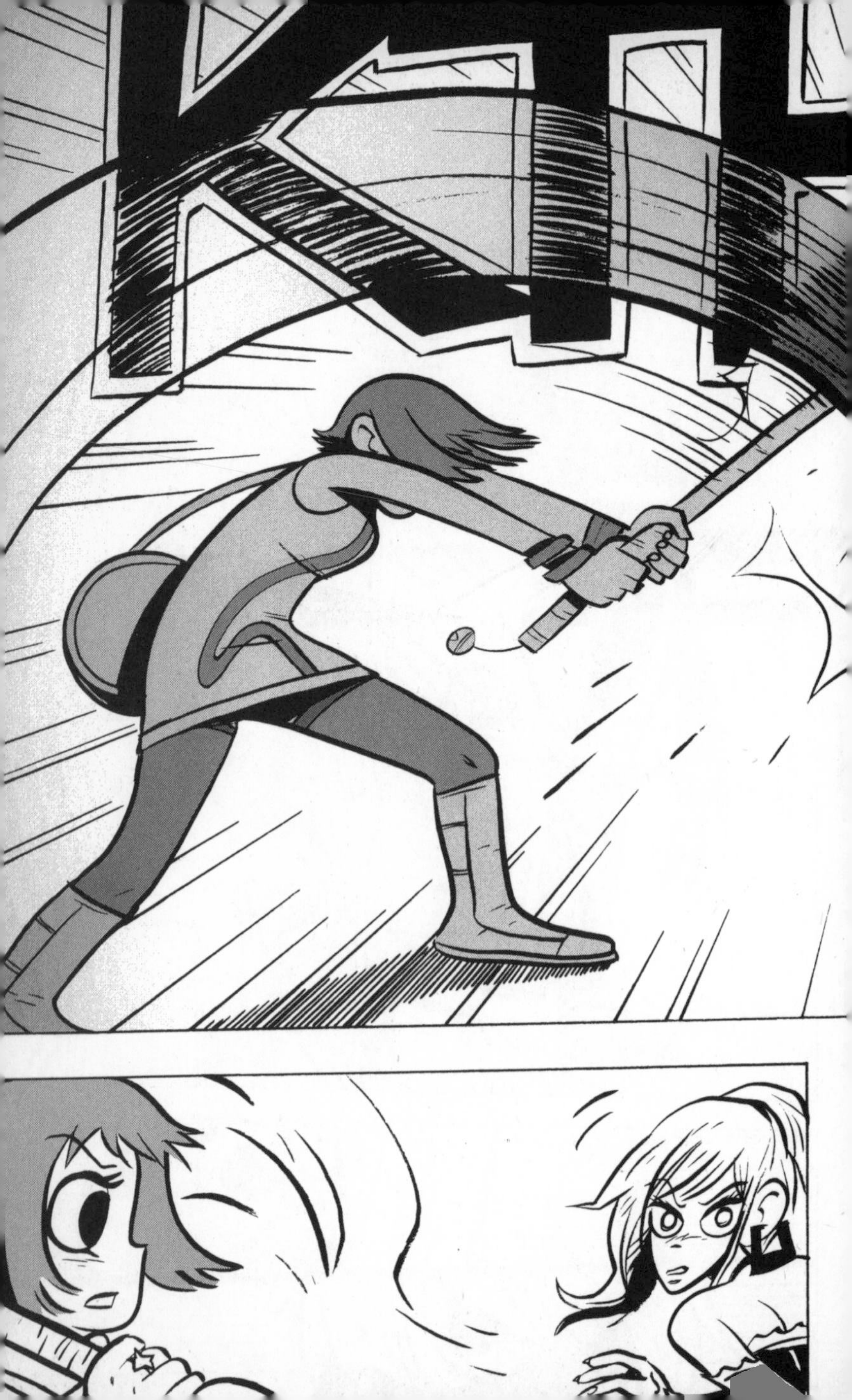

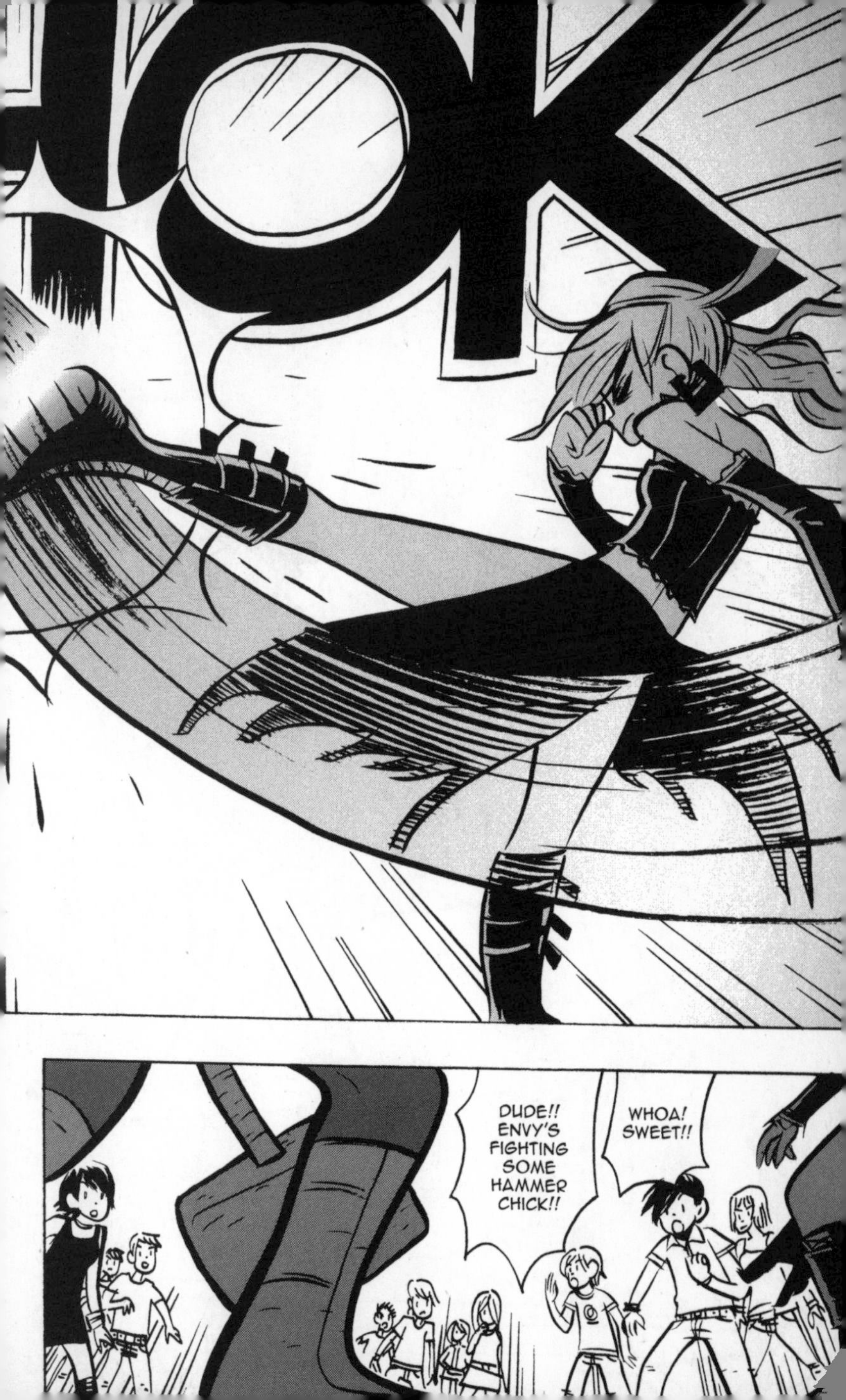
KOK
DUDE!! ENVY'S FIGHTING SOME HAMMER CHICK!!
WHOA! SWEET!!

17 the infinite sadness

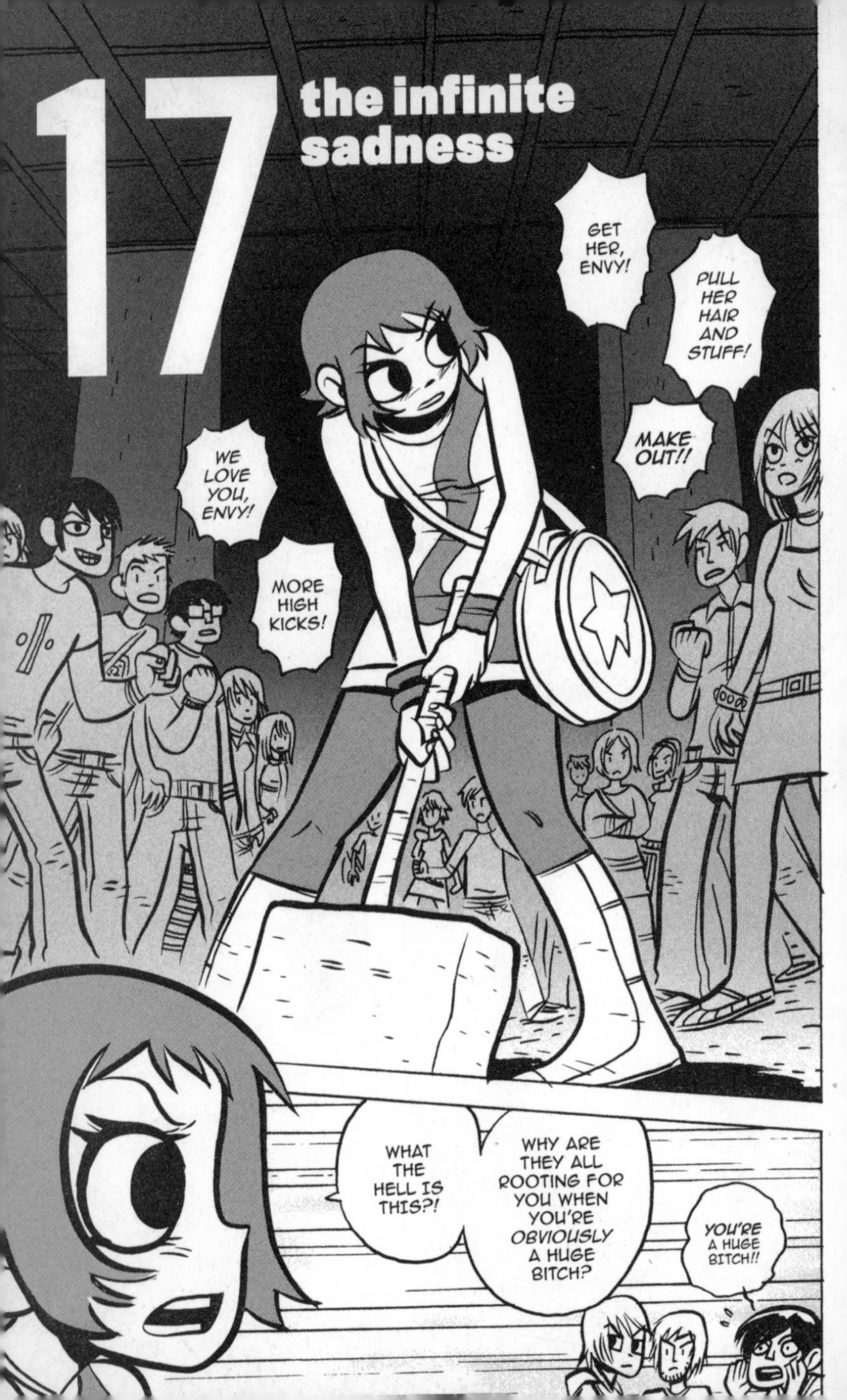
GET HER, ENVY!
PULL HER HAIR AND STUFF!
MAKE OUT!!
WE LOVE YOU, ENVY!
MORE HIGH KICKS!
WHAT THE HELL IS THIS?!
WHY ARE THEY ALL ROOTING FOR YOU WHEN YOU'RE OBVIOUSLY A HUGE BITCH?
YOU'RE A HUGE BITCH!!

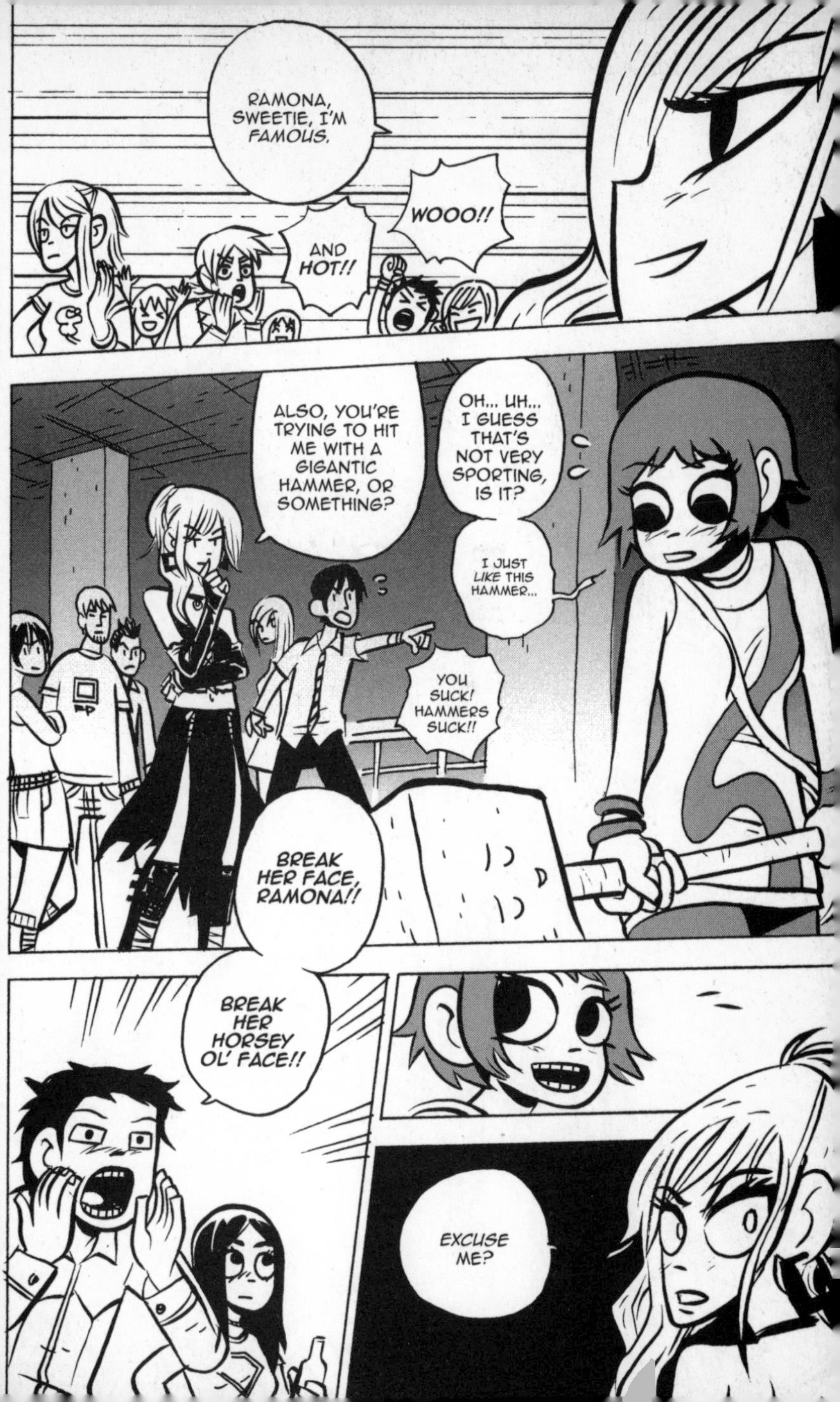

RAMONA, SWEETIE, I'M FAMOUS.
AND HOT!!
WOOO!!
ALSO, YOU'RE TRYING TO HIT ME WITH A GIGANTIC HAMMER, OR SOMETHING?
OH... UH... I GUESS THAT'S NOT VERY SPORTING, IS IT?
I JUST LIKE THIS HAMMER...
YOU SUCK! HAMMERS SUCK!!
BREAK HER FACE, RAMONA!!
BREAK HER HORSEY OL' FACE!!
EXCUSE ME?

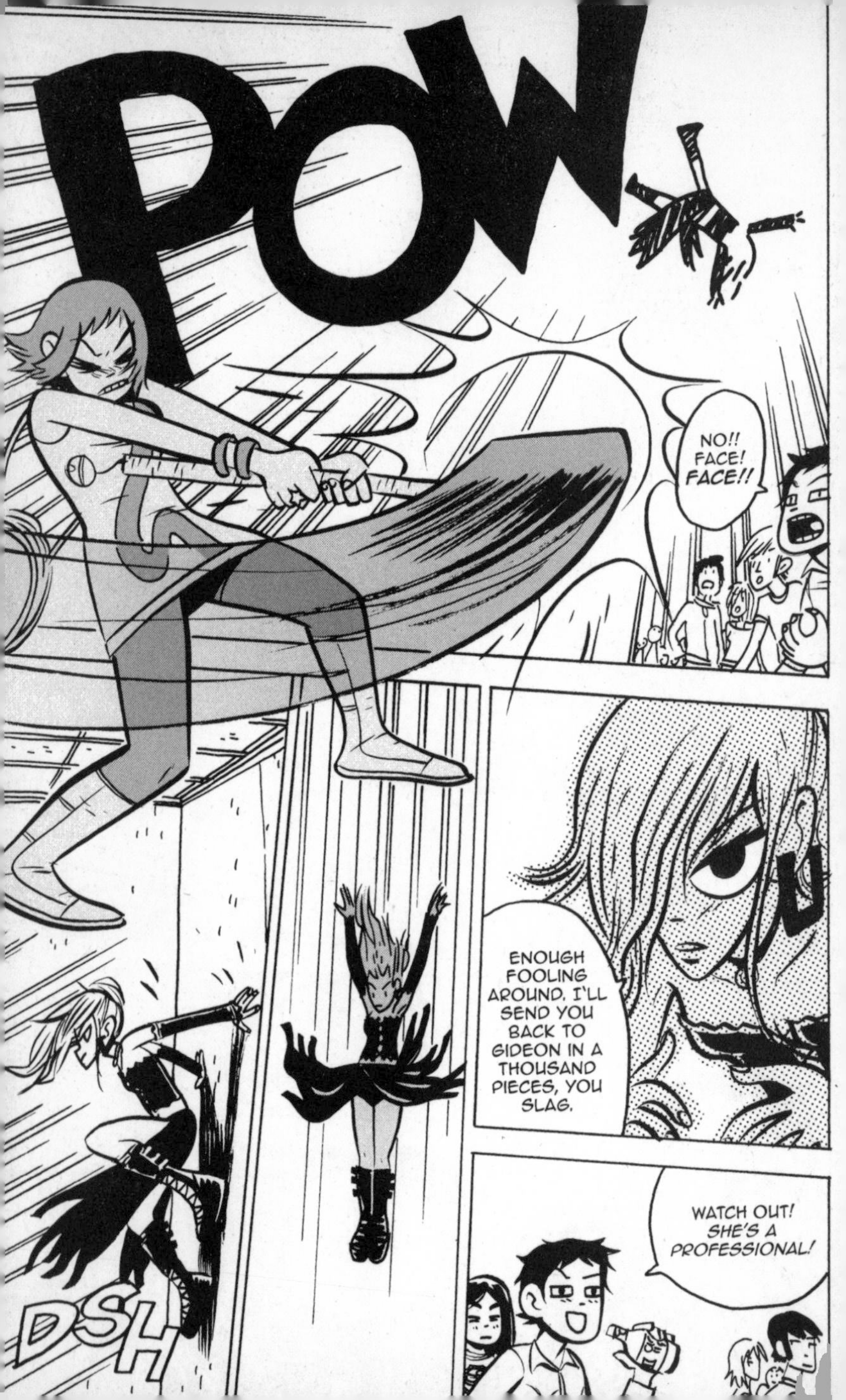
POW
NO!! FACE! FACE!!
DSH
ENOUGH FOOLING AROUND. I'LL SEND YOU BACK TO GIDEON IN A THOUSAND PIECES, YOU SLAG.
WATCH OUT! SHE'S A PROFESSIONAL!

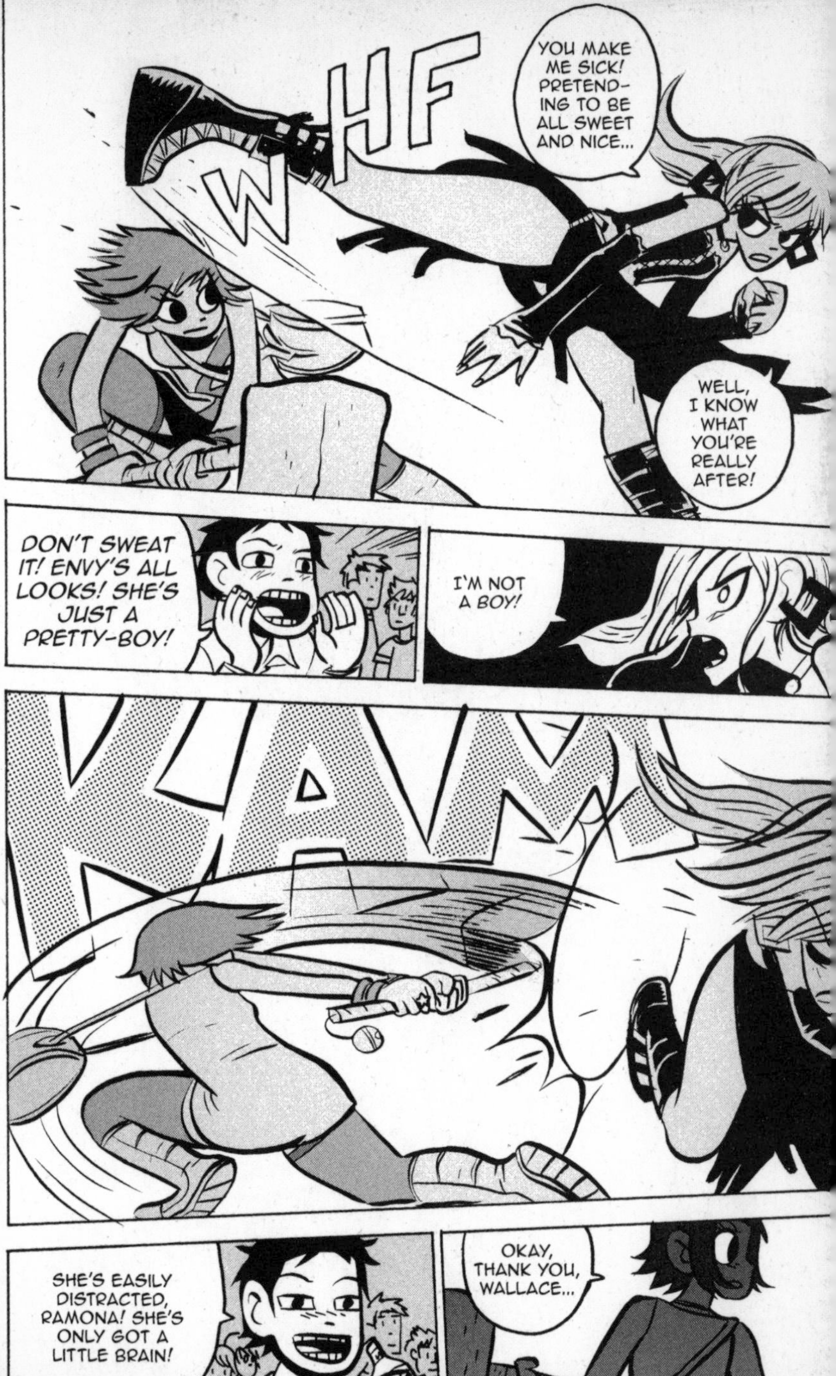

WHF
YOU MAKE ME SICK! PRETENDING TO BE ALL SWEET AND NICE...
WELL, I KNOW WHAT YOU'RE REALLY AFTER!
DON'T SWEAT IT! ENVY'S ALL LOOKS! SHE'S JUST A PRETTY-BOY!
I'M NOT A BOY!
WAM
SHE'S EASILY DISTRACTED, RAMONA! SHE'S ONLY GOT A LITTLE BRAIN!
OKAY, THANK YOU, WALLACE...

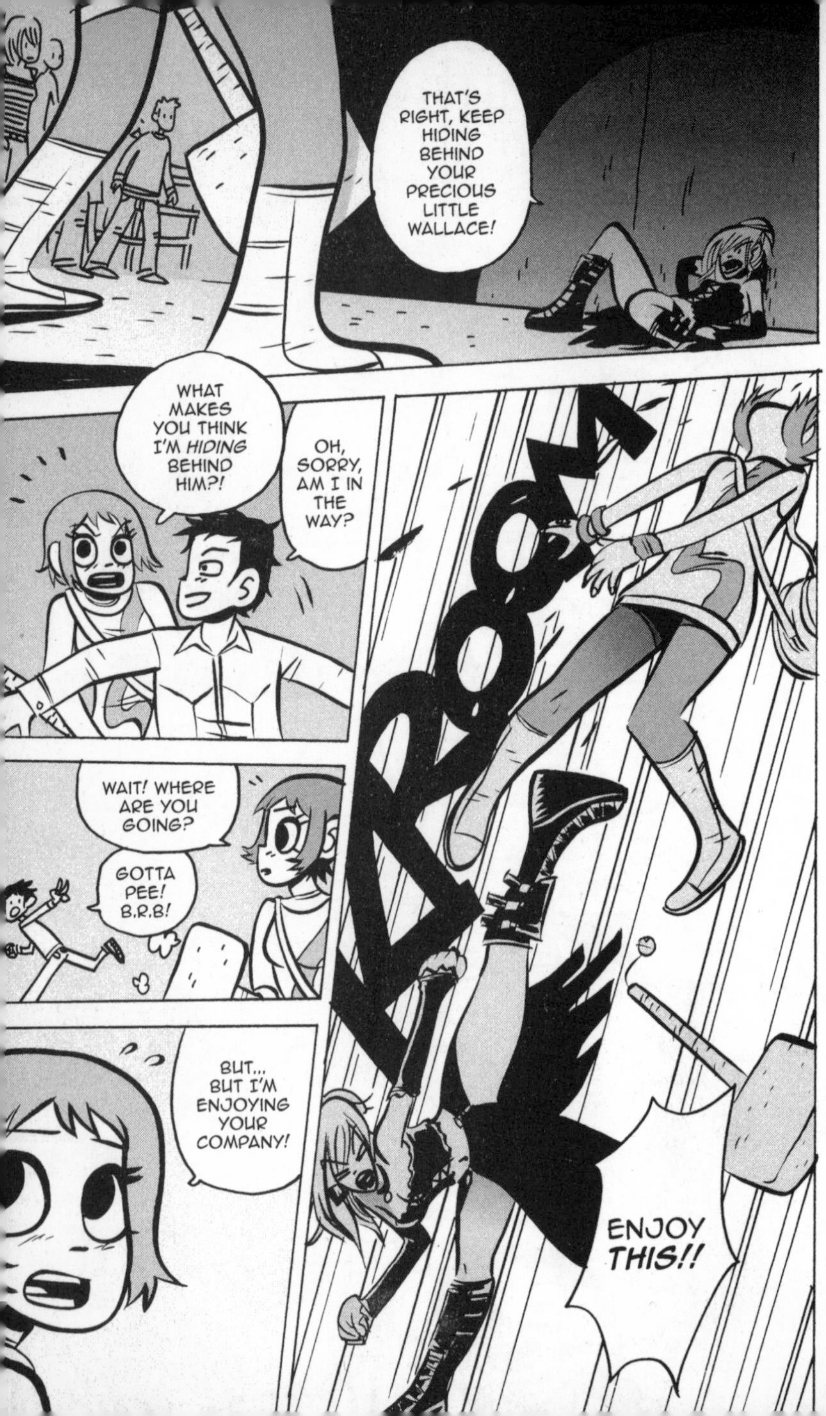
THAT'S RIGHT, KEEP HIDING BEHIND YOUR PRECIOUS LITTLE WALLACE!
WHAT MAKES YOU THINK I'M *HIDING* BEHIND HIM?!
OH, SORRY, AM I IN THE WAY?
WAIT! WHERE ARE YOU GOING?
GOTTA PEE! B.R.B!
BUT... BUT I'M ENJOYING YOUR COMPANY!
KROOOM
ENJOY *THIS!!*

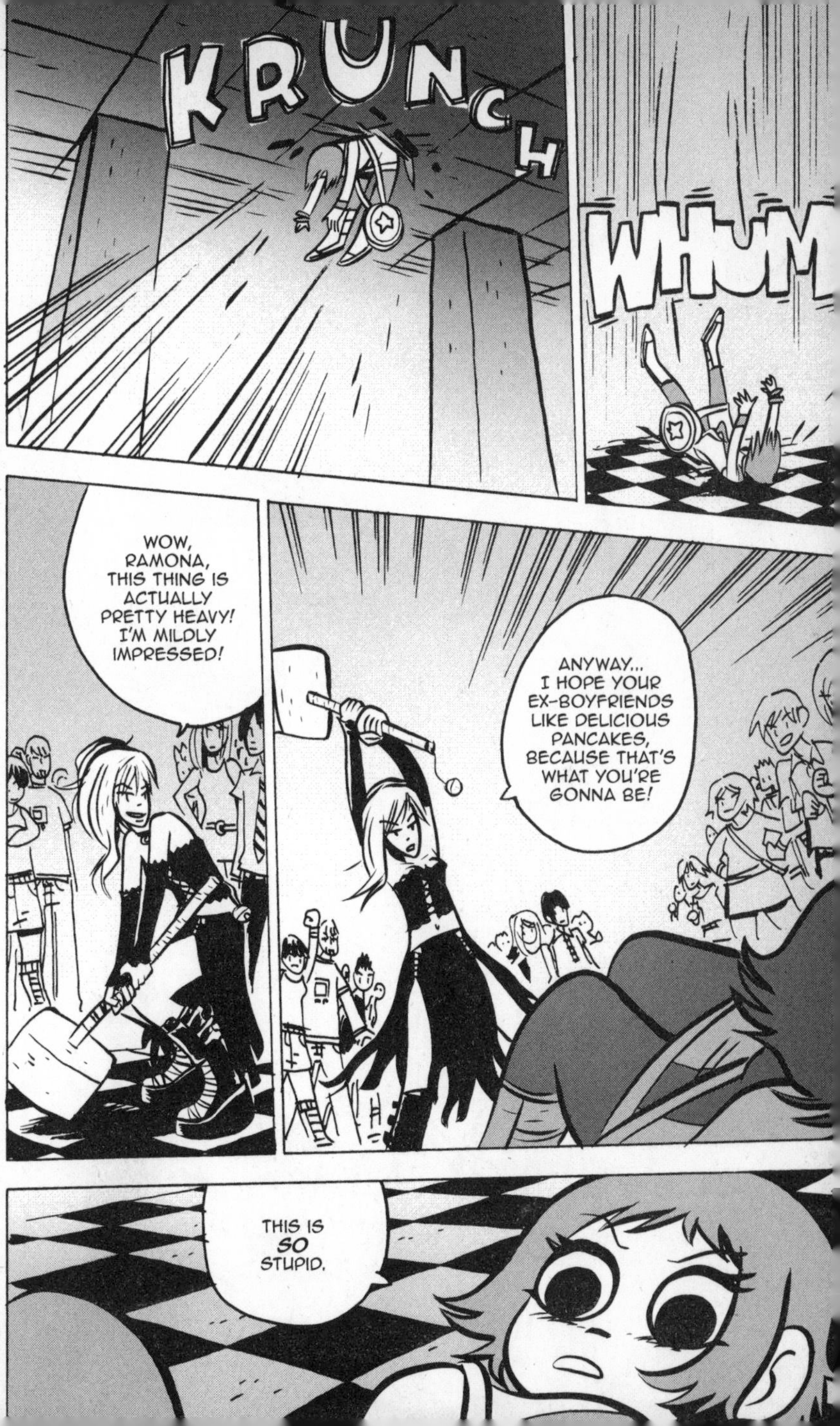
KRUNCH
WHUM
WOW, RAMONA, THIS THING IS ACTUALLY PRETTY HEAVY! I'M MILDLY IMPRESSED!
ANYWAY... I HOPE YOUR EX-BOYFRIENDS LIKE DELICIOUS PANCAKES, BECAUSE THAT'S WHAT YOU'RE GONNA BE!
THIS IS SO STUPID.

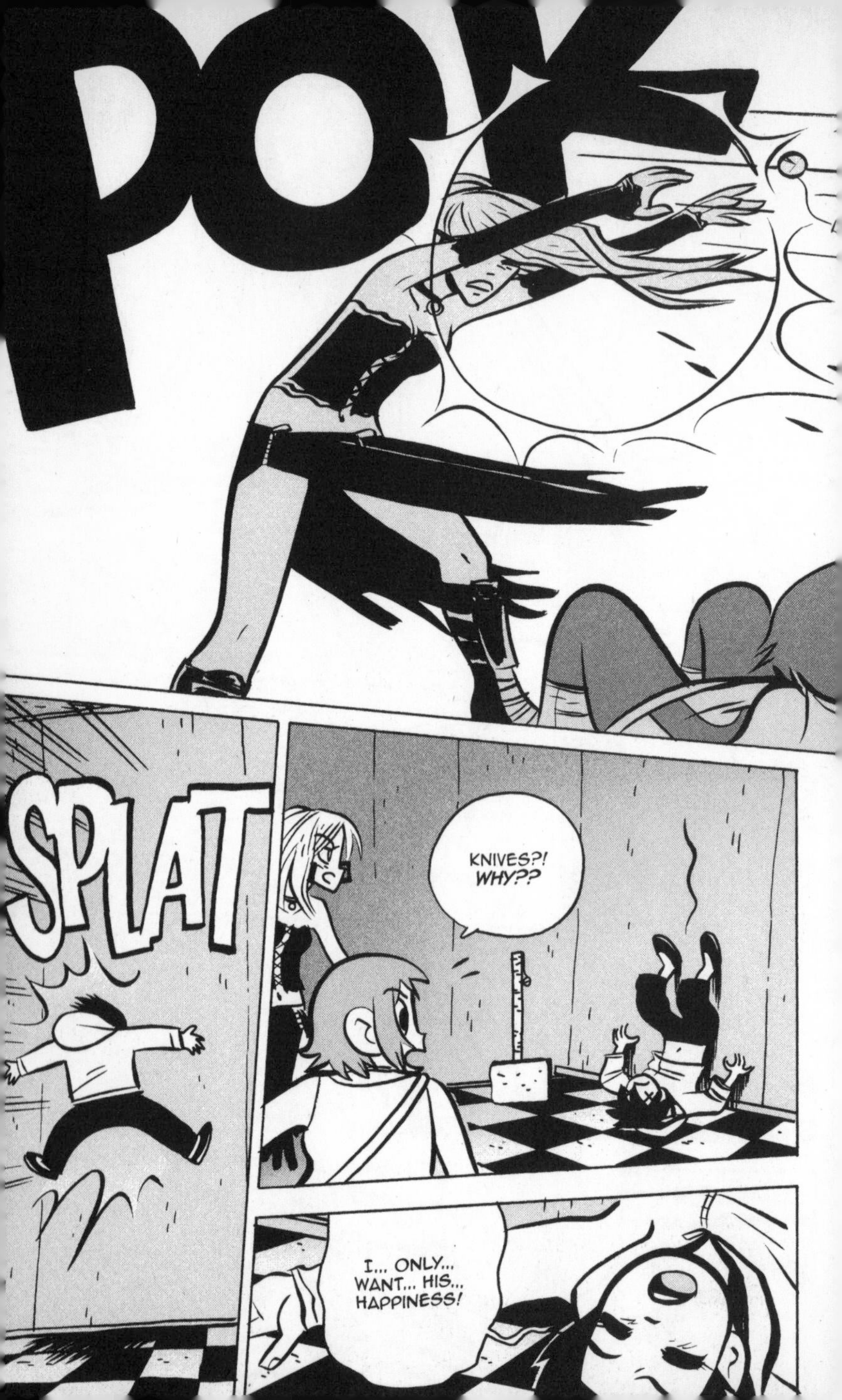
POK
SPLAT
KNIVES?! WHY??
I... ONLY... WANT... HIS... HAPPINESS!

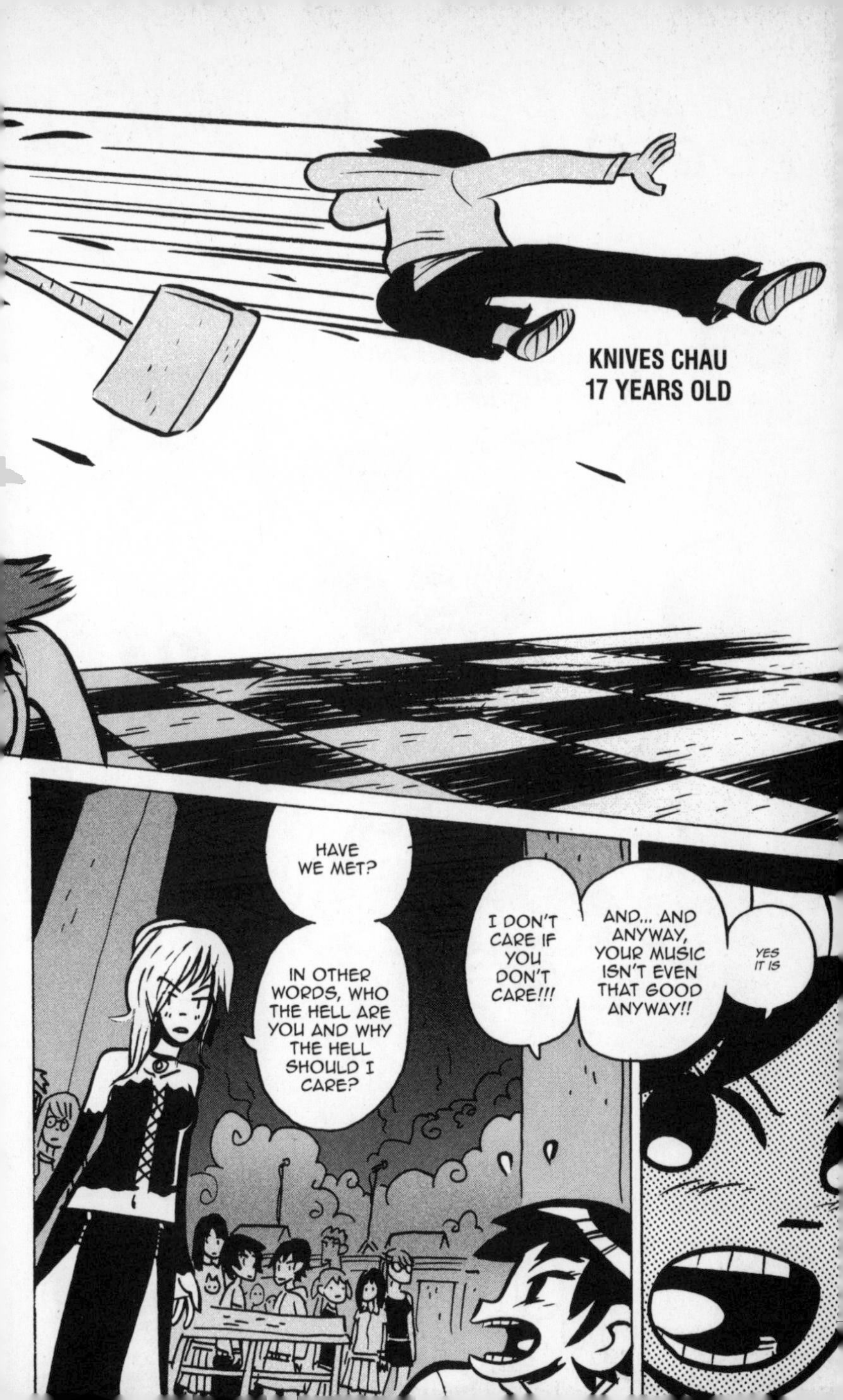
KNIVES CHAU
17 YEARS OLD
HAVE WE MET?
IN OTHER WORDS, WHO THE HELL ARE YOU AND WHY THE HELL SHOULD I CARE?
I DON'T CARE IF YOU DON'T CARE!!!
AND... AND ANYWAY, YOUR MUSIC ISN'T EVEN THAT GOOD ANYWAY!!
YES IT IS

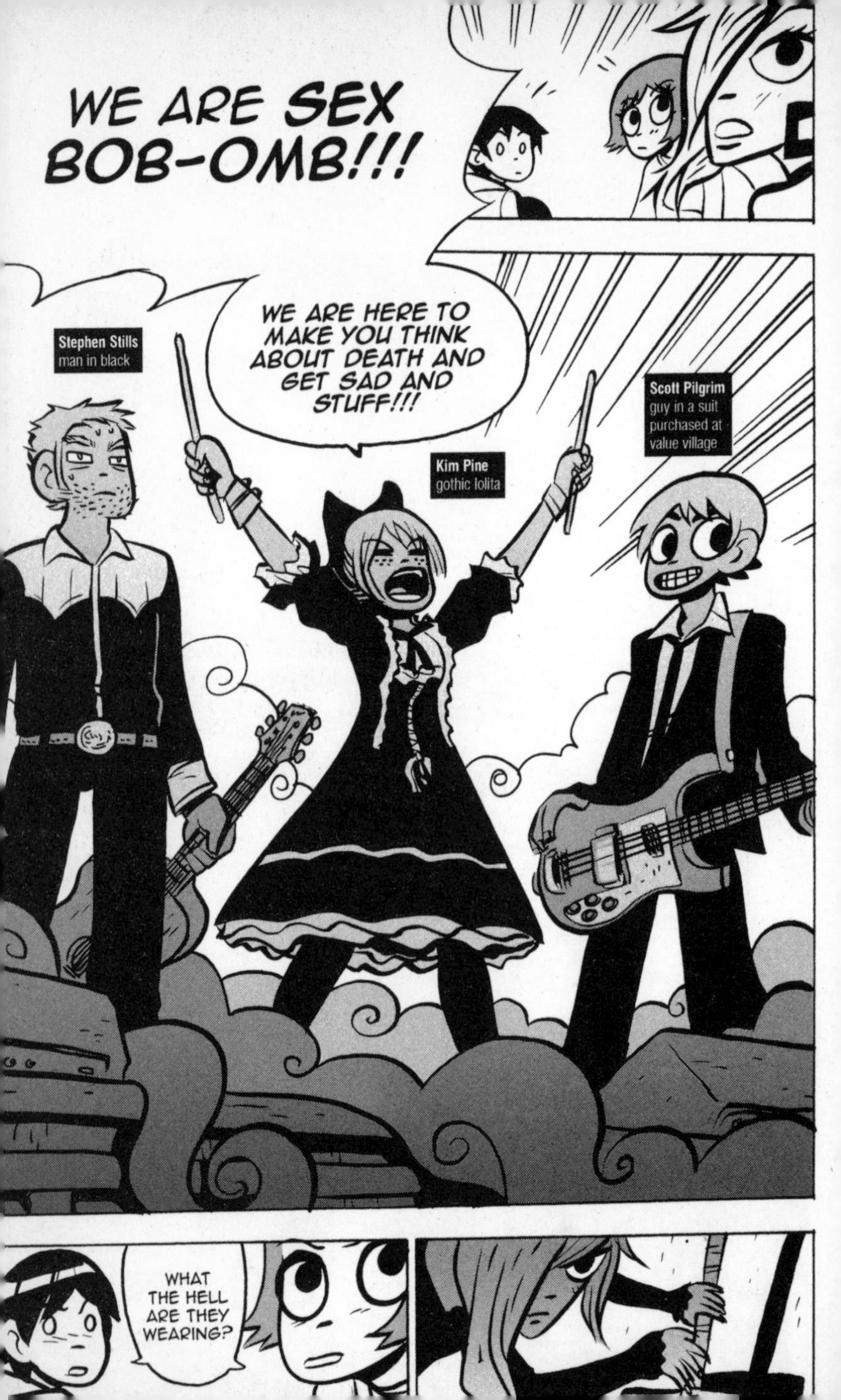

WE ARE SEX BOB-OMB!!!
WE ARE HERE TO MAKE YOU THINK ABOUT DEATH AND GET SAD AND STUFF!!!
Stephen Stills man in black
Kim Pine gothic lolita
Scott Pilgrim guy in a suit purchased at value village
WHAT THE HELL ARE THEY WEARING?

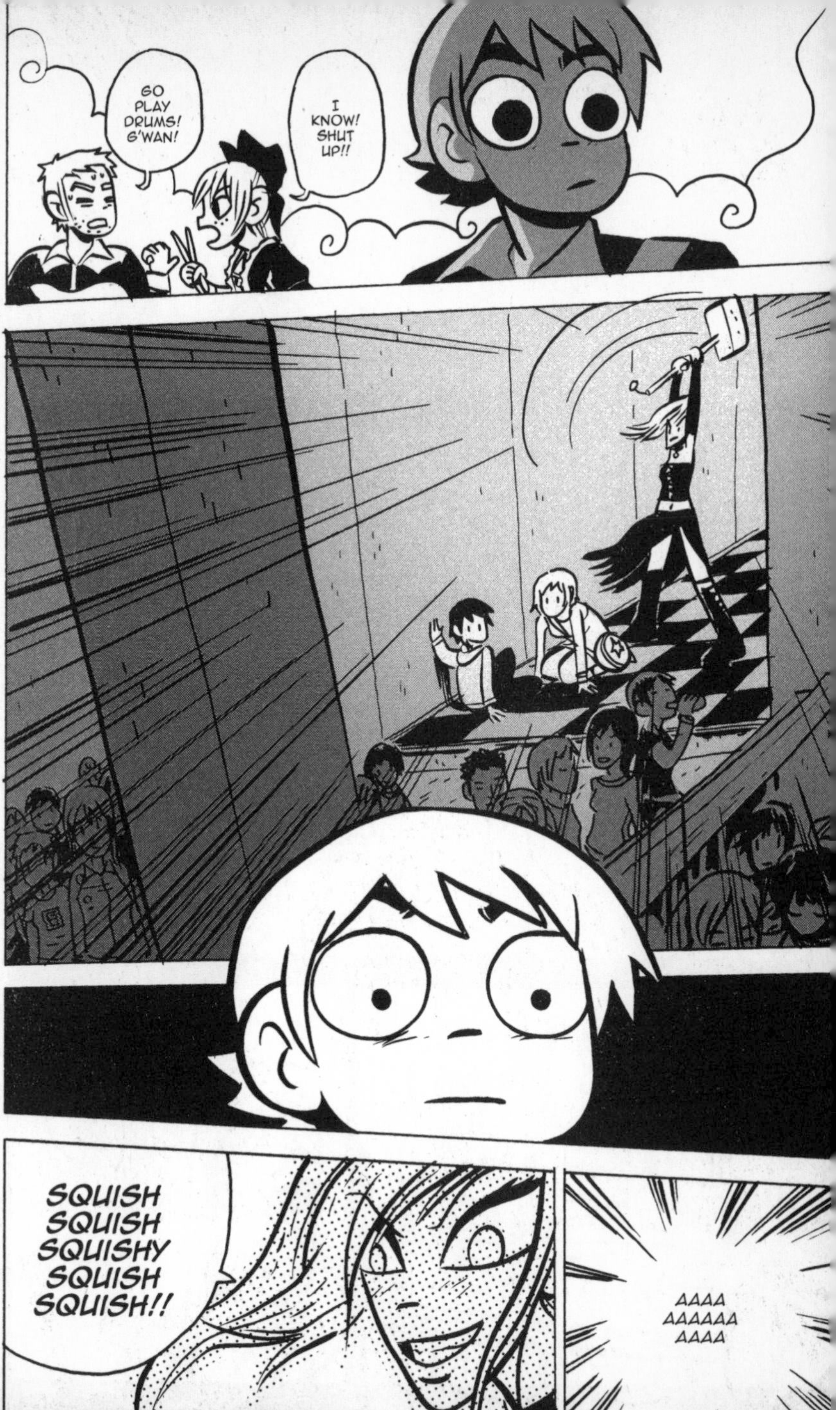
GO PLAY DRUMS! G'WAN!
I KNOW! SHUT UP!!
SQUISH SQUISH SQUISHY SQUISH SQUISH!!
AAAA AAAAAA AAAA

ENVY, ARE YOU THERE? COME ON, PICK UP.
WELL, I WAS JUST, UH... I WAS JUST THINKING ABOUT YOU, AND I THOUGHT I'D TRY CALLING.
BUT, UH, I GUESS I'LL TRY AGAIN LATER.
IING RIIING RIIIING
CLICK
WH- WHAT WAS THAT? WHO IS THAT?
OH... GOD... IT'S THIS GUY JACOB...
HE CALLS SOMETIMES...
DID YOU USED TO DATE HIM OR SOMETHING?
SORT OF... NOT REALLY...
ARE YOU...
...CHEATING ON ME?

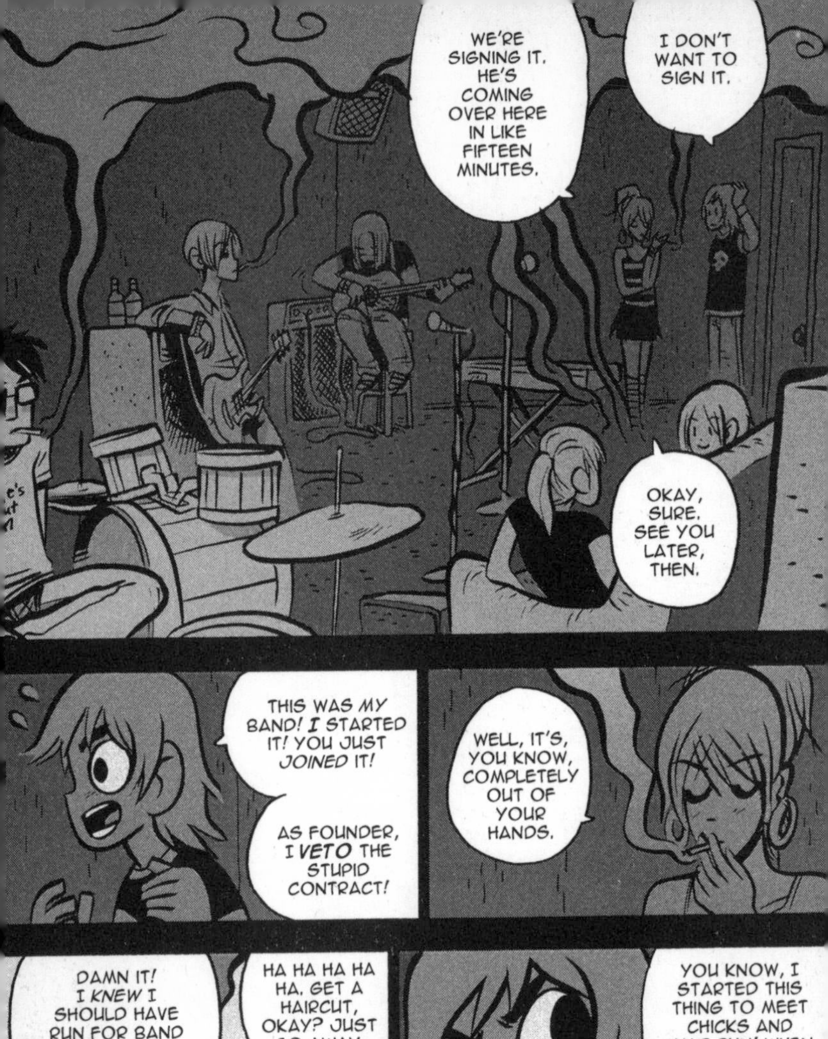
WE'RE SIGNING IT. HE'S COMING OVER HERE IN LIKE FIFTEEN MINUTES.
I DON'T WANT TO SIGN IT.
OKAY, SURE. SEE YOU LATER, THEN.
THIS WAS MY BAND! I STARTED IT! YOU JUST JOINED IT!
AS FOUNDER, I VETO THE STUPID CONTRACT!
WELL, IT'S, YOU KNOW, COMPLETELY OUT OF YOUR HANDS.
DAMN IT! I KNEW I SHOULD HAVE RUN FOR BAND PRESIDENT INSTEAD OF SECRETARY!!
HA HA HA HA HA. GET A HAIRCUT, OKAY? JUST GO AWAY.
YOU KNOW, I STARTED THIS THING TO MEET CHICKS AND HAVE FUN! WHEN DID IT TURN INTO A "BAND"? DID I JUST MEET THE WRONG CHICKS??

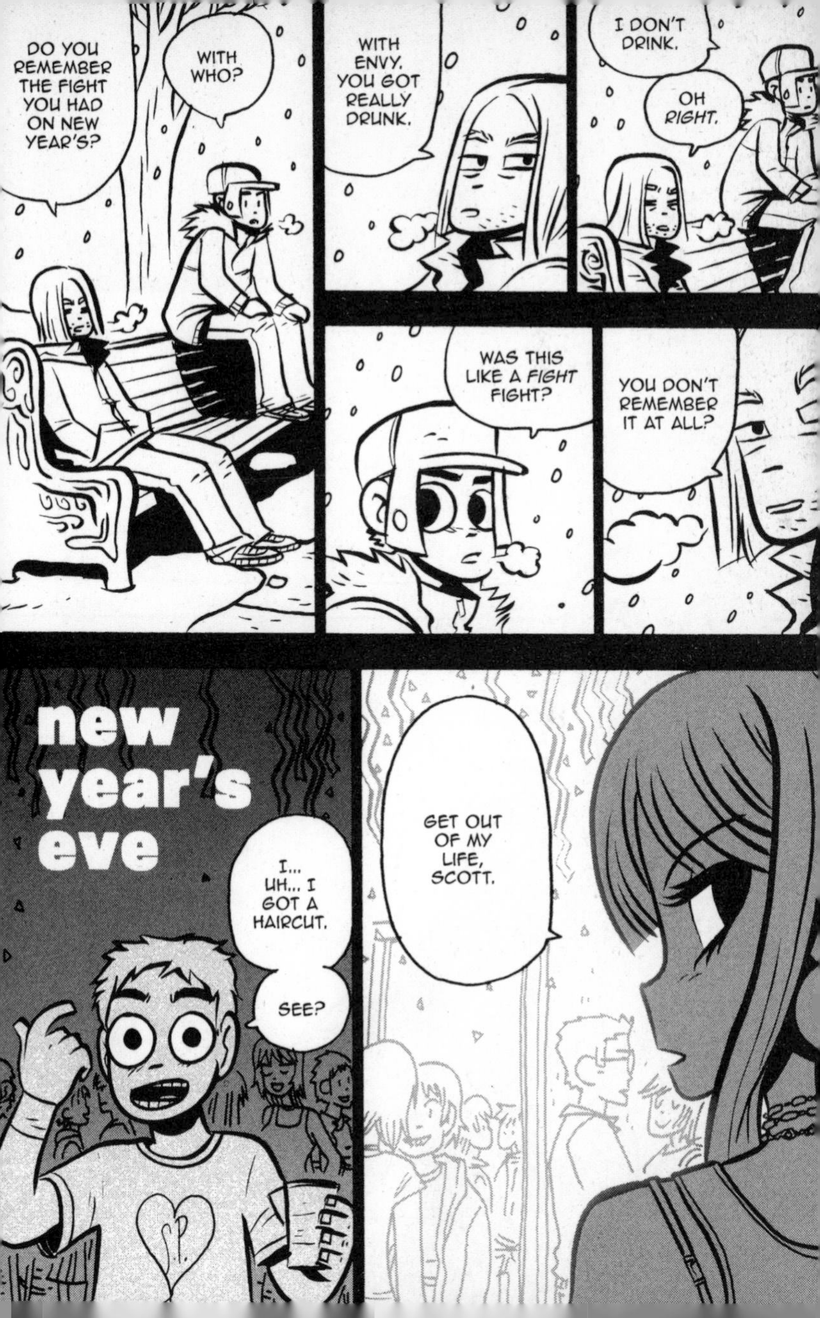
DO YOU REMEMBER THE FIGHT YOU HAD ON NEW YEAR'S?
WITH WHO?
WITH ENVY. YOU GOT REALLY DRUNK.
I DON'T DRINK.
OH RIGHT.
WAS THIS LIKE A FIGHT FIGHT?
YOU DON'T REMEMBER IT AT ALL?
new year's eve
I... UH... I GOT A HAIRCUT.
SEE?
GET OUT OF MY LIFE, SCOTT.

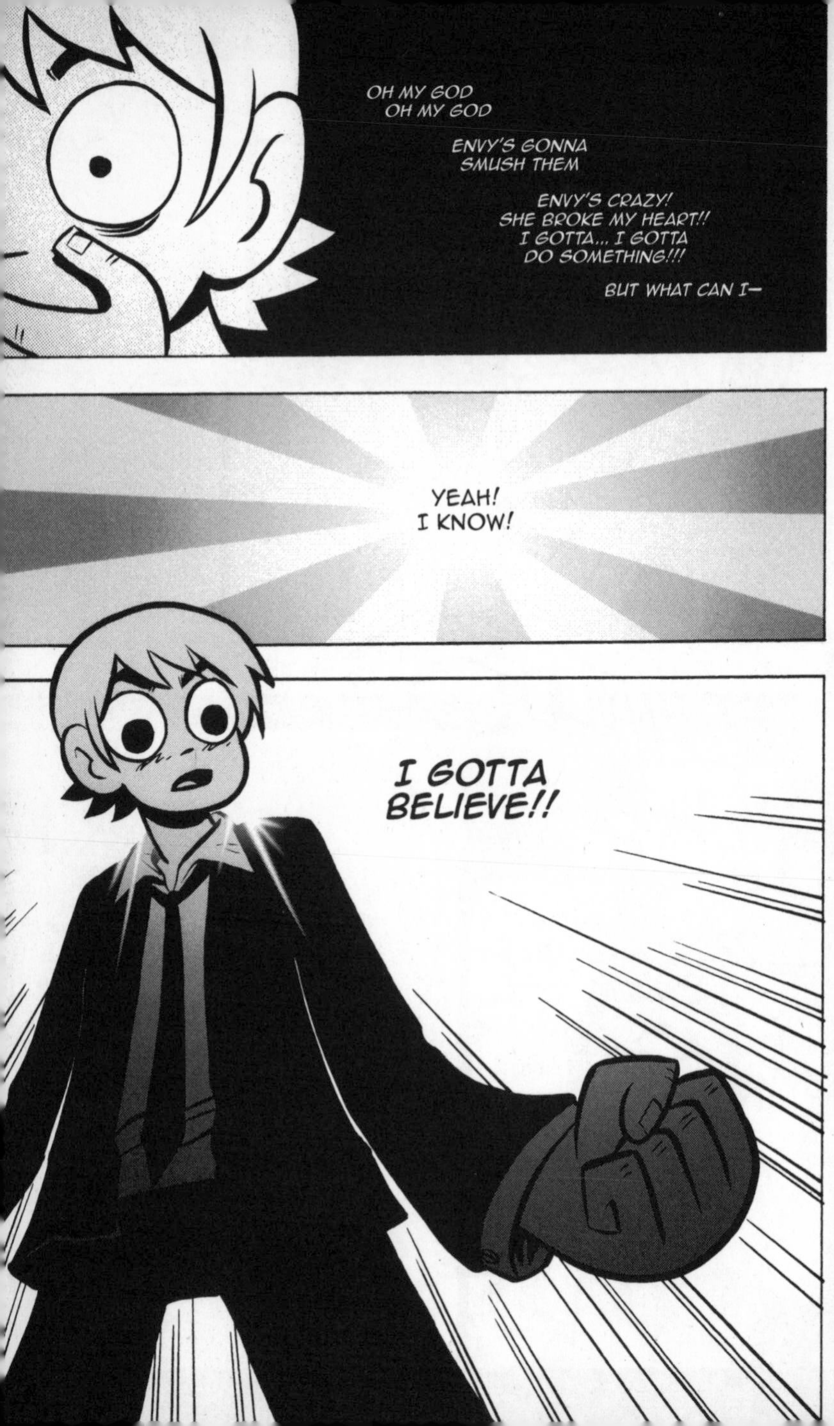
OH MY GOD
OH MY GOD
ENVY'S GONNA SMUSH THEM
ENVY'S CRAZY! SHE BROKE MY HEART!! I GOTTA... I GOTTA DO SOMETHING!!!
BUT WHAT CAN I—
YEAH! I KNOW!
I GOTTA BELIEVE!!

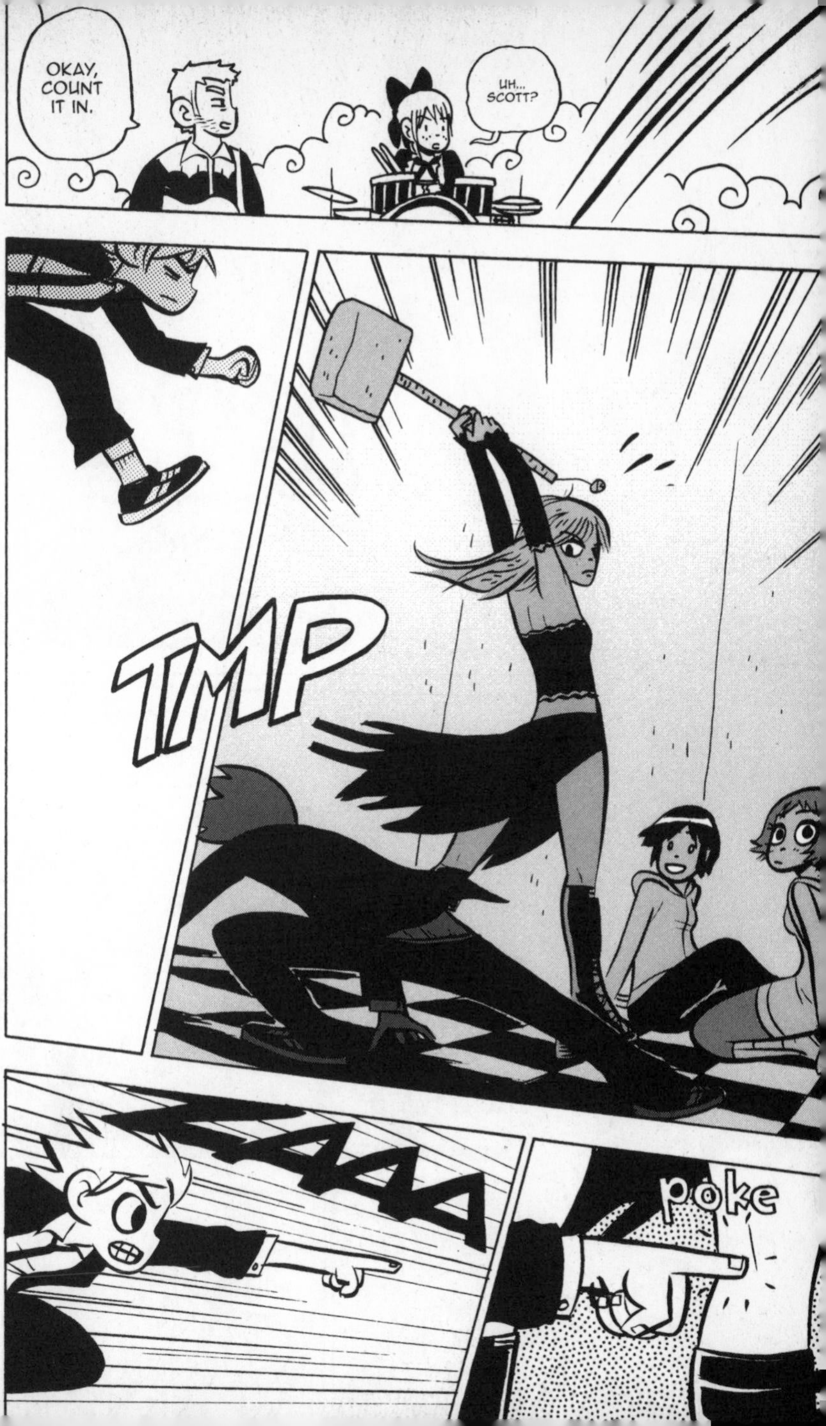
OKAY, COUNT IT IN.
UH... SCOTT?
TMP
poke

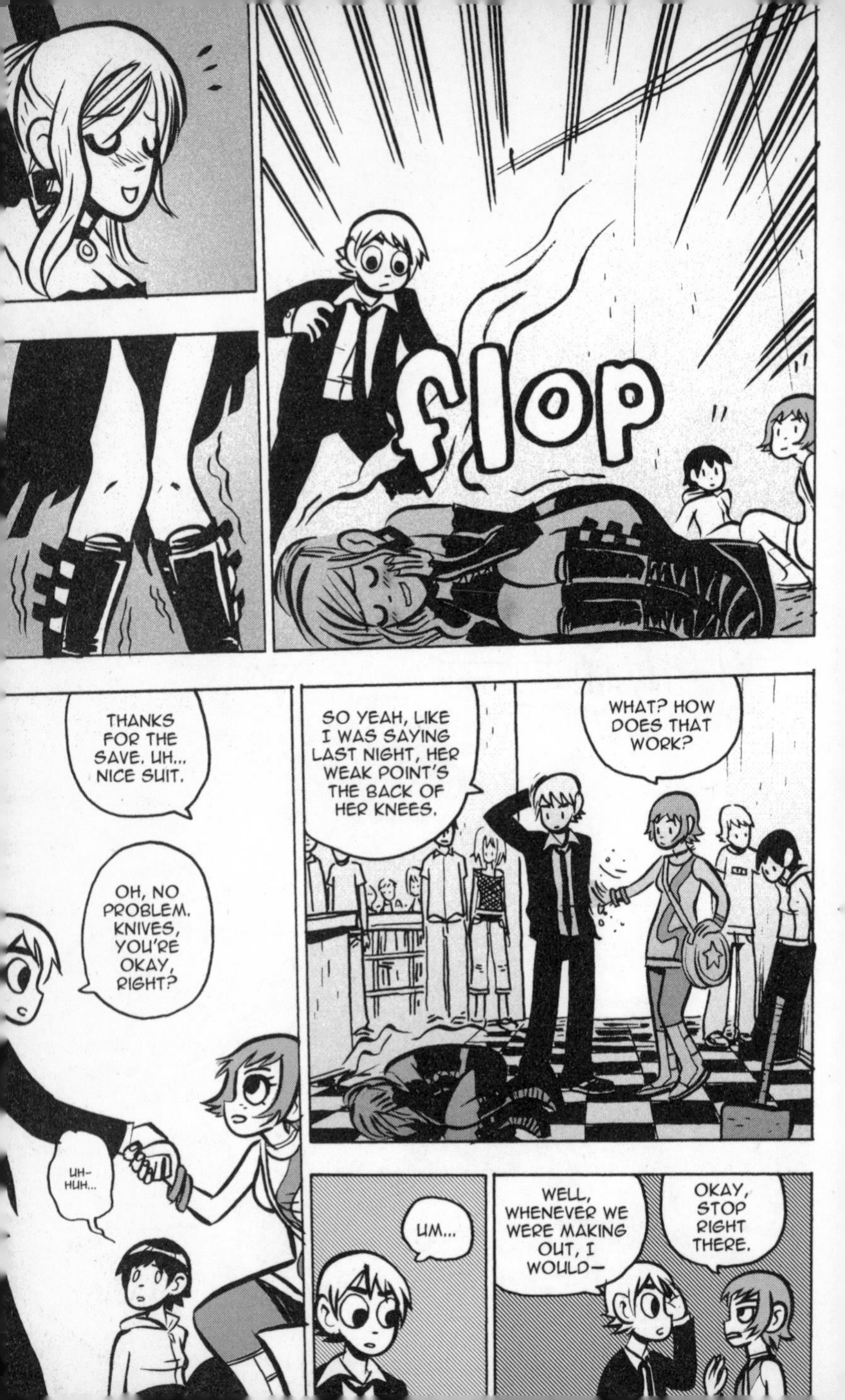
FLOP
THANKS FOR THE SAVE. UH... NICE SUIT.
OH, NO PROBLEM. KNIVES, YOU'RE OKAY, RIGHT?
UH-HUH...
SO YEAH, LIKE I WAS SAYING LAST NIGHT, HER WEAK POINT'S THE BACK OF HER KNEES.
WHAT? HOW DOES THAT WORK?
UM...
WELL, WHENEVER WE WERE MAKING OUT, I WOULD—
OKAY, STOP RIGHT THERE.

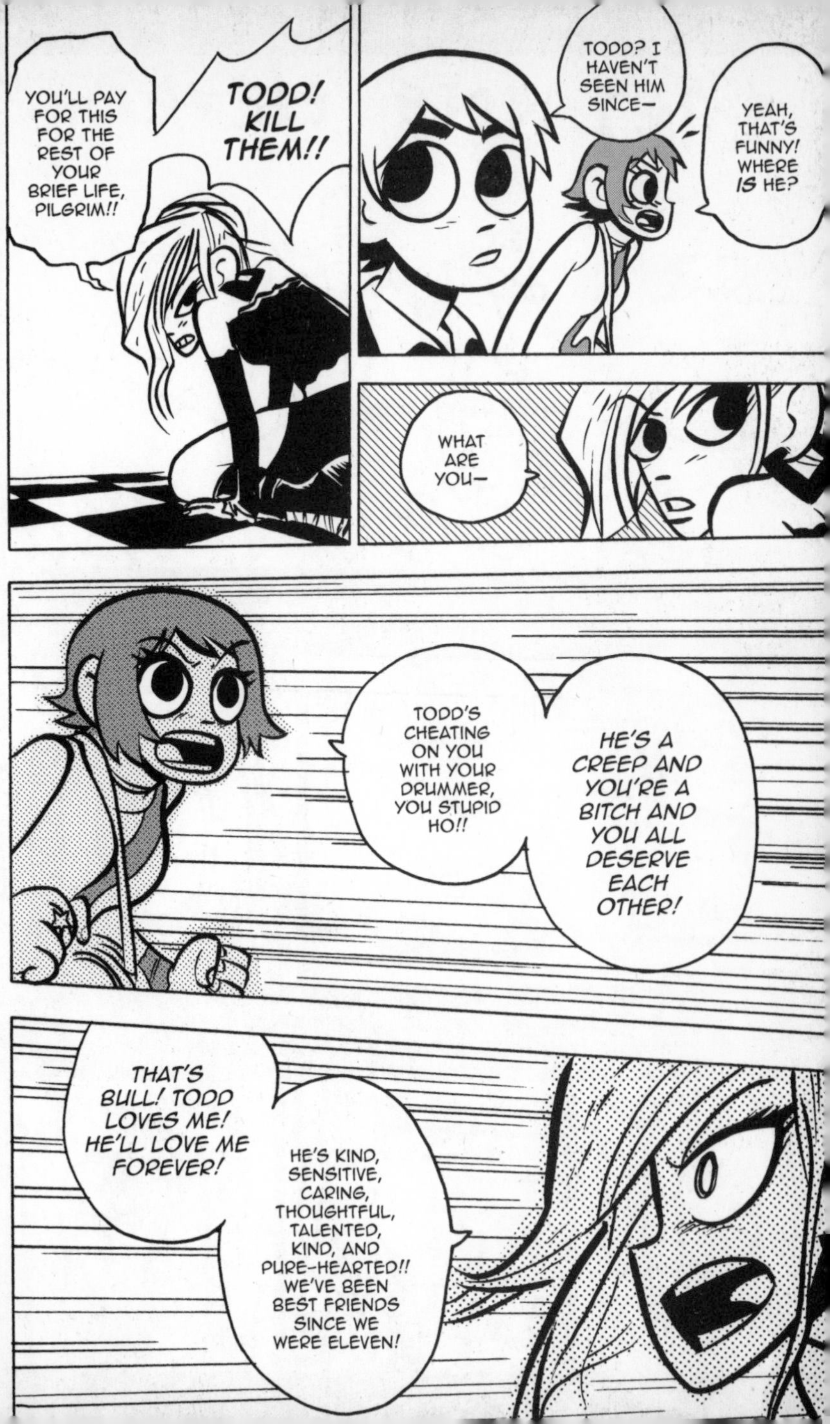

YOU'LL PAY FOR THIS FOR THE REST OF YOUR BRIEF LIFE, PILGRIM!!
TODD! KILL THEM!!
TODD? I HAVEN'T SEEN HIM SINCE—
YEAH, THAT'S FUNNY! WHERE IS HE?
WHAT ARE YOU—
TODD'S CHEATING ON YOU WITH YOUR DRUMMER, YOU STUPID HO!!
HE'S A CREEP AND YOU'RE A BITCH AND YOU ALL DESERVE EACH OTHER!
THAT'S BULL! TODD LOVES ME! HE'LL LOVE ME FOREVER!
HE'S KIND, SENSITIVE, CARING, THOUGHTFUL, TALENTED, KIND, AND PURE-HEARTED!! WE'VE BEEN BEST FRIENDS SINCE WE WERE ELEVEN!

they were eleven

Once upon a time, there was a boy and a girl. They lived as next-door neighbours in a small town called Montreal, and their love was as pure as pure can be.

But it was not to last. One day, the boy and his family moved away to a distant land of mountains and dairy cows. The girl grew up alone, and never found another she could truly love, though she tried her hardest.

GRADUATION

A nd then, at last, when all seemed lost, the boy returned.

Promising they would never again part, the boy displayed his affection in a most remarkable and *unprecedented* fashion...

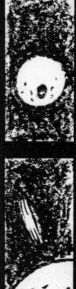

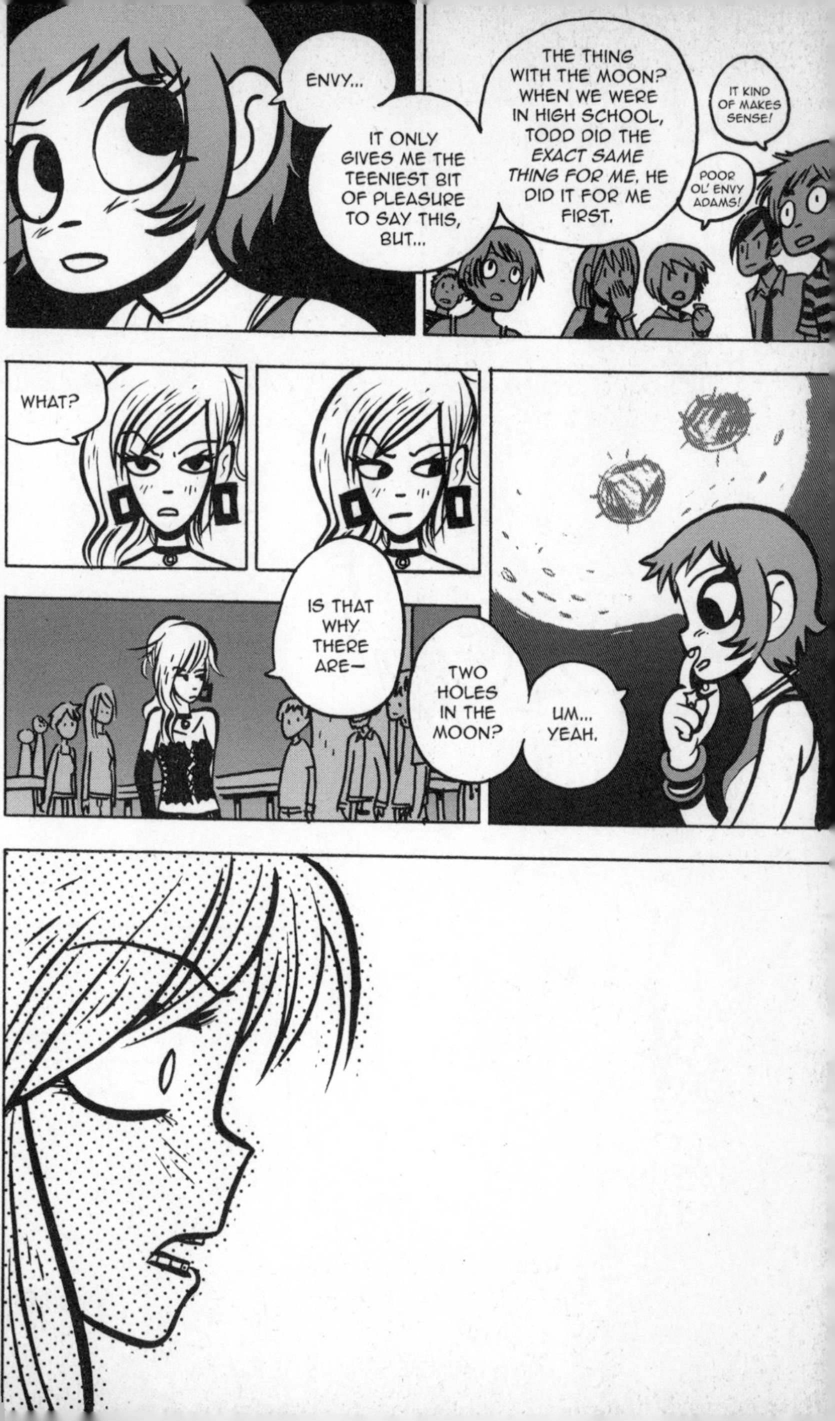
ENVY...
IT ONLY GIVES ME THE TEENIEST BIT OF PLEASURE TO SAY THIS, BUT...
THE THING WITH THE MOON? WHEN WE WERE IN HIGH SCHOOL, TODD DID THE *EXACT SAME THING FOR ME.* HE DID IT FOR ME FIRST.
IT KIND OF MAKES SENSE!
POOR OL' ENVY ADAMS!
WHAT?
IS THAT WHY THERE ARE—
TWO HOLES IN THE MOON?
UM... YEAH.

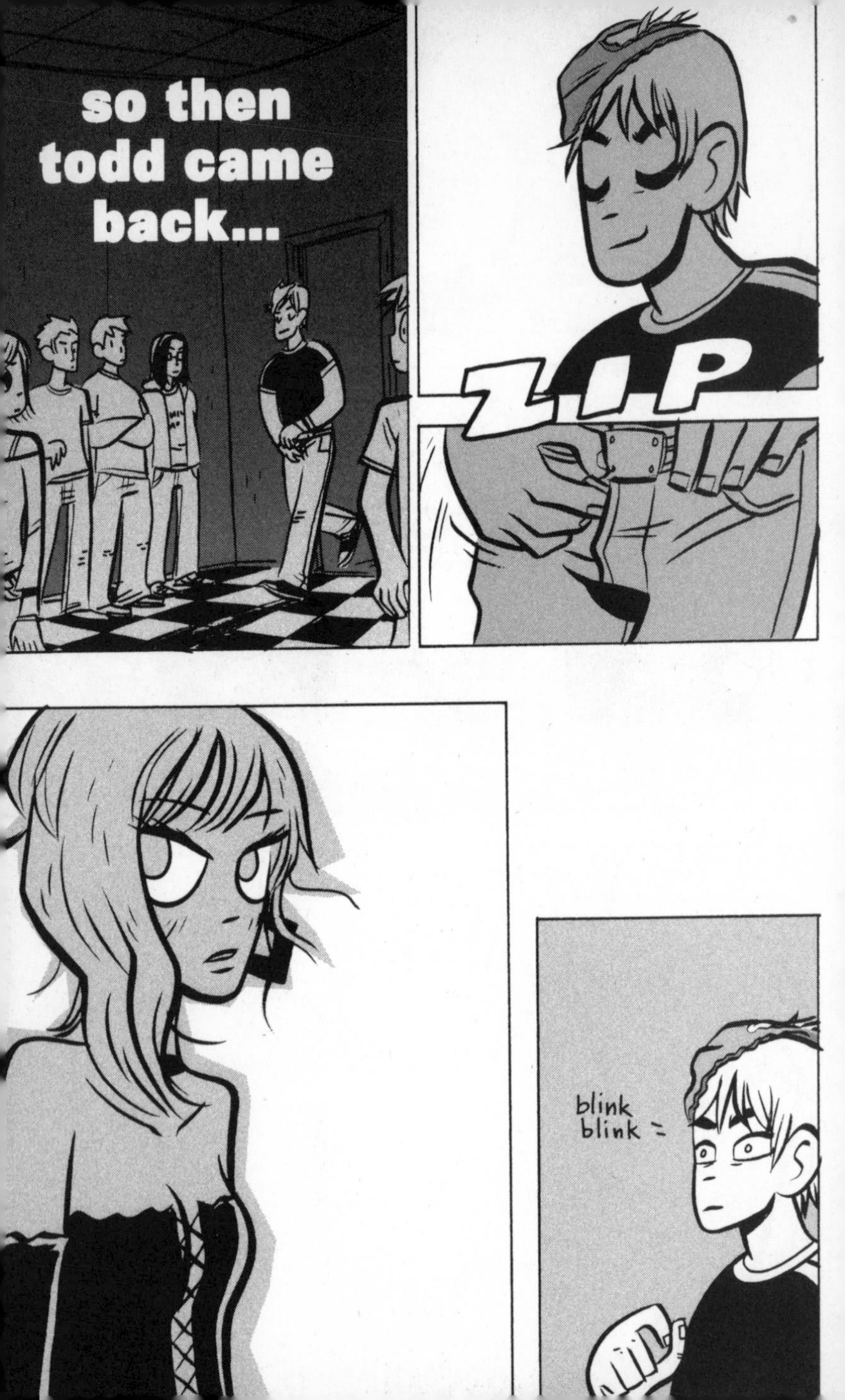
so then todd came back...
ZIP
blink
blink

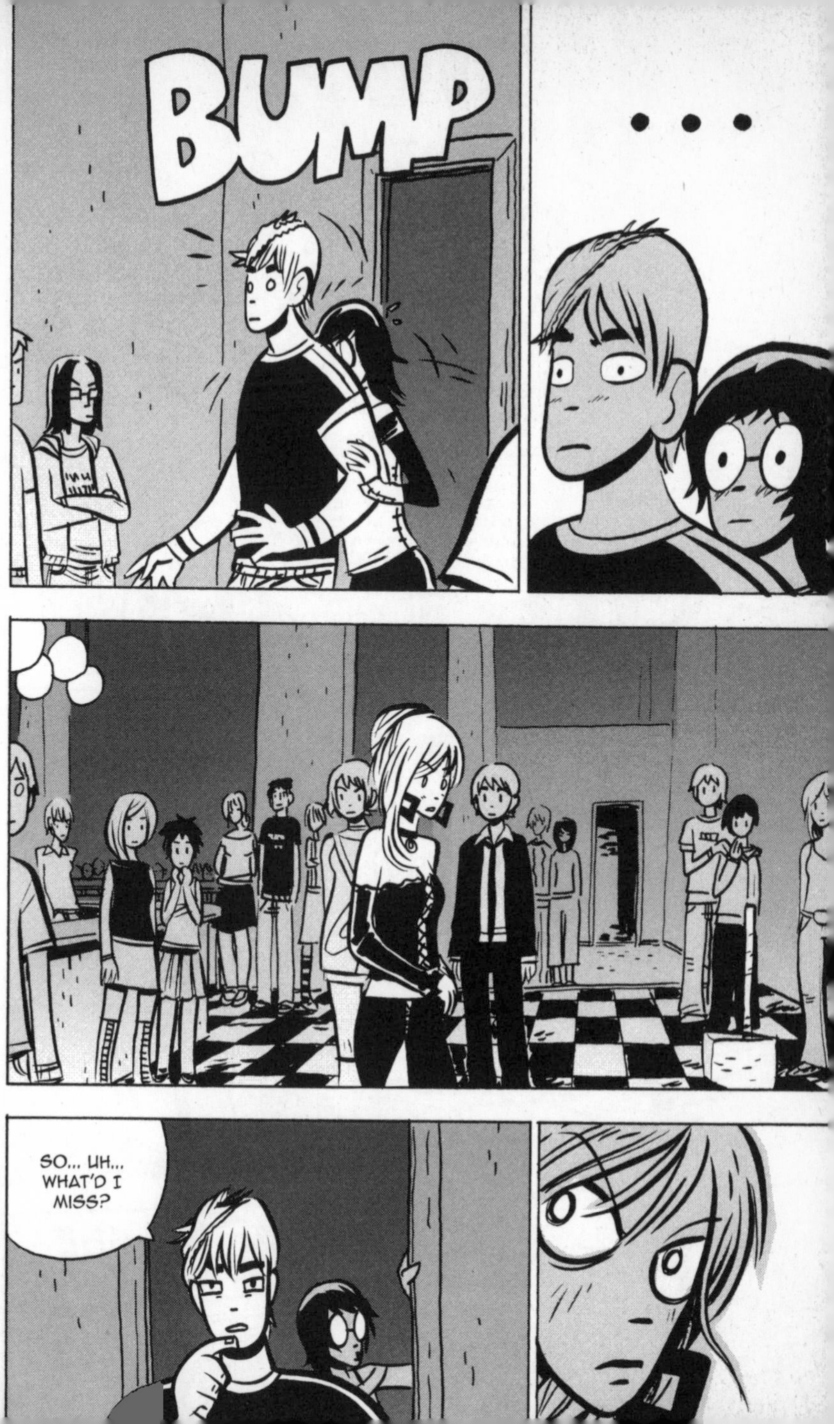
BUMP
...
SO... UH...
WHAT'D I
MISS?

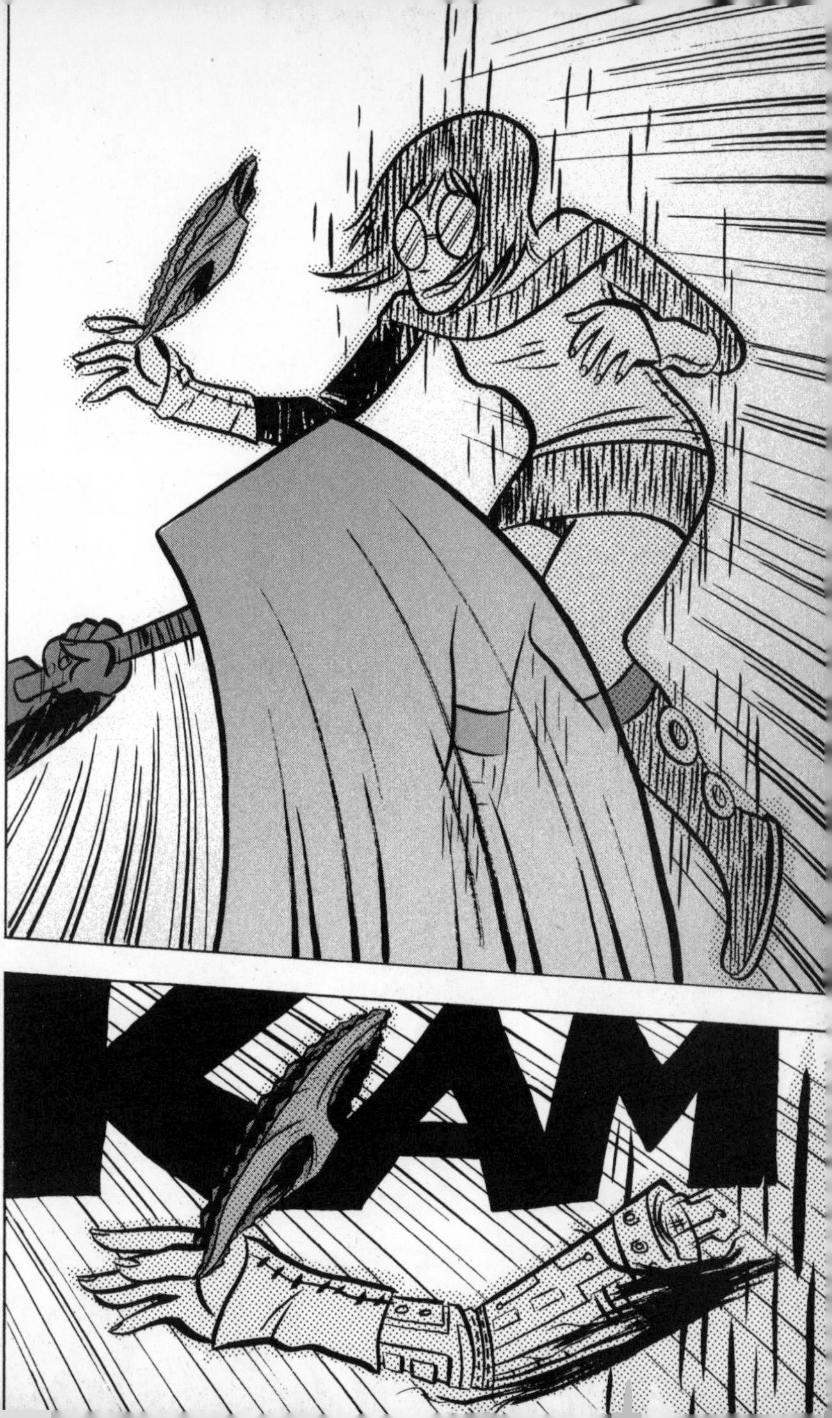
KAM

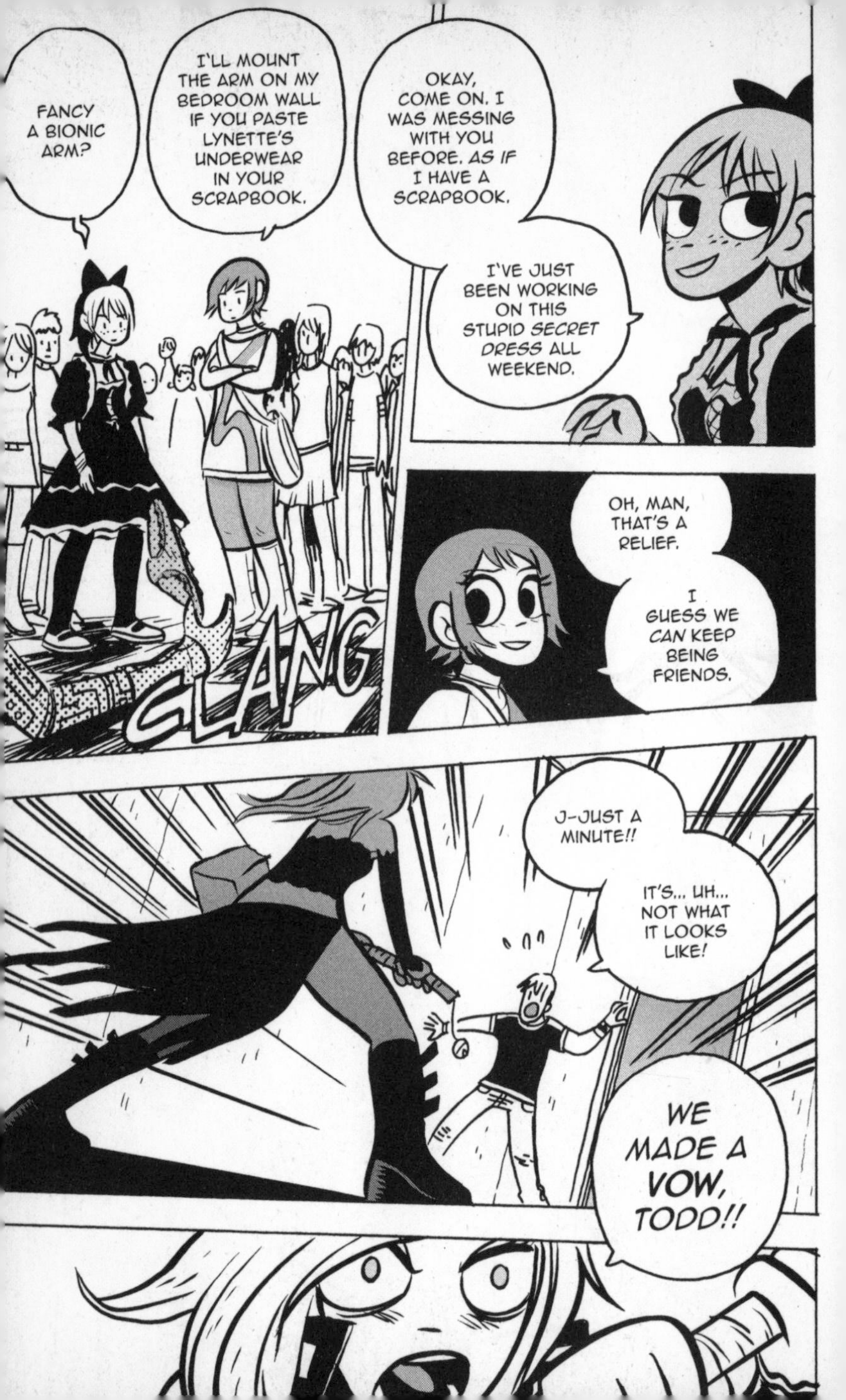
FANCY A BIONIC ARM?
I'LL MOUNT THE ARM ON MY BEDROOM WALL IF YOU PASTE LYNETTE'S UNDERWEAR IN YOUR SCRAPBOOK.
OKAY, COME ON. I WAS MESSING WITH YOU BEFORE. AS IF I HAVE A SCRAPBOOK.
I'VE JUST BEEN WORKING ON THIS STUPID SECRET DRESS ALL WEEKEND.
CLANG
OH, MAN, THAT'S A RELIEF.
I GUESS WE CAN KEEP BEING FRIENDS.
J-JUST A MINUTE!!
IT'S... UH... NOT WHAT IT LOOKS LIKE!
WE MADE A VOW, TODD!!

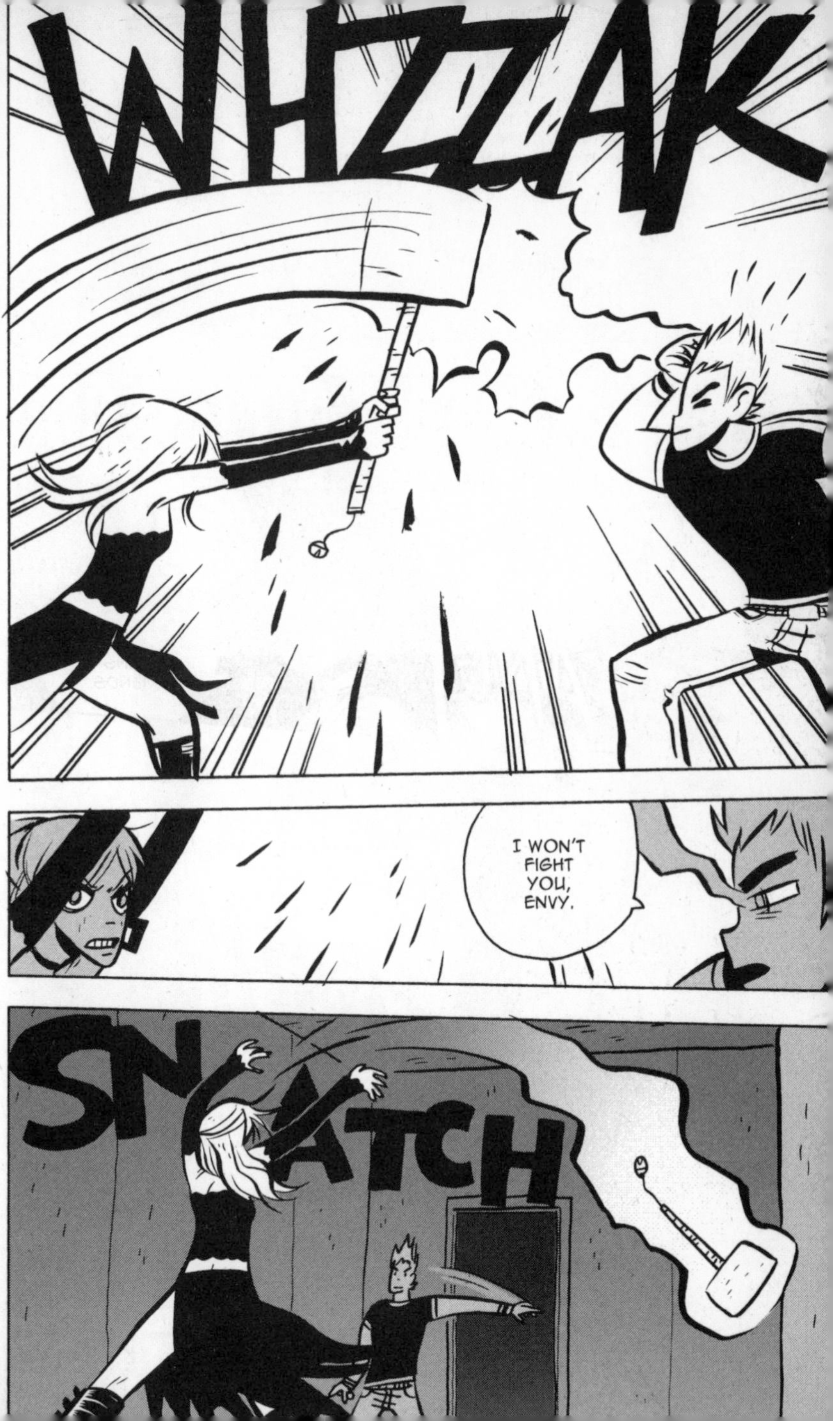
WHZZAK
I WON'T FIGHT YOU, ENVY.
SNATCH

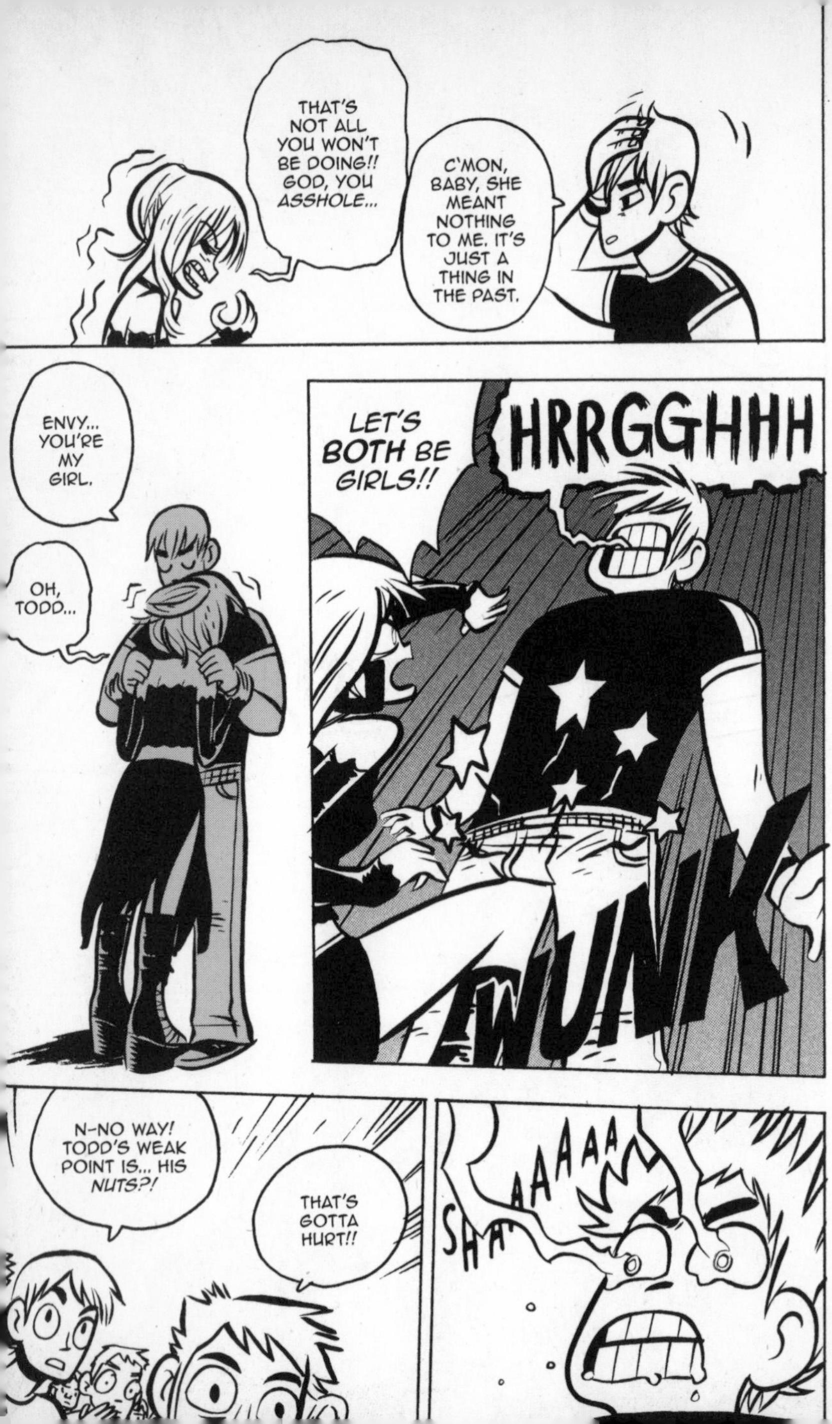
THAT'S NOT ALL YOU WON'T BE DOING!! GOD, YOU ASSHOLE...
C'MON, BABY, SHE MEANT NOTHING TO ME. IT'S JUST A THING IN THE PAST.
ENVY... YOU'RE MY GIRL.
OH, TODD...
LET'S BOTH BE GIRLS!!
HRRGGHHH
WUNK
N-NO WAY! TODD'S WEAK POINT IS... HIS NUTS?!
THAT'S GOTTA HURT!!
SHAAAAAA

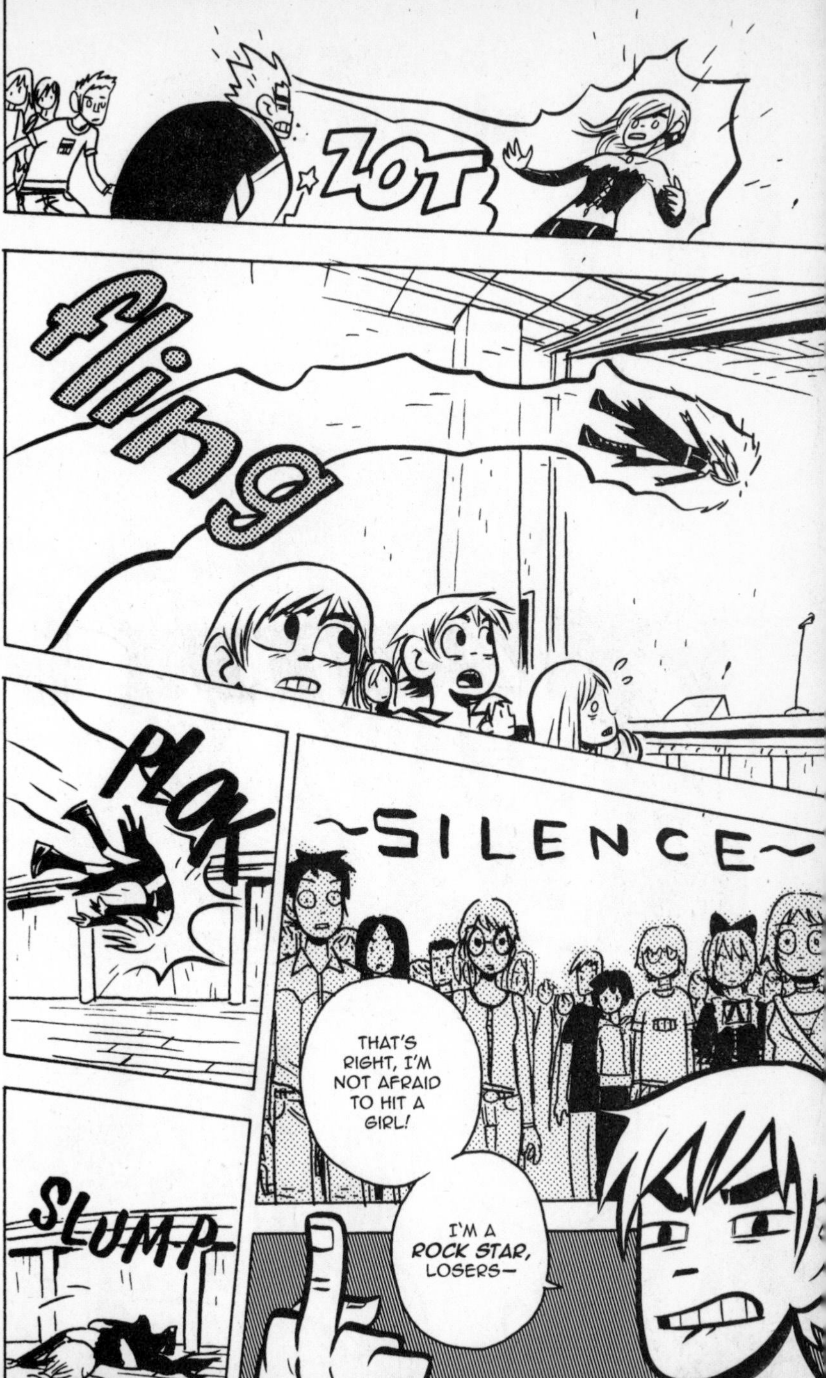
ZOT
fling
PLOCK
~SILENCE~
SLUMP
THAT'S RIGHT, I'M NOT AFRAID TO HIT A GIRL!
I'M A ROCK STAR, LOSERS—

18 destroy all vegans

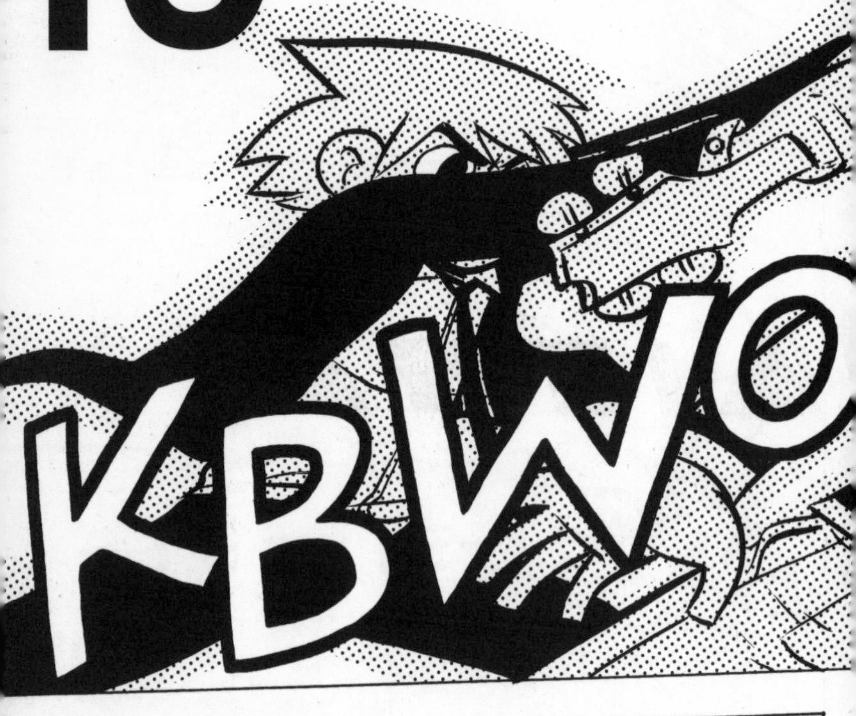

KBWO

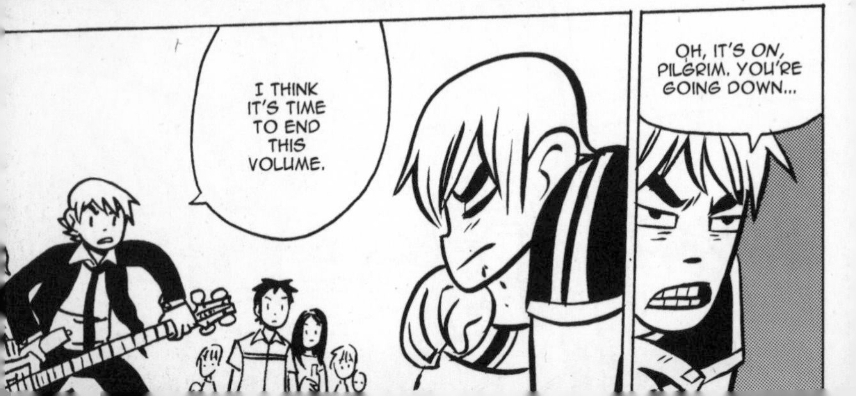

I THINK IT'S TIME TO END THIS VOLUME.
OH, IT'S ON, PILGRIM. YOU'RE GOING DOWN...

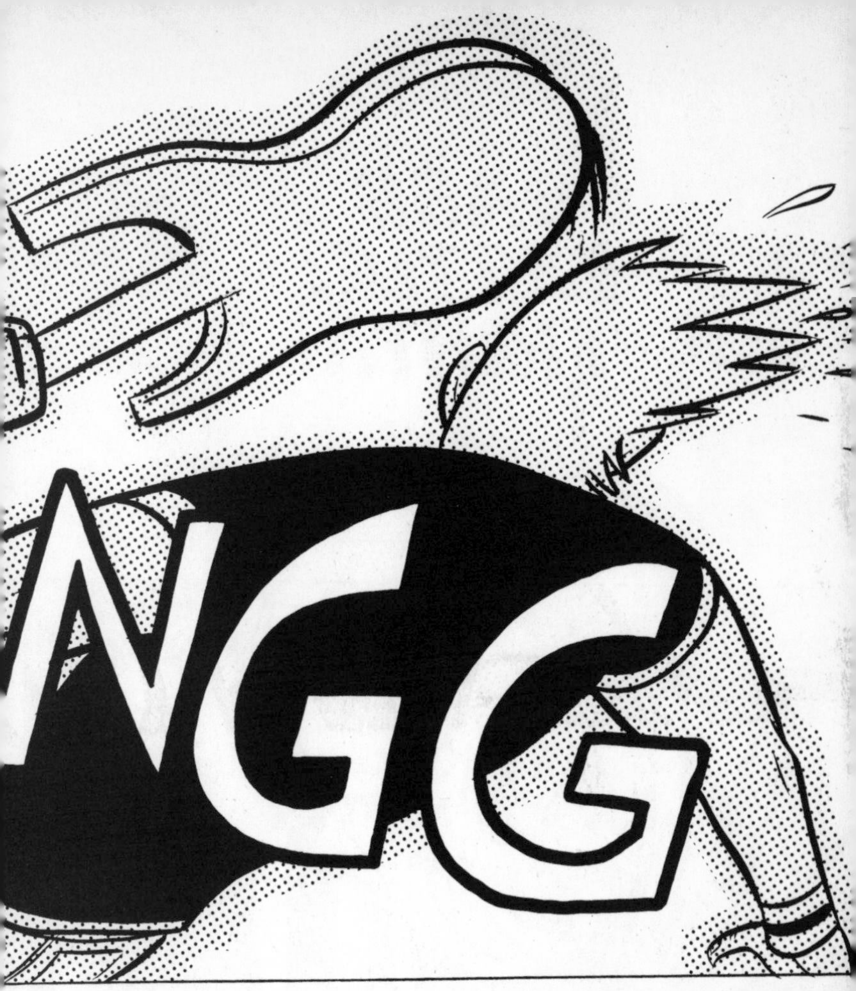
NGG

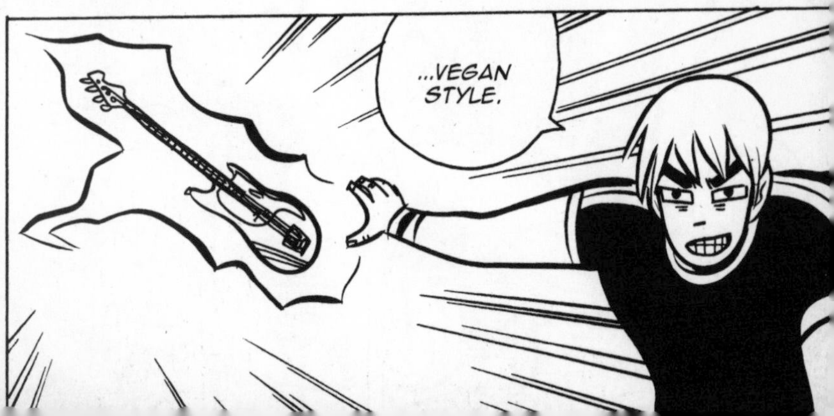
...VEGAN STYLE.

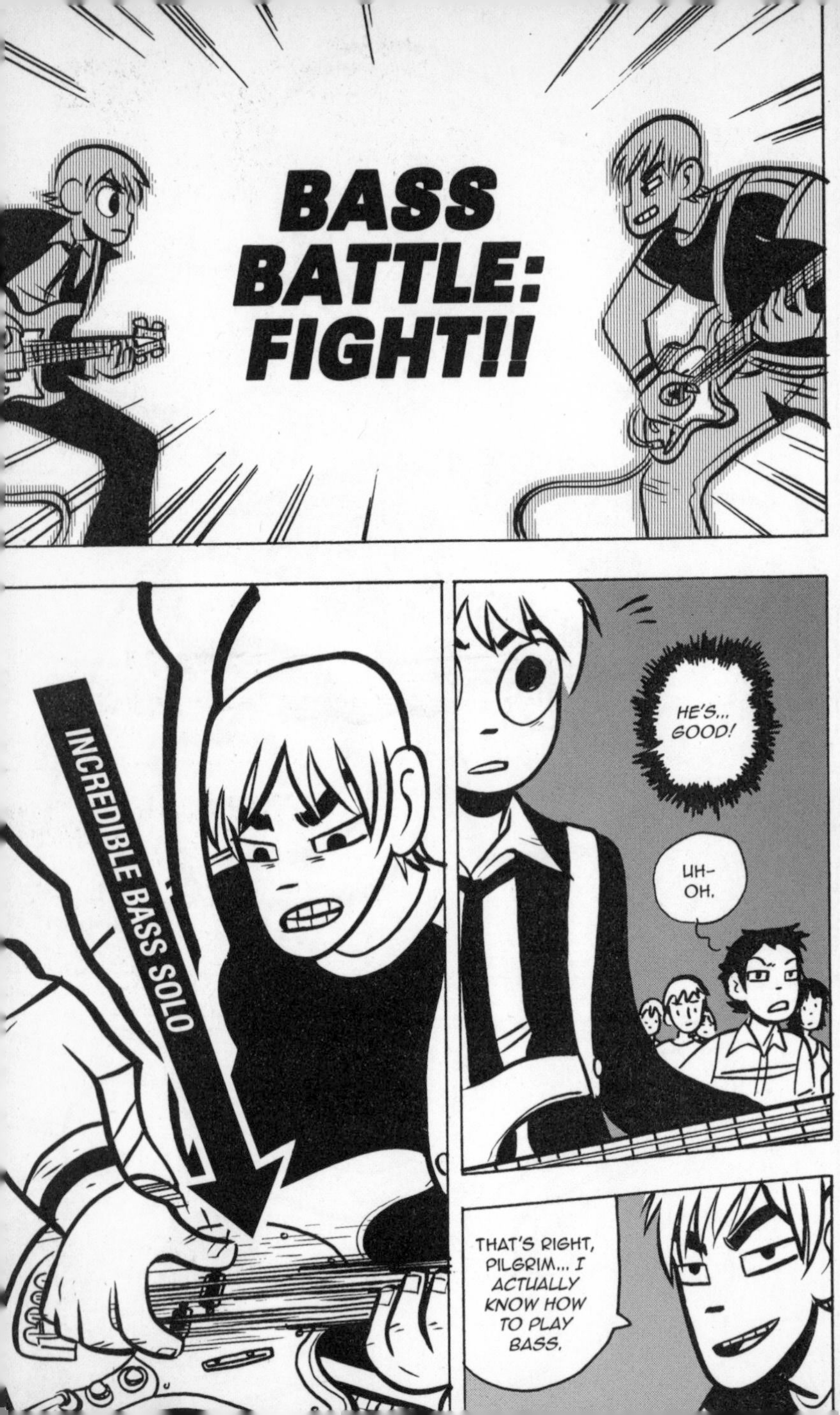
BASS BATTLE: FIGHT!!
INCREDIBLE BASS SOLO
HE'S... GOOD!
UH-OH.
THAT'S RIGHT, PILGRIM... I ACTUALLY KNOW HOW TO PLAY BASS.

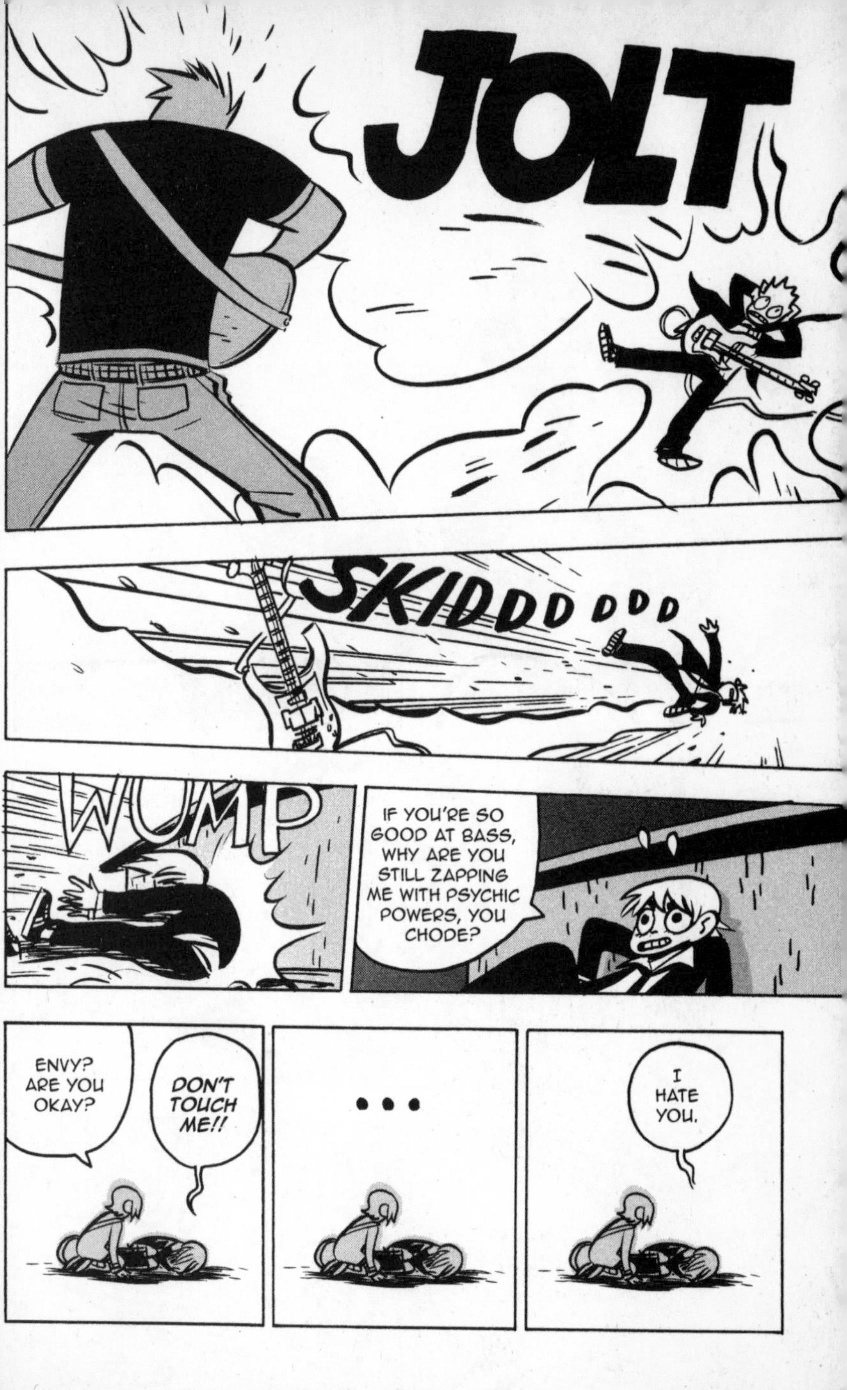
JOLT
SKIDDDDDDD
WUMP
IF YOU'RE SO GOOD AT BASS, WHY ARE YOU STILL ZAPPING ME WITH PSYCHIC POWERS, YOU CHODE?
ENVY? ARE YOU OKAY?
DON'T TOUCH ME!!
...
I HATE YOU.

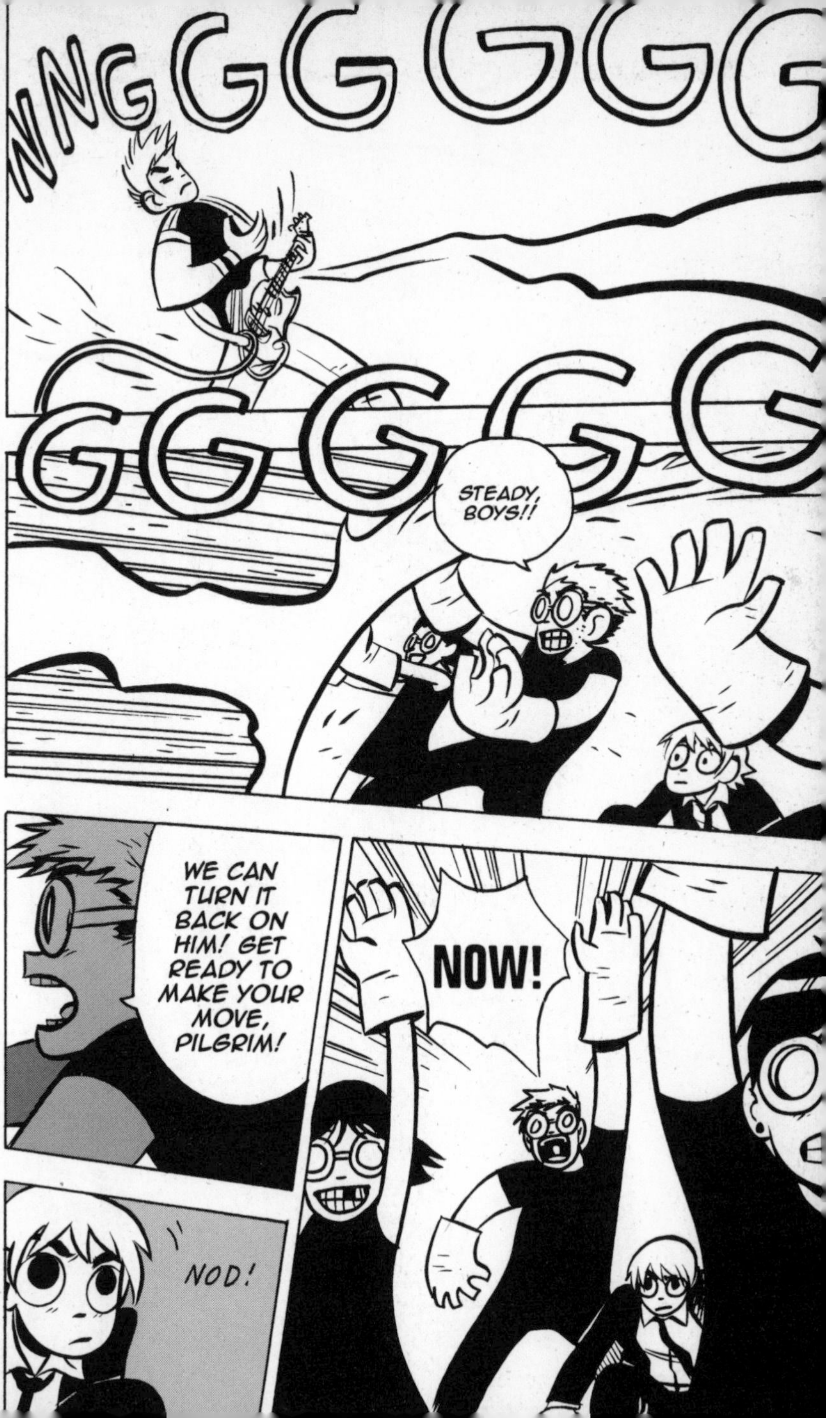
WNGGGGGG
GGGGG
STEADY, BOYS!!
WE CAN TURN IT BACK ON HIM! GET READY TO MAKE YOUR MOVE, PILGRIM!
NOW!
NOD!

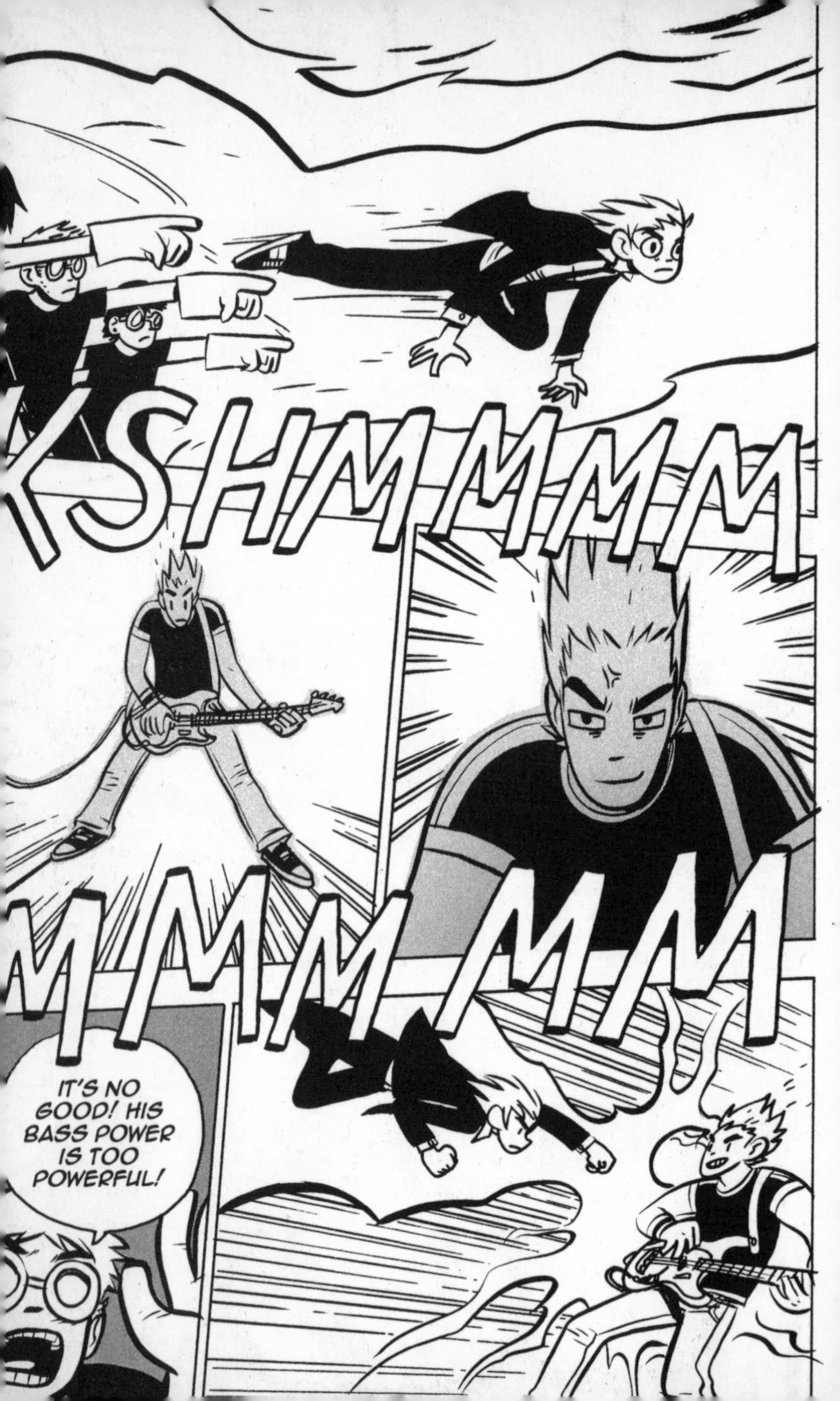
KSHMMMMMMMMMM
IT'S NO GOOD! HIS BASS POWER IS TOO POWERFUL!

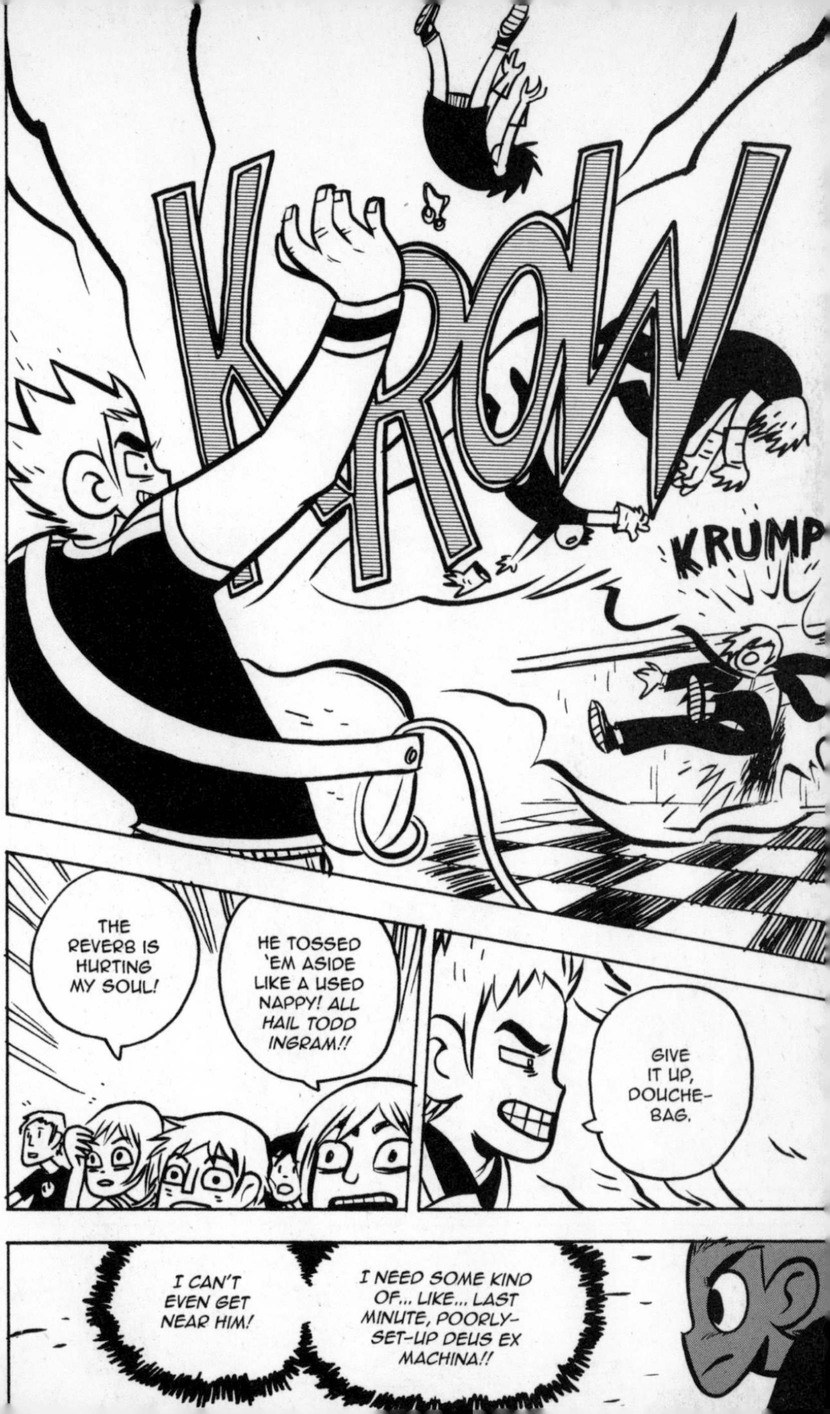
KRROW
KRUMP
THE REVERB IS HURTING MY SOUL!
HE TOSSED 'EM ASIDE LIKE A USED NAPPY! ALL HAIL TODD INGRAM!!
GIVE IT UP, DOUCHE-BAG.
I CAN'T EVEN GET NEAR HIM!
I NEED SOME KIND OF... LIKE... LAST MINUTE, POORLY-SET-UP DEUS EX MACHINA!!

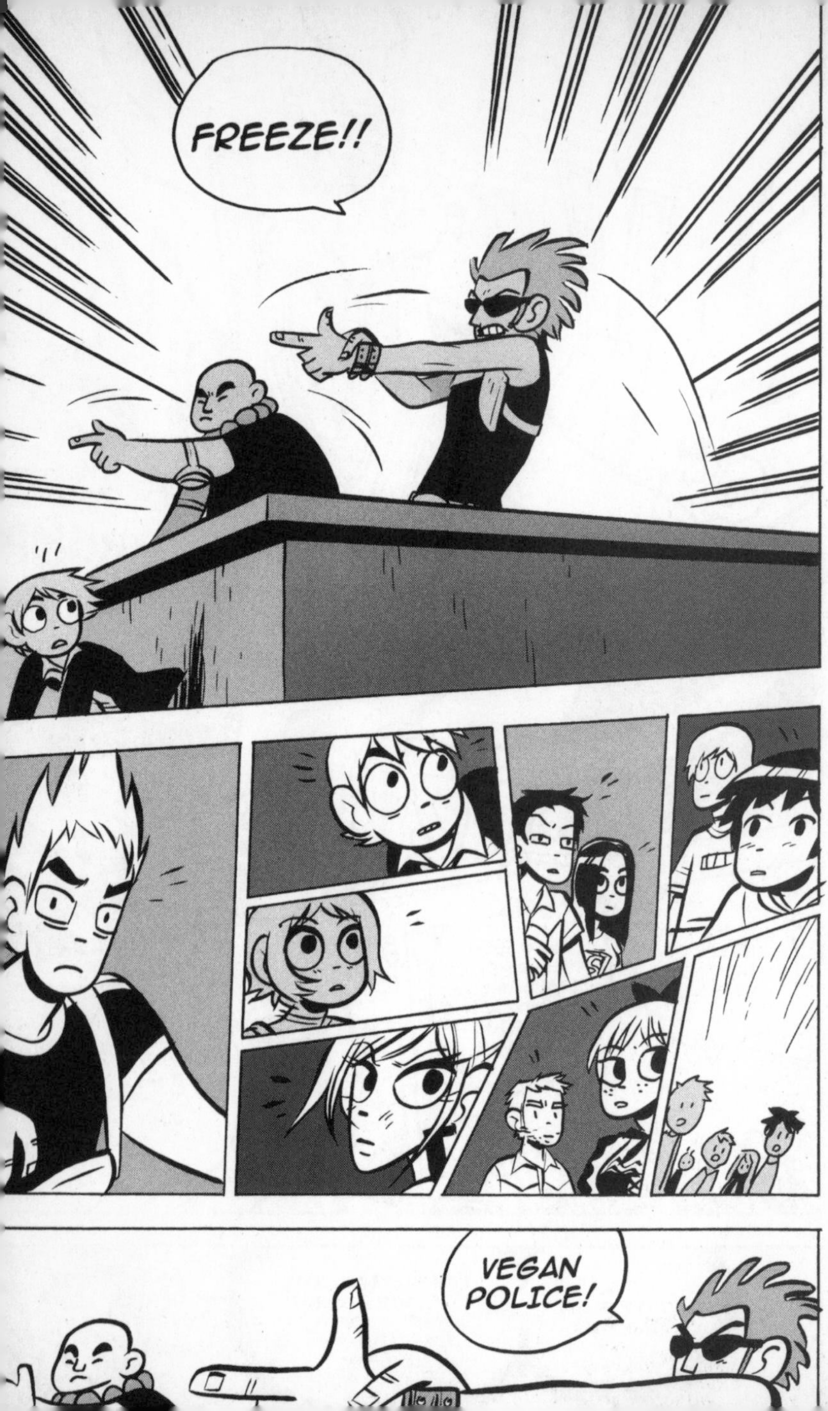
FREEZE!!
VEGAN POLICE!

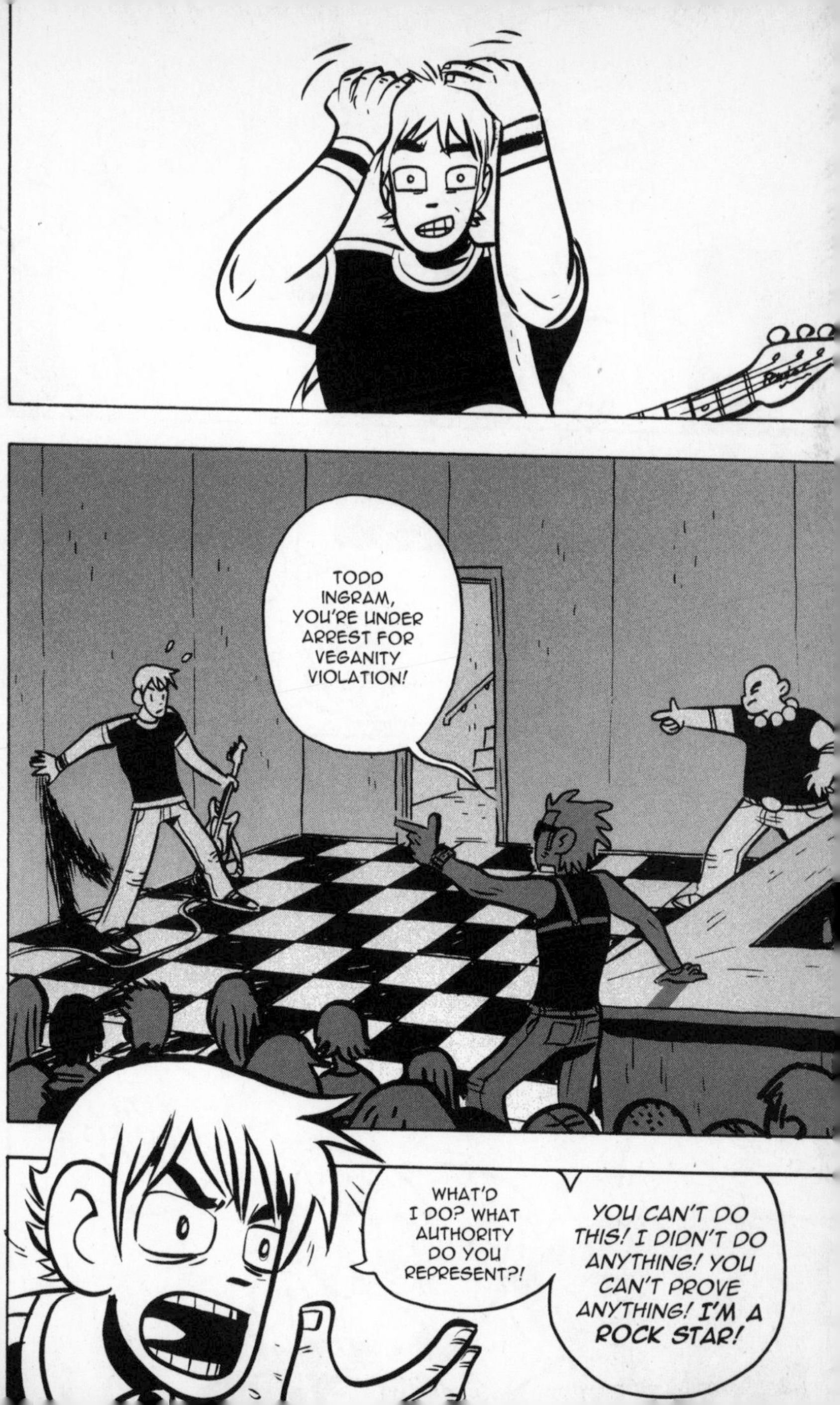

TODD INGRAM, YOU'RE UNDER ARREST FOR VEGANITY VIOLATION!
WHAT'D I DO? WHAT AUTHORITY DO YOU REPRESENT?!
YOU CAN'T DO THIS! I DIDN'T DO ANYTHING! YOU CAN'T PROVE ANYTHING! I'M A ROCK STAR!

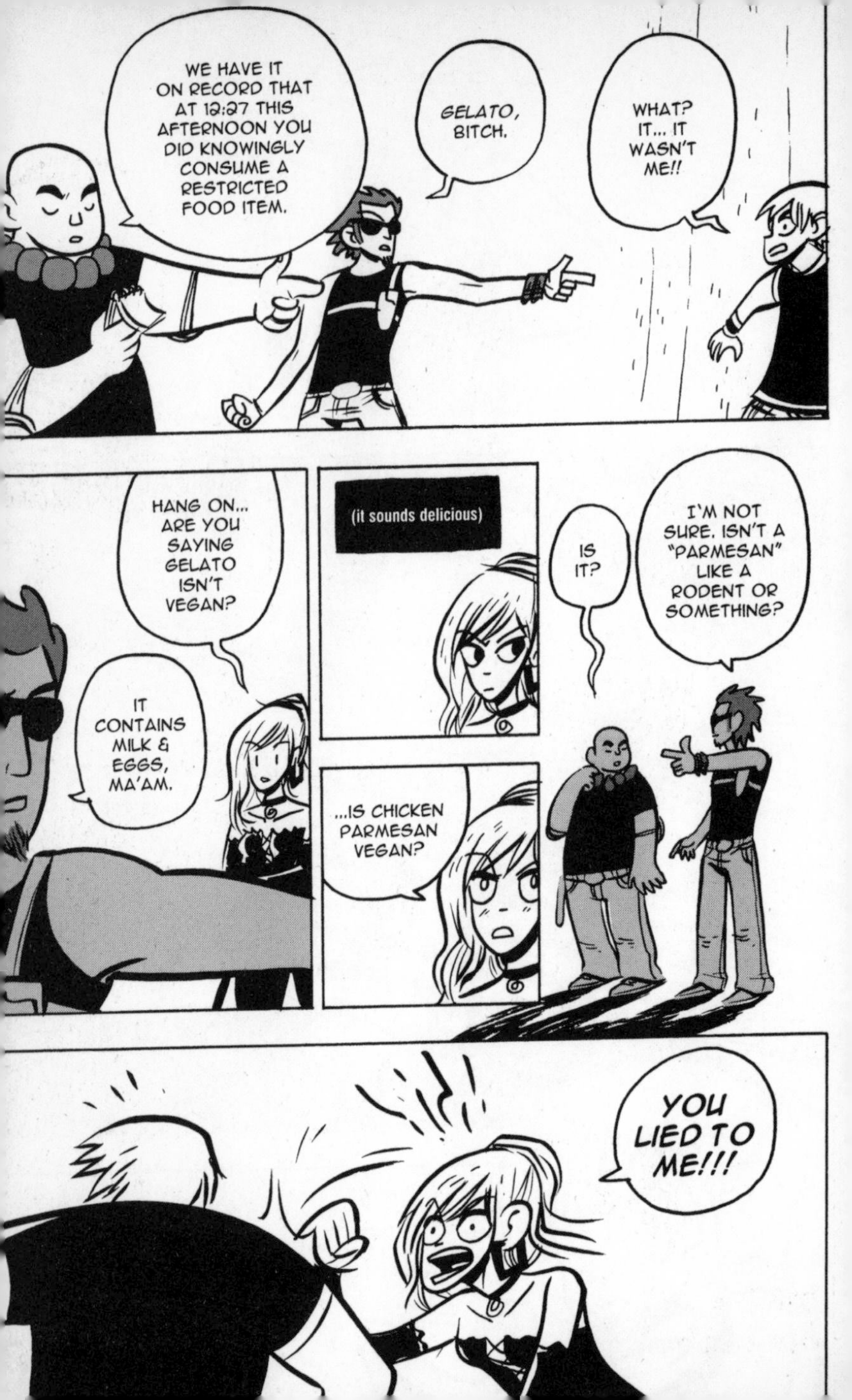
WE HAVE IT ON RECORD THAT AT 12:27 THIS AFTERNOON YOU DID KNOWINGLY CONSUME A RESTRICTED FOOD ITEM.
GELATO, BITCH.
WHAT? IT... IT WASN'T ME!!
HANG ON... ARE YOU SAYING GELATO ISN'T VEGAN?
IT CONTAINS MILK & EGGS, MA'AM.
(it sounds delicious)
...IS CHICKEN PARMESAN VEGAN?
IS IT?
I'M NOT SURE. ISN'T A "PARMESAN" LIKE A RODENT OR SOMETHING?
YOU LIED TO ME!!!

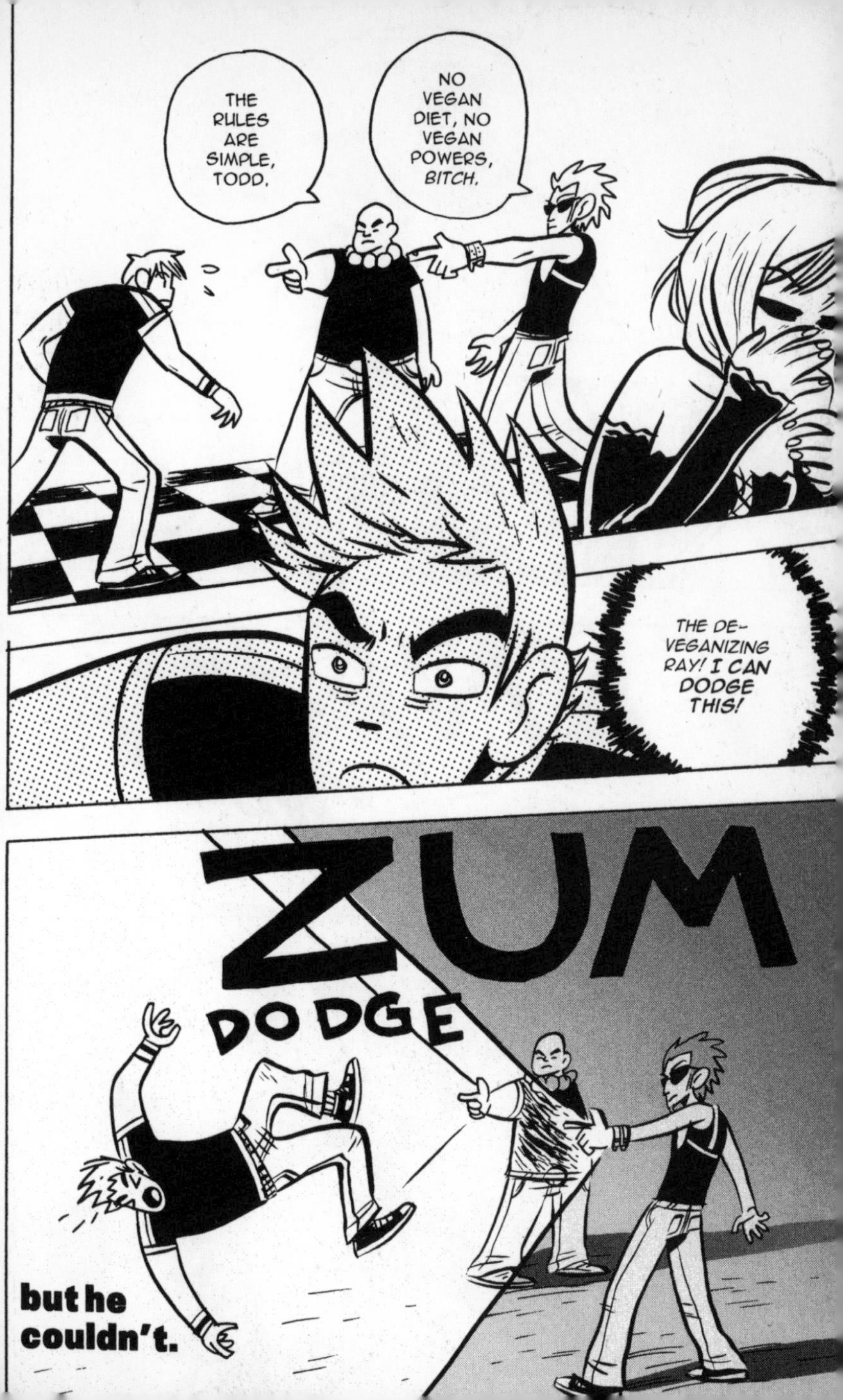
THE RULES ARE SIMPLE, TODD.
NO VEGAN DIET, NO VEGAN POWERS, BITCH.
THE DE-VEGANIZING RAY! I CAN DODGE THIS!
ZUM
DODGE
but he couldn't.

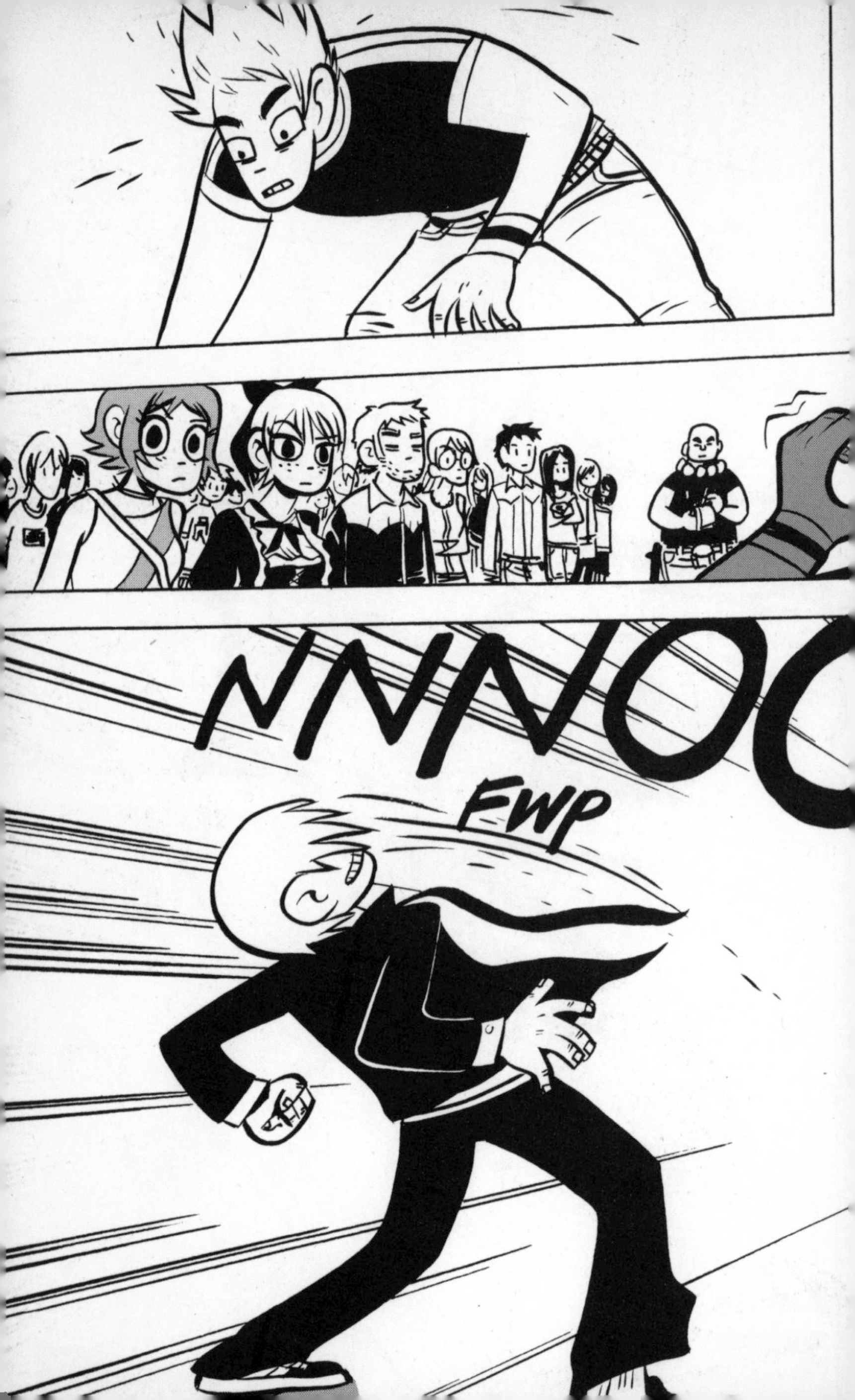
NNNOO
FWP

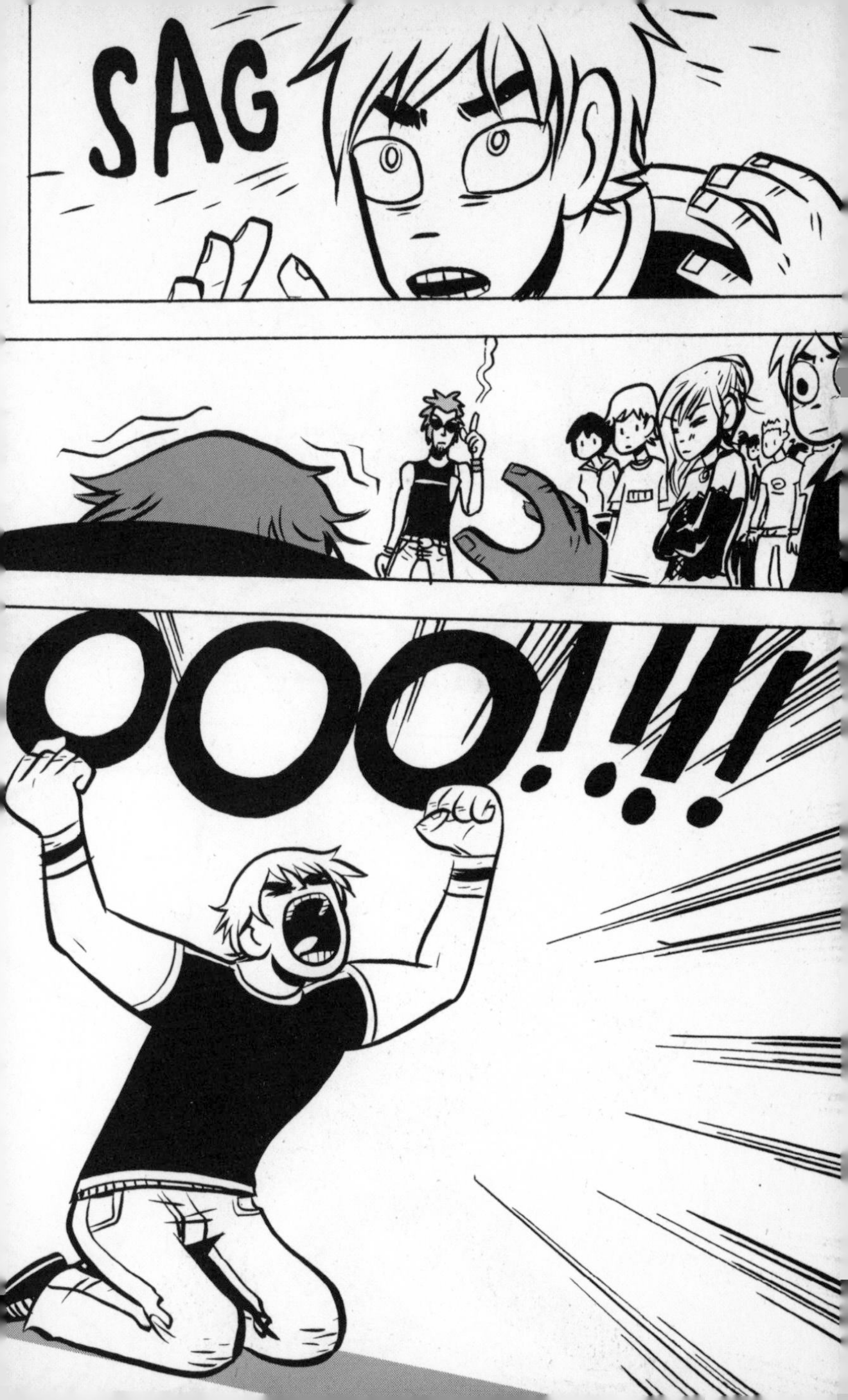

SAG
OOO!!!!

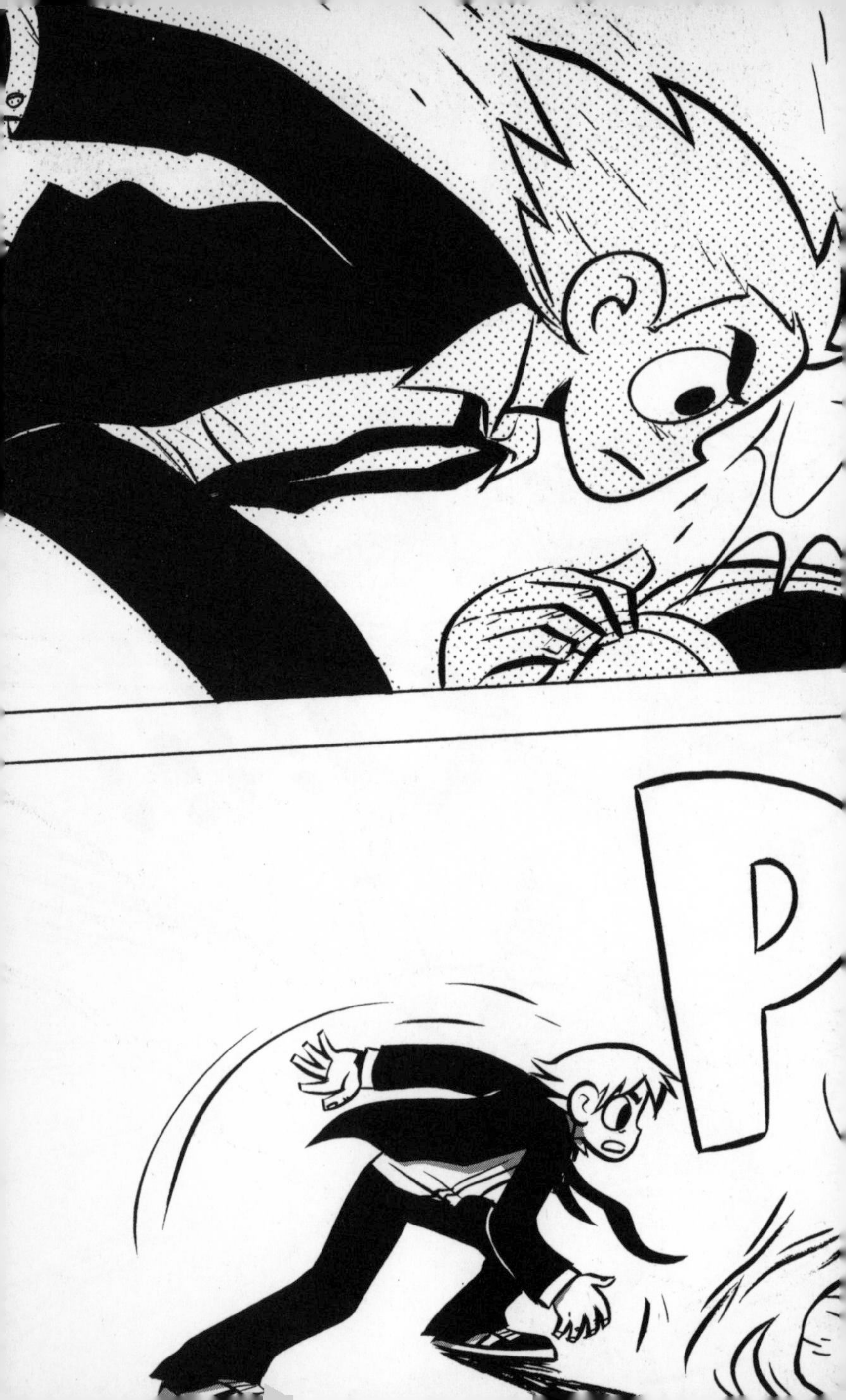

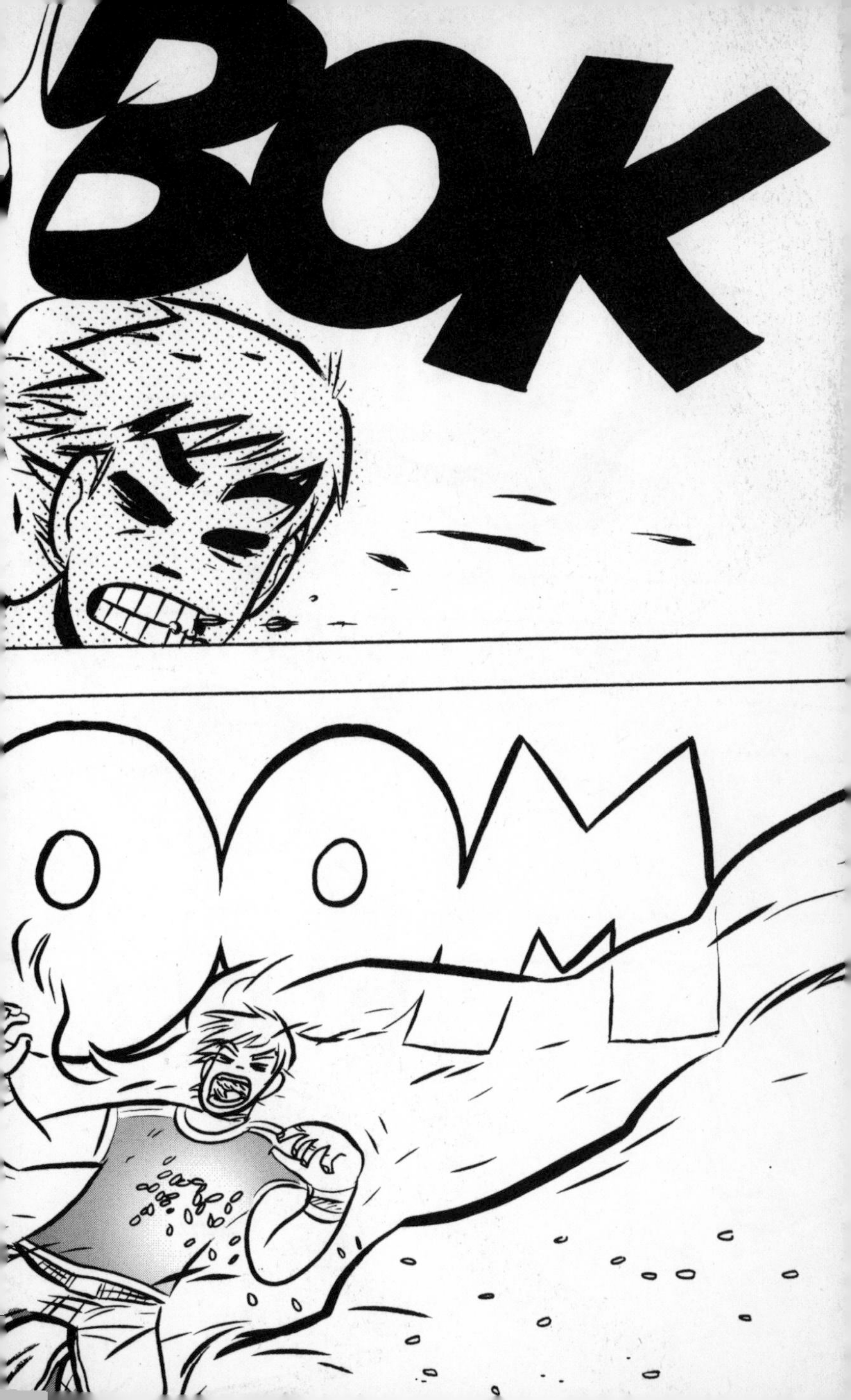
BOK
OOM

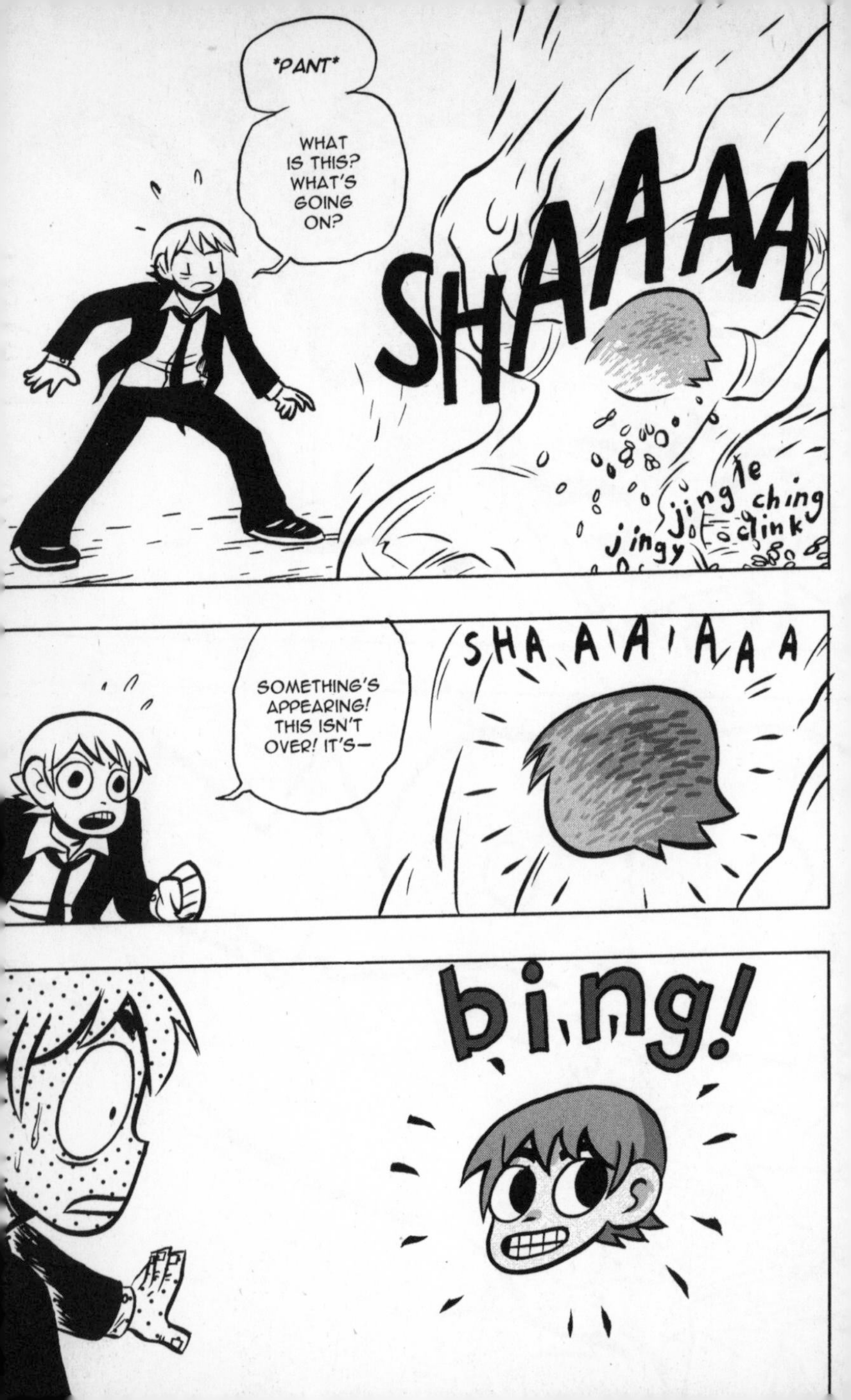
PANT
WHAT IS THIS? WHAT'S GOING ON?
SHAAAAA
jingle ching
jingy
clink
SHAAAAAA
SOMETHING'S APPEARING! THIS ISN'T OVER! IT'S—
bing!

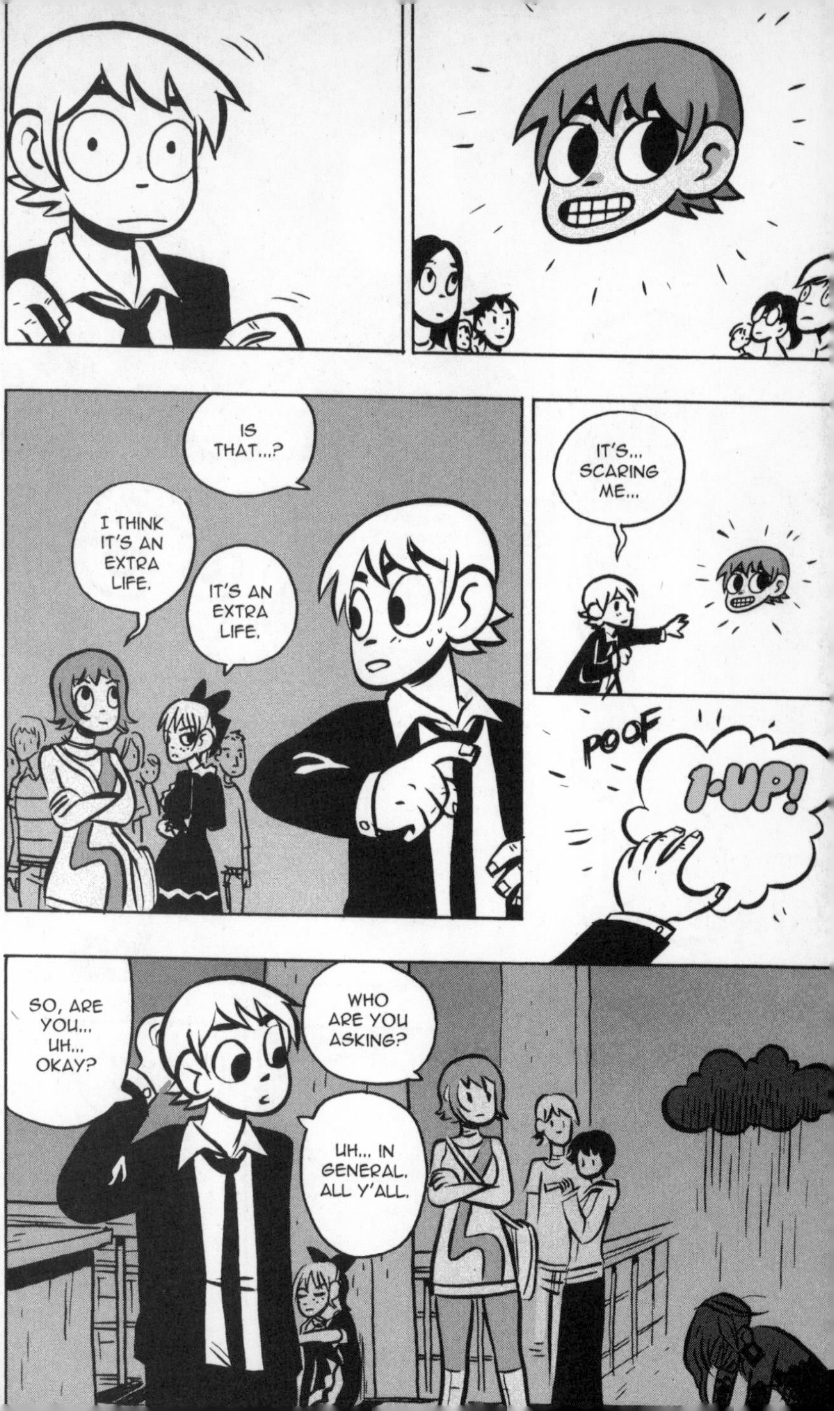
IS THAT...?
I THINK IT'S AN EXTRA LIFE.
IT'S AN EXTRA LIFE.
IT'S... SCARING ME...
POOF
1-UP!
SO, ARE YOU... UH... OKAY?
WHO ARE YOU ASKING?
UH... IN GENERAL. ALL Y'ALL.

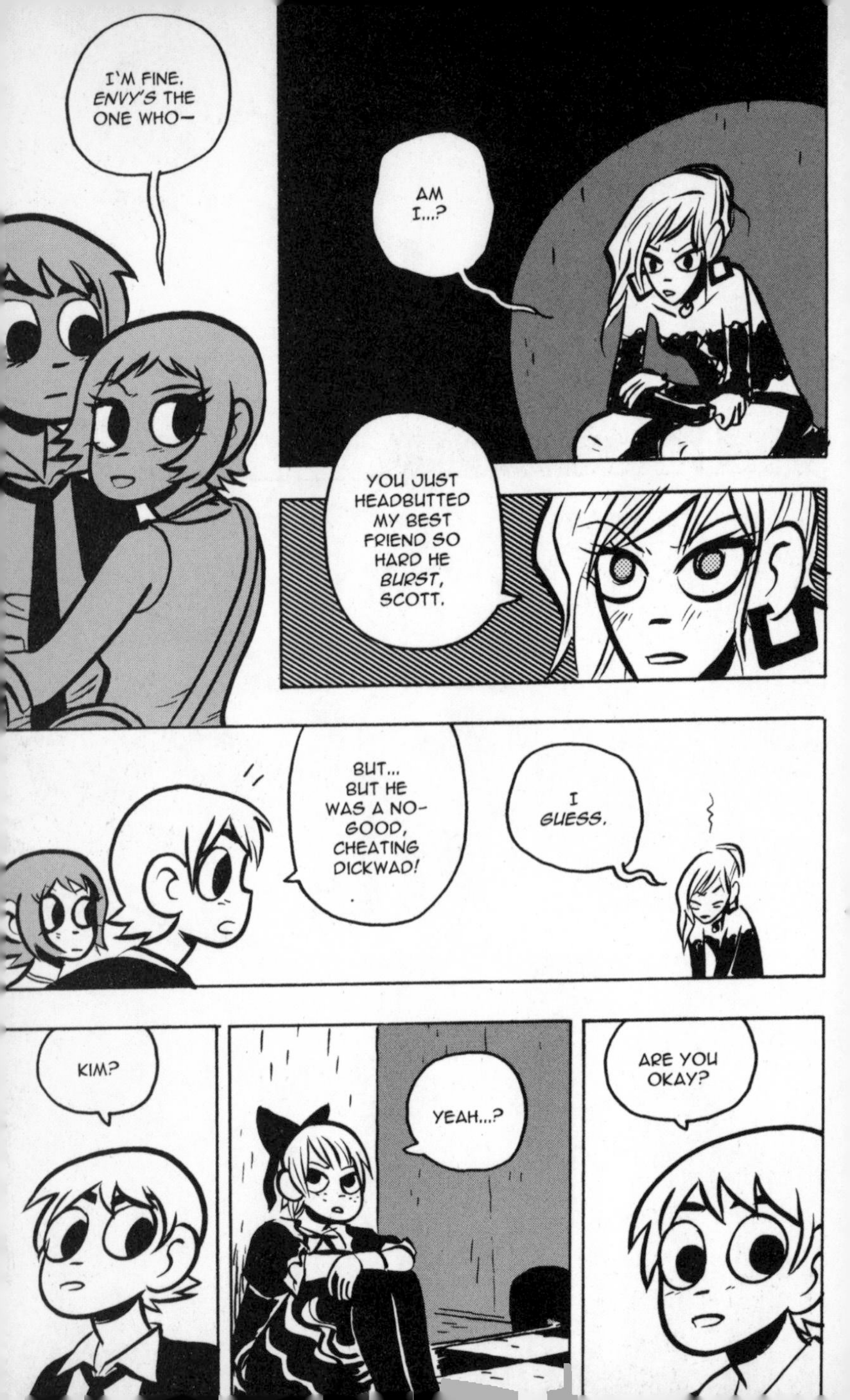

I'M FINE. ENVY'S THE ONE WHO—
AM I...?
YOU JUST HEADBUTTED MY BEST FRIEND SO HARD HE BURST, SCOTT.
BUT... BUT HE WAS A NO-GOOD, CHEATING DICKWAD!
I GUESS.
KIM?
YEAH...?
ARE YOU OKAY?

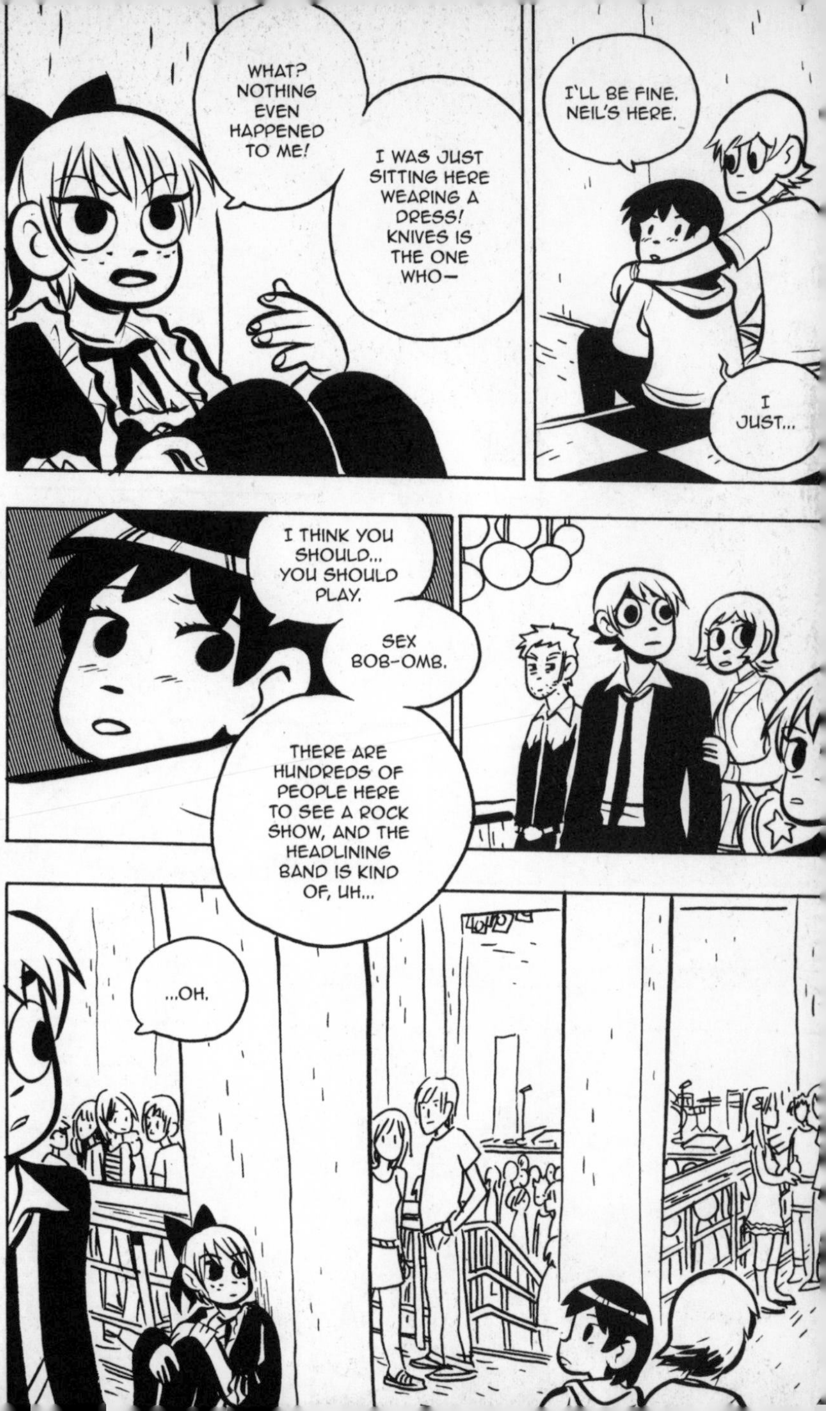
WHAT? NOTHING EVEN HAPPENED TO ME!
I WAS JUST SITTING HERE WEARING A DRESS! KNIVES IS THE ONE WHO–
I'LL BE FINE. NEIL'S HERE.
I JUST...
I THINK YOU SHOULD... YOU SHOULD PLAY.
SEX BOB-OMB.
THERE ARE HUNDREDS OF PEOPLE HERE TO SEE A ROCK SHOW, AND THE HEADLINING BAND IS KIND OF, UH...
...OH.

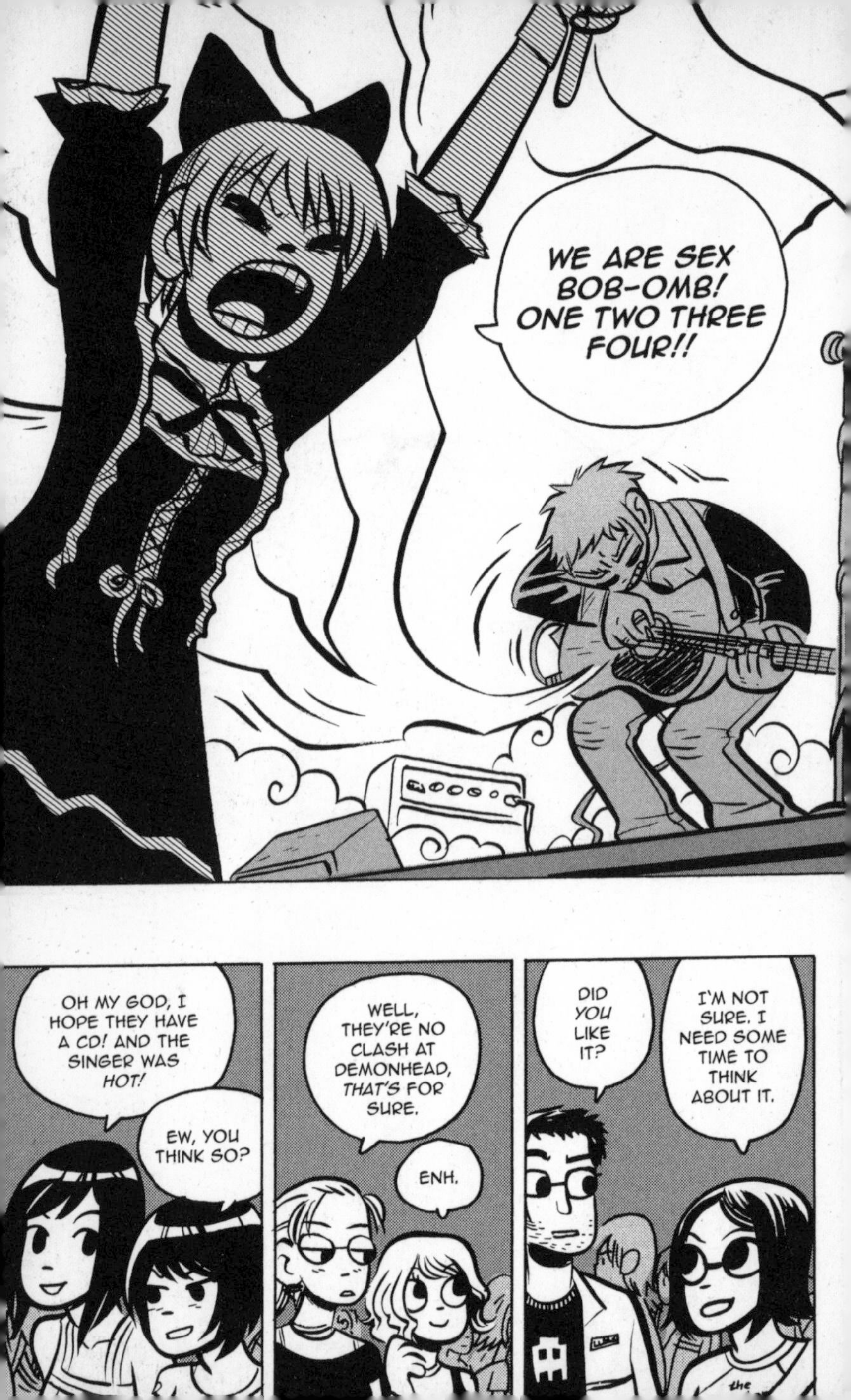
WE ARE SEX BOB-OMB! ONE TWO THREE FOUR!!
OH MY GOD, I HOPE THEY HAVE A CD! AND THE SINGER WAS *HOT!*
EW, YOU THINK SO?
WELL, THEY'RE NO CLASH AT DEMONHEAD, *THAT'S* FOR SURE.
ENH.
DID *YOU* LIKE IT?
I'M NOT SURE. I NEED SOME TIME TO THINK ABOUT IT.
the

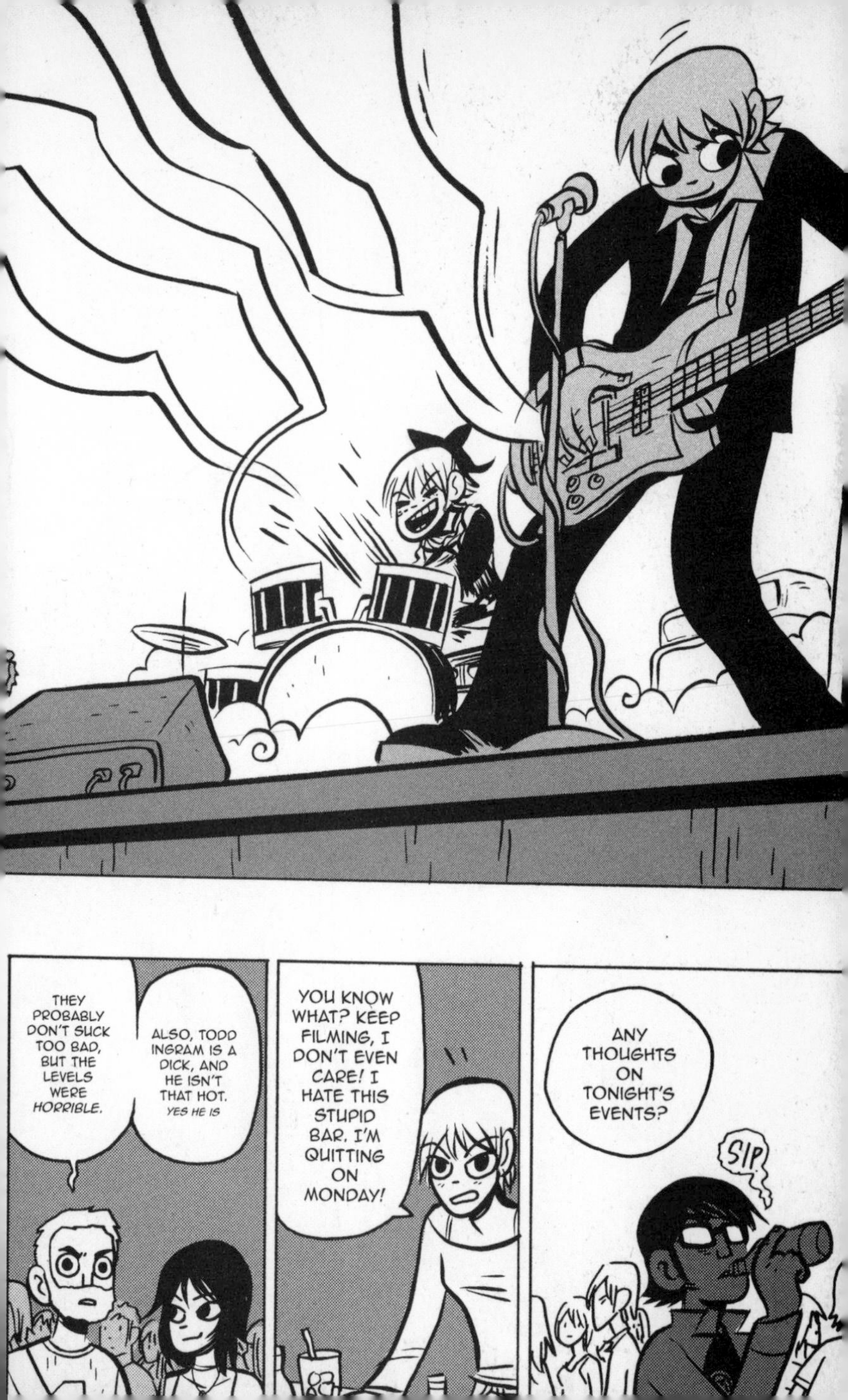
THEY PROBABLY DON'T SUCK TOO BAD, BUT THE LEVELS WERE HORRIBLE.
ALSO, TODD INGRAM IS A DICK, AND HE ISN'T THAT HOT.
YES HE IS
YOU KNOW WHAT? KEEP FILMING, I DON'T EVEN CARE! I HATE THIS STUPID BAR. I'M QUITTING ON MONDAY!
ANY THOUGHTS ON TONIGHT'S EVENTS?
SIP

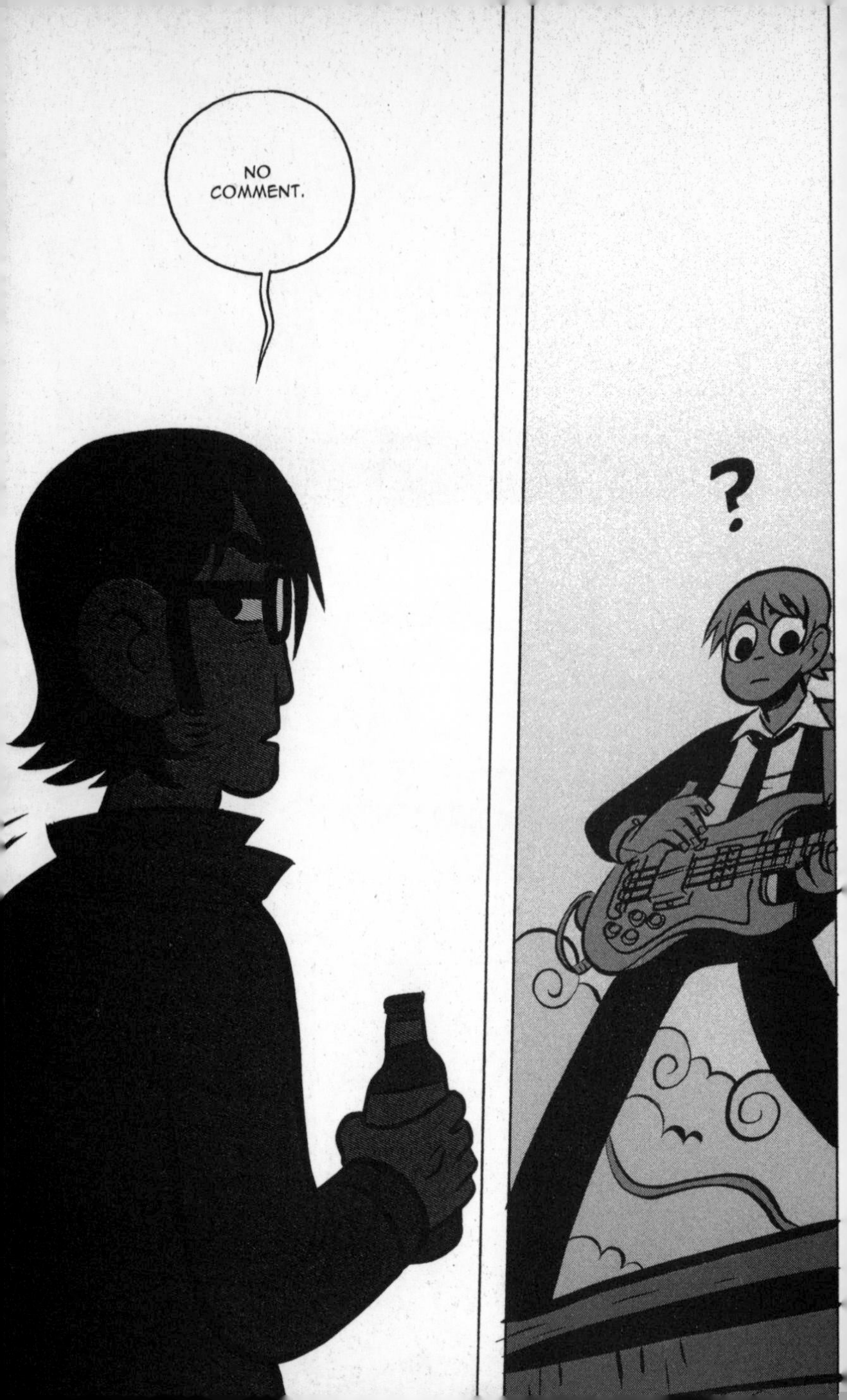
NO COMMENT.
?

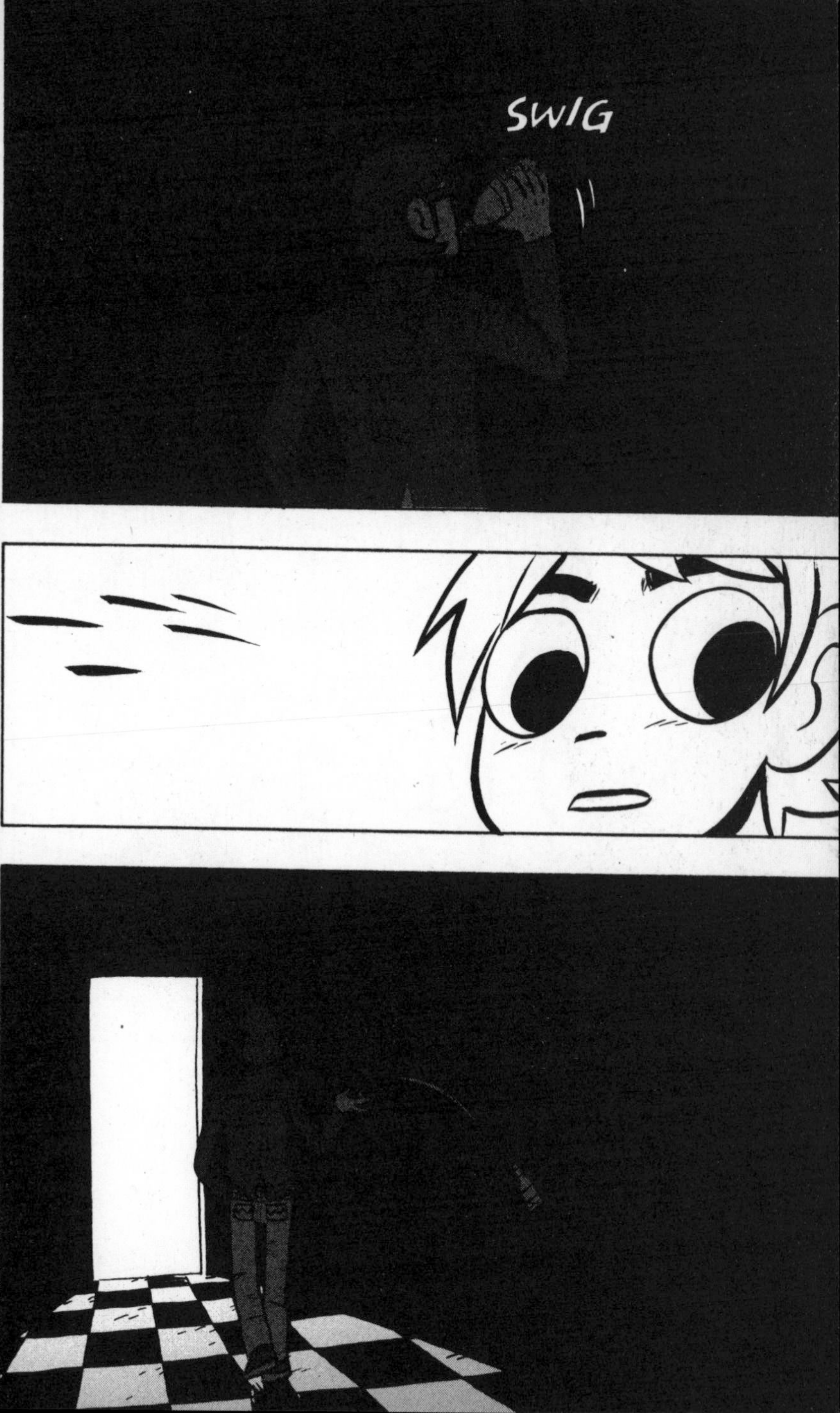
SWIG

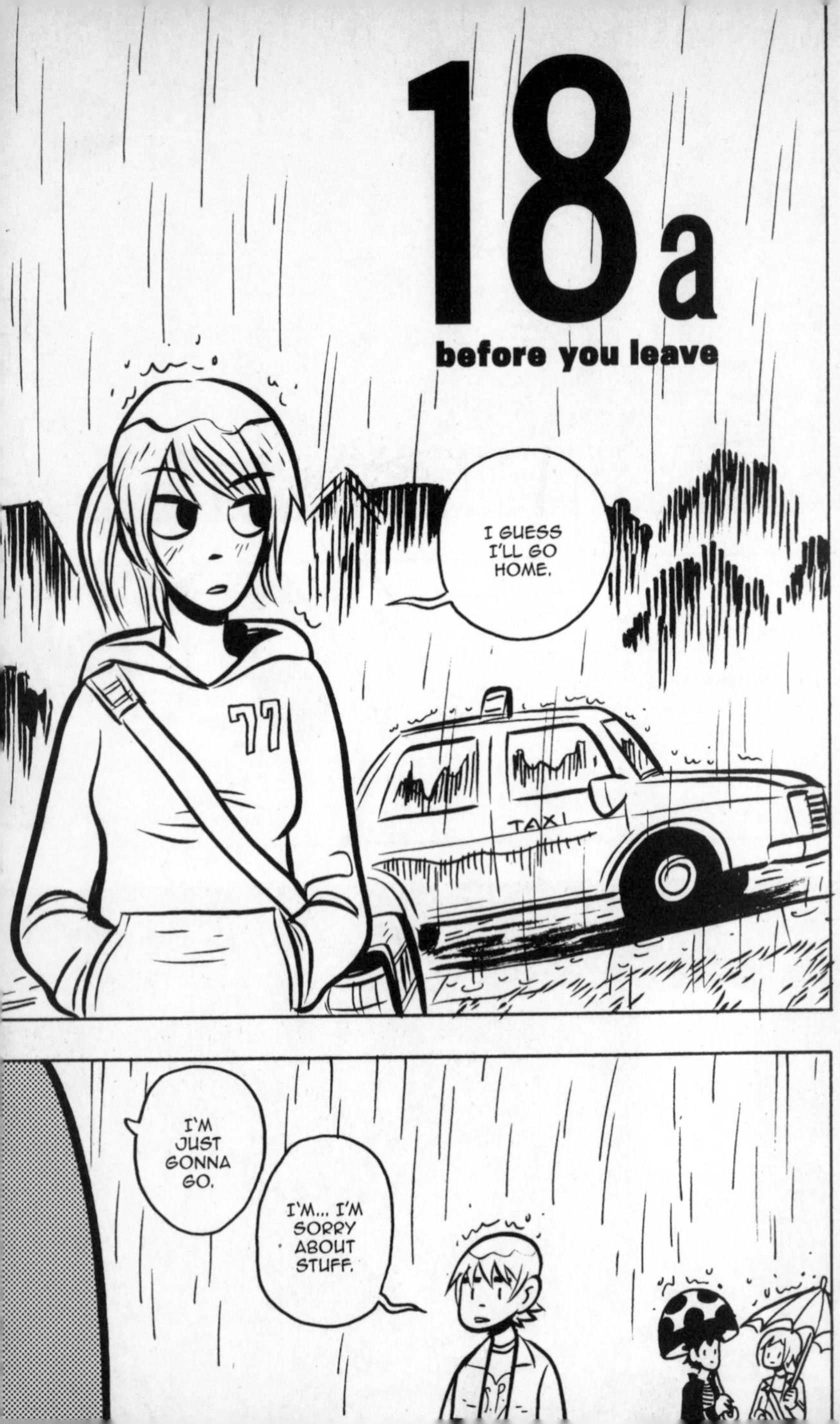
18a
before you leave
I GUESS I'LL GO HOME.
77
TAXI
I'M JUST GONNA GO.
I'M... I'M SORRY ABOUT STUFF.

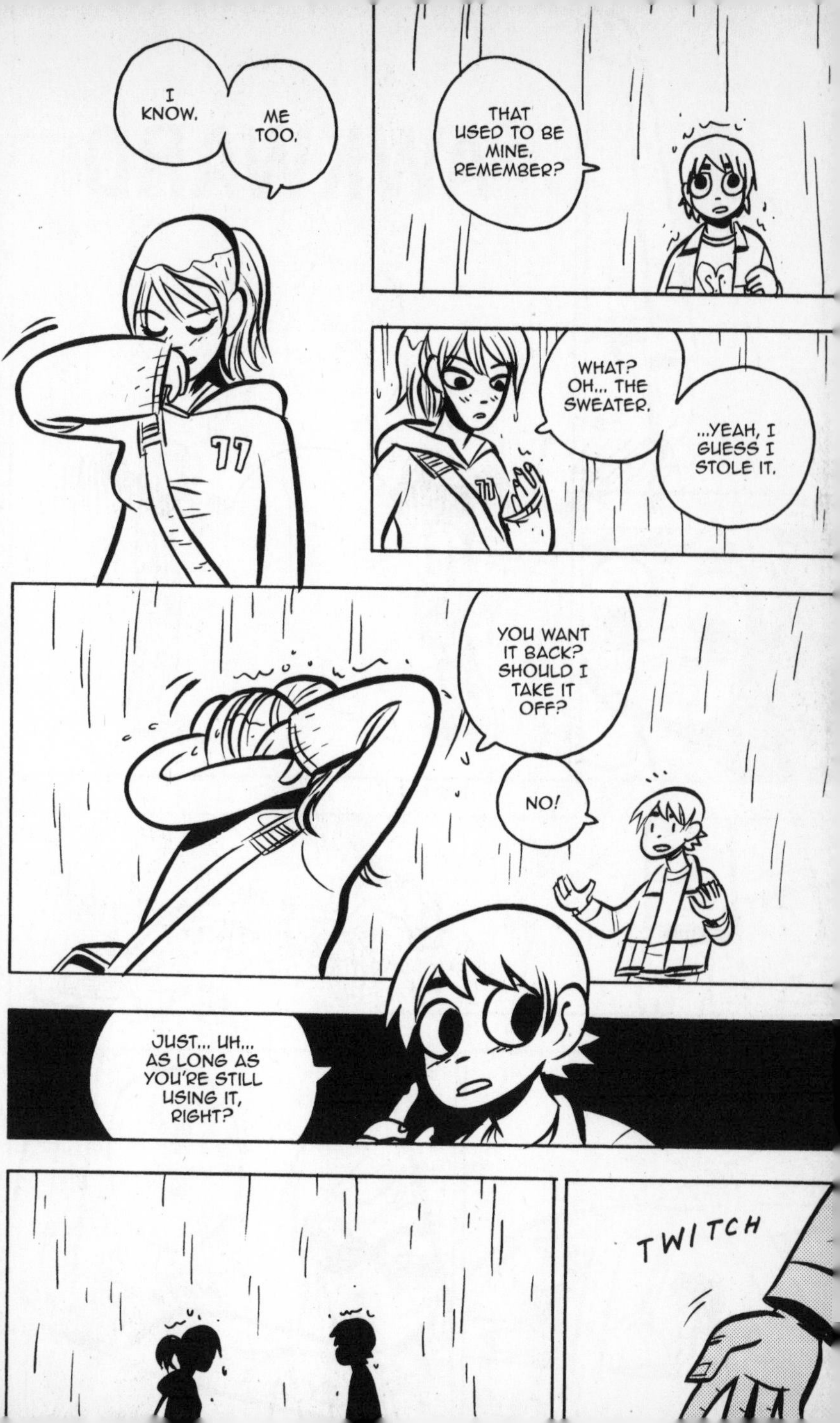
I KNOW.
ME TOO.
THAT USED TO BE MINE. REMEMBER?
WHAT? OH... THE SWEATER.
...YEAH, I GUESS I STOLE IT.
YOU WANT IT BACK? SHOULD I TAKE IT OFF?
NO!
JUST... UH... AS LONG AS YOU'RE STILL USING IT, RIGHT?
TWITCH

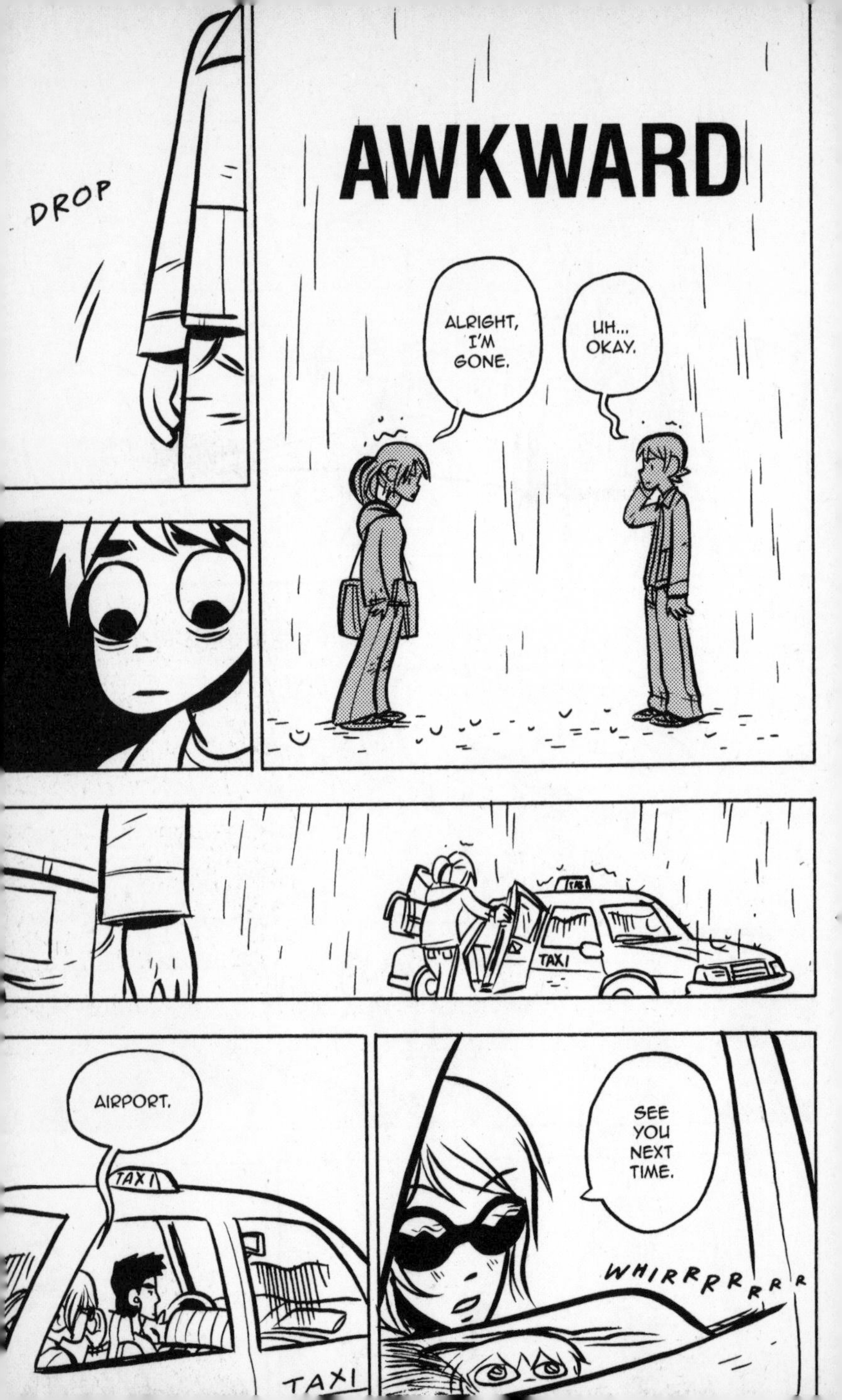
DROP
AWKWARD
ALRIGHT, I'M GONE.
UH... OKAY.
TAXI
AIRPORT.
TAXI
TAXI
SEE YOU NEXT TIME.
WHIRRRRRRRR

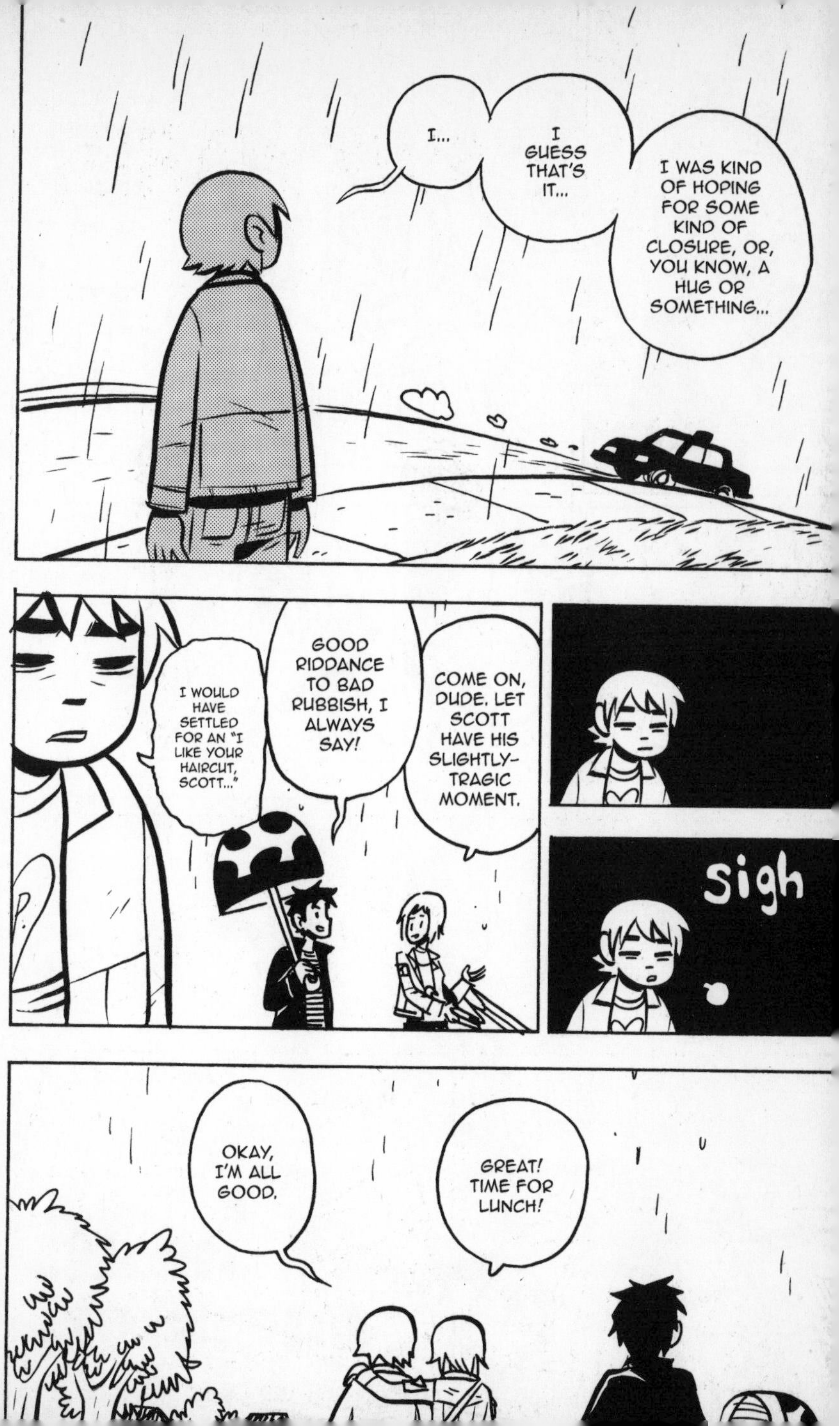
I...
I GUESS THAT'S IT...
I WAS KIND OF HOPING FOR SOME KIND OF CLOSURE, OR, YOU KNOW, A HUG OR SOMETHING...
I WOULD HAVE SETTLED FOR AN "I LIKE YOUR HAIRCUT, SCOTT..."
GOOD RIDDANCE TO BAD RUBBISH, I ALWAYS SAY!
COME ON, DUDE. LET SCOTT HAVE HIS SLIGHTLY-TRAGIC MOMENT.
Sigh
OKAY, I'M ALL GOOD.
GREAT! TIME FOR LUNCH!

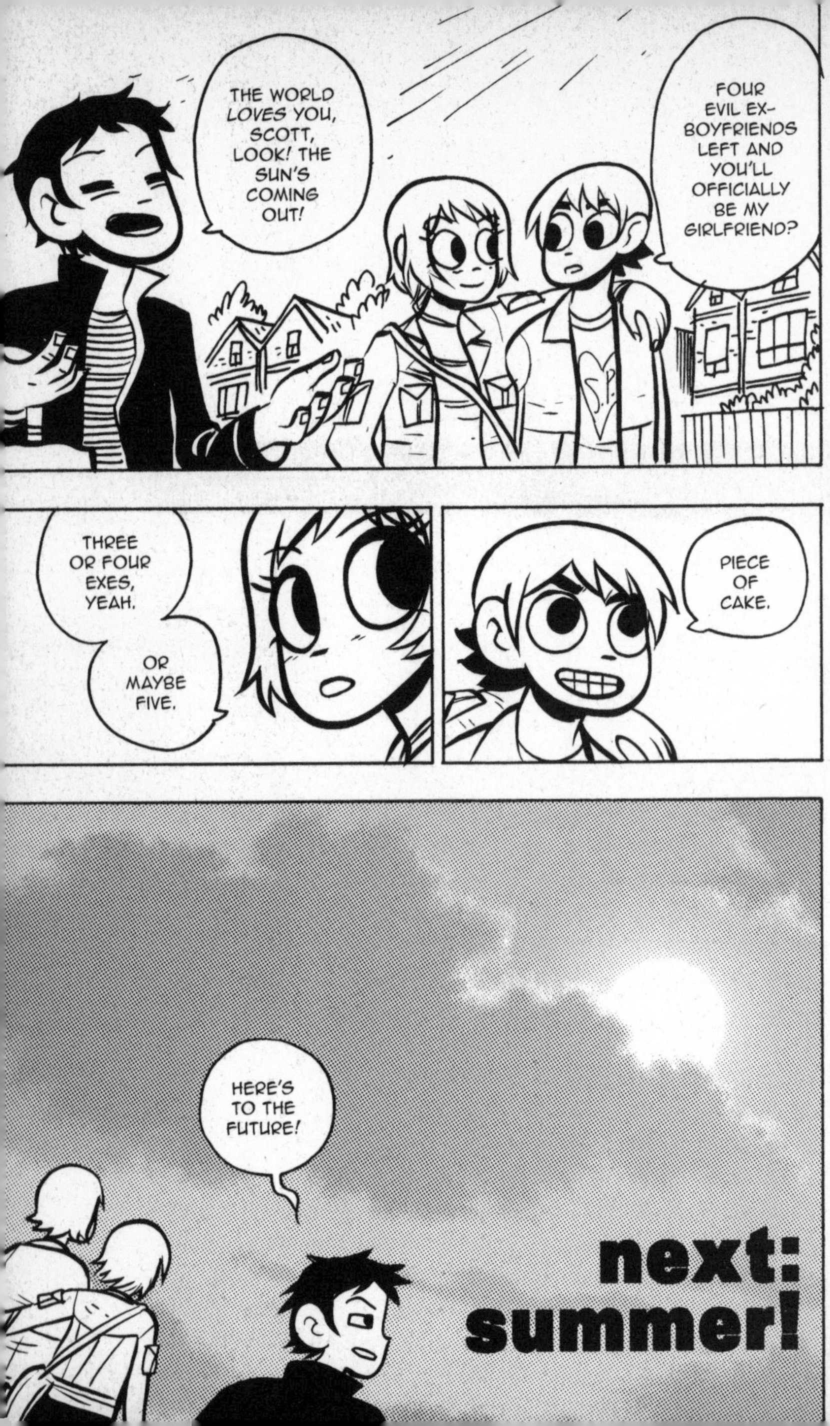
THE WORLD LOVES YOU, SCOTT, LOOK! THE SUN'S COMING OUT!
FOUR EVIL EX-BOYFRIENDS LEFT AND YOU'LL OFFICIALLY BE MY GIRLFRIEND?
S.P.
THREE OR FOUR EXES, YEAH.
OR MAYBE FIVE.
PIECE OF CAKE.
HERE'S TO THE FUTURE!
next: summer!

I wasn't sure what direction to take with the Vegan Police, so I asked my friend Nathan Avery to help me out. These are his original designs. I chickened out and simplified them a lot, but the spirit is there.

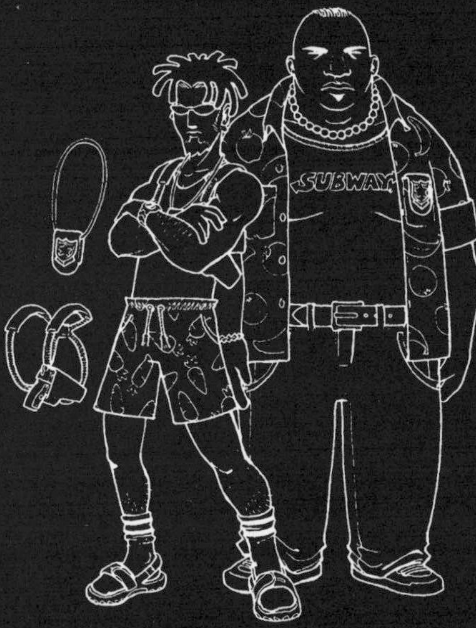
SUBWAY

BONUS SECTION

I THOUGHT IT WOULD BE NICE (OR AT LEAST INTERESTING) TO ASK SOME FRIENDS TO CONTRIBUTE A FEW LITTLE THINGS FOR THE BACK OF THE BOOK, AND HOPEFULLY I CAN GET A FEW MORE THINGS FOR THE NEXT BOOK. THE IDEA IS THAT IT'S FUN FOR THEM (THE CREATORS) AND YOU (THE READERS) AND WE ALL GET TO SEE DIFFERENT INTERPRETATIONS OF THE CHARACTERS OR WHATEVER. ANYWAY, PLEASE ENJOY.

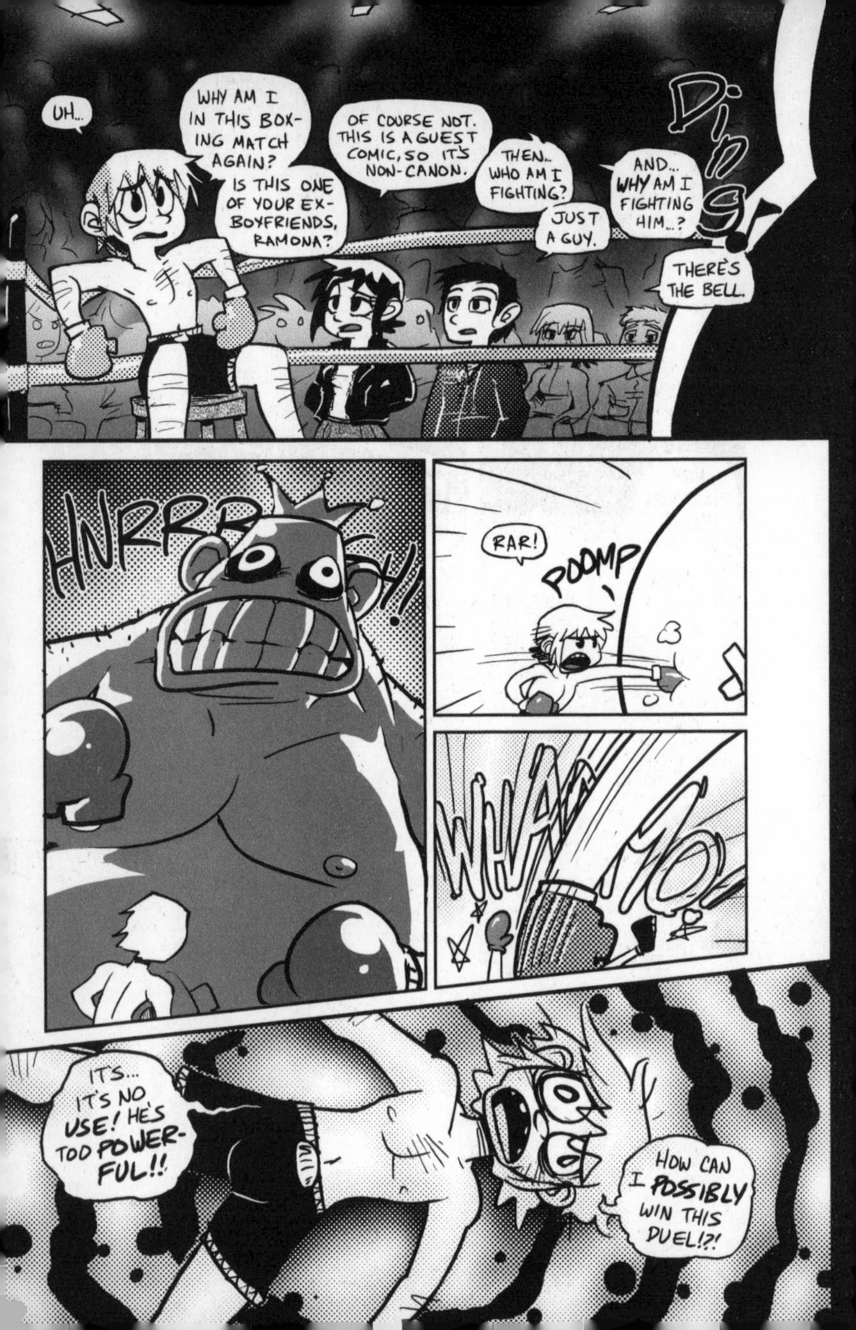
UH...
WHY AM I IN THIS BOXING MATCH AGAIN?
IS THIS ONE OF YOUR EX-BOYFRIENDS, RAMONA?
OF COURSE NOT. THIS IS A GUEST COMIC, SO IT'S NON-CANON.
THEN.. WHO AM I FIGHTING?
JUST A GUY.
AND... WHY AM I FIGHTING HIM...?
Ding!
THERE'S THE BELL.
HNRRRGH!!
RAR!
POOMP
WHAMO!
ITS... IT'S NO USE! HE'S TOO POWERFUL!!
HOW CAN I POSSIBLY WIN THIS DUEL!?!

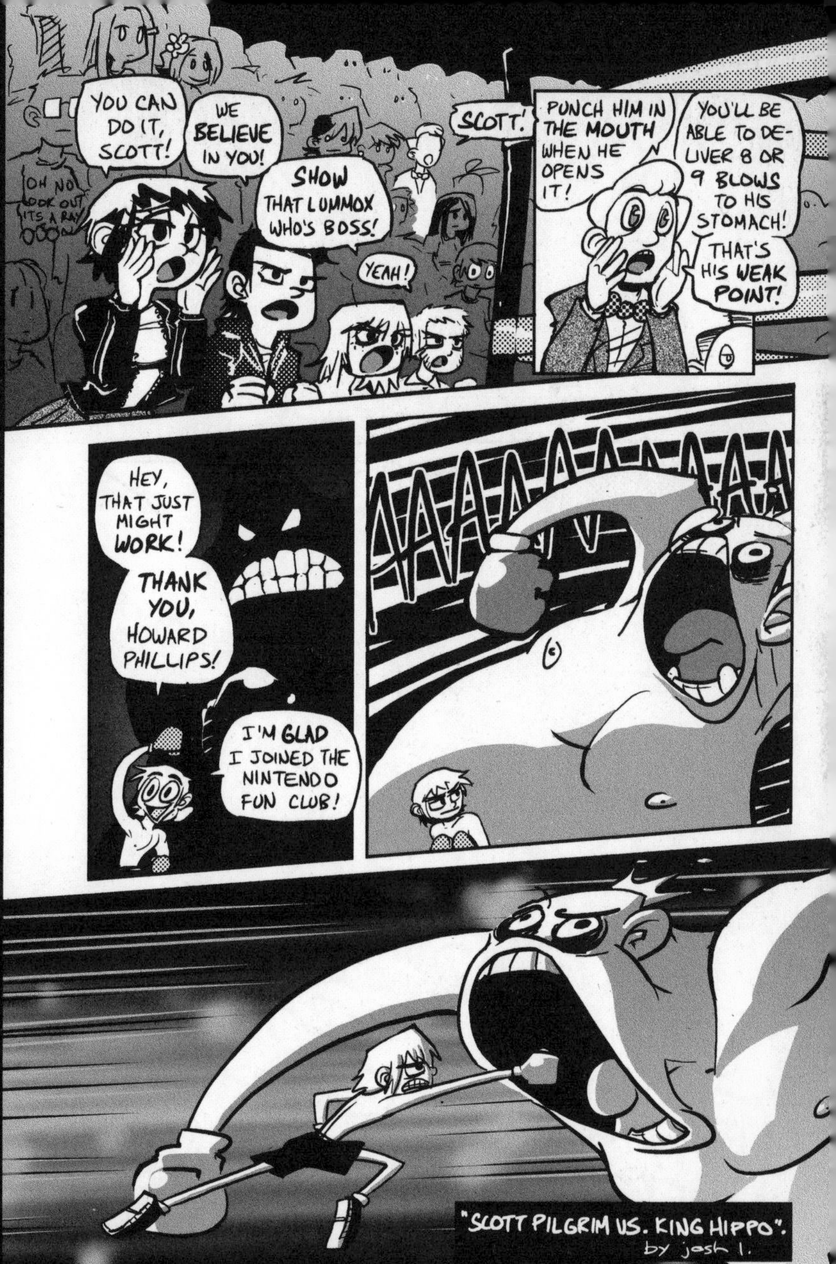
YOU CAN DO IT, SCOTT!
WE BELIEVE IN YOU!
OH NO LOOK OUT ITS A RAY
SHOW THAT LUMMOX WHO'S BOSS!
YEAH!
SCOTT!
PUNCH HIM IN THE MOUTH WHEN HE OPENS IT!
YOU'LL BE ABLE TO DELIVER 8 OR 9 BLOWS TO HIS STOMACH!
THAT'S HIS WEAK POINT!
HEY, THAT JUST MIGHT WORK!
THANK YOU, HOWARD PHILLIPS!
I'M GLAD I JOINED THE NINTENDO FUN CLUB!
AAAAAAAAAAA
"SCOTT PILGRIM VS. KING HIPPO".
by josh l.

JOSH LESNICK draws the webcomic **Girly** ***(www.go-girly.com)*** and I have known him since the first day I went on the internet or something.

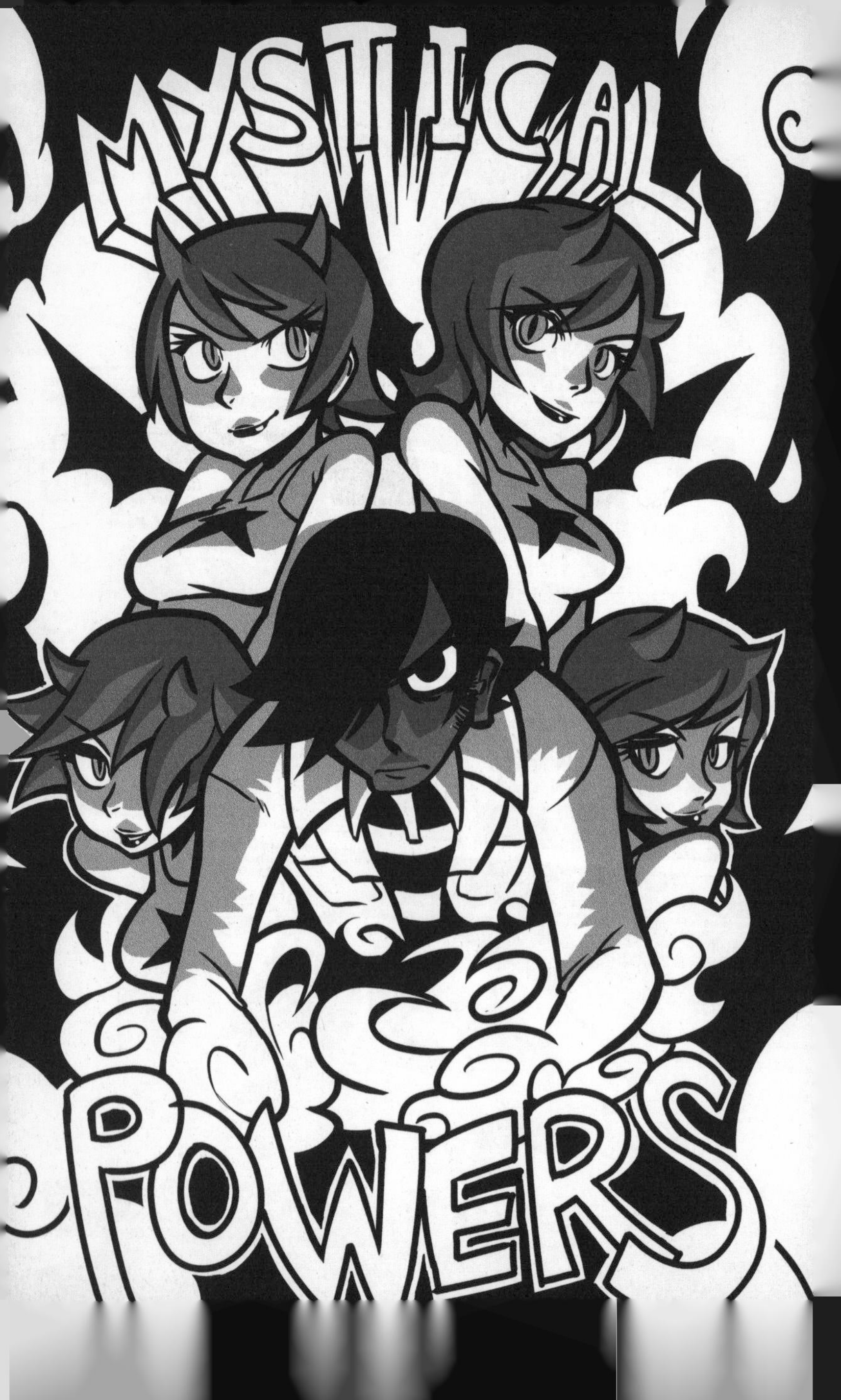
MYSTICAL
POWERS

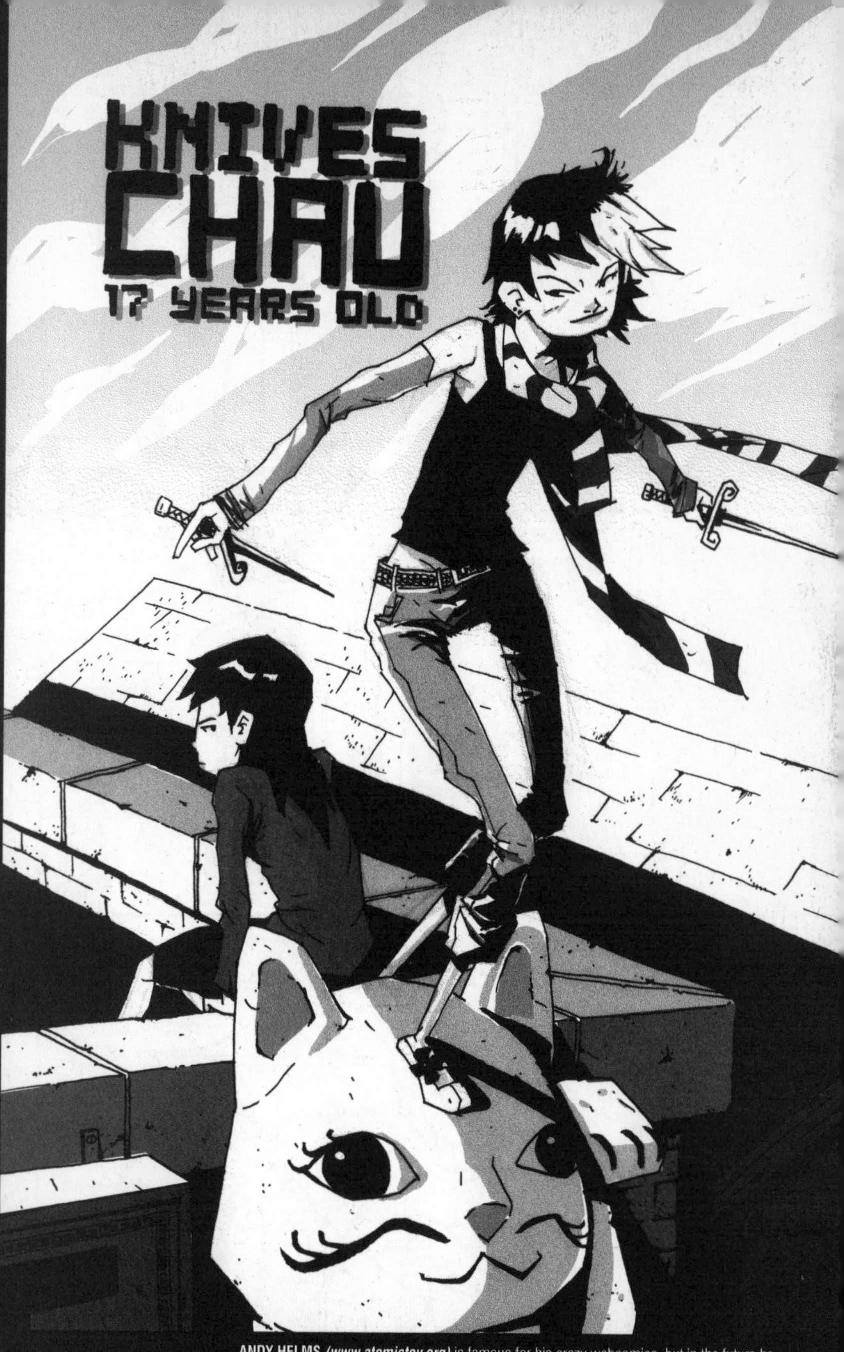
KNIVES CHAU
17 YEARS OLD

ANDY HELMS ***(www.atomictoy.org)*** is famous for his crazy webcomics, but in the future he will be even more famous for **FEARLESS GRIGGS**, coming from Oni Press in 2006.

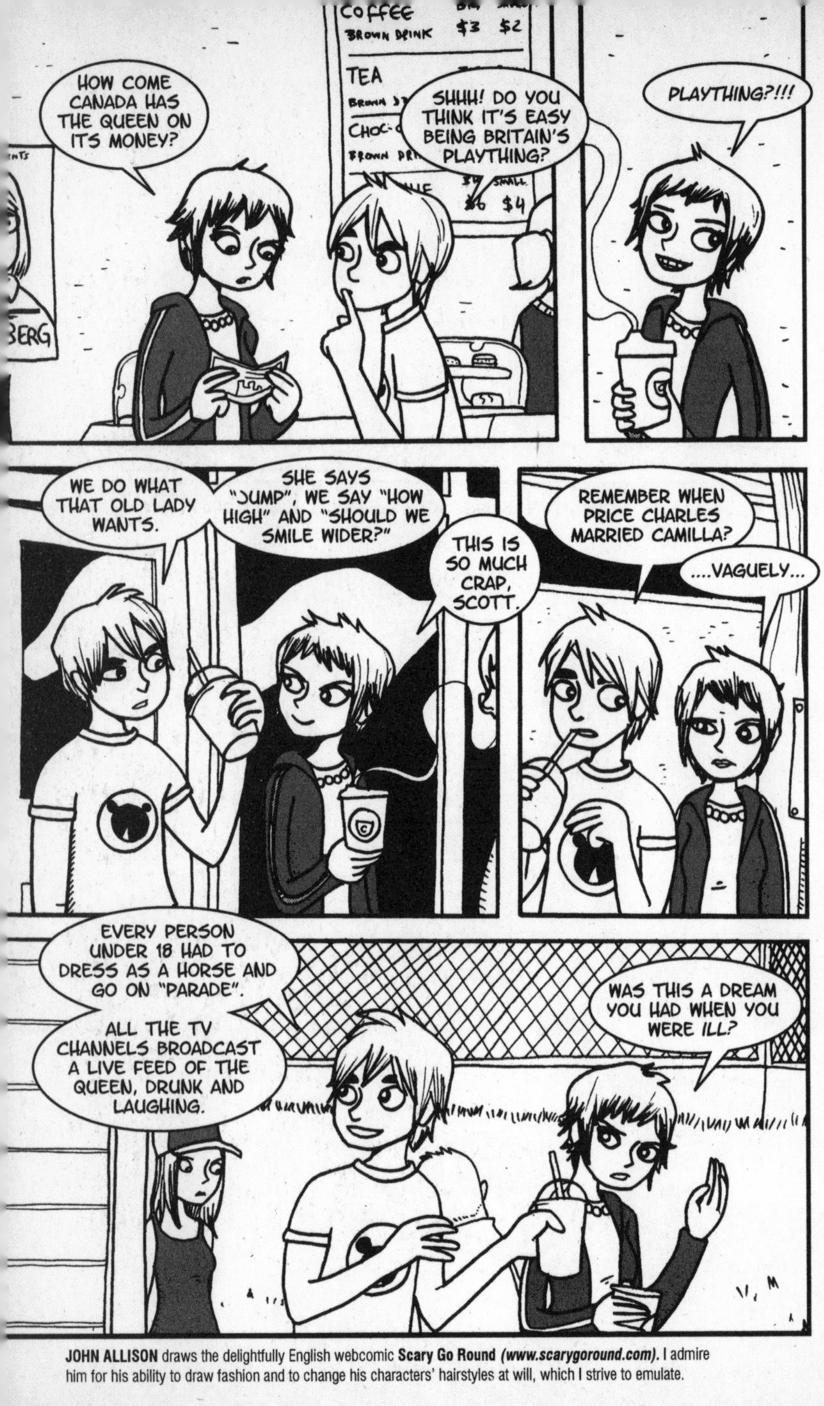
COFFEE
BROWN DRINK $3 $2
TEA
HOW COME CANADA HAS THE QUEEN ON ITS MONEY?
SHHH! DO YOU THINK IT'S EASY BEING BRITAIN'S PLAYTHING?
PLAYTHING?!!!
WE DO WHAT THAT OLD LADY WANTS.
SHE SAYS "JUMP", WE SAY "HOW HIGH" AND "SHOULD WE SMILE WIDER?"
THIS IS SO MUCH CRAP, SCOTT.
REMEMBER WHEN PRICE CHARLES MARRIED CAMILLA?
....VAGUELY...
EVERY PERSON UNDER 18 HAD TO DRESS AS A HORSE AND GO ON "PARADE".
ALL THE TV CHANNELS BROADCAST A LIVE FEED OF THE QUEEN, DRUNK AND LAUGHING.
WAS THIS A DREAM YOU HAD WHEN YOU WERE ILL?

JOHN ALLISON draws the delightfully English webcomic **Scary Go Round** ***(www.scarygoround.com).*** I admire him for his ability to draw fashion and to change his characters' hairstyles at will, which I strive to emulate.

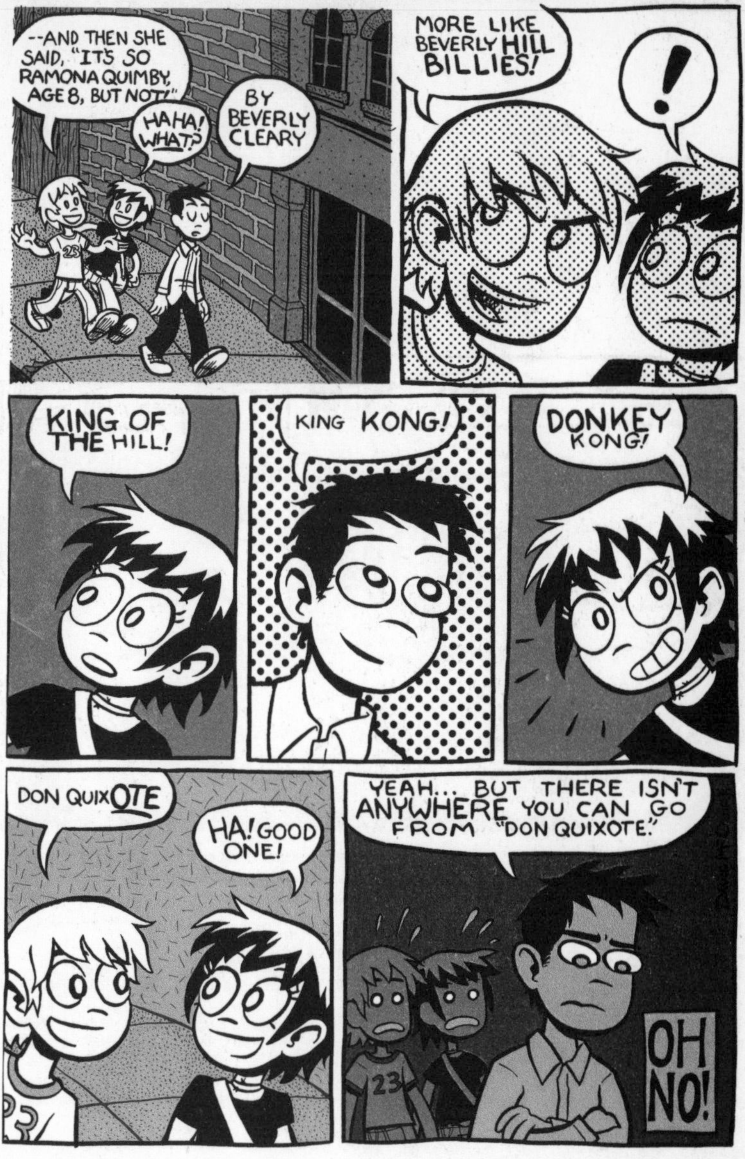
--AND THEN SHE SAID, "IT'S SO RAMONA QUIMBY, AGE 8, BUT NOT!"
HAHA! WHAT?
BY BEVERLY CLEARY
MORE LIKE BEVERLY HILL BILLIES!
!
KING OF THE HILL!
KING KONG!
DONKEY KONG!
DON QUIXOTE
HA! GOOD ONE!
YEAH... BUT THERE ISN'T ANYWHERE YOU CAN GO FROM "DON QUIXOTE."
OH NO!

DAVID McGUIRE ***(davidmcg.com)*** is famous to me and to everyone who knows him, and one day everyone in the world will know him. He is a cartooning prodigy from another world.

author's portrait by Vera Brosgol

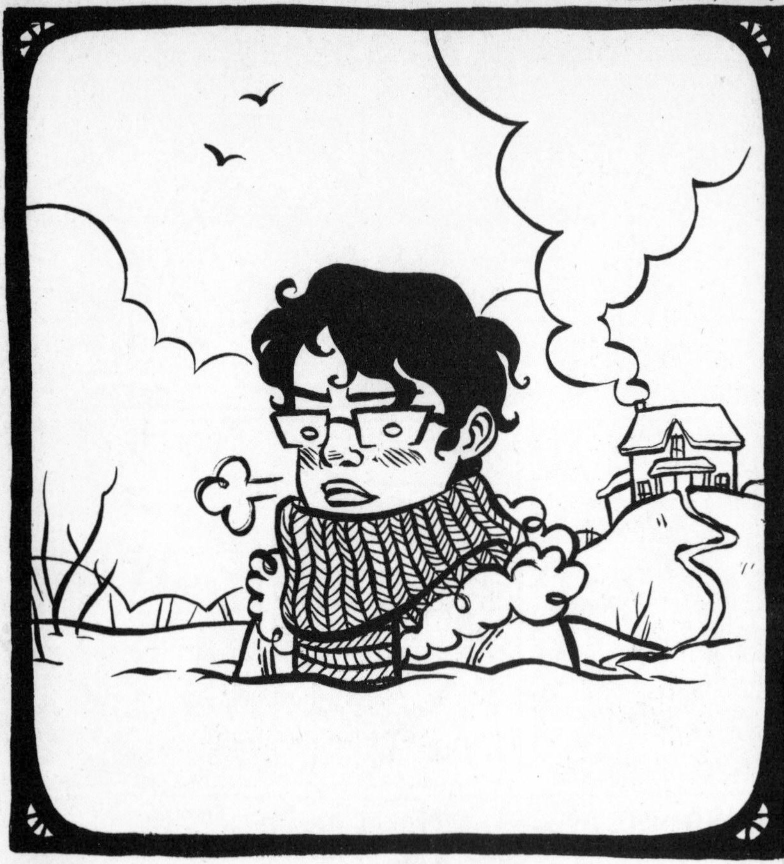

ABOUT THE AUTHOR Bryan Lee O'Malley *(born 21 February 1979)* is a Canadian cartoonist and occasional musician. He lives in the wilderness with Hope Larson (**www.hopelarson.com**) and three cats, and has an extremely great website at **www.radiomaru.com**.

this is kind of like a blog

I got re-obsessed with manga while I was working on this book. Here's some stuff that I can remember reading, in no particular order, that I more or less recommend: **BERSERK** (Kentaro Miura), **GANTZ** (Hiroya Oku), **DEATH NOTE** (Tsugumi Ohba & Takeshi Obata), **AZUMANGA DAIOH** (Kiyohiko Azuma), **LIVING GAME** (Mochiru Hoshisato). There's a lot of good stuff out there if you can get past the fanboy/fangirling...

Some people have been asking about the music I listen to while working on Scott Pilgrim. For each book, I tend to make one mix CD of songs that capture the right mood. I don't have much space here, so I'll just list a few major songs...

PLUMTREE - "Scott Pilgrim" - this is the song that inspired the book in general, by a great Canadian indie girl-rock band from the 90s. Plumtree rocks forever!

JOEL PLASKETT - "When I Have My Vision", "Written All Over Me", etc - he's a guy whose music has had a huge influence on me and Scott Pilgrim. He was also in a great 90s band called Thrush Hermit whose defining album "Clayton Park" is an overlooked classic.

THE FLYING BURRITO BROS - "To Ramona", etc - this legendary band fronted by Gram Parsons in the early 70s is the soundtrack to Scott's mind.

BEACHWOOD SPARKS - "By Your Side" - a swirly cosmic countrified cover of a Sade song. It's the ultimate Scott Pilgrim love song. I secretly love the original, too.

THE REPLACEMENTS - "Left of the Dial", "Can't Hardly Wait", etc - they wrote amazing songs. I always think of them as Ramona's favorite band. They're one of mine.

UNCLE TUPELO - "Grindstone" - the original alt-country band. I equate them with the character Stephen Stills.

NEIL YOUNG - "Borrowed Tune" - and every other Neil Young song. Scott also 'borrowed' a tune from the Rolling Stones in this book, in case you missed it...

SPOON - "Waiting For The Kid To Come Out" - gets me moving every time. This is an old b-side but it screams Scott Pilgrim to me. Rockin' and ramshackle.

OLD 97s - "Let The Idiot Speak", etc - they're a bouncy pop-country-punk-something band from Texas and they've given this comic a lot of juice over the years.

TOM PETTY - "American Girl" - this song plays over the credits of every episode of Scott Pilgrim in my mind. Check out that guitar in the intro! *CLASSIC ROCK!*